This is a work of fiction. Names, characters, places, and incidents either are the product of the author's imagination or are used fictitiously. Any resemblance to actual persons, living or dead, events or locales is entirely coincidental.

Cover Design by Miblart

www.miblart.com

First edition December 2025

ISBN 9798992238976 (Paperback)

ISBN 9798992238969 (E-Book)

Also by Torie Gaylord

Three Seconds
Three Seconds and Gone
Blink and You Miss It
Whispers of Moments
Torn Between Times

Watch for more at toriegwriting.com.

For the survivors, the ones who have had to endure things no one should – this one's for you. May you have the courage to not let those things hold power over you.

Val's journey has been far from easy. In the following pages, Val will continue to experience hardship with themes such as sexual abuse, violence, and death. Please proceed with caution and make sure to take care of yourself. If you, or someone you know, has been a victim of sexual violence, RAINN can provide support and resources that can be found on their website (RAINN.org) or by calling their national hotline (1-800-656-4673).

TORN BETWEEN TIMES

TORIE GAYLORD

Chapter 1

Warrick's face paled to a shade I didn't think was possible. I glanced over to Lou who kept his eyes trained on Warrick's mysterious family member. Everyone else was watching very carefully, not daring to make a sound.

The new man clapped his hand on Warrick's shoulder again, chuckling, before moving to pull up a chair. Before he settled into it, he made a big show of pulling off his leather jacket revealing more than just the one tattoo I recognized from the photo. There was a whole sleeve of wolf-themed tattoos covering his arm and continuing across his chest (the white v-neck stood no chance of hiding his ink). He leaned back, spreading his legs and rested one of his hands on the back of Warrick's chair. He looked at each of us, his gaze lingering a little longer on me before he returned his focus to Warrick, "Well, are you going to introduce me, brother?"

I whipped my head around to Lou, mouthing, "Brother?"

Lou just shook his head. I didn't need him to say anything for me to know he had no idea Warrick had a brother nor had he seen Warrick like this before. Pure fear was a rare expression for Warrick.

"Everyone," Warrick quietly started. He cleared his throat to shake whatever had a hold over him, "This is Azrael, my brother. Az, you have Joe and Bev at the end there. That's Jennie across from Lou. And this is Val."

Azrael gave each of us a smile making my skin crawl. He leaned towards me reaching out to tuck my hair behind my ear, "Hi, Val-pal. Fancy meeting you here, it's been a while since I've seen that beautiful face of yours."

Warrick's head snapped up to look at his brother, "What did you ca – "

I cut Warrick off, "How do you know me?"

Azrael dropped his hand back to his lap, feigning hurt, "Do you not remember me?"

"What are you talking about?" I asked, confused.

He leaned forward to rest his forearms on his knees, "That hurts, Val, especially when we have so much history."

"Can you please bring me up to speed, Az?" Warrick asked between clenched teeth.

Azrael turned his head towards Warrick, "You don't know? I'm surprised she hasn't said anything considering this isn't the first time we've seen each other in this world."

"Get to the point," Warrick said.

"You're no fun, little brother," Azrael chided. "I'll get back to that in a moment. What does it take for a guy to get a drink around here?"

"I got it," Lou grumbled.

I threw a hand out, stopping him from getting up, but didn't dare take my eyes off Warrick and Azrael, "No, I'll take care of it."

I grabbed a few other empty glasses and headed over to the bar. When I started going through the motions to pour the drinks and set them on a tray, I observed the scene playing out in front of me: Warrick looking scared shitless while also somehow looking like he was ready to kill this man claiming to be his brother; Lou watching Warrick closely, my friends keeping their eyes trained on the table to avoid conflict; and Warrick's brother taking in the scenery like everything is normal. The thing that was getting me was this man claiming to know me, and he even used my father's nickname for me, yet I couldn't place where I knew him. At all. There was only a hint of familiarity. It was killing me.

I brought the drinks back to the table, everyone mumbling their thanks. I took a long swig of my beer, closing my eyes, when Azrael opened his mouth again, "I've missed you, Warrick. Could've used your brains a couple of times, but I ended up getting things figured out."

"Why are you here?" Warrick asked.

"I'm giving you another chance to join me. Be on the winning side for once," Azrael said before taking a sip of his beer.

Warrick shook his head, "Not a chance in hell."

"You're a lot like dad, you know that? And quite frankly, it pisses me off," Azrael countered.

Warrick's face paled again, but this time, he looked sick to his stomach rather than scared. It was almost as if Azrael knew what kind of reaction he was going to get from Warrick by saying that.

Doing one more glance at the two of them, it was hard not to see the similarities in how they looked, except Azrael's hair was a little longer, he was covered in tats, he had hazel eyes, and he didn't keep himself as clean shaven as Warrick. *No doubt about them being related, though.*

Azrael turned his attention to me reaching out to stroke my face, but continued talking to Warrick, "What if I said you could bring your little plaything, too? I mean, I wouldn't mind having another shot. As long as you're willing to share, that is. Plus, it should sweeten the deal. All the previous offers still stand. You just get a little bonus now."

I jerked my head back, my lip curling in disgust, "Who the hell do you think you are?"

"I think you need to leave," Lou cut in.

Azrael let out a bark of laughter then downed the rest of his beer. He leaned across me shoving his glass into Lou's hand, "Make yourself useful while the adults are talking shop."

"I'm serious, Az," Warrick warned. "I'm not joining you, Val's not going anywhere with you, and you need to keep your hands off her."

"Or what?" Az cocked his head. "You'll hurt me? You didn't stand much of a chance of doing that the other night."

Blood drained from my face. Everything connected in that moment. Azrael was the one who attacked Warrick. He's also the reason why Warrick wouldn't tell me anything about the enemy because *Az* is the enemy. And on top of that, my memories suddenly came rushing back: Azrael was the first man I was in an actual relationship with after Gabriel's death. He was the first person to drag me out of the darkness to enjoy life again, then he disappeared.

"You've got to be fucking kidding me," I said.

Warrick furrowed his brows, "What's going on, Val?"

Az burst out laughing, "Oh, this is great. She just remembered."

"Remembered what?" Warrick asked.

Lou slammed down Azrael's beer splashing some in his face, "Are you going to start filling in some of the gaps?

Az wiped the beer off his face then pointed at Lou keeping his tone serious, "You're a nuisance, but you could be of use for me in the future, especially if what I heard is true."

"Don't fucking count on it," Lou scoffed as he settled back into his seat.

Az turned back to me, "You have benefits. Some that I know very well, and you were about to share with the class."

"Please, love, tell me what you remembered," Warrick said looking at me with a worried expression.

"You're kidding right, Warrick? You're using that 'love' shit on her? Aren't you tired of wrapping women around your finger with one little word?" Azrael asked in disbelief.

Warrick slammed his hand down on the table making all of us jump, "Cut that shit out, Az! I'm sick of your damn games and want to hear what an honest person has to say."

"Fine," he responded, holding his hands up. He gestured to me, "The floor is yours."

I sighed pinching the bridge of my nose and closing my eyes. No one was going to like what I had to say, especially Warrick. I didn't want to see another fight break out after the injuries Azrael caused last time. It was too soon for me to risk losing Warrick again. Yet, he did ask about what I remembered.

When I opened my eyes, I looked at Jennie hoping she knew what I was about to say. She subtly nodded her head while taking a small sip of her beer. Recognition was written all over her face which was all I needed from her to know she remembered the same thing I did, and the reassurance I needed to start explaining. She knew I had a history with Az and it wasn't just a few months of sleeping together, either.

I brought my attention back to Warrick, "Your brother and I had a thing for a little while."

"That's it?" Az scoffed, eyes wide. "A *thing* for a little while?"

I ignored Azrael trying to stir the pot more than he already had. He clearly had a new-found love for the dramatics. Warrick narrowed his eyes at me making panic creep in. He's been better lately, but I know he's still a loose cannon and he hasn't held back when it comes to taking it out on me. I started to reach for him across the table, but stopped thinking the last thing he'd want would be for me to touch him. Instead, Warrick directed his fury towards Az, "Was dating her a part of your scheme?"

Az feigned shock, "I'm insulted. How dare you think I'd use someone as beautiful and sweet as Val. Especially after her fiancée died. How very tragic."

My eyes slowly made their way over to the man who crashed our evening. If he truly is behind this war, he's the reason Gabriel died and there was no way of knowing if he had planned that or not. Knowing how Warrick is, Az was probably just as good at scheming or better. Head games run in this family judging how Az is carrying himself tonight.

"Did you target Gabriel? Was I just a pawn in your plan?" I asked doing my best to hold back my rage.

Az turned back to me holding my hands in his and bringing his face within inches of mine. His voice was serious as he said, "There's no way I would've intended for you to go through that kind of pain. I'm a twisted person, but even I wouldn't do that to someone like you."

I snatched my hands back, "To someone like me. So, you're saying you would do that to someone else?"

He shrugged, "I wouldn't take it off the table."

"I can't believe you," I said.

"Did you change Chris?" Jennie blurted suddenly.

We all jumped a little at the sound of her voice since the conversation was primarily me, Warrick, and Az. I watched a slow, sinister smile inch its way across his face, "Now we're asking the right questions. That, my dear, is a question that will get answered in a little bit."

"You're sick, Az," Warrick said. He knew with absolute certainty Azrael had changed Chris. Azrael knew that would change Chris' demeanor and throw a wrench into things. I would even bet he knew Warrick and Lou would be on the lookout for Chris the night they changed, which gave Az the perfect opportunity to lure Warrick away to attack him.

I needed to put some distance between myself and this stranger sitting next to me. The Az I dated was nowhere near this cold and calculating. He took care of me in a time of need. He was sweet and loving, always showing up with flowers in hand. Sure, he could be a little reckless when we went on rides, but that side of him was always tucked away when we wandered up into my apartment for the night. He never showed any signs of violence or malicious intent.

I stood behind the bar filling up my glass again knowing no amount of alcohol was going to erase the past, but I'd sure like to try. Az was distracted for a moment, so I caught Warrick watching me. There wasn't any anger or frustration in his eyes to make me worry. Instead, there was sadness in knowing what his brother did to me and how I was taken advantage of.

"While you're at it," I heard a voice purr from behind me. I jumped, not realizing Az had left his seat. I shot a look back at Warrick to see he hadn't noticed the sudden movement either. Him and Lou were both tense, poised to jump from their chairs at any moment.

Azrael leaned against the bar right next to me, propping himself up on his arm, "I'd like a refill myself. You got some good beer here, Lou."

"Thanks," Lou forced out.

Az looked at the two other wolves and scoffed, bringing his attention back to me, "Look at them. They think I'm going to do something to you. How cute."

I placed our now full glasses on the bar unable to look at him, "Well, are you?"

"I can if you want me to," his voice lowered to a dangerous level.

"Excuse me, I would like to sit back down," I said trying to change topics and to get out from behind the bar to put space between us. I started to take a step around him, sliding his beer towards his hand while grabbing mine. Az stood up like he was going to let me pass when he yanked both of my arms behind my back and placed his other hand around my throat. He applied a gentle pressure, enough to remind me he could kill me in a second, but not enough to interrupt my airflow.

My glass smashed around my feet sending beer everywhere while Lou and Warrick jumped up and my friends all let out a scream. I felt the low rumble of laughter building in Az, "Tsk, tsk. If you two take another step, I will snap her neck. I really don't want to do that, though. It'll spoil my fun tonight."

Warrick took a step towards us, "I told you not to fucking touch her."

Az's grip instantly tightened making my wrists groan in protest. I tried gasping for air, and after seeing that, Warrick slowly sunk back into his chair motioning for Lou to follow. Once they were both situated in their seat, Az loosened his grip, "Good. Glad to see you two actually have some common sense. Now, where were we. Oh, that's right. My fun for this evening. Doesn't this bring back memories, my beautiful Val?" He started humming – it was a familiar song, but I was having a hard time placing it. Lowering his voice, Az leaned in, "We're having a Celine moment. Remember those?"

"What are you talking about?"

"Celine Dion? C'mon, Val. Don't let me down," Az chided.

I tried to turn my head to look at him, but was finding it hard to move with how he was holding me. Az continued humming, now gently swaying us to the rhythm of the song. When I still didn't show any signs of recognition, Az tsked, "Really? 'It's All Coming Back to Me Now'? It surprises me you're not recognizing it considering how often we listened to it. Besides, it's fitting for this moment, don't you think?"

"Stop," I choked out, still trying to catch my breath. It may have only been an instant that I couldn't breathe, but the panic was drawing out my reaction.

"Stop, what?" he asked, his lips now brushing against my ear. "Your friend over there, Jennie, is it?"

She nodded and Az continued, "She asked if I changed Chris. Let me ask you something, Val. Does the way I'm holding you remind you of anything?"

He lowered his hand from my neck to my breast, but still didn't let go of my wrists. Anger and recognition flashed across Lou's face when he was taken back to the night in the club when Chris was all over me. Even before this, the three of us knew Azrael was the one behind Chris' change. Anything he was doing now was just for show.

When I didn't answer, he brought his hand back up to my neck giving me a little shake, "Answer me."

"Yes," I responded a little too quickly.

I could feel him smiling as he turned his attention back to his audience, "Good. So, long story short, the answer is yes, Jennie, I turned Chris. I even showed him some of the ropes hoping he would be able to get Val to join our cause. Unfortunately for me, these two knights in shining armor had to ruin things."

Jennie turned away. It pained me to see her having to relive something she buried away. Joe and Bev started to console her making me wish I was over there too.

"You made your point, now let me go," I said squirming a little to try to get out of his grasp.

Az lowered his voice to a volume only myself, Warrick, and Lou could hear, "I'm afraid I haven't. There's still something I want to see with my own eyes."

"What is it?"

"I want to know if my little brother and my ex, who I wish wasn't my ex, have something between them," he chuckled.

I gave my wrists one more tug in the hopes he had loosened his grip enough for me to slip out, "Why does that matter?"

"That's for me to know and not for you to find out," Az answered as I felt his fingers tapping against my wrists. As soon as I felt his hands let go, I tried to cross my arms over the front of me for comfort, but realized the tapping I felt was him tying something around my wrists. "It's cute you thought I was just going to let you go. You forget, Val, I know you well enough to understand the fire that burns in you."

Az still kept one of his hands around my neck while he took a sip of his beer with the other. He cleared his throat when he was finished, wrapping his free hand around my waist, "Going back to the Chris question for a moment so we're not here all night. I changed him because I saw the potential, plus he asked me to. We met at a coffee shop one day after I heard him asking Jennie if she ever wondered what it would feel like to be a wolf. When she dismissed him and ran off to do her Christmas shopping, I couldn't pass on the opportunity to swoop in to answer all his questions. It wasn't me who made that decision for him. No, sweet Jennie, it was Chris who practically begged me to change him. As for what happened after that, I had a minimal part to play in his actions. He cheated on you because he wanted to. Hurts, I know, but nothing you can do to change that now. I only asked him if he knew Val because I recognized Jennie. When he said yes, I asked him to try to bring her over to our side. Clearly, that didn't work the way I wanted it to. I miscalculated who Val may have gotten involved with."

"What does that have to do with you holding her hostage right now?" Lou asked holding back his anger.

Az lowered his voice again, "I didn't quite believe my sources when they told me Warrick was all over Val. I also had a hard time believing Warrick would beat someone to a pulp over some woman, but when I came to Val's house and saw

Warrick standing guard, I knew there was something precious he was protecting. I've never seen him act that way. I also couldn't believe I was standing outside the house belonging to the parents of the last woman I had dated. Brought back memories."

"That didn't answer my question," Lou said.

"So impatient," Az sighed. "Work with me, Lou."

Lou let out a growl, threatening to stand back up. Warrick shook his head, "Sit, Lou. There's nothing we can do right now if we want Val to make it out of this."

He sounded awfully calm for someone watching his brother try to make a move on the person he's apparently fated to. Azrael picked up on that, chuckling. He turned his attention to me, "Val, I need you to clear some things up for me."

"What, Az?" I said between clenched teeth.

Azrael breathed my scent in, "How I've missed you calling me that. Not necessarily in that tone, but I digress. Let's start with this: tell me, does Warrick call you 'love'?"

I nodded, "You should know this. You already called him out on that."

He tsked, "Classic Warrick move, as I was saying earlier. He's been pulling that since he was a kid. Now, for my last questions. Did he give you the whole fated speech? Does he whisper sweet nothings to you as you lay in bed? Did he give you the whole speech about his one, true love? I forget her name, but maybe that's because he changes it every time."

The blood drained from me once again as my world tilted. Az felt my knees give out and he held me up, "Hang in there. I know this isn't the easiest thing to hear, but judging by your reaction, I would say the answer to both of those are yes. Ah, what a treat."

Those questions were dripping with the implication this was something Warrick did all the time. I was just another woman to sleep with, to fill an emptiness for a short period of time. Maybe Lou and I were right all along in that Warrick was just using me to get closer to my dad and get the information he wants. But that doesn't change the fact that I fell, and I fell hard.

"Tell me, Val," Az continued. "Does he know where to touch you to drive you wild? Does he know how to take care of you when you wake up feeling all alone? Because I remember every inch of your body and what makes you tick. I remember the way you moaned and arched your back when I did this and how my touch seemed to cure everything for you."

The hand around my waist inched down between my thighs as his other hand worked its way up my shirt to my breast. The feeling of his skin against mine almost made me throw up between the memories of a person I used to know and what was happening in this moment. Az let out a soft moan when he felt the lace of my bra, but that didn't slow him down from his final destination. Once he got both of his hands where he wanted them to be, he worked them in a way I hadn't felt in years, slowly at first then picked up the pace. My body instinctively arched against his, my head falling back and eyes closing. It took everything in me not to moan in response, but he already had me right where he wanted me.

"See," Az purred in my ear directing this towards Warrick. "Val and I were close at one point. Really close, and I didn't have to play her. I just had to learn what she likes so she can feel like her needs are being met. Then, I had to pass that along to an eager student, like Chris. It made me so proud to see him executing everything according to plan. Anyways, your tricks are old, Warrick. Let's face it. Val's coming with me now that she knows the truth, you'll move on to the next woman walking down the street if you haven't already, and – "

Az was cut off by Warrick slamming into him. *I guess Az isn't the only one who can move that fast.* I was thrown to the end of the bar, further away from my only exit. I collapsed against the back wall, my body erupting in pain from hitting the bar, but I didn't have a chance to focus on that. I curled in on myself to offer some sort of protection as all the glass bottles came raining down on me, glass shattering everywhere.

At some point, Az had released my arms that were now instinctively coming up to protect my face. Cuts on my exposed skin felt like fire as alcohol coated them. I peeked out from behind my arms finding Warrick pinning Az by his neck against the wall, "I told you to leave. Her. *Alone*!"

Az let out a cough followed by a laugh, "Aw, little baby brother's upset. Now he thinks he can be the hero after putting her through the wringer. You think this is going to make up for what you did?"

Warrick screamed, throwing wild punches and kicks. Every time one of his blows connected, a sickening crunch filled the space. Blood splashed on to me, and yet, Az was still laughing. He managed to get free, slamming Warrick against the wall. This time a shelf came crashing down narrowly missing me as Az sneered, "My turn."

Az reeled his head back before knocking Warrick out with the hit. He took full advantage of having a lifeless opponent, throwing nonstop punches. Az lifted Warrick and slammed him down into the bar. Wood cracking rang out as I watched Warrick's body twitch from the impact.

"Everyone, upstairs now!" Lou yelled out.

I stayed rooted to my spot out of fear I'd be caught in the middle of the brutal beating Az was giving his brother. I heard chairs scooting back and the quick pace of feet as my friends did what they were told. Just when I thought I was stuck here, Lou thrusted a hand into my line of sight, "C'mon, Val."

I hesitated a little too long. Lou wiggled his fingers in front of me, "Take it. This is the only way you're getting out of here."

As I reached out for Lou's hand, Az snapped, "I don't think so."

He left Warrick and headed straight for Lou. Az picked up one of the broken bottles and nearly stabbed it through Lou's hand on the bar top. When he realized he missed, Az snagged Lou's outstretched hand, "This isn't your fight. I suggest you walk away, now."

"Fuck off," Lou smacked him away. "She's got nothing to do with this rivalry you have with your brother."

"She's got *everything* to do with this," Az hissed in response.

There was motion out of the corner of my eye. I slowly turned my head in that direction, my eyes darting back to Az every now and then. Warrick was conscious, silently moving towards the other two wolves. He saw me watching him and motioned for me to stay quiet. He didn't have to tell me twice. I pressed myself against the back of the bar as much as I could to stay out of whatever was about to unfold.

Az and Lou were almost at each other's throats when Warrick grabbed Az's shirt, yanking him back. He kneeled down on Az's chest, Warrick's hand reaching for Az's throat, "Lou, this is my fight, not yours."

As soon as he heard his name, Lou snapped out of whatever trance he was put in from being drug into a fight. He reached towards me again. Before Lou could order me to take his hand, I placed my hand in his, no hesitation this time. He pulled me over the bar and we ran for the stairs. As we passed Warrick and Az, Lou called over his shoulder, "Bar repairs are being added to your tab, Warrick."

I glanced over my shoulder to get one last look at the fight still going on. Az was holding Warrick up by the neck and slammed him against the bar again. This time, the bar top completely broke and Warrick ended up on the ground. I couldn't stop myself as I yelled out, "Warrick!"

Only it was Az who looked up, giving me a smile that would haunt me.

Chapter 2

Lou shoved me through his front door. I stumbled forward only to be caught by Bev. I mumbled a thanks before whirling around to Lou, "What the hell?"

"A thank you would suffice," he grumbled, his attention still focused on downstairs.

"Why'd you shove me, Lou?"

I became more frustrated when he didn't answer. I stormed up to him grabbing his chin so he was forced to look at me, "Why did you shove me?"

He leveled his grey eyes on me, his voice serious, "I couldn't trust you wouldn't bolt back down there to try to save Warrick. He can handle this, and before you try to argue that, it's better for him if you aren't there as a distraction. Besides, I didn't want to leave Azrael any chance to take you."

"I would've been fine," I said in an even tone in an effort not to scream.

"Go get cleaned up," Lou ordered with another glance down the stairs. When I didn't move, he threw me over his shoulder ignoring the protests from my friends, "I'm not dealing with your stubbornness right now, Val. Azrael is dangerous. He's currently down there destroying my restaurant and I can't do anything about it. I watched as he assaulted you then let you get buried by more bottles than I'd like to count. Then, on top of all that, he was ready to grab you and run."

He tossed me on the bed, blocking the doorway. I looked away not wanting him to see the tears forming in my eyes now that all my fight was leaving me. Lou had a point. Not only did I get an unwanted trip down memory lane, but I watched as the man who almost killed Warrick was going at it again just when Warrick was feeling better. I knew Az was playing head games to try to get in between me and Warrick, but everything he said still bugged me. And for the icing on the cake, everyone just witnessed me getting felt up in a way I fully intended to keep behind closed doors.

"Damn it," I finally let out. The tears followed the words and Lou crouched in front of me wiping them away. I met his concerned gaze, but instead of blurting out every thought running through my head, I reached out to trace the scar running through his eyebrow. Warrick had done so much to him, convinced us all he was invincible, and yet he's getting his ass handed to him again.

Lou closed his eyes leaning into my touch. He started to bring my hand towards his lips, but dropped it when he realized what he was doing. "You okay?" he asked in a gravelly voice.

"Did I make a mistake?" I asked with a shaky voice.

"Hey," he said coming closer as he dropped his voice to a whisper. "You did what you thought was best. It wasn't going to be easy, I said that from day one, but believe me when I say things have a way of working out."

I shook my head, "It's so hard to believe literally everything in my life has been going south. Gabriel dying, being transported here only to get tortured by Warrick, almost dying by the hands of some vampires, having Warrick proclaim his love for me out of nowhere, and now this? Azrael coming back out of the blue and worming his way into my head? It's too much, Lou."

He glanced towards the living room and then the open apartment door. I followed his gaze seeing Jennie, Joe, and Bev watching us with concerned expressions. Lou sighed as he turned back to me, "At the end of the day, it's your choice. You don't know how badly I wish for this all to be a bad dream that we'd wake up from after dancing the night away in my living room. But, I do know one thing. I know a lot of Warrick's history and I know I've never seen him act the way he does when he's with you. Anything he's said to you, he's meant it."

The commotion coming from downstairs had finally ended. I sat there a few moments longer trying to quiet everything telling me Az was right while Lou stood up. He put a hand on my shoulder, "Get cleaned up. I'll get you back to your place."

When he turned, I had a full view of his entry way again. My eyes widened. Warrick was standing there, his chest heaving from how hard he was breathing, and watching the two of us very closely. He didn't look happy, making me feel the instant need to run. I slowly stood up, and as I did so, Warrick started to make his way towards me, one slow step at a time matching my pace. I glanced towards Lou's bathroom door trying to determine if I had time to make it there before Warrick could get his hands on me and decided to take the chance.

I bolted in that direction, knowing Warrick picked up his pace, too. I barely made it behind the safety of the door when I felt him slam against it. A sob escaped my throat as I slid to the floor. Warrick may have kept any negative feelings towards me in check when Az was present, but now that he's gone, all bets are off.

"Val, don't shut me out," Warrick shouted from the other side of the door. "Please don't do this to me."

"Warrick," Lou started.

"Give us space, Lou. I'm just going to talk to her," Warrick snapped at him.

I heard a sigh followed by Lou's voice starting to fade as he walked away, "Just know the way you chased her in there isn't doing anything to build her confidence that you aren't going to try to hurt her. You guys have a history and it's starting to have an impact."

A soft thud sounded and I assumed it was from Warrick now resting his head against the door. I couldn't bring myself to move, anxiously waiting for Warrick to start talking again.

"Val, love," Warrick finally started after what felt like an eternity. He was talking in a hushed, calm tone that did nothing to hide the tiredness and sadness. "I'm sorry, I know there's so much running through your mind right now and you're thinking you can't quite trust me anymore. What I'm about to say is the truth. Az hasn't been around me in a long time and he has no idea what's been going on in my life. I've only ever been in one serious relationship, which you know about. Even then, I didn't sleep around. I don't go calling every woman 'love' nor do I tell them I'm fated to them. I take that topic incredibly seriously."

He sighed then went on, "This is what Az does. He plays head games to get an upper hand. He wants to drive you to him because he wants what we have, but he's also convinced you're the key to this war. Why? I don't know. Maybe it's something your dad told him or something Az pieced together on his own. It all boils down to the same thing, which is getting an edge. This is telling me we're getting close to being able to take him down and he's getting scared. Otherwise, he wouldn't have shown his face and he wouldn't have put on that fucking show. Az, like always, got what he wanted. He shook you up, got me to fight him, and caused chaos then left like nothing happened."

I took that in trying to trust his words, but I was still having a hard time trying to determine who to believe. I looked towards the ceiling, "Playing head games must run in the family, then. What I have a hard time believing is that someone who looks the way you do, has the kind of money you have, and plays his cards close wasn't surrounded by women."

"I can see that," Warrick responded thoughtfully. "I stuck to myself a lot, though. Then Az started this war and that became my focus. I didn't care about dating or having sex. I didn't care if someone saw me with women on my arm. Very much the opposite of Bruce Wayne."

That one got me to smile a little bit and I'm sure he knew it.

"Please, love, open the door. I want to make sure you're okay."

I took a deep breath to steady myself before asking, "If I open this door, I'm not going to end up with your hands around my neck?"

"No, I promise. I was never planning on hurting you. I realize my reaction that trapped you in here was wrong," Warrick said with a hint of emotion in his voice.

I turned my head pressing my cheek against the cool, wooden surface of the door, "Why did you do it, then?"

"I was feeling wild and crazed. My wolf wasn't happy with that fight and he was a little too close to the surface for comfort. Not a good excuse, I know," he sighed.

"Warrick, you can't do that to me. Not after everything that's happened between us."

"I know and I'm sorry," he responded quickly.

I sat there contemplating my next move. I could take a risk and open the door to face him, or I could lock myself in here for the rest of the night until Warrick left. While the latter option sounded more appealing, I listened to the small voice telling me to let him in. I put some space between myself and the door as I opened it a crack. Warrick's icy blue eyes widened with surprise the moment he saw me. He scrambled so he was on his hands and knees facing me. It was surprising seeing him still covered in bruises and blood. His nose must have been broken because he still had black eyes, and if I looked close enough, his nose was slightly crooked.

I dropped my gaze, fully opening the door so he could come in. I wasn't expecting him to rush me, crushing me into a hug, but there we were. Warrick had me completely wrapped in his arms, his face buried into my neck, and I was curled against his body. The only thing keeping us up was the tub.

"I love you, Val. Your past doesn't change that. I don't ever want you to think that'll change or that I'm just using you," Warrick breathed into my neck.

I ran my fingers through his hair, "I love you, too, Warrick. There's a part of me who knows what Az was doing, but the other part of me who's been terrified this whole time was louder."

Warrick pulled back a little cradling my face, his eyes searching mine, "It didn't help he took advantage of you, putting you in a dangerous situation. Are you okay, love?"

I took another deep breath, "Yeah, just more shaken than anything. I'm embarrassed. I'm scared. I'm just feeling all the things right now."

"You have cuts all over," Warrick observed.

I looked at my arms taking in the small cuts. I had completely forgotten about those until now. I looked back up at him, "They're small, but I should get cleaned up. So should you."

"I'm fine," Warrick said caressing my cheek.

"Warrick, your nose is still broken. You're covered in blood."

He rested his head on my shoulder, "I know. I'll take care of that when I get home."

Warrick sat back on the floor, and we sat there in silence, watching each other. A few more minutes passed then Warrick stood up offering me his hand, "I should go, love."

"Okay," I said finally on my feet.

He gave my hand a squeeze as he gave me a quick kiss on my forehead. When he pulled away, Warrick said, "Get cleaned up. I'll see you in the morning."

As he walked away, I suddenly felt alone. My arms wound their way around my stomach as I sank back down the ground. *What the fuck happened tonight?* Az stirred some things up in me I had kept tucked away. It surprisingly hurt to see him as a completely different person from who I thought I knew.

Warrick, thankfully, proved he's different, but it was still conflicting to watch him tonight. I mean, I was definitely feeling like I made a mistake there. If I were with Lou, I'd probably have avoided all of this and maybe I'd have a shred of sanity left in me.

I groaned letting my head fall back to rest on the edge of the tub.

"You okay?" Lou asked.

"Yeah, just coming down from everything that happened. Is everyone still out there?" I asked.

"They all went back to your house," he answered. Lou sat next to me on the floor, "I take it things are good between you and Warrick again? He left looking better than when he came in."

I sighed turning my head to look at him, "I guess, but it's still a little murky."

"A lot of feelings must've been stirred up tonight."

A laugh escaped my lips as I went back to staring at the ceiling, "What did Jennie tell you?"

Lou ran a hand through his hair, "Quite a bit, actually. You and Azrael have some history."

"Yeah, we do," I agreed.

"Do you think he misses you and that's why he was acting the way he was tonight?"

I sat up, wringing my hands together, "Maybe? I've never seen that side of him. I just don't know how much of what he said was true and how much was just to stir the pot."

"That's fair," Lou nodded his head. "You may have thought you made a mistake, but I don't think we would ever work out in that way."

"What do you mean?"

"You have a type, you know that, right? And I definitely don't fit in that picture," Lou gently elbowed me.

I snapped my head up at him to find him grinning. I laughed again, shaking my head when I realized he was messing with me, "What? Dark, moody, and unstable?"

Lou shook his head, "I don't know how Gabriel was, but I wasn't going to put a label on your preference of men."

"Whatever," I shook my head, getting up smiling. "I should head back and see how everyone else is doing. They shouldn't have been forced to see all that. Can I have a ride?"

"Sure," Lou said following me towards the exit. "Just know you aren't going to be able to shelter them forever, especially if they're joining you on this journey."

"I can still try."

Lou dropped me off at the house and I walked in to find Jennie and Bev still up sharing a bottle of wine. Bev pointed to an empty glass, "Gonna join us?"

"Yeah, but let me get cleaned up first. I'm tired of smelling like alcohol and there's blood that doesn't belong on me," I answered.

I took a quick shower hissing at the sting from the cuts, and was back downstairs before Jennie and Bev could finish off what was in their glasses. Jennie patted the space in between them while she filled my glass with a little more than usual. I started to protest, but she shook her head, "You need this more than we do tonight."

"I'm sorry you guys had to see that," I blurted. I was embarrassed by what went down and could only imagine how they felt.

"Why?" Bev asked. "You didn't do anything wrong. It should be Azrael apologizing to us, not you."

"I can't believe Az changed that much," Jennie said before taking a sip.

"Yeah," I nodded. "I'm with you there."

"How was he before?" Bev asked.

"He was honestly my favorite out of all the guy's Val had seen before shit hit the fan," Jennie started. She polished off what was left in her glass and refilled before continuing, "Az was so kind and loving. He took care of Val in every way possible. She was really grieving at the time, but he never made her feel bad. He never told her to move on. Val's parents loved him. Everyone approved, even Daryl, who was always the hardest one to convince."

We sat there in silence for a moment missing our friend. Jennie was the first to break the quiet moment, looking at me, "On a lighter note, can I just say you know how to find the sexiest men?"

I let out a bark of laughter and drank about half of my glass before responding, "They may be hot, but they have *a lot* of issues. Can't forget about the red flags. I mean, Warrick and Az are walking red flags, and yet, I can't seem to stay away. You know Lou mentioned I have a type?"

Jennie giggled, "Yeah you do."

"Okay, catch me up here. What's your type?" Bev asked.

Jennie held up a finger and ran upstairs. When Bev looked at me confused, I just shrugged my shoulders. Jennie didn't leave us for too long, returning with a couple of pictures in her hand. She spread them on the table, pointing to the one on the left then moving to the right, she said, "Let me introduce you to Gabriel. Az. And now, Warrick."

Looking at the three of them next to each other, I instantly knew what Lou was talking about. They each had dark hair, handsome faces, were built, and looked like they had a darker side. Bev let out a whistle, "Damn, Val, you like the bad, brooding type. I could see that by looks alone, but personalities? Are they really all the same?"

"I think two out of the three are pretty similar considering they're brothers and all," I said. "But, Gabriel was very different from the rest of them."

"In what ways? If you don't mind me asking," Bev looked at me.

I sighed, "He was the kindest person you could meet. He wouldn't hurt a fly and was one of the hardest workers I knew. That man never did anything toxic or abusive or anything that falls under the red flag category unlike the other two, clearly."

Bev stared into her glass before looking back up at me, "Not trying to be mean, Val, you could just have a little bias. Jennie, is that really how he was?"

"Oh yeah," Jennie nodded her head vigorously. "I mean those of us close to Val weren't happy when he got her riding bikes, but that man had the sweetest soul."

Silence settled around us. We all took a few more sips waiting for someone to start the conversation again. Deciding to be that person, I reached over to Jennie's hand, giving it a squeeze, "I really am sorry about Chris."

She stared at her glass playing with the stem, her face and tone matching in seriousness, "Before you came home tonight, Bev and I were talking about everything that's happened since the bombing, but we were mostly focused on what's happened since being back here this time. How do you handle all of this?"

"Handle what?" I asked, not quite following where she was going.

Jennie brought her eyes up to mine, tears threatening to spill over, "How do you handle all the death, threats, and attacks so well? I mean, out of all of us, you've definitely gone through it. Despite all of that, you're still standing and moving forward. How?"

"Oh," I said taking my turn to focus on the glass in front of me. I gave it a twirl thinking about how I was going to approach this. I didn't feel like I was handling anything. I felt like I was a rope finally fraying, approaching the end of what I can take. "Bear with me for a minute because I know you're going to try to dispute me. I'm not handling it well. I've honestly felt like I've been chewed up and spit out, literally and figuratively. It started when I got Daryl's head delivered to me wrapped up with a fucking bow. Then, I got out of this world and felt like I was living in paradise with Lou until Warrick showed up. Between him and Lou, I got beat up pretty good. Add in Lou getting close to Melody sending me into a reckless spiral that ended with me almost dying and I just about broke. Jennie, you saw how I was. I still have nightmares and jump when anything goes bump in the night. Hell, in the fae world, I almost got dragged under the sand. Then, I come back here and I feel like I broke up your engagement. Add in the shit from tonight, and we have the perfect disaster that is me."

I paused to take a sip then jumped right back in, "I haven't hardly been here for you guys. I haven't been around to talk about how you all have been feeling with the world falling down around us. I'm not the only one who feels like home is no longer home. I'm lucky to have this house jumping with me, but I don't feel like I can live life back in that world anymore. I can't even imagine what's been running through all your minds when it comes to figuring out what life looks like after this is all said and done. I find a way to keep going because I feel like the best gift I can give in return for everything you guys have done for me is to try to get you back to some sort of normalcy. I've felt so lucky to be able to find you as quick as I have when there are so many places you could've ended up."

"Well," Bev said after she was sure I was done. "Joe and I appreciate all you've done for us because it's been a lot. We've been thinking of planting our roots here because, like you, we don't know what we'd be going back to in our world. Even if our house was still standing, I don't know that I'd want to live in a world so boring after seeing all of this. You've brought more excitement into our lives than anything we could've done. Yeah, it's sucked losing people along the way and dealing with crazies like Az, but we're still standing, right, Jennie?"

Jennie swiped at her eyes, "Yeah. I know I haven't said the best things to you, but you've been fighting like hell for all of us. You make it look so easy; I had no idea you were still feeling like that. The only time you ever showed how you were truly feeling was after Melody rescued you. I guess my question was more coming from a place of struggling with all these crazy changes at once while losing those we love."

"Well, I for one, am glad Chris is now out of the picture," Bev said leaning back in her chair taking a long drink.

"That's harsh," I muttered under my breath.

"That's because Jennie has a shot at Lou now, right?" Bev asked cocking an eyebrow.

Jennie's jaw dropped and I burst out laughing. Bev stood up to grab another bottle, "If I were in your shoes, I wouldn't complain."

"Does Joe hear you talk like this?" I asked, giving Jennie a chance to piece some sort of response together.

Bev giggled, "Yeah. He doesn't mind. He actually agrees. It's like we're watching our favorite reality shows play out in front of us with all the relationship drama. You don't need to worry about us, Val. We're happier than we've ever been."

"Hold on," Jennie finally said. "What makes you think I'd have a shot at Lou? He's still so wrapped up in Val. You saw him tonight."

I shook my head, "I think you've had some blinders on when it comes to him. Lou and I have already made it clear we aren't ever going to work out in that capacity. It's only the friend zone from here on out."

"He's also become super protective of you, Jennie," Bev said settling back in her chair. "And don't think I don't catch the little glances you steal of him and vice versa."

A smile slowly crept across my face as I said, "Being with a werewolf will change your life. There's no going back after that."

"Val!" Jennie blushed giving me a light smack on the arm.

"Let's not forget that one of your wishes came true," I teased.

Confused, Jennie asked, "What are you talking about?"

"As intense as it may have been, you not only got to see Warrick naked, but you got to see Lou, too," I casually took a sip of my wine finishing what was in the glass.

Jennie's faced turned redder than a tomato while Bev burst into a fit of giggles. When she composed herself, Bev joined in, "That's right! You're already one step closer to getting with him."

"You guys are relentless," Jennie said trying her best to hide a smile.

"Busted," I called her out. "That smile tells us everything we need to know."

"And what exactly is that?"

Bev laughed, "You enjoyed what you saw."

Jennie shook her head but didn't say anything to deny it. A few more giggles escaped from us as Bev and I kept giving Jennie a hard time. She eventually got over whatever was making her embarrassed and joined in.

"Oh, this has been a great way to end a weird night," Bev smiled.

"We really haven't had girl talk like this in a while," I observed.

"It has been nice," Jennie nodded her head. "Val?"

"Hmm?"

"I'm glad you're doing okay, even if things still feel really hard to keep moving forward," Jennie gave my arm a squeeze.

"Thanks. I'm glad you two are hanging in there, too," I reached for both of their hands.

We talked a little more about Joe and Bev starting to try for kids and the plan to try and get Jennie and Lou on a date. Bev moved to put her glass in the sink, yawning. When she turned back around, she yawned again, "I think it's time to sleep. Goodnight, ladies. Thanks for hanging out."

"Goodnight, Bev," Jennie and I called in unison.

I pulled out my phone to shoot a text to Warrick to let him know I'd be coming over whether or not he wants me there. The conversation with Jennie and Bev stirred up questions of my own and I knew I wouldn't be able to wait for answers.

"Booty call?" Jennie asked with raised eyebrows.

"Actually, no," I put my phone on the table. "More like I have questions that I want answers to. I can't think of having sex after the stunt Az pulled."

"Well, I'm going to head up to bed, too," Jennie moved to get out of her chair. "Take that bottle with you."

"Aye, aye, captain," I gave her a little salute.

I checked my phone not surprised to not see any response then checked outside. The roads were dry and it didn't look like there was any threat of inclement weather, so I threw on some riding gear and rode over to Warrick's apartment. It may not be the smartest thing to do right now, but I can't ignore this tugging feeling in my gut. I tested the door handle finding it unlocked. I cracked open the door giving a little knock, calling out to the dark apartment, "Warrick?"

He still had the Christmas decorations up, the glow of the lights keeping the place from being completely shrouded in darkness. I stepped in closing the door behind me, "Hello?"

I took one more step into the space but froze the moment my foot crunched on glass. I crouched down to try to see what I had stepped on and was greeted with the smell of whiskey. I scanned the rest of the space before taking any further steps. It looked like some of his furniture was out of place. There were a few more broken things littered about the living room. I shot a text to Lou letting him know I was over at Warrick's and that something was up. *Shit, I hope he's not losing it right now or worse.*

My phone buzzed with a response from Lou: *Are you surprised? He's having to face the only person who can hurt him.*

My fingers flew across the screen: *No, something's really wrong. I don't think he's at his place and things are smashed up. I can't get ahold of him either.*

How smashed?

Broken glass on the floor. Furniture out of place.

Maybe he's just been drinking and taking his anger out on his stuff.

Maybe.

Staying in my spot, I listened for anything to indicate any signs of life only to be met with silence as I shoved my phone in my pocket. Rolling my shoulders back and taking a deep breath, I took a few more steps into his place, "Anyone home?"

I finally heard footsteps approaching from the hallway. I put my helmet and my bag holding the bottle of wine on the counter and turned to face the dark space, "Is everything okay?"

"Of course, I'm doing fine, but I have no idea where you chased Warrick off to," Az answered.

Chapter 3

"What the hell are you doing here, Az? And how did you even get in here?" I asked taking a step back and running into the island.

He was out in the light now, his sinister smile on full display, "I don't think that's what you should be concerned about right now."

He was right. I was in Warrick's apartment alone with Azrael. I was no match for his strength and he could do whatever the hell he wants to me without anyone trying to stop him. I glanced at the front door. I wasn't that far away and there was still some good distance between myself and Az, but I had a hunch he would be able to catch up to me before I could make it. I had to take that chance because if I didn't, he would definitely get his hands on me.

I grabbed my helmet bolting towards the door. Hope ignited in me as my fingers grasped the handle. I was going to make it out of here before Az could catch me.

The second I twisted the door handle he slammed into me. I was pressed up against the door trying not to panic any more than I already was as I felt any hope slip away.

"You hesitated a little too long," Az laughed in my ear. "What are you going to do now that Warrick isn't here to stop me?"

"What do you want with me?"

To my surprise, he got off me. Much to my dismay, on the other hand, Az still had a tight grip on my wrists pulling me away from the door. He pushed me onto the couch in the living room grabbing the bottle of wine as he joined me. Az worked the cork out then took a swig. When he offered me the bottle, he said, "Now, that's a loaded question. We really need to work on getting more specific in your asks. Drink."

I shook my head no and he grabbed the back of my head yanking my hair back. My mouth opened to protest only to be filled with the bottle. Wine rushed down my throat, the sweet drink turning sour on my tongue. "That wasn't a question," he snarled.

By the time he let me go, I was coughing, struggling to catch my breath. Az took another swig then set the bottle on the table. He leaned back sighing and throwing his arms along the back of the couch, "That's more like it. Don't let me drink alone tonight, Val."

"What the hell is wrong with you?" I asked with a raspy voice, my hand rubbing my throat. There was still wine stuck back there threatening to send me into another coughing fit.

"A lot of things. Where do you want to start?" Az cocked an eyebrow at me.

"What did you do to Warrick?"

He stroked his facial hair bringing his gaze to meet mine, "I don't remember you asking this many questions. Relax, take a load off."

I rolled my eyes at him and looked out the window, "You better not have hurt him."

"What are you going to do if I did?" Az shot back, poison lacing every word. "Besides, he wasn't even here when I arrived, and before you make assumptions, this was how I found his place."

"You've given me no reason to believe you," I said looking back at him.

"I see you still ride," Az jerked his head towards my helmet on the floor. He pointed to the bottle, "Remember, don't let me drink alone tonight."

"I don't want any more and of course I still ride," I said scooting away from him. If I moved slowly enough without revealing my intentions, I might be able to make it out of here.

"I told you to drink, Val. I know you can," Az thrust the bottle into my hand while closing the distance I just created. *Damn it.* It was too much to hope for him not to catch on to what I'm doing.

I glared at him while taking a long drink from the bottle. I slammed it back down on the table, "Happy?"

"Very."

"You still never answered my question," I pointed out.

He rested his head on the couch closing his eyes, "Which one?"

"Any of them, but the first one is the one I need to know the answer to."

Az grinned and chuckled, "There's a lot of things I want to do with you. Things that would make most blush, but I also want information out of you. Don't bother asking anymore questions tonight. I'm done with that game."

Warrick was right about one thing. Someone encouraged Az to go down the path that led to me. Why? I had no idea. He hadn't moved for a little while, so I pulled out my phone to send texts to Jennie, Warrick, and Lou. They needed to know what was happening in case Az makes me disappear tonight.

"You text anyone and I will make your worst fears come true," he threatened. Az sat back up, polished off the wine and headed into the kitchen to try to find another bottle. When he called me out, I pretended to put my phone away, but his back was turned to me. This was my chance. Az pinned me down to the couch as soon as my fingers started typing out a message to Lou, catching me off-guard with how fast and quietly he came back over to me. He ripped my phone out of my hand and threw it against the island, my smashed phone adding to the debris already littering the floor.

A growl ripped from his throat, "You really don't know how to listen, do you?"

He forced me to drink more wine, not getting off me. Az took another sip then started unzipping my jacket, "We'll be here for a while, might as well get comfortable."

I grabbed his hand stopping him. There was no way I was going to let him take off any of my clothes tonight, "I'd like to leave this on."

"I'm sure you would, but you don't have a lot of say in that, do you?"

Panic gripped my throat making it hard to speak. Forcing the words out, I said, "Just tell me what you're going to do, Az. I can at least mentally prepare for this shit show."

"I'm hurt, Val," Az said in a mocking tone. "First, you don't remember me. Now, you won't even enjoy some time with me."

I squirmed underneath the weight of him, "You're starting to hurt me."

"Good," he sneered, his face within inches of mine. "You hurt me, Val. This is only fair."

"Hold on," I countered, anger starting to overtake the panic. "You were the one who left me without anything. You were just gone. Disappeared. Don't start this fucking pity party with me especially when you show back up in my life like this."

A popping noise rang out through the apartment. I was now staring at the bottle on the table, my cheek burning. I didn't even see his hand move before it connected with my face. "I'm getting tired of this bullshit. Let's liven things up, shall we?" Az mumbled.

Still in shock, I didn't realize he was back to unzipping my jacket. This time, he wasn't as gentle. He pulled me by my shirt, "This is my game now. Do as I say and it shouldn't be too bad."

"Can I at least have more wine?" I forced out.

"Here," he shoved the bottle back in my mouth. At least this time I was a little more prepared. I swallowed about half of the almost full bottle by the time he yanked it away and finished it.

He pushed me back onto the couch as his lips crashed into mine. I closed my eyes wishing for the wine to hit me. Wishing for someone to knock on the door when the only person who knows how to get here is the one who disappeared. Wishing for this to already be over.

Az pulled back, "You know what would be even better? If I *fucked* you on my brother's bed. He'll be stuck smelling our scents entangled in one another."

"No, you're not fucking me tonight," I said. I knew he wasn't going to listen to my protests, but I had to try.

"Nice try," he laughed, a wicked sound that made me want to be sick.

Az got off me and I started to scramble away from him. I was almost off the couch when he grabbed my ankles. He dragged me over to the kitchen pausing to grab yet another bottle of wine. I took advantage of him being distracted trying to crawl away again. I heard him chuckle before he yanked me back to him, "This is going to be fun."

On our way to Warrick's room, Az didn't take any care to keep me from going over the glass on the floor adding to the cuts already on my body. I started to scream for help the closer we got to Az's desired destination. I thought I had a chance, but now that my only escape was out of my line of sight, I had to find another way out of here. I had to try to get some of the other residents' attention.

"With the money Warrick pays for this apartment, no one's going to hear you. This place is soundproof," Az said as he tossed me on the bed.

I kicked a leg out hitting him between his legs. He grunted in pain and doubled over. I scrambled off the bed and tried running for the door, but the wine made my legs feel like noodles. There was no way they could support my weight with how fast I wanted to move.

"I could work with this. Come back here," Az grasped my hair to pull me on the bed. I let out another scream, this time from pain rather than trying to get someone's attention.

Az was back on top of me, lips finding their way back to mine. Not kissing him back earned me another slap, "You're only going to make this harder on yourself if you don't play along."

"I can give you information," I blurted. "I'll tell you whatever you want to know if you just stop."

"We're way past that, but that was a nice attempt," he smirked. "I changed my mind about what I want from you tonight, and most importantly, I changed what tactic I wanted to use to get under Warrick's skin. I want him on my team more than whatever information it is you think you have."

Az studied me for a moment, "Now, where were we?"

His hands rubbed up and down my sides then over my chest until his fingers gripped my collar. He yanked and the sound of my shirt ripping filled the room. I watched his pupils dilate at the sight of my nearly naked torso beneath him. Az skimmed my bra making my nipples harden to a point. With a husky voice, he said, "Look, you even dressed for the occasion. Will I find the matching thong?"

I tried to shove at his chest, but despite my best efforts, he didn't budge. I tried again, "Get off of me, Az."

He shook his head, "No can do. If you just relaxed, you know I could make this feel good."

"I don't want to feel this. I want you off me."

"Fine," Az said as he slowly backed off the bed. His fingers hooked into the waistband of my pants trying to yank them off. They didn't budge earning a frustrated growl, "I can appreciate these pants looking like they were made for you, but they have to go."

Az managed to unbutton my pants, my legs exposed in an instant and a happy look back on Az's face, "I should've known what the answer was to my question."

"Please stop," I forced out. I couldn't breathe any more.

He stood up and I felt my panicked heart rate slow for a little bit. I tried to flip over to make another escape attempt, but he grabbed one of my arms out from under me. I fell on my face and was flipped over, pinned on my back. He wagged his finger scolding me for once again trying to run. Az leaned over me placing his forearm across my throat. I picked up on the silent warning: try to run and he crushes my throat, stay and all I will feel is a slight pressure against my windpipe.

He pulled his shirt over his head with one arm, replacing the arm holding me down with the other one so as to not chance me running away. All his tattoos were on full display now along with his muscles. Az looked stronger than the last time I had seen him, the hard lines showcasing that strength. Another somber reminder I stood no chance at getting out of here on my terms.

Az watched me with anticipation as he undid his belt and unbuttoned his pants, arm still holding its position on my throat. Tears came spilling out as I continued to plead with him. Every time I opened my mouth, I was met with cruel laughter. The Az I knew was completely gone at this point.

He reluctantly lifted his arm away from my neck so he could completely undress. Even though I knew I wasn't going to be making it far, I tried to crawl away again. This time I got to the other side of the bed almost to the edge.

"You're the perfect piece of prey," his words washed over me, coating me in slime. "Every time you run, you just make me want you more."

Then he was grabbing my waist from behind. Az jerked my arms behind me, my shoulders screaming in pain at the sudden movement. He pressed a knee into my back burying my face into the comforter and filling my nose with Warrick's scent while he secured my wrists with some piece of fabric, making me cry harder. Satisfied with the security of the restraint, Az lifted off and moved so he was directly behind me.

I flipped my head to look out the window. The sun was just starting to rise, filling the sky with purples, oranges, and pinks. I told myself to focus on this and Az's torture would soon be over. He slid my thong down exposing me to the cool air. Az moaned while he slid his fingers in between my legs.

Sobbing at this point, I begged him to stop. He pushed my head down into the bed. "Shut the fuck up or I'll make it hurt," Az hissed into my ear.

I whimpered in response. His cock teased my entrance, but he stopped when I was expecting him to thrust in. Az was still pressing my head down when I heard a click.

"I will kill you, Azrael. I will fucking kill you right *fucking* now if you don't get off her," Warrick calmly said.

That only earned a laugh from Az, "You think you're going to kill me with that? What? It has a few silver bullets? Try me."

Az moved so he was closer to me. The hand holding my head down moved to my neck and yanked me up. I felt as his lips curled into a smile, "I dare you to try me."

Warrick looked insane. His hair was everywhere, those blue eyes wild. Yet, he held the gun steadily, aimed at Az and me. I watched as his hand squeezed the trigger. The bang made my ears ring. I let out a scream and felt blood splatter on to me. Shaking, I looked down as far as Az's hand would let me. The blood wasn't coming from me, thankfully. It was coming a large hole in Az's arm.

"That stung," he hissed in my ear. "Too bad it won't last for long."

I couldn't believe my eyes as the bullet slid out of the wound and his skin closed. Warrick had started to drop the gun confident he had made a point, but when he watched the same thing I did, his eyes widened and he quickly took aim again. Several more shots rang out only to end up with the same results. Az instantly healed like nothing had happened.

"Thanks to Holly and some other friends, I now have an advantage against those special bullets you made," Az said with a cocky air to his voice.

Warrick shot at Az until the gun ran out and all we heard were clicks. Knowing the coast was clear, Az came out from hiding. Still holding me by the neck, he sneered at his brother, "Well, this has certainly been a fun experiment. Since you can't beat me right now, why don't you join in on the fun?"

More tears ran down my cheeks, "Please stop, Az. I'm begging you."

"I like when you beg," Az responded in a husky voice as he traced my jawline.

"Get the fuck out of my house!" Warrick screamed. He bounded over to the bed in a blink of an eye grabbing Az by his hair and bashing the gun into his head. Blood trickled on to my shoulder from where Warrick hit Az.

"Alright," Az mumbled massaging the already healed spot. "Don't have to be so aggressive."

Warrick and I were stunned as Az let me go, slowly exiting the apartment. He was so close to getting something he wanted, but Az just walked away. No questions asked. No protesting. He just left.

"Warrick? Talk to me," a voice said from the phone.

"Is that Lou?" I croaked.

Warrick locked eyes with me as he lifted the phone closer to his mouth, "Yeah, Lou. I'm here. I got in at the right time."

"Do you have eyes on Val? Is she okay?" Lou asked.

Warrick moved closer to me, "I'm looking right at her. She'll be fine. Just shaken up more than anything."

There was a sigh on the other side of the line, "I can't tell you how relieved I am she's still there. I'm assuming Az walked out unscathed?"

"Unfortunately. Look, I'll tell you more in our meeting later after I've gathered my thoughts and taken care of a few more things. The important thing is that I handled the situation. By the way, put distance between yourself and Holly. My hunch was right. Pass that message along."

He didn't give Lou the chance to say anything else. The phone clicked ending the call. Warrick tossed the gun aside, cradling my face and ignoring my flinch at his touch, "What are you doing over here, love? What happened?"

I smelt the alcohol on his breath, but he wasn't nearly as drunk as what he had been back on Sarind's island. There was no sign of the asshole I had seen before. Nothing to add to the panic already running through me. My voice wobbled as I asked, "Where were you?"

He wiped away the new tears and sat next to me, "Clearly I had an outburst, but then I decided I needed to run some errands."

"In the middle of the night?" I asked trying to cover myself with shaky arms.

Warrick saw what I was trying to do and went over to his closet. When he came back to where I was sitting, he handed me one of his hoodies keeping his eyes on the ground. I tossed it on instantly grateful for the warmth and comfort it provided. He sat back down and looked out the windows, "Not the typical errands. I'll explain more about that later, but what were you doing here? Why did you come to my place? And what happened?"

I drew in a shaky breath twisting the sleeves around in circles trying to calm my nerves. I followed Warrick's gaze out the windows, "I was worried about you. I wanted to make sure you were okay and I wanted to talk through what had happened at Lou's with, with Az. How was it even possible for him to get in here?"

"He's upped his game. By a lot," Warrick sighed. "It shouldn't be a surprise that he's good with tech, too. Az bypassed all my security systems before I had a chance to make any upgrades."

Warrick started to reach for me, but stopped when I flinched again. I stood up, his hoodie doing more than enough to cover me, "I think I'm going to try to sleep. I'm sorry, Warrick, I just can't talk about this right now. I'm sorry for adding one more thing to your plate to worry about. I'll head out of here when I wake up. I just can't drive right now."

"Val, stop," Warrick stood up. "There's nothing for you to be sorry for. Take as much time as you need. You don't need to run off, love."

I nodded. The tears wouldn't stop now, so I turned and made my way to his guest room. He was slowly trailing after me, but when I closed the door and locked it, he left me alone.

I curled up on the bed staring out these windows not letting myself think. I eventually fell asleep, but my dreams were filled with Az's sneering face and the feel of his rough hands on me.

I jolted up in the bed when I heard yelling coming from Warrick's home office. He sounded pissed, and as much as I wanted to stay in the safety of this locked room, curiosity got the better of me. I wandered down the hall still only wearing his hoodie and paused when I was outside of his office. I had no idea how long I had been out for, rubbing the sleep out of my eyes as I leaned against the wall.

"Stop playing that innocent game, Holly. I'll be heading in there soon. So help me if I see your ass still in that chair," Warrick said through clenched teeth.

There was some stammering coming through the speaker of his phone as he furiously typed away on his computer. When there was a pause in Holly's protests, Warrick slammed a fist on his desk, "I don't give a fuck! You should've thought about that before you partnered with Az. If I see your face anywhere near the office, the pizza place, or Val and her friends, I will kill you. No hesitation, and I won't make it quick either."

Warrick ended that call immediately jumping on another one. A man's voice answered. Warrick didn't waste any time with pleasantries, "You need to roll out the upgraded system now. New badges for everyone, except for Holly. She's terminated effective immediately. I also emailed you a list of people the system can't let in."

"Do you need it installed at your place, boss?"

Warrick shook his head, "No, I already have that taken care of. Also, we're going to have some visitors. Their information is contained in a separate email that you should have in your inbox."

"Got it."

"Thank you," Warrick ended the call. He ran a hand through his hair smoothing it back. I don't know if he had slept at all, but he looked much more refreshed than what I had seen in the early hours of this morning. He turned back around so he was facing the door, straightening when he saw me, "Hi, love. How are you doing?"

"I don't want to be alone," I said in a quiet voice. "I can't sleep. I just see his face."

He crossed the room, "Can I put an arm around you?"

I nodded. Warrick wrapped a comforting arm around me, leading me to a chair to sit. He returned to his desk chair, sighing, "You know I have security cameras in here, right?"

"Not until now," I answered unable to meet his gaze.

His voice softened, "I'm only telling this to let you know that nothing happens in here without me knowing."

"Then where the hell were you? Why didn't you get here sooner?" There was no hiding the anger in my voice.

Warrick dragged a hand down his face, "My signal was spotty. I didn't get the notifications until I was already almost at the door."

"Why were you on the phone with Lou?" I asked wanting to change the focus of the conversation.

He rummaged in a drawer for a second, pulling out a box as he said, "Lou wouldn't stop calling me, so by the time I had a strong enough signal, I finally answered. He was in a panic not knowing how to get to you and your phone was going straight to voicemail. The broken phone on the ground explains that, so here, take a new one before Lou loses his damn mind."

I accepted the box Warrick had just pulled out, turning on the new phone. It was exactly like my old one, phone numbers included. I looked back up at him, "How?"

"I was able to rescue the sim card."

"Well, thank you," I said putting the phone down.

He leaned on the desk, "Val, I'm not going to let that happen to you again."

"And how exactly do you plan to do that? I know I'm being harsh right now, but I'm being realistic. Unless you're with me 24/7, you're not going to be able to make that promise. Even then, you haven't been a match for Az and I don't want to risk you dying for the sake of me. Not when there's so much at stake," I leaned back in my chair.

He winced, but nodded, "Just felt like the right thing to say, I guess, but you do have a point."

"Warrick, I'm hurting right now. I'm scared shitless, but I will be fine. I always recover," I assured him. "We can't change what happened, we can only move forward. At least I'm not bleeding out this time."

He shook his head, "Fair enough."

"What's the plan now?" I asked successfully changing topics this time.

"Are you up for going into the office? I need you at a meeting," Warrick asked returning his attention to his computer.

While I was trying to decide how to respond, he typed for a little bit until he looked at me waiting for an answer. I reluctantly nodded, "I have no clothes to wear unless I go back home."

"I have you covered, if you trust me," he said moving to stand up. I gave him another nod following him into his closet. Out of the corner of my eye, I noticed he had completely new furniture in here, and I couldn't help but wonder if he replaced everything else with Az's scent on it while I was asleep.

Warrick handed me a hanger with clothes fit for a business meeting: an airy, long-sleeved white blouse and black dress pants. He dug around his closet producing a shoe box containing grey pumps. I took what he was holding out to me and started working on changing in the bathroom. While my back was turned, he snuck in a fresh pair of underwear and a bra.

I met him out in the living room in the fresh clothes he provided, noting the new furniture in here, too. *Guess he wanted to get rid of any reminders of what his brother attempted.*

"Ready, love?" Warrick asked, handing me my riding gear.

"Yeah, I guess," I quietly answered. I had no idea what kind of meeting I needed to be present for, but I'm hoping it doesn't take that long. I'm also hoping he isn't sliding me in as the replacement for his assistant.

I followed Warrick into the parking garage and pulled my bike into the empty space next to him. Throwing all my gear into my bag and putting on the heels, we made our way up to the top floor walking through the last door before getting to Warrick's office, stepping foot into a boardroom. I almost tripped, and when I looked up, I felt all the blood drain from my body. Liam gave me a little finger wave while Cian glared at me. I turned around to leave only to run into Warrick's chest. "Is this some sort of sick joke?" I hissed at him.

"You're safe here, love. Please, turn around," Warrick said in a calm and quiet tone. "They aren't the only ones in this room."

"No," I shook my head. "I can't do this. Not after what just happened. I can't breathe, Warrick."

"Val?" a familiar voice asked.

Warrick watched me as my eyes widened. I slowly turned in the direction of the voice to find my dad standing there in his military attire.

Chapter 4

Nothing could've prepared me to see my dad standing in front of me. My legs slowly moved towards him, my hand covering my mouth as more tears threatened to spill over. The moment I was within arm's length, I reached out, letting my fingers settle on the crisp fabric of his uniform. "You're really here," I whispered.

My dad softly placed his hand over mine offering me a kind smile, "I really am."

He pulled me into a hug, temporarily lifting all the pain off my shoulders.

"This family reunion is nice and all, but can we get this started?" Cian asked impatiently.

My dad and I pulled back. I shot the two vampires a glare. Warrick cleared his throat, "James, Val, please take a seat."

I scanned the room seeing several pairs from different worlds seated around the table. Sarind and her second were there next to Liam and Cian. There were four other unfamiliar faces, though. Two looked like humans dressed in Medieval times clothing, insignias with dragons on their shoulders while the other two looked like elves from *Lord of the Rings*. My eyes finally landed on Lou who was sitting across from me on the other side of Warrick.

"Thank you all for coming on such short notice," Warrick started in a very business-like tone. "There's been some recent unfavorable developments and we need to think about moving fast. I've come to find the silver, venom coated bullets don't work on Az and I have my team diving into other potential weapon options. I've never seen a wolf heal like that from something that should do some serious damage. Az is a much bigger threat than what we originally thought and we need to take him down fast. The last thing we need to do is give him more time to become even more powerful. James, please fill us in on the changes from your world."

"Right," my dad nodded. As he spoke, he looked at everyone around the table, "Our world has seen a lot of destruction up to this point. I've tried to relocate as many people as possible without raising suspicions, but it's now getting to a point that I have to be very selective. Based on the damage and how fast we're losing our military strength, we'll be losing our world soon. His attacks are starting to get out of hand. He's no longer just focusing on major military bases. Now, he's targeting anyone and anything in his path relishing in the chaos he's causing."

"We need each of you to make sure you have your people ready on a moment's notice. When you leave today, you'll be given larger devices that have a bigger reach to allow you to transport more at once," Warrick cut in.

Cian tapped his fingers on the table, "Have you been able to recruit anyone else outside of who's here?"

"Unfortunately, no," Warrick shook his head. "I have one more world to visit, sooner rather than later, but that's my last target."

Everyone sat there in silence letting this information soak in. I could feel the tension in the room, but was tired of no one saying anything. I kept my eyes trained on the table surface as I asked, "How do you know your next round of weapons are going to have any shot of working?"

Warrick stood up and walked over to the wall of windows. It was a cloudy day, I'm sure something Cian and Liam are appreciative of, but no signs of any storms. Warrick stood there contemplating how he wanted to respond. He sighed, "I don't. There's no way of testing these. I'm just hoping to take a chance with what I have. Thanks to you, I have blood samples so the best I can do is test them to see if the weapons cause any sort of reaction."

I only nodded my head. It made sense he's going that path, but there's still a lot at risk in that not working.

"She *does* serve more of a purpose than just warming your bed, Warrick," Cian said. "Poor Liam was hoping to get his shot this time around."

My head snapped up to find Liam grinning at me. Warrick's head whipped around, a growl rumbling low in his chest as he stalked back to his seat at the head of the table placing his hands on the table, "This is neither the time nor the place for that shit, Cian. Move on from what happened. Val has, you can too."

My dad was watching me carefully. "What is he talking about, Val?" he whispered.

Not daring to take my eyes off the two vampires, I answered, "We have a lot to catch up on."

"Your little girl isn't as innocent as you think," Liam chuckled.

"Can I circle back to something?" Sarind calmly interrupted from her seat. Everyone's heads turned to her, the tension fading away.

"Be my guest," Warrick said sitting back down in his chair.

"You mentioned our enemy has gotten more powerful. When you first came to me, you asked if I could see what the outlooks are or if I could try to see what would happen with him. There was a little bit of time where I could see those things, but now they're gone," Sarind explained furrowing her brows.

"What do you mean?" Warrick asked leaning forward.

"Anything I try to see that pertains to him results in nothing. I'm worried he might've gotten involved with an incredibly powerful group to help strengthen him," she hypothesized.

Cian turned to Warrick, "Which world did you say you were going to visit?"

Warrick ran a hand through his hair, "I didn't. I'm planning on going to the witch world. They would be a major advantage, but with what you're saying, Sarind, I'm worried he may have beat us there."

"I wish I could tell you if that were the case or not," Sarind mentioned.

"Don't worry about it," Warrick waived her off. He turned to Lou, "Do you have any issues with making a jump two days from now?"

"Why not sooner?" Lou asked.

"I'm trying to give you time to get your affairs in order before leaving again," Warrick said unable to hide the impatience.

"Sure," Lou nodded keeping his answer short.

"What's after the witch world?" one of the elves asked.

"We'll be heading to James' world," Warrick answered with no hesitation.

I sucked in a breath. I wasn't sure if I was ready to head back home yet, especially if it was as bad as my dad was saying.

No one said anything else, so Warrick stood back up, "Thank you all again for taking this time to talk through some strategy. Stick around a little longer if you can. I'd like to catch up with each of you to see how we can continue to support your groups."

Everyone joined him with getting out of their chairs. I couldn't wait to get out of this room away from Cian and Liam. I glanced at Warrick who nodded for me to come over to him while the others started talking amongst themselves. He placed a hand on my arm glancing at my dad approaching from behind me, "How are you holding up, love?"

"I'd like to get out of here. You don't need me anymore, do you?" I asked.

"No," he shook his head. Warrick removed his hand from my arm, extending it towards my dad, "Thank you, again. You helped drive the message home."

"Happy to help, Warrick. If you don't mind, though, I'd like to have a moment alone to catch up with my daughter," my dad said.

"By all means, please use my office. It's about the most private space you'll get," Warrick moved so we could make our exit.

I muttered another thanks and led us into his office, hung up on how formal Warrick was acting around my dad. I gave one last look towards the room we were just in. I guess Warrick was bringing everyone here last night which explains why his signal was spotty. After shutting Warrick's office door, my dad and I moved chairs over to the corner farthest from any doors to minimize any chances of being overheard. My dad studied me for a moment before looking around the space, "This place is a lot nicer than I thought it would be."

"The office or the world?"

"Both," he answered still looking around. He finally brought his attention back to me when he asked, "How are you holding up, Val-pal? You were pretty anxious getting into that boardroom and don't think I didn't notice those scars you've tried hiding under the makeup."

My dad has always been quick to pick up on when things were wrong with me. I let out a nervous laugh, "You don't miss anything, do you, dad?"

"Nope, so start filling me in," he ordered.

"What do you know so far?"

"Warrick only filled me in on who's with you, who we've lost, and what Az has been up to."

"Okay, I sighed. "I need you to promise me that you're not going to get all wound up and try to make things right. Like Warrick said back there, we've moved on and are leaving that shit in the past where it belongs."

My dad held out his hand for us to shake on it. I rubbed my hands on my legs, "Alright. I guess I'll go in order. I'm sure you're aware of Warrick attacking me once he found out I was trying to get info out of him."

"Unfortunately, yeah, and I'm sorry if I ever gave the impression I was okay with him killing you. That was all a ruse to get Az off my back. I am proud of you for finding ways to get into my system and get everything you need," he smiled at me.

"Took me a second, but Lou helped me eventually get it figured out. Anyways, I'll skip through reliving all that part and just jump to where Cian and Liam came in," I started. I took another steadying breath because my nerves were still wreaking havoc on me, then continued, "I decided to take out some of Cian's vampires and he didn't like it, so he got ahold of me with Warrick's help and put me through some torture."

"Is that why you have the scars?" he asked with a stern tone.

I slowly nodded, "Unfortunately. Cian basically decided to bleed me out and Liam got to have some fun. Nothing really happened in Sarind's world, thankfully. At least nothing crazy negative, but what are your thoughts on Warrick?"

My dad leaned back crossing his arms, "He's a loose cannon, let's his anger take hold of him too quickly, and he's aggressive. I can't leave out the fact he's crazy powerful and smart. He knows how to use those things to his advantage. He's also related to Az who's been a pain in my side ever since I found out he's the one behind this damned war."

It was very rare for him to throw any kind of explicative, big or small, into a sentence. I raised my eyebrows at him, but he ignored me as he continued his assessment, "But that man has been more instrumental in us making progress than anyone else. We would've been done for if he hadn't reached out to me. I can tell he really cares about you, too, Val. It's written all over his face, in how he carries himself, and in what he says about you. Why do you ask?"

"Well, because there's a werewolf tradition, I guess that's what you'd call it, that basically means him and I are destined to be together," I responded holding my breath for his answer.

All he did at first was nod. Then, he leaned forward looking at me, "If you're asking if I'm okay with you being with him, the answer is yes. Although, I don't know why you'd need to ask me. You're on your own now. You take care of yourself. I'd support you in just about any choice of man. Well, except for Az, but I think that one's a given. So, anyways, what had you all shaken up before that meeting? It's very unlike you to show that side."

I dropped my gaze to my lap, "Az tried to pay Warrick a visit last night, but I guess Warrick was out trying to round you all up. I stopped by his apartment and Az greeted me."

"What did he do to you?" my dad asked, his voice dropping to a dangerous tone.

I held up a finger, "You promised me you wouldn't try to do anything. I can't lose you too, okay?"

"I keep my promises."

My fist clenched as I prepared to talk about what Warrick had walked in on. I dug my fingernails in the palm of my hand to help distract me from needing to throw up as I said, "Az tried to rape me. He almost did, too, if Warrick hadn't come in and shot him with those bullets."

My dad's face paled, but remained serious. He got out of his chair to start pacing the room. With his back to me, he asked, "Did Liam try this, too?"

"He didn't get as far as Az, but yeah, the intent was there," I answered.

"And you said Cian tried to bleed you out. What did you mean by that?"

I pinched the bridge of my nose, "Beat the crap out of me and cut me so I could add to their blood supply."

"All this after everything Warrick did to you?" he asked.

"Can you please get to the point? Reliving all this shit isn't exactly easy," I muttered.

He came back to his chair, settling in, "You've lived too many lives since that air raid."

"Isn't it all a symptom of war?" I asked.

"Yes, but that doesn't change the fact I hate it. Val, you really shouldn't have had to go through all this," he shook his head. "That wasn't my intent for getting you out of there."

I put a hand on his knee, "Dad, it's not your fault. These were things out of our control."

"I don't know if that's necessarily the case. I was the one who may have hinted to both Warrick and Az that you were the key to a lot of the information they kept harassing me for. I needed to do something to get them off my back and I mistakenly directed them to you. I did have a hand in sending you to this world without the intention of Warrick going after you the way he did, but fate had other plans. I asked him to look out for you, not attack. I'm so sorry, Val," my dad said with remorse in his eyes.

It was my turn to stand up and pace around the office. That explains why Warrick was so obsessed with me, holding on to any and all things that mentioned my name. That would also explain why Az is so hell bent on coming after me, proving that Warrick was right. I looked back at my dad who was watching me closely waiting for my response. I went back to walking around, my attention focused on each step I took. There were two paths I could take: be mad at him for being the catalyst in this situation or move on because this all probably would've happened anyway since I'm fated to be with Warrick. Well, at least all the things that happened with Warrick.

I made my way back to my seat taking my time with getting comfortable. When I was finally ready, I looked up at my dad, "I don't know that this is entirely your fault. I think these things would've happened regardless of what you said or did. Either way, I'm looking past it because, as you've heard, I've made it through worse. How's mom?"

He turned his head away from me so fast after that question, but I swear I saw some tears in his eyes. His shoulders subtly shook and I instinctively reached out to rub his back, "Dad? Are you okay?"

He sniffled, wiping his nose with the back of his hand, "Before Warrick showed up, I just got news that your mom's body was found."

I stopped. I could feel my world starting to turn upside down. I was thankful to already be sitting because if I weren't, I'd probably collapse to the ground. The door leading to the hallway slowly opened with Warrick poking his head in. He must've known something was wrong with how fast, but silently, he moved into the room. Lou was behind him keeping quiet as well. My dad hadn't noticed they were there. He started sobbing at this point and I reached back out to him again. "Dad," I started with a voice full of emotion. "What do you mean her body was found?"

I saw Warrick stiffen out of the corner of my eye, but willed myself to focus on the distraught man in front of me. He sucked in some air to calm down enough to talk, "Your mom's body was mauled. She was murdered and barely recognizable."

I couldn't hold back the emotions anymore. Sobs wracked my body and the two wolves standing in the background finally moved towards us. Warrick crouched down in front of me holding out a tissue for me to take, "Do you know who did it, James?"

"Yes," he forced out.

"Was it Az?" Warrick asked.

"Yes," my dad said again.

"That asshole!" I screamed. My mom, who was one to always go out of her way to make sure everyone in her life was cared for, was gone. There would be no more bone-crushing hugs, no more midnight laughter over her freshly baked cookies, no chance of her going wedding dress shopping with me, no chance of experiencing what life would be like as a grandparent.

Warrick pulled me into his chest as I became consumed with grief. Lou had handed my dad his own tissue. After a few more minutes like this, my dad finally composed himself, "She wouldn't want us to be like this, Val-pal. You know one of the last things she said to me?"

I wiped at my eyes, "What?"

"She told me that she knew you'd find a great love again and you were the best thing that's ever happened to us. She went on this whole, long speech about how we never needed to worry about you because you always landed on your feet. She even laughed remembering back to when you got that bike of yours. We were both so worried about you, but she was the first one to come to terms with it."

"I already miss her so much, dad," I said looking at him through the tears. "There's been so much death."

"We're going to make it through this," he said giving my hand a squeeze. "We always do, and we have to now. For her."

I nodded. I swiped at a few tears thinking of what my dad had said about my mom not wanting us to cry over her. As I finished wiping the last of them, my dad stood up, "I hate to do this after dropping that news on you, but I do really need to get back. My phone has been buzzing nonstop which means something bad is going down."

"So soon?" I asked. I wasn't ready for him to leave yet. He may have been here for longer than how much I've seen him, but I wasn't ready for my dad to go again. I had no idea when I'd be able to see him again.

"Yeah, it's a cruel world out there, but listen to me," he said grabbing both of my hands. I stood up with him to make it easier to talk, nodding for him to go on. He cleared his throat, "No matter what happens, you keep finding a way to move forward. Do that for me, okay? And if anything happens – "

"Don't talk like that, dad," I cut him off.

He shook his head charging forward with what he was about to say, "If anything happens to me, I want you to know that I approve. Of what we were talking about earlier. I know you'll be conflicted, just know mom and I will always be watching over you, willing love to find its way back into your life. I love you."

My dad was being cryptic since Warrick was standing right there, but I followed everything he said. I was yanked into a tight hug. "I love you, too, dad," I mumbled into his shoulder.

He pulled away and made his exit. For all I knew, that would be the last time I would see him. Warrick put an arm around me tugging me close to him, "Are you okay, love?"

"My heart has been shattered in pieces, and after going through what Az put me through last night, I don't know which end is up anymore," I stared out the door.

"We're going to kill him, right?" Lou asked.

Warrick nodded, "That is the goal."

Before we could say anything else, Cian and Liam walked through the door. Lou let out a small growl, but Cian ignored him. Instead, he walked straight up to me and stuck out a hand. I glanced down at it then back up at his face before slowly shaking it. He looked a little relieved at me returning the gesture, "I'm willing to call a truce if you are."

"I don't have any plans to take out any more vampires," I said.

"Thank you, and I'm apologizing on Liam's behalf even though he should be the one doing this part," Cian jerked his head in Liam's direction.

I looked over at the other vampire who just rolled his eyes. "I guess it's fine," I responded.

"That settles it. Warrick, we're out of here. A lot of work to do," Cian said giving Warrick a little salute.

When they left and we were sure no one else would be coming in, I collapsed back into my chair while Warrick took up his usual seat at his desk. Lou sat in the chair my dad had been using studying me for a moment before asking, "What exactly happened to you last night?"

Warrick jumped in with a question of his own, "Is it okay if I review the security footage with him?"

I glanced away. I didn't want Lou to see me like that, but I also knew Warrick was more asking so he could show Lou Az's upgraded speed and healing. I rolled my shoulders back, "It's fine."

"Thank you, love," Warrick said then turned the computer monitor so the three of us could see. He started the footage from when he came home. Warrick threw back two glasses of whiskey then started destroying things. He checked his phone and left the apartment. It wasn't too long after that when Az made his appearance.

Az walked around the empty apartment looking for Warrick then moved to his office to start digging through all the files in there. He slammed a fist on the desk apparently not able to find what he was looking for. It was right after that when I walked through the door. I swallowed, afraid of seeing what happened next. I felt every movement I made, every breath I took as I relived these moments. When it got to the first time Az forced me to drink, Lou sucked in some air, "Shit."

The rest of the night played out on the screen in front of me. As the footage progressed, Lou's fist clenched tighter and tighter. I also watched the muscles in Warrick's jaw twitch out of rage. He was starting to understand what Az was able to accomplish before he walked through the door. Meanwhile, I was sitting there fighting the bile working its way up my throat. The fact I was watching this all happen not even a full day after it meant I was a hell of a lot stronger than I gave myself credit for.

When it got to the part where Warrick shot Az, Lou's eyes widened as he watched the bullets slide out of the holes put in his arms. "You've got to be fucking kidding me," Lou mumbled.

"We're dealing with a truly untouchable enemy," Warrick noted. His icy blue eyes slid over to me, "I'm sorry you had to relive that, love."

"It's fine," I replied in a small voice. I looked down at my hands, "You were right by the way."

"About what?"

"My dad admitted to telling both you and Az I was the key for information," I said able to bring myself to meet both of their eyes.

"Shit," Warrick cursed.

Lou looked between the two of us, "What does that mean?"

"It means that Az is going to try to grab Val at some point to get as much of an upper hand as possible. It's no longer him trying to mess with me by using her," Warrick explained.

"Do you have any way of knowing if Az is still here in this world?" Lou asked, urgency increasing in his tone with each word.

Warrick flipped the screen back towards him typing furiously. His eyes scanned the screen, but he only ended up shaking his head, "Nothing is showing up, but that doesn't mean anything. He could've jumped or he could be hiding out. Either way, we need to go ASAP. Lou, how fast can you get things ready to go?"

"I can probably get things settled tonight," Lou answered.

Warrick turned to me, "Are you okay if I call all your friends up here?"

"Why?" I asked, confused.

"To see if they all want to join us or if we could help Lou get ready a little faster," Warrick explained pulling out his phone.

"O-okay," I stammered still confused.

He hung up the phone as fast as he was done with it and stood up, "They're on their way. I'm going to meet them downstairs to speed up the check in process."

Lou and I watched him leave. As soon as the coast was clear, Lou whipped around to me, "Are you okay, Val?"

"I sure am getting asked that a lot lately," I said bringing a shaky hand up to run through my hair.

Chapter 5

Lou tried to get as much out of me about last night as he could, but I wasn't willing to budge too much. He finally got the hint I was done talking about this when I was only giving him single word answers. I let out a sigh of relief when Warrick returned with Jennie, Joe, and Bev in tow. He closed the door behind all of them and returned to his desk.

"What's going on, Warrick?" Joe asked.

"We're going to the witch world and we need to leave now. I'm not going to beat around the bush on this one. Their world is harsh and there's a good chance we'll walk away without getting them to join our cause. There's also a good chance we won't find the remaining two of your group. The climate is cold. It's often dark there. I need to know if you three are planning on joining us. I'll throw this out there before you make the call: Lou could probably use some help running his pizza place while we're gone and I'm sure he can bring any one of you up to speed on what needs to be done. Plus, you'll have Raf as a resource in case you need help. Thoughts?" Warrick looked at them expectantly.

Jennie didn't hesitate with speaking up, "I'm planning on going. If Mark and Lilly are there, I'll be able to help Val get them to join up with us. Since they've been in their world the longest, it might be harder for them to want to leave if they've made good connections."

"Okay. Joe and Bev?" Warrick asked.

Bev gave Joe a look and he nodded. She turned back to us, "We'll stay here. You all know we're trying for kids and I don't know what jumping worlds will do for those chances. Besides, we can keep an eye out for anything suspicious."

"I thought that might be the case," Warrick nodded. "Can I see your phones?"

"Why?" Joe asked.

"I want to make sure we'll be able to get ahold of each other if we need to. I'm going to add some hardware in here that I have in my phone to make sure we're good to go," Warrick said. He turned to look at me, "I'll need yours, too."

I tentatively handed it over. Warrick added my phone to the pile, "I don't know that I'm going to be letting you out of my sight all that much, but it's better you have this in case you need it."

"What about Lou's?" I asked.

"His already has the upgrade," Warrick mumbled.

I shot a glare over at Lou who only shrugged, "Perks of being promoted, I guess."

"Promoted to what?" I shot back at him.

Warrick cut in, "If you didn't notice, love, everyone had their seconds in that room with them. You happen to be your dad's and Lou happens to be mine."

I was getting ready to ask another question, but was cut off by Warrick handing back Joe and Bev's phones. I had no idea how Warrick worked that fast, but I was genuinely impressed. He clapped his hands together, "Alright. Lou, go do whatever it is you need to. Jennie and Val, I need you two to take care of getting the things on this list." He handed me a piece of paper, "We're leaving tonight as soon as I get done here."

And that was that. I followed everyone else across the street to grab some food. Lou kept glancing at me while I sat leaning my head against the wall in the booth we were in. The lack of sleep was catching up to me, but I avoided every question thrown my way about how I was doing or where I went last night. Thankfully, Lou didn't give away anything either.

Jennie moved out of the booth looking at me, "Well, you ready to tackle this shopping list?"

"Yeah, just give me a second," I said heading back to the kitchen.

Lou followed me in there blocking the doorframe in case any of my friends got curious. He studied me for a little longer then shook his head, "You're an enigma, you know that?"

"Just call me the Riddler," I mumbled as I splashed water on my face.

"What?"

I waived Lou off, "Don't worry about it. What's up?"

"I just wanted to check on you. You looked like you were about to pass out while we were eating. You know you could use my apartment to take a nap, right?" Lou said looking worried.

"I'm fine. If I closed my eyes, I'd just see Az anyways."

He crossed his arms over his chest, "Do you really think we stand a chance against him?"

"Lou," I sighed. "I really don't know. I hope Warrick has some massive trick up his sleeve he's not telling anyone about because Az's strength? His speed? His healing? There's nothing that can stand up to that."

"Yeah," Lou looked over his shoulder. "I should let you go. Jennie looks ready to kill me."

I moved towards the door, Lou sidestepping out of my way. I gave his arm a squeeze, "Thank you for not saying anything, about last night or my mom."

His gaze softened, "I figured that's your business to tell, not mine. Now, get out of here."

I met up with Jennie and took a picture of the list. There were so many things on here from food and water to supplies like rope, portable battery chargers, and extra blankets. I was getting my riding gear on, "We should divide and conquer this. I have a feeling Warrick's gonna be at my place sooner than we think and I don't want to keep him waiting."

"Are you sure that's a good idea?" Jennie asked cocking her head to one side.

"Why?"

"Well, it just seemed like Warrick wasn't wanting you to do things alone. I don't know why that is, and I honestly feel like you're keeping something from me, but we should stick together," Jennie explained.

"I'll be fine, Jennie. There's a lot of shit he needs us to get. You take the top half, I'll take the bottom."

"Fine," she huffed then marched out to her car.

I gave her a little wave as I walked into the parking garage to my bike. I headed out to the first spot on the list and had no problem finding the item Warrick noted. The rest of the list turned out to be just as easy. As I was getting ready to head back home from the last stop, I took a look around me. I wasn't entirely sure where I was at, but the landscape looked a little familiar. I started inching out of the parking lot, but instead of turning right to go home, I turned left following the sign pointing to the ocean. It wasn't long before I pulled up to the shack Warrick took me to. I ordered enough food for those of us jumping and found a way to secure it in my bag with everything else then finally started the trek back.

I was getting closer to the city when I heard another bike behind me. *Odd, I've never seen anyone else ride around here.* Then it dawned on me. Az also had a bike. I threw a glance over my shoulder and sure enough it was him. He rode a sleek, black bike that packed a lot of power from what I remembered the few times he let me drive it. I didn't recognize the manufacturer since it was a brand from this world, only that it was the same one he had always ridden – he always tried to cover up the logo with one from my world while he dodged my questions. It was weird, but I always brushed it off since the fight wasn't worth it. He was gaining on me fast. I picked up the pace only for it to not be enough. Az pulled up next to me and gestured for me to pull over. I shook my head. We went through those motions a few more times.

Az eventually got frustrated and tried to run me off the road. I hit my brakes, the squeal of my tires on the pavement screeching until I came to a full stop. He whipped around and stopped next to me, "Don't run from me, Val. We've been over this."

A memory flashed in my mind from last night. I ripped my helmet off to throw up in the grass. I wiped my mouth, scowling up at him, "What do you want?"

"I just wanted to say hi. Is that so bad?" he asked using that mocking tone of his.

"I'm not playing these games right now. If you're going to grab me, just fucking do it. I know I can't outrun you," I crossed my arms over my chest.

I felt my arms start shaking when he slowly got off his bike and removed his helmet. Az walked over, setting my helmet on my bike. He held my chin in between his thumb and his forefinger, our lips almost brushing, "It makes me so happy to see the effect I have on you. Don't think I forgot about what we started."

Another wave of nausea rolled over me. I tried to pull my head back to put some space between us to get some air, but that only made him grip me harder. I clenched my teeth, "I just want to know one thing, Az. Did you kill my mom?"

A slow, sickening smile crept along his face, "Yes."

Before I could say anything else, he kissed me. I shoved against his chest despite knowing he wouldn't budge. I felt him laugh against my lips at my feeble attempt to get him away from me and then a sharp pain erupted in my side. Az released me, "See you soon, Val-pal."

He put on his helmet and gave me a little wave before speeding off back in the direction of the coast. I was rattled. If his goal was to get in my head, he's doing a damn good job.

"What the hell?" I asked trying to find the source of the pain. I lifted my right arm to discover a knife wedged into my ribs. I ripped one of my gloves off to check for blood not finding any. Yet.

"Shit, shit, shit."

I started panicking. I was nowhere near the city. I knew I would start bleeding the more I moved around. I pulled out my phone sending a quick text to Raf to let him know I would be stopping at the hospital to talk to him really quick and to make sure he didn't mention it to anyone else. He responded with instructions on where to go to sneak into the building. I sped off towards the city thankful for his quick response. The hospital was going to be faster than driving all the way to Lou's or my house. Plus, I'd be able to get patched up and hopefully not need stitches. All I knew was that I couldn't let Warrick find out what had just happened. I couldn't let Jennie find out, either. I had to pretend like everything was okay until I could have a moment to myself. Then, I could break.

I cut the engine of my bike when I got close to the hospital, pushing it the rest of the way meeting Raf outside the back entrance. He made sure we were hidden from any cameras, "What's with the surprise visit, Val? Everything okay?"

"I wish I could say so, but unfortunately not," I said lifting up my arm to show the knife.

Raf's eyes widened and he ushered me through the door. He took me through a series of winding hallways until we entered into his office. He shut the door then pulled out a small suture kit, "I'm going to pull this knife out. Apply pressure as soon as I'm out of the way."

I nodded. He gripped the hilt of the knife and pulled. I bit down on my lip to fight the pain then followed Raf's instructions. I worked my way out of my jacket, lifting the shirt Warrick gave me to give Raf a better look at the wound.

"It's pretty small and doesn't look like it went too deep. You can thank your jacket for that. Do you feel like telling me what happened?" he asked while getting to work with bandaging the spot Az stabbed me. "You didn't really even get blood on that nice shirt of yours."

"I'd rather not dive into what happened if that's okay with you," I said.

Raf finished what he was doing and I bundled back up. He poked his head out of his office to make sure the coast was clear then led me out the same way we came in. Back outside, I gave Raf a hug, "Thank you for patching me up and being discreet about it."

"Anytime, Val. Make sure you take a shower when you get home to get whoever's scent that is off you. Oh, and Lou mentioned you guys are about to jump. Be careful, okay?"

"Okay," I promised. He had no idea how hard I was going to work to keep my head down in the next world. The last thing I needed was to spend any more time in the hospital.

Raf watched as I sped away. I felt my phone buzz with what I'm assuming is an impatient text from Jennie. I pushed my bike even harder until my house came into view. I pulled into the garage, walking in the house to be greeted by Jennie tapping her foot and Warrick chilling at the island.

I put my bag on the island unloading all the chicken wraps and fries. Warrick smiled seeing the bag of food, but Jennie started scolding me, "Where the hell have you been? Do you know how angry Warrick was when he came in here not finding you?"

"I was getting us some dinner tonight. Figure I'd make it easy since we're going to be leaving the moment Lou walks through that door," I said avoiding eye contact with either of them. "Now, if you'll excuse me, I need to take a shower."

I didn't give Jennie the chance to say anything else as I ran up the stairs. I hustled into the bathroom after grabbing a fresh pair of clothes and stripped down to my underwear. I dug through my clothes to pull out the extra gauze and tape Raf gave me and hid that in a drawer. I started the water, stripping down so I was completely naked. I slowly pulled away the bandage. It may not have been bleeding a lot back at the hospital, but it definitely was now. The gauze was almost soaked through and there were no signs of it stopping.

A knock came from my door making me jump, "Love, Lou just showed up. We're going to make the jump. Just wanted to let you know since you're getting cleaned up."

I scrambled to hide everything from Raf and buried the bloodied gauze in the trash then hopped into the shower. I winced as I poured out some of my body wash, but I had to do it to try to hide Az's scent. I poked my head around the shower curtain and called out, "Thanks for the head's up!"

"Anytime," Warrick said.

I watched as the door opened a crack. Panic crept up into me. "Can I have a few moments alone, Warrick?" I blurted.

The door stopped moving. I held my breath waiting for his response. Instead, the door started closing again and Warrick was gone. I sank to the floor letting the warm water wash over me and let it all out. I was mad. Mad I hadn't been given a chance to stop or breathe until now. Mad my dad had painted a giant target on my back. I hated that a part of me wanted the old Az back because maybe I could handle that version of him. I couldn't ignore the grief lurking in the background, either. I had to watch my dad deliver news he hadn't ever thought he would have to say. My mom, who always knew what to say and how to provide comfort, was gone. I didn't even get a chance to say goodbye or tell her I loved her one more time. Most of all, I was scared. This new version of Az was crazy strong and very unpredictable. He was very much using me. By going after me, he was not only getting under Warrick's skin and distracting him, but I'm positive this would come around to distract my dad, too.

I stood up to start getting clean so they weren't waiting on me for too long. The air immediately got sucked from my lungs and I had to brace myself against the wall until everything felt normal again. There would be some new scenery when I stepped out of the shelter of my bathroom. I checked the wound one more time breathing a little easier now that the blood flow was slowing then got to work with getting the rest of myself cleaned. I put a fresh gauze pad over the hole in my side and wrapped myself in the comfort of my robe.

I paused at the balcony door to see if I can get any ideas as to where we ended up. The blizzard raging outside made it impossible to see anything. Add in the dark, and there was no hope of seeing anything. The wind was howling and a gust would shake the house every now and then. I pressed my hand against the window, immediately drawing it back because of how cold it felt. *We landed in the arctic. Great.*

Sighing, I finally made my way downstairs. Lou ended up behind me coming from my dad's office where I'm sure he was down in the lab hiding the device again. "Warrick's upset. What happened?" he asked me in a quiet tone.

I paused looking at him over my shoulder, "I have no idea, but we'll probably find out soon enough."

"Where did she get this food?" Jennie asked, her voice carrying up to Lou and I.

"A place outside of the city," Warrick mumbled.

When we both joined them at the island, Jennie smiled at me, "Thank you for picking up dinner."

I returned the smile, "Of course."

Lou joined Jennie on the opposite side, raised his eyebrows at me then glanced at Warrick, and got to work warming up the now cool food. Lou had Jennie distracted giving Warrick the opportunity to nudge me. He jerked his head towards the basement indicating for me to follow. Warrick kept his back to me as he said, "Want to explain how this knife ended up in the bag of food?"

Ah, there it is. That would explain why Warrick's upset. I gently took the knife out of his hand and he turned around to face me. There were storms raging in those blue eyes of his. I examined the knife a little bit debating if I wanted to try to play it off or if I should just tell the truth.

Sighing, I gave the knife back to him, "Az decided to pay me a visit."

Truth won out. Warrick inhaled deeply as he ran a hand through his hair. He closed his eyes as he let that breath out, finally looking at me, "Why didn't you stick with Jennie?"

"I figured you would want to leave as soon as possible, so I thought dividing the list between the two of us and splitting up would help us get through it faster," I explained.

Warrick took a step closer to me, our bodies almost touching. My dear friend panic started creeping back in, sending warning signals. I looked up at Warrick hoping he couldn't sense how I was feeling right now in case that would only set him off more. He caressed my cheek, cocking his head to one side, "Where are you bleeding?"

"I-I don't feel like showing you r-right now," I stammered, my voice betraying me.

His other hand came up to my waist tracing my robe's belt to where it tied in the front. My legs started shaking first, but Warrick ignored that, "It's nothing I haven't seen before, love."

"That's n-not the problem," I swallowed.

Warrick sighed. I thought he was going to back down when he dropped both of his arms, but the rush of cool air against my naked skin told me otherwise. I stiffened and avoided his gaze, focusing on a spot on the wall behind him. He pushed one side of the robe out of his way inspecting for any signs of a wound then moved to the other side, dragging his fingers lightly against my skin. I felt the goosebumps rise to the surface and the shaking came back.

"You paid Raf a visit," Warrick observed when he found the patch of gauze.

"Dinner's ready!" Lou called.

"We should eat," I said, my voice barely a whisper.

Warrick covered me back up, yanking the belt tight. He pulled me even closer to him using the collar of my robe. His face was inches from mine, "You don't know how lucky you are that you're standing in front of me right now. Az could've grabbed you right then and there. From now on, you don't go venturing by yourself. You stick with one of us."

Warrick let me go and went back upstairs. I heard him and Lou talking in a light-hearted tone, a stark contrast to how he just was with me. I slowly dropped to the ground, keeping my cries silent as I curled in on myself. He shouldn't be taking his anger out on me. He should be finding Az and taking it out on him.

"Val?" Jennie asked.

I quickly wiped my eyes and nose before plastering a smile on my face. I stood up to face her, "Hey, what are you doing down here?"

"Are you okay?" she rushed up to me, lowering her voice. Concern was written all over her face.

I nodded. If I said anything, I'm almost positive I would cry again.

She pulled me into a hug, "I don't know what that asshole upstairs said to you or what's going on, but so help me, if he makes you cry again, I'll find a way to hurt him."

I let out a weak laugh, "Thanks, Jennie, but you don't have to do that." I pulled back and started moving towards the stairs, "Let's go eat before the food gets cold again."

We joined the guys at the island. They kept their conversation going with Jennie jumping in every now and then. I sat there quietly eating, staring at the spot where the Christmas tree was not too long ago. I hadn't even realized the decorations were down, but Jennie, Joe, and Bev must've done that before we had to leave.

"Love?" Warrick asked wiping the corner of his mouth and putting a hand on my knee.

"Hmm?" I said slowly bringing my attention back to those in front of me.

"We were just talking about how different it feels without Joe and Bev here," Jennie filled me in, watching me carefully.

"Oh," I nodded. I couldn't muster up the energy to change the tone in my voice, so it remained monotone as I said, "It does. Where are they staying, by the way?"

"I offered up my apartment," Lou answered keeping an eye on Warrick.

"How thoughtful," I said pushing my empty plate away. "Well, considering I may have gotten only a couple of hours of sleep over the last couple of days, I'm going to head up to bed. Goodnight."

They each mumbled goodnight as I wasted no time ascending the stairs. I locked the door behind me and threw on a pair of pajamas before crawling into bed, letting the howling wind lull me into a dreamless sleep. A loud thud outside my door startled me awake. I sat up pulling the covers around me. There was another thud making me jump again. I couldn't bring myself to move hoping my door would hold against whatever was trying to beat it down.

"Val, love, please let me in," Warrick slurred.

I blew out a breath thankful it was just Warrick, but I knew he was drunk which was a wild card in terms of which side I would get.

He gave a polite knock, "Please. I need to talk to you about something."

I swung my legs to the ground, grabbing my robe I left on the bed. I pulled it tight around me and hesitated before I finally opened the door. Warrick stumbled into the space mumbling something under his breath. I looked down the hall to find Lou watching from his room. I shook my head telling him he didn't need to come down here. Lou turned back into his room, quietly shutting the door behind him. I did the same making sure I didn't make too much noise so Jennie didn't get woken up then whirled around to face Warrick. "What the hell is wrong with you?" I hissed.

"What?" he cocked his head to the side. "I figured I would come and sleep with you."

"Are you kidding me? I locked the door for a reason. I wanted some privacy especially after you proved you weren't going to listen to me when I told you no," I scolded, taking a few steps closer.

"I didn't like the thought of Az having his hands on you again," Warrick pouted. At least I was getting a more light-hearted version of drunk-Warrick.

"I don't either, but we can't change that now, can we?"

"I guess not," he said reaching out for me.

I held my ground staying just out of reach. Crossing my arms, I asked, "Do you always drink this much when your brother comes around?"

His face suddenly became dark and he sprang to his feet. *That was the wrong question to ask.* He held my chin forcing me to look at the anger brewing in his eyes, "You don't know the half of it, love."

"Then tell me. Tell me the full story," I said holding his gaze.

Chapter 6

Warrick dropped my chin with a growl and stalked over to the balcony door. He placed his hands on either side of the door watching the blizzard rage around us.

"Don't go backing out of this now," I said.

Warrick didn't move as he started, "You really want to know the reason why Az gets under my skin so easily, love?"

"I think I've already answered that question," I crossed my arms again.

He dropped his head then looked back out the door before pushing from the wall and standing in front of me. Warrick took one more step so our bodies were touching, something he apparently needed tonight, then sighed, "Ever wonder how my parents died?"

I gestured for him to get on with it. He pursed his lips for a moment before continuing, "Az is a couple years older than me and had been working already. Our parents were proud of his fancy job in the nicest building in the city. I don't know what the real reason is for his actions because it changes every time I try to ask him, but he came back from work one day all wound up. As you know, he and I both have a temper, although his is slightly worse than mine. I was home sick that day, laying on the couch watching a movie. My mom had some cookies in the oven so they were ready for him by the time he got home while she took care of the laundry upstairs."

Warrick swallowed squeezing his eyes shut and I knew he was about to barrel through to the hard part of the story. When his eyes opened again, they were almost glowing, "Az burst through the door and threw his bag across the room. He demanded to know where mom was, but she was upstairs. My dad came out of the kitchen from getting a snack and Az rushed him, breaking his neck. He had no time to react to Az's speed. I had never seen him move that fast."

Beads of sweat were starting to form along his forehead. I could tell by the way he was starting to shake, the way his eyes were changing, that his wolf was threatening to come out. I reached up to touch his cheek, "Is it possible for wolves to change when there's not a full moon?"

Warrick shook his head easing that concern. He leaned into my touch calming his breathing. His skin was warmer than usual to the touch, making me doubt whether or not he could change on command, but I didn't want to press the issue. Warrick picked up his head, recounting the memory, "My mom came running downstairs after hearing me screaming. When she saw my dad's lifeless form on the floor, she started screaming at us to know what happened. Az only laughed at her. She dropped to her knees next to my dad's body, crying her eyes out. I remember trying to get off the couch, but freezing when Az just shook his head at me. Then, he grabbed her by her hair and dragged her to the middle of our living room. Az all of a sudden had a knife, I don't even know where he got it, and started yelling obscene things at her. Blaming her for all the shit that was wrong in his life. Blaming her for having me and ruining his life. He had completely lost any semblance of sanity at this point."

I watched tears threaten to spill over and entangled my fingers with his. Warrick immediately tightened his grip taking away any opportunity for me to take my hands back. He closed his eyes again, "He started cutting her. Blood was going everywhere. It was almost as if our mother's pleading voice and her screams encouraged him to keep going. The Az I knew was gone, a feeling I'm sure you're coming to know. Anyways, he started cutting away body parts until he finally ended her life. I didn't care how sick I felt, I bolted. I ran to the neighbors we always spent time with, and they took care of me from there."

"Warrick," my voice wobbled. "That's awful. Did anyone ever do anything to him?"

"No," he answered, no emotion left in his voice. "He got away with it. I found out later that he had just been changed and wasn't coping well with it, but no one thought to keep him tucked away until things settled down, which is why I changed that process the minute I became alpha. Before you ask, yes, Az found ways to come back and torture me off and on. Now, he upped his game and is threatening to take away everything from everyone. Since that day, I made a promise to take him down the minute I got the chance. That's why I'm so focused on being the strongest and having the latest and greatest technology so I can take him out. It's not for pride, despite what everyone may think."

A lot of things clicked in place in that moment. Warrick hasn't been power hungry, he just wants to eliminate an evil that's been hanging over him for his whole life. Warrick's been a little bit of a loose cannon because of the demons he's been battling. I wondered how many times he lost his shit because Az chose to mess with him that day. Then I come along to use him and stab him, probably triggering painful memories from his past.

Warrick took a step back from me, shaking his head. He brought his hands up to his eyes then dragged them down. He tracked my movements as I came closer to him. "Knowing Az is trying to target you – if he ever did anything," he kept struggling to find the right way to start his sentence. A growl ripped from his throat and he turned his back to me again, "All I keep picturing is you being cut up into pieces with Az standing over you and laughing. Seeing that knife scared me shitless, love. It was like my worst fears were starting to come true."

"Hey," I gently tugged at his shoulder to get him to turn around. "It's already better. He didn't cut me deep."

"That was a message for me," Warrick said looking at the spot on my side he found earlier. I guided him over to the bed and sat him down. I lifted up my shirt just enough to reveal the gauze, "Take it off. You'll see."

I may not have had any idea how it was looking, but it had been feeling so much better. Warrick carefully lifted the gauze away. Looking at the gauze he set on the bed, I was happy to see there wasn't any more blood on there. He let out a breath, relieved at what he found. I lifted his chin up so we could look at each other, aware of his hand lingering on my skin, "I told you."

"How was it not worse?"

"Be thankful for my riding gear," I explained.

Warrick pulled me into a tight hug. I felt his warm tears coat my skin as he let out everything he had been holding in. I kept running my fingers through his hair not wanting to make him feel like he couldn't have this release. Warrick finally let me go, wiping at his eyes. I sat next to him on the bed and put my head on his shoulder, "Thank you for sharing."

"I think I'd like to try to sleep now," he mumbled.

I stared at him caught off-guard by the sudden decision. He didn't wait for me to say anything. Warrick crawled up to the pillows settling in under the covers, clothes and all. I pulled off my robe and climbed in next to him, his arm instantly wrapping around me. It didn't take long for his breathing to slow and I wasn't too far behind him, falling asleep.

A soft knock woke me up. My head jerked up and fell back down on my pillow. Warrick's heavy arm still kept me close to him. I was starting to think I imagined the sound when I heard it again. I gently lifted his arm off, pausing to make sure I didn't wake Warrick up then grabbed my robe. I opened the door a crack to find Lou's grey eyes staring back at me, "Hey, up for joining me?"

"Sure," I answered making my way out of my room. I made sure the door closed quietly behind me following Lou down to the basement. Apparently, that's the meeting place of choice.

He settled in one of the chairs gesturing for me to do the same before handing me a warm cup of tea. I took a sip and got comfortable, "What's up?"

"I wanted to ask you something, but I first wanted to check with you to make sure you're okay. Warrick got pretty drunk after you went to sleep and chased Jennie off being his typical asshole self. As soon as I saw him stumble his way to your room, I got worried. Especially after what happened with Az," Lou said with his eyebrows furrowed in concern.

"Oh," I said staring down into my mug. "Yeah, I'm okay. He actually didn't do anything. We just talked."

"Really?"

"Surprisingly, yes."

Lou leaned forward, "Anything you care to share?"

"I don't think it's really my information to share," I noted.

"Got it," he said sitting back. "I don't know if I've really had a chance to talk to you after what happened."

Lou didn't have to explain for me to understand what he was talking about. I waived him off, "Don't worry about it."

"Jennie also told me about your relationship with Az," Lou said, his tone serious now. "There's a lot between you two."

"What are you hinting at?" I asked bringing my gaze back to him.

He held up a hand signaling me to wait, "Raf texted me before you got to the house saying you showed up at the hospital, too."

"Damn it," I muttered under my breath.

Lou raised his eyebrows at me, "Would that play into why Warrick was in such a mood yesterday?"

I took another sip of my tea, wrapping my hands tighter around the mug. There was no getting out of this one. I dropped my shoulders, "Yeah, he wasn't happy I went off on my own. When I was coming back from grabbing the food, I was a ways out of the city. I was the only one on the roads for a bit, then Az joined me. All Warrick knows is that Az stabbed me. What he doesn't know, and what I don't want him to find out, is that Az also kissed me."

Lou sucked in a breath, "I'll keep it between us. Warrick's been losing his mind and we don't need to add anything to that."

"Exactly," I nodded my head. "Anyways, what's your question?"

"Oh, yeah, that," Lou said starting to fidget. "I think that can wait."

"You might as well get it out there or I'm going to find out anyways," I teased him.

He chuckled at that, "Yeah, you probably will. Alright, here it goes. Would you be okay if I dated Jennie?"

"That's your question?" I asked trying to not to laugh. "You made it sound so much more serious."

"I mean, it kind of is. I didn't want to step on any toes. I also don't know if she would be interested in me like that," Lou mumbled.

"First of all, Jennie has been crushing on you since day one. Second of all, I don't care who you date or do whatever with. We're friends, remember? Nothing more. We've established that," I leaned forward putting my hand on his knee. "Take a chance. You've already gotten to know her pretty well."

"Thanks, Val," Lou smiled at me.

We talked a little more about everything that's happened since we celebrated Christmas trying to piece the puzzle together when Warrick came running down the stairs, eyes wild. Lou's defenses instantly went up. I whipped my head around, "Why are you running around here like that?"

"Where'd you go?" Warrick asked. Worry was laced in every word and in every muscle of his body.

I slowly stood up putting my mug down, "I've been talking with Lou about Jennie. That's all. I haven't stepped foot out of this house."

Warrick ran over to me bringing both hands to my shoulders. Instead of saying something, he inspected every part of me. My brows knit together and I tried to take a step back, "I'm fine, Warrick. You need to take a deep breath."

He pulled me into him, whispering, "All I could see was you cut up."

"I'm safe. There aren't any cuts on me," I pulled away. "Go take a shower and get cleaned up. I'm not planning on going anywhere, okay? I'll be in this house."

"Warrick," Lou stood up. "I won't let anything happen to her either."

"Right," he said nodding his head and stepping away. "Right."

As quick as Warrick had stormed down the stairs, he left. Water started running and I was able to breathe easy. I turned back around to Lou, grabbing my mug as I did so, "Have you ever seen him like that?"

"No. I'm worried about him, too," Lou said watching the spot Warrick was standing in just moments ago. "He needs to regain his composure if he has any hope of getting the witches on our side."

I nodded, "Yeah, and he's going to have to be okay with leaving me when he goes to find the person he needs to talk to."

"Speaking of leaving, are you and Jennie going to try to find your other friends?" Lou asked.

I headed upstairs with Lou trailing me. Jennie was already at the island making some breakfast. Her head snapped up when she heard the sound of our feet approaching, "Do either of you know what the hell is going on with Warrick?"

"Yeah," I cut Lou off. "He's just too stressed out for his own good. We need to help him regain his composure and focus on what we came here for."

"Fair enough," she said putting the last pancake on a plate. I could tell she wanted to ask more questions, but thought better of it when Warrick joined us, "What are we helping me with, love?"

I winced, "Trying to get you more composed again so you have the best chances at getting the witches on our side."

"Ah, yes. Sorry about my outburst earlier. I should know better than to drink that much," Warrick acknowledged each of us. "Thank you for breakfast, Jennie."

"Anytime," she replied tersely watching as he grabbed a plate then moved to the dining room table. Jennie looked back at me and I shrugged. Warrick and his mood swings were unpredictable, so there was no justifying what happened unless I told Jennie and Lou about what Warrick confessed to me last night.

We all ended up at the table taking turns with watching the snow whip around the house. It didn't look like the storm had let up from what it was last night. Jennie scoffed after taking another look outside, "Well, this is depressing. I'd like to go back to the island, please."

I chuckled, "I hear you there."

"When we're done here, Val and Lou, I need to talk to the both of you since you're both involved in the main group I've pulled together. Jennie, you're more than welcome to join, too," Warrick cut in.

"What are you going to be talking about?" Jennie asked.

"Going over some strategy and my plans for while we're here and for what's next," Warrick explained in between bites.

"Sure. I have nothing better to do," Jennie said.

I finished swallowing the food I had in my mouth then said, "I thought we already covered that."

"There's a few things I haven't shared with you yet," he pushed his seat back from the table and started heading upstairs. "Meet me in the office."

We watched him walk away. "Well, that's a fast change from where he was at this morning," Lou observed.

"No kidding," I muttered. I grabbed everyone else's empty plate and put them in the sink. We headed up as a group each taking our seats across from where Warrick sat behind my dad's desk. Warrick leaned forward resting his elbows on the shiny surface, diving right in, "Alright. As you know, we have the vampires and fae on our side. You might've picked up on the elves joining us as well, and the last group we have is the dragon riders. In case you get stuck alone with any of these leaders, I want you both to know the name of their worlds so you're being respectful."

"Okay," Lou said slowly.

I glanced at Lou to see he was just as confused as I was. Turning back to Warrick, I asked, "This feels a little out of the blue. Why are we jumping into all of this so quickly and why do we need to know now?"

Warrick leaned back impatiently tapping his fingers on the desk, "You both need to know these things because after our meeting, several of the leaders came up to me expressing their doubts about you two. Val, love, you're already at a disadvantage because of Cian's comments. The rest, besides Sarind and your dad, didn't like the fact that we're romantically involved. They felt the only reason you were at that table is because of us and your relationship with your world's representative. As for you, Lou, they didn't even know I had a second so I need to make sure you're prepped in case you get drilled with questions. They need to know you're on my level in order to establish a greater sense of trust in me. We're doing this now because this world is unforgiving. There may be times where I'm gone for a couple of days, so I don't know when I'll be able to go over this with you next and I want to make sure we cover all the bases before we have to spring into action. Got it?"

We both nodded our heads. Warrick looked relieved that we didn't ask any further questions, so he pulled out a map he had stowed under the desk, "Alright, world names." He pointed to my world, "Earth which is Val's world and the one currently under attack. Next one is ours, Lupusantha, where the werewolves roam. We then went over to Cian's world, Stragairel. The wonderful paradise where the fae hide out is Flamediocris. We're now in Frigusmada. The elves' call Nudryadales home and you'll find the dragons at Validracos."

I watched as he slid his finger from one world to the next, nodding my head. *I really hope this is written down somewhere.*

Warrick rolled the map back up continuing, "As you know, we're here because we're trying to get the witches on our side. However, with Az's latest upgrades, it's looking doubtful. I have no idea where to find the leader of this hell hole, so my time will be spent searching for them. I have a couple of packets outlining the weapons my team built and stashed back home which you both need to read through. Not like those weapons are going to do anything but it's worth a shot. Each of the world leaders are equipped with their own devices as I mentioned. I also mentioned that we'll likely be heading straight to Earth after we're done here. When we get there, we're going to take some time to get the lay of the land and try to see where Az is holing up. This will also give us the chance to prep everything and finalize our attack.

"For the time we're here, I've updated each of your phones so you can get ahold of one another, even though it is a weak signal. Val, you are not to leave this house without either Jennie or Lou with you. Preferably Lou, but I get that won't always be possible. Other than that, you're stuck in this house."

I clenched my fists under the table but maintained my composure, "Do we know if Az is here or not?"

Warrick shook his head, "No, but I don't want to take any chances."

"You're locking me up because – "

"Listen, love, I'm not risking you getting hurt or worse. End of discussion. I have to head out," Warrick stood up abruptly and left the office.

I stormed out after him towards my room. He was grabbing a few things from his main bag and putting them in a smaller duffel bag. I closed the door behind me even though I knew Lou would be able to hear us if he wanted to. Warrick glanced at me for a second then went back to what he was doing, his tone still business-like, "Is there something on your mind?"

"You're kidding me, right?" I scoffed. "No ifs, ands, or buts about it. My house has now become my prison and you're just leaving me here after saying you wouldn't let me out of your sight. We can't get a day together?"

That got him to stop. He flinched now realizing the effects of what he said earlier, "I'm sorry, love. My goal is to come back every night, but I have to start this search as soon as I can. We don't have a lot of time based on what your dad said, and if Az hasn't made a stop here, he likely will. I'd like to beat him."

"Is this how our lives are going to be?" I blurted. This question had been sitting in the back of my mind ever since I decided to accept the fact that Warrick and I were fated.

He crossed the room lifting my chin so I was forced to look him in the eyes, "We will have some time to ourselves, I promise. Take this as some time to recover from the mental strain Az put on you the other night."

"Just go," I said yanking my head back, walking over to the door. I now felt like a pawn in his master plan, no longer feeling like someone he cared about and I was pissed. I ripped the door back open and made my way downstairs.

Jennie and Lou were talking by the island, but stopped when I pulled up a seat. I rolled my eyes, "Don't stop just because I showed up."

"Someone's in a good mood," Lou huffed.

"Sorry," I sighed dropping my head. "Just frustrated with Warrick and I shouldn't be taking it out on you guys."

Jennie put a hand on my arm, "I'd be frustrated, too, especially since you have your own focus here."

"Thanks," I said giving her a weak smile.

Warrick came down the stairs dropping his bag and walking towards us, "I'm hoping to be back tonight." He lifted my chin up, "We'll go out when I get back, okay, love?"

"Sure," I said still holding his gaze. He leaned in for a soft kiss not quite pulling away. A few beats passed by the time he ended the kiss. Warrick's face was still pressed against mine as he said, "I'm really not trying to punish you, love. Give it a few days."

"Okay," I whispered.

Then, he left. I stared after him wishing for him to be back tonight like he said. Jennie clapped her hands, "So, who's up for exploring?"

"What do you have in mind?" Lou asked.

"Try to find a bar later?" she suggested.

They went back and forth a little longer while I zoned out. I wasn't a fan of my freedom being taken away because of a worry, and even though he's trying to come from a place of concern, that's no excuse. There's no evidence of Az being here and I'd like to at least explore this new space since I probably won't be seeing it again after this. I'm sure the blizzard raging outside is going to make sightseeing next to impossible, but I'd at least like the choice.

"That settles it. We're going to the first bar we can find tonight. We're not going to let you stay cooped up in this house, Val," Jennie said smiling at me.

We spent the day playing boardgames. I did my best to ignore the pitying looks in my direction, but they still bugged me. The sun started to set and Jennie dragged me upstairs to get ready. The storm wasn't as bad as it was when we first got here, but the snow was still obscuring a lot of our view. We bundled up then braved the cold, getting smacked by the wind as soon as we stepped out of the house. There was no way we were going to be able to talk to each other over the wind, so hand signals it was. Lou led the way while Jennie was behind me until we forced a door open on the first building we came across.

Turns out we found a bar. Brushing ourselves off, Jennie asked, "How did you know we wanted to come in here?"

"Lucky guess," Lou chuckled.

We tucked ourselves in an empty corner so our backs weren't facing anyone. There was a surprising number of people in here considering how miserable it was outside. Even though we didn't have to walk far, I was already dreading the walk back and had a hunch I'd be staying in the house most of the time anyways.

Jennie pranced over to the bar to get us some drinks. I glanced at Lou who watched after her, "How do we have the right currency to buy things here?"

"Thank your boyfriend," Lou said turning his attention to me. "Apparently, he's loaded no matter what world we go to."

"Have you asked her out yet?" I tilted my head in Jennie's direction.

Lou instantly blushed, "Not gonna lie, Val, it's kind of weird talking to you about dating your best friend."

I laughed a little, "Suck it up, Lou. I'll be asking about how things are going as long as you two have something going on."

He laughed in response, "Fine, then, I haven't. Maybe soon."

"Why don't you guys have a date tonight?" I threw out there.

"What?"

"I'm serious. I'll go find another table that's still within eyesight, but offers you two privacy. Get to know her a little," I said.

"Warrick will kill us," Lou tried to object.

"We're not breaking his rules. I'm still out with the two of you, and like I said, I'll be in your line of sight," I grinned.

He shook his head, "You're always up to something whether you know it or not."

Jennie returned with a couple pitchers of beer and some glasses, "What did I miss?"

"You two are going to have some alone time while I go sit at the table over there," I pointed to a table a few spots away where I would still be facing the door and I was clearly in their line of sight. "Have fun you two."

"Wait," Jennie started. I didn't give her the chance to finish as I grabbed one of the pitchers and a glass then moved to my new spot. They stared after me. I gave them a finger wave once I settled in. Lou shook his head at me again while Jennie mouthed, "What are you doing?"

I motioned for them to start paying attention to each other breathing a sigh of relief when they did. I pulled out a book I had tucked away in my coat, but before I started reading, I took a scan around the room trying to find any signs of a familiar face. My phone buzzed making me jump and I scanned the notification. Warrick texted me letting me know he wasn't going to be back tonight, but he's rain checking our date. *Figures*. I only sent him a thumbs up in response deciding it was time to get lost in someone else's story.

About an hour had passed. I glanced over at Jennie and Lou feeling happy when I saw them sitting closer together, laughing. I poured the last beer from this pitcher then went over to grab their empty one. Might as well refill since we'd probably be here a while. Jennie and Lou seemed like they were having such a good time that I didn't want to cut it short. While I was waiting at the bar, a hooded figure shifted closer towards me. I shuffled to put a little distance between us, but he only followed me.

"Can I help you?" I asked worried someone was going to try to attack me.

"Depends," he mumbled. "Do you know if there's a cure for the Val-effect?"

Chapter 7

Those words froze me. There was only four people who knew that term. One was dead, one was back in the werewolf world (*I have to remember to call it Lupusantha*), and one was a wolf that should be back in that world, too.

"Excuse me?" I asked.

The man removed his hood and I did a little jump, "Mark!"

There was no hesitation as I pulled him in a hug. He wrapped his arms around me letting out a soft laugh, "You have no idea how happy I am to see you."

"The same could be said to you. I've been missing your goofy self," I said as I pulled back. "Come join me."

"Anyone else with you?" he asked as he followed me back to my table.

I gestured towards Jennie and Lou, who were still very much engrossed in each other, "Just Jennie, but I know where Joe and Bev are at."

"Who's that?" Mark asked furrowing his brows.

"There's *a lot* I need to catch you up on, but you first. Where's Lilly?" I asked. Being around him was already lifting my spirits, but it didn't seem like I had the same effect. In fact, I had never seen Mark look this down in all the years I've known him. He was pale with dark circles under his eyes. He looked like he lost a lot of weight, too. I put a hand on his arm, "Are you okay?"

Mark rubbed his face with his hands and pointed towards the pitcher, "May I?"

"Be my guest."

He filled his glass then downed half of it before topping it off. He leaned forward on his elbows sighing, "Lilly and I ended things." He paused then looked at me, "Wait, how did you know she was here with me?"

"I'll explain more later, but it's a trend I noticed."

"Okay," Mark said not quite wanting to drop his question, but moving on anyways. "This is a fucked up place, Val. I'm really happy to see you here, but if you have any way of getting us out, we need to do that sooner rather than later."

It was my turn to be confused, "What do you mean?"

Mark scanned the room then leaned in closer, dropping his voice to a whisper, "There's a lot of powerful witches here, and not the good kind. They feed off your pain and sadness, basically anything negative. If they even catch a whiff of those emotions, they'll try to suck you dry until there's nothing left of you."

"I know about the witches," I nodded. I stared at the thin line of foam topping my beer, "I didn't know they were like that, though."

"It's pretty brutal. This is about the only bar where the witches don't come in. It's been my safe haven."

I brought my eyes back up to his, "Is that what happened to you? The witches, I mean? Because you honestly look awful."

A weak attempt at a smile formed on his lips, "Thanks. I needed to hear that, I guess, but yeah."

"Please tell me they didn't kill Lilly," I said watching him very carefully to see if his body language betrayed him.

He shook his head, a shadow crossing over his features, "No, but she became one of them."

My jaw dropped, "What?"

Mark threw back the rest of his beer and filled his glass up. He nodded his head, his tone now one filled with disbelief, "Yup, and what better way to try out your newfound magic than on your now depressed ex."

"Oh, Mark. I'm so sorry. Do you even know how she got her magic?"

"No," he said closing his eyes. "She just came home one day and said she had something cool to show me. Before she showed me, though, she ended it. Said she just wanted to have sex with me and that was it. She went on to tell me that the apartment was hers, but I could stay there. I didn't question that. I mean, where was I going to go? Then, she attacked me. I had never experienced anything like that before."

Mark swallowed fighting back the painful memories. I scooted closer to him, bumping him, "Hey, you don't have to keep reliving this if you don't want to. I think I got the picture, and from what I can see, it's pretty fucked up. Just tell me you're not staying there now."

"No," he shook his head sounding relieved he didn't have to tell me anything else. "I've been crashing here. The bartender's been nice enough to set up a cot after closing. I just have to help with dishes."

"Would you like someplace else to stay?" I asked.

He looked at me, confused, "What do you mean?"

"I have my house. You're more than welcome to crash with us," I offered then took a long swig of my beer.

"Really?" Mark asked, his face finally lighting up.

"Yup," I smiled. "No questions asked."

"Let me grab my things and break the news," he said leaping to his feet. Mark wasted no time talking with the bartender then heading into the back where his things were stored. He came back tossing his bag at my feet, "When do we go?"

"When those two are done with their date," I nodded in the direction of Jennie and Lou.

"Right," he slowly nodded, the light in his face that was just there starting to fade. "Which reminds me. Who's that?"

I sighed, "I wish I could say you were the only one who went through hell and back, but hopefully this brings you some comfort in knowing that we all went through some shit."

"I guess? Sorry to jump off track for a moment, but are you and Daryl still a thing?" Mark asked tilting his head.

I shook my head and finished what was in my glass. I poured what was remaining from the pitcher back in and watched the foam settle down a little bit. When I was finally ready to talk, I let out a breath, "Daryl died."

"What? How?" Mark's eyebrows shot up.

"Here we go. I'll get to that in a second. That guy with Jennie? His name's Lou. He's an alpha werewolf and has been traveling with me between worlds," I paused.

Mark jumped in, lowering his voice and looking around again to make sure no one was listening in, "Werewolves? Worlds?"

"Yup. Just like witches are real, so are werewolves, fairies, vampires. You name it. Anything we thought was just a myth exists in their own little world. Literally. I woke up in the werewolf world, Jennie and Chris found themselves in the vampire world, and Joe and Bev were in the fae world," I explained. I held my hand up to keep him from asking more questions as I went on, "Basically, the bombs had little devices in them that could transport us to different places. Bombs that were built by my dad, by the way. Don't worry, he's not actually the bad guy in this story, but I'll get to that in a minute.

"There's another alpha traveling with us, Warrick. He's the one who killed Daryl. I'll spare you the details because it's messy, but we've all moved past what Warrick did. You will, too, even though you probably don't believe me now," I said watching as Mark shook his head.

I went on, "Keep in mind, I'm giving you the Cliff notes version. If I went into every little detail, we'd be here all night. Anyways, Lou's been helping me through this whole mess. We were able to create a device and jumped to the vampire world where I got reunited with Chris and Jennie. Not without troubles, though. My dumbass decided to try out the *Buffy* lifestyle which ended up with me nearly dying. This is after Warrick essentially tortured me."

"Is that why you have scars all over?" Mark said gesturing around his face.

I nodded, "Yup. The only reason I'm alive is because Warrick hatched a plan to save me. This is where he turns into the good guy. We moved on to the fae world finding Joe and Bev. I found out Warrick and I are fated which means exactly what it sounds like. Him and I are destined to be together. After that, we headed back to the werewolf world to celebrate Christmas and to recalibrate a little. Come to find out Warrick has a brother who's not someone you really want to even meet. Ironically, I dated his brother back home years ago, but his brother didn't forget that. Oh no. He definitely remembered and decided that he was going to try to rape me partly because he wasn't over me, another part of him has been trying to get in Warrick's head, and the icing on the cake is that my dad told him I'm the key to the information he needs for the war. Did I mention that Warrick's brother is the person behind the war?"

"Holy shit, Val. This is like a crazy TV show or something," Mark said, eyes wide.

"Oh, one more thing," I started. I looked over towards Jennie, "Chris and Jennie got in a relationship, got engaged, then broke up all because Chris wanted to be a werewolf and cheated on her. I think that brings you up to speed."

"Fuck," Mark shook his head.

"Mmhmm," I nodded drinking more. "So, needless to say, we're all a little messed up now. You should fit right in, and the best part? You won't even have any pressure to be your old self."

"Sounds like a party," he said sarcastically. "There's one thing you didn't explain, though."

"What's that?"

Mark looked towards Jennie and Lou, "How do you know that Lilly and I came here together?"

"Ah, that. We figured out that if two people were in the same room at the time of the transfer, then they ended up in the same place. Daryl and I were in a room and wound up in the werewolf world. Jennie and Chris were together and so were Joe and Bev," I explained.

He nodded, "Makes sense as much as it can, I guess."

Mark was about to say something else when the door slammed open. A tall figure walked in, dressed in all black. He scanned the space before making his way to the bar, but when he looked in our direction, I froze. Thankfully, the newcomer kept walking and didn't make a move in our direction.

"That was a little aggressive," Mark mumbled. He grabbed the empty pitcher and moved to stand up, "I'll go grab us some more."

My hand closed around his arm. "No, we gotta go," I choked out.

"What?"

"Don't act suspicious, just grab your shit and let's get Lou and Jennie," I said still watching the newcomer. He was waiting for his order, casually looking around the bar. His hazel eyes landed on me and winked before returning his focus on the bartender.

"Fuck, fuck, fuck," I whispered.

We made our way over to where Jennie and Lou sat. Mark lowered his voice, looking over his shoulder, "Who is that?"

I ignored his question along with the look of surprise on Jennie and Lou's faces, "Mark, Lou. Lou, Mark. I'll explain later, but we have to go now."

"Uh, nice to meet you," Lou said extending a hand. His brows knit together in confusion, "What's going on, Val?"

"Az. Fucking *Az* is here right now and he knows I'm here, too," I said, the anxiety very present in my voice.

"Where?" Lou asked suddenly getting very serious.

"That doesn't matter," I said tugging at their arms. "We have to go now."

"Val, I have to close out the tab," Jennie said, eyes darting between Lou and me.

"I got it," Lou mumbled. Jennie handed him the money. He walked over to the bar, head on a swivel. The rest of us got bundled up to head back to the house watching Lou the entire way to the bar.

"Shit," I mumbled.

Jennie looked at me, "What's wrong?"

I nodded towards the table Mark and I were sitting at, "I left my book."

"I got it," Jennie said, no hesitation. "You stay here."

The bar was packed at this point. She was swallowed up by the crowd and panic gripped my throat when I could no longer see Lou. I leaned into Mark, "Is it normally this crowded?"

"Yeah, we're in prime time now," Mark noted. "I don't think I've ever seen you this freaked out before. What did you say this guy's name was? Ass?"

A laugh escaped me, "Close enough."

I glanced up at Mark happy to see his smile coming back. *His jokes are just what we need right now.* An arm circled around my waist, and at first I thought it was Mark, but his face had gone serious. I was pulled away from him and felt lips against my ear, "I've missed the sound of that laugh of yours."

I stiffened. I don't know what was taking Jennie and Lou so long, but they had been gone long enough for Az to slip in. He let me go. I backed into Mark who put a protective hand on my shoulder. Az smirked, "Sneaking around now that dear little brother is running errands?"

"Hey, man, I don't know who you think you are, but it's time to go," Mark said.

Az held his hands up, "Tough guy."

Mark's hand tightened on my shoulder. I was getting to see a whole new side to him. He's typically all jokes and smiles.

Az did a little mocking dance and then closed the distance between us so we were almost touching. He brought his hand up to my chin, his thumb pressing against my bottom lip, "Told you I'd be seeing you soon, beautiful."

He faded into the crowd just in time for Lou and Jennie to get back. *Of course he has that timing down.* Jennie saw how tense Mark was and looked at me, "What happened?"

"Az popped out of the ground. Didn't do anything, just showed his face," I said staring in the direction Az disappeared.

Lou looked over his shoulder, "Let's go."

The three of them circled around me as we pushed our way out the door. We kept that formation, this time Lou in the rear as we made the arduous journey home. No one made any sounds or any conversation until we were back within the safety of my house.

"Want to fill me in on what just happened? We were gone for minutes and neither of us saw anything," Lou said.

Surprisingly, Mark was the one who answered Lou, "He showed up right after Jennie went to grab Val's book. Wrapped his arm around her waist and whispered something to her. I didn't catch what he said the first time, but he didn't hesitate to throw shots at me. Then he gave Val an 'I told you so.' Said something about him proving he'd see her soon."

Jennie came up to me, "When did he tell you that? I feel like I'm missing way too much."

I looked at Lou from the corner of my eyes only to get a shrug in return. *A lot of help he is.* "Let's sit down," I motioned towards the couch.

Lou and I got comfortable while Jennie had her loud, excited reunion with Mark. She skipped over to join the two of us with Mark in tow, "I was so caught up in everything else that I didn't get a chance to say hi to Mark."

"I see that," I grinned. "I had a hunch I wasn't going to need your help with persuading him to come back here with us."

"But where's Lilly?" Jennie pouted.

Mark ran a hand through his hair as he explained to her the same story he did to me. Jennie's hand moved towards her opened mouth. When Mark finished, she shook her head in disbelief, "She would never do something like that."

"Really, Jennie?" I asked, unable to keep the annoyance out of my voice.

"What the hell do you mean, Val?" Jennie threw back at me looking hurt.

"She isn't exactly the nicest person."

"Anyways," Mark said, cutting back in before Jennie and I could fight. "You'll be stuck with yours truly because Lilly has no intentions of leaving here. Now, Val, I believe you were going to answer Jennie's question."

I was staring at Mark in disbelief. There was a sternness behind his tone that was new. Jennie wore a shocked expression, almost as if she'd been slapped. I don't blame Mark for reacting that way when Jennie is defending the woman who tormented him. Lou just raised his eyebrows. He may not have the full story, but he can pick up on the context clues.

"The floor is yours," Mark made a grand gesture.

"There's a few things we left out in the chaos of getting here," I started slowly bringing my focus from Mark to Jennie. "That night after you and Bev went to sleep I headed over to Warrick's."

She nodded, "Right."

"Well, he wasn't there. I walked into the place looking like it had been robbed. Turns out Az was there looking for Warrick, too," I swallowed knowing I'd be getting to the part of the story I would much rather keep to myself.

Lou put his head in his hands, reliving the video footage. Jennie saw this movement and brought her eyebrows together. I squared my shoulders and continued, "He wouldn't let me leave. He forced me to share a few bottles of wine then forced himself on me. By the time Warrick got back, Az had almost gotten what he wanted. Then, Warrick shot him about six times with no effect. Az just laughed it off and left."

"How did none of you say anything to me?" she asked incredulously.

Lou still holding his head in his hands answered, "It wasn't something you needed to worry about."

"You knew?" Jennie asked.

Lou finally sat back up nodding his head, "I watched it."

Jennie looked horrified, "What do you mean?"

"Warrick has cameras throughout his apartment. We watched the footage back," he said keeping his tone somber.

I couldn't meet anyone's eyes at this point, but I cut back in, "Then, I was stupid and suggested we split up to take care of the shopping. Az caught up to me, stabbed me, then kissed me before telling me he'd see me soon."

"Hence the reason why Warrick doesn't want Val to step foot outside this house, and if he hears ab – "

"Hears about what?" Warrick's cool voice asked from behind us.

We all jumped. Mark looked Warrick up and down then kept his eyes trained on the floor. Warrick put a hand on my shoulder, "Who'd we bring home, love?"

"This is Mark, one of our missing friends," I gestured towards the man now folding in on himself.

Warrick extended a hand in his direction, "Nice to meet you. Glad Val could find you."

Mark hesitated before shaking the outstretched hand. He didn't dare look in Warrick's direction or say anything, earning a chuckle from Warrick, "I guess Val caught you up on things. Don't worry, I'm not the one you should be scared of."

"Warrick," Lou started. "Az is here."

The hand on my shoulder gripped harder causing me to let out a small whimper. He immediately loosened it, "What happened?"

"He snuck up on Val just to show he was there. Met Mark, too."

Mark cleared his throat, "He didn't make a move on her. Just said some things then left."

"Love?"

"Yeah," I nodded. "Just playing more head games."

"That wasn't what I was asking," Warrick said as he moved in front of me. He crouched down examining what he could see, "Are you okay?"

I nodded my head, "Just a little freaked out, that's all."

"Seems like it's more than that," he observed.

"She just got done telling me what happened after the restaurant," Jennie jumped in. "I had no idea."

"It wasn't pretty," Warrick said not taking his eyes off me.

I met those icy blue eyes and reached out to push his hair back, "I thought you weren't coming back tonight."

"Something was telling me you needed me," Warrick said.

"Did you make any progress?"

"No," he shook his head. "It's only the first day, so not surprising. Did you all eat?"

"No," Lou said. "I'll cook."

Warrick stuck a hand out, "I got it." He started making his way over to the kitchen, "Glad you're here Mark."

"Thanks," Mark mumbled.

Everyone except for Mark and I got off the couch. Jennie and Lou got to work helping with dinner and I elbowed Mark, "I've never seen you so quiet."

"Is he always that intimidating?" Mark asked in a hushed tone.

"You get used to it," I said. "C'mon, would alcohol help loosen you up a little bit? Bring out the old Mark?"

He gave me a goofy smile, "You know my language."

We joined everyone else. Jennie pushed a glass of whiskey towards Mark who gratefully accepted. I stuck with water while Jennie moved to wine and Lou stuck with beer. We kept the conversation light, but I could tell Warrick wasn't happy hearing about the run-in with Az. I had followed his instructions, even added someone else to watch over me, and he still had to worry about me.

Warrick started moving around the kitchen, throwing back a glass of whiskey as he started cooking. Jennie and Mark were catching up on everything that happened to her while Lou quietly approached me keeping one eye trained on Warrick, "Want a beer?"

"Sure," I nodded.

He came back with a couple of bottles, clinking them together before taking a long sip. Lou grabbed a chair and sighed as he got comfortable, "Nice surprise, huh?"

"What are you talking about?"

"Warrick," he nodded his head in the chef's direction.

"Music anyone?" Mark asked.

"Go for it," I said.

Jennie smiled, "Yes, please. Something to lighten the mood. You all are way too serious for me right now."

Mark gave her a salute then followed her instructions. He came back over doing a little dance, holding his hand out to Jennie. She made a show about accepting his invitation and then they were twirling around the room, Jennie's infectious laugh filling the air. I turned back toward the island where Warrick was consumed with what was in front of him on the stove. I don't know why I thought I'd turn around and he'd be offering a dance to me, but that didn't weaken the sting. I shook my head taking another sip when Lou tapped my arm. He offered his hand out, jerking his head towards the living room where Mark and Jennie were, "C'mon."

"Okay," I said sheepishly.

Lou led the way over and pulled me close. He was careful not to pull me too close so as to not set off the beast who was doing his best to ignore us. "Just because he's in a mood doesn't mean you should miss out on having some fun," Lou said keeping his voice quiet.

I smiled, "Thank you. I keep feeling like I'm constantly screwing up."

"You're not," Lou said turning us so Warrick was out of my line of sight. "You have no control on what's happening, only on how you react. You're doing nothing wrong."

"Thanks," I said resting my head on his chest. My body suddenly felt heavy and I appreciated Lou being there to hold me up. "How was your time with Jennie tonight?"

"It was good, just not sure where it's going to go," Lou drifted off.

I lifted my head up to see his features filled with uncertainty. I put my head back down, "The good thing is that nothing is set in stone. You're just feeling it out."

"Exactly," Lou responded.

We let the music fall on us ending our conversation. The next song started and I heard someone clear their throat behind me, "Mind if I cut in?"

"Sure thing," Lou let me go. "I'll take over the cooking duties."

Warrick gently pulled me into him, a hand on my lower back while the other held my hand. I draped my free arm around the back of his neck and rested my head on his chest as I had been doing with Lou moments ago. He gave me a soft kiss on my head, "I'm sorry, love."

"For?" I asked.

"The way I've been acting," he said softly.

I closed my eyes, "You've been doing what you think is best. It's not your fault your brother is being an asshole."

"But it is my fault he's getting under my skin," Warrick said cooly. "I can control how I react and I've been doing a poor job at it."

The words escaped my mouth before I had a chance to stop them, "I wasn't going to say anything."

Warrick stiffened then relaxed again, "I deserve that."

I lifted my head so I was looking at him, "Look, I'm sorry for lashing out. You should know by now that I don't like to be restricted. I was very conflicted on whether or not I should listen to you, but that was before Az showed up here. I know he's dangerous. Hell, I think you and I have had the most intense interactions with him. All I'm saying is, know I'm not going to be leaving the house anytime soon unless it's absolutely necessary, especially with this weather. I found what I came here for. There's no need to risk things."

"Thank you, love," he visibly relaxed. He opened his mouth to say something, but Lou announced dinner was ready.

We all loaded up some plates of curry and got comfortable around the dining room table. Warrick lifted his refilled glass in Mark's direction, "I'm glad you're here."

Everyone else followed his motions, nodding. Mark's smile inched across his face, "Thanks, man. You have no idea how happy I am to be able to see the light at the end of the tunnel."

It warmed me seeing Mark come back to life a little bit. His smile was taking on its usual spark and color was coming back to his cheeks. Plus, Mark was happily throwing jokes around now that he stopped letting Warrick scare him so much. Lou grabbed us a couple more beers while Jennie took a refill on her wine. She started batting her eyelashes at Lou more and more as the night went on. I felt myself loosening up and knew Lou was, too. Warrick was leaning back in his chair, an arm draped across the back sharing the rare, genuine smile that fills me with warmth. Lou looked relaxed. Seeing all this made me smile.

These moments of normalcy were hard to come by, especially lately, which makes me enjoy them even more.

I grabbed the empty plates and started cleaning up. Warrick came up behind me wrapping his arms around my waist, resting his chin on my shoulder, "Is this okay, love?"

My body tensed at first, but relaxed when I reminded myself I wasn't under attack here. I nodded, "Yeah, thank you for asking."

"I made a surprise for you," he mumbled into my neck.

"What's that?"

Any extra heat I was getting from him left as he walked over the fridge. I finished with the dishes as I watched Warrick pull out a container. He set it down next to me and took off the lid to reveal his chocolate cake. My mouth watered just looking at it earning a smile from Warrick, "Dessert."

I stared down the cake as Warrick came back behind me. He pulled me into him, his voice dropping to a whisper, "If there's any left, maybe we can take it up to bed with us tonight."

I didn't need his body heat this time. His words were doing just fine at warming me.

Lou came up to grab everything shaking his head, "Just remember there's other people here, you two."

That snapped me out of it and I got back to helping take things over to the table. I knew what to expect with this particular chocolate cake, but I don't think anyone else at this table knew. Jennie's eyes widened then closed after the first bite, "This is the best damn cake I've ever eaten."

Even Lou looked impressed, "I didn't know you made things like this, Warrick."

Warrick chuckled, "I'm a man of many talents, what can I say?"

Mark was sitting there humming to himself as he devoured his piece while it was taking everything in me not to moan. Warrick knew how hard I was trying judging by the smile tugging at the corner of his lips every time he glanced in my direction. Mark leaned back in his chair patting his stomach, "I haven't had this much to eat in I don't know how long. Thanks."

"Welcome back," I smiled at him.

Mark returned the smile then pushed back his chair, "I'm feeling pretty beat, so if you all don't mind, I'll be getting some shut eye."

"Goodnight," we all said in unison.

The four of us sat in silence until we heard a door close. Jennie sighed, "Lilly really did a number on him."

"I was shocked when I first saw him," I said staring into my bottle.

"What happened?" Warrick asked leaning forward.

Jennie recounted Mark's story and I filled in the blanks. When she was done, I glanced over to Warrick, "The man you met tonight was like a shell of who we knew and loved. Mark's a goofball by nature, but it's like she sucked that all out of him."

"She really did," Jennie agreed.

I could see the gears turning in Warrick's head, but he never said what was on his mind. Instead, he put a hand on my knee, "I have an early morning tomorrow, care to join me, love?"

"Sure," I said. Turning back to Jennie and Lou, I gave them a wave then led the way to my room. The minute we closed the door, Warrick leaned against it, arm above my head and face inches from mine, "Don't think I forgot about grabbing the rest of that cake, as long as you're up for it?"

He had no idea. I reached up to caress his cheek watching his pupils dilate, "Of course I am."

Warrick slowly came in for a kiss, gentle at first but then needy. He led us from the door over to the bed laying me down. I watched as he slowly unbuttoned his shirt, removing that and his undershirt to reveal his hardened body. I ran my hand over the muscles noting the new scars, letting my hand drift closer to his pants. Warrick grabbed me, stopping it before I was able to tease him, "I'll be right back."

"I'll be here," I responded.

Warrick gave me another passionate kiss before leaving the room. I rolled over on my side and propped my head up as I watched the door. Warrick had wasted no time with grabbing what was left of the cake along with a couple of forks. When he saw my raised eyebrows, he smirked, "Still up for this?"

"Bring it on," I answered.

Warrick was all over me in an instant. His lips were kissing everywhere while his hands roamed my body making me wish I were already naked. I barely brushed my hand over his hardened cock, but that was enough to make him stop what he was doing. In a husky voice that sent shivers down my spine, he said, "You have no idea how much I've missed this, love."

I lifted his chin to look at him, "Me too."

Our lips collided while he sat me up. I angled myself so we could deepen the kiss earning a moan from him. Warrick's fingers grasped on to the hem of my shirt, but not without grazing my skin that instantly erupted in goosebumps. When he had my shirt off, he stepped back to admire then came back to remove the rest of my clothes. Once I was naked, I stood up and pushed him back on to the bed. I crawled up to kiss his neck while working on removing his pants. I trailed kisses down his body until I reached the waistline.

Warrick started to work himself out of his pants, but I put a stop to that. I wanted to take some control of this process. I took my sweet time removing his pants leaving kisses as I went. He scooted further back on the bed and I climbed back on top of him, teasing his tip with my tongue. His moans of pure pleasure rang out as I filled my mouth with him. I gave him one more kiss down there before making my way back up to his lips.

Warrick flipped me under him caressing my cheek, "I've missed you so much, love."

"Show me," I said, my voice laced with desire.

He dragged his fingers down my body barely touching me. One hand came up to palm my breast, rolling my nipple between his fingers while the other found its way between my legs. He moved his fingers at the same time making me arch into him, eyes closing. Warrick lowered himself to tease me with his tongue, and when I opened my eyes to grip his hair, I saw hazel eyes staring back at me instead of blue.

Chapter 8

My body tensed and I froze. I couldn't breathe as my senses were flooded with all things Az. His scent, the feel of his skin on mine, the rumble of his voice.

Warrick came back up to me, worried, "Are you okay, love? What's wrong?"

I scrambled away from him, "I can't."

"We can stop," he said trying to follow me.

I curled in on myself while throwing a hand up, "Don't! Just don't touch me. I can't breathe right now."

My chest became tight, air struggling to reach my lungs. I was in a full blown panic attack trying to get it under control.

The worry was replaced with a mask of anger. Warrick kept his voice collected as he said, "I'll be right back."

He threw his pants back on and grabbed the cake before heading to the door. I lifted my head up to see he was watching me very carefully. "I'm sorry," I croaked.

He only shook his head and left. I still couldn't bring myself to move. I guess Az wormed his way into my mind after all. We were having a perfectly good moment, one where Warrick wasn't angry for once and I had to go and ruin it.

The door softly closed, the lights flicked off. I heard Warrick rummaging around in my closet before the bed dipped from him getting back in. I felt soft fabric against my back, "Here, love."

I reached behind me still not exposing myself and felt the tears spring into my eyes as I looked at the Christmas pajamas he had gotten me. I sat up, my back still facing Warrick, slowly pulling the clothes on. My head fell into my hands as the tears no longer wanted to be held back. "I'm so sorry, Warrick," I wiped at the onslaught of tears. "This is not how I wanted to spend my time with you."

"There's nothing you need to be sorry for. It was too soon and I should be sorry for rushing you into physical intimacy after what happened," he paused. "You saw Az, didn't you?"

I nodded then turned around, crawling into his arms. Warrick held on to me tightly running a comforting hand over my hair. Neither of us said anything else as we let the weight of what we both realized settle on us: Az had us right where he wanted. He was impacting our relationship enough to where Warrick would start to put more focus on repairing things between us rather than the war. Az was also so far in my head that I would eventually go to seek him out to get some sort of peace, and that is when he would strike.

"What do we do?" I asked in a weak voice.

Warrick tightened his hold on me resting his cheek on top of my head, "We don't let him win. We don't give in to what he's trying to do. It's not going to be easy, love, and we have to be okay with hitting some bumps in the road as long as we stay true to each other."

"Don't leave," I croaked out.

He shook his head, "I'll make sure to come home every night, love. We'll dance in the kitchen and hold each other as we fight off the demons that come to haunt us. I'll make you a chocolate cake just to hear those moans of yours until you're ready to go to bed with me. I'll go to battle each and every day to keep those tears from staining your beautiful face ever again. Most of all, I'll love you until the day I die. Then, I'll wait for you so I can keep loving you in the afterlife."

I looked up at him, wiping away the stray tears on his face, "I'll always love you, Warrick. This day and the next and forever after that."

Warrick gave me a tender kiss holding me for as long as I'd let him. When we pulled apart, he lifted the covers, "Let's try to get some sleep, love."

And we did just that. I cuddled into him letting his scent wash over me, the steady rhythm of his heart lulling me into a deep sleep. I startled awake a couple of times thanks to Az popping up in my dreams, but Warrick was there still holding me, tightening his grip every time I woke up to remind me I was safe here.

The last time I woke up Warrick had to start getting out of the bed. Cold air suddenly rushed in where he was laying making me wide awake. I propped up on my elbows to see him getting ready to leave, but without a bag this time. Rubbing the sleep out of my eyes, I asked, "Have to go so soon?"

"I need to get a head start on my day. Hopefully I can find some leads," he grunted as he forced his legs through his pants.

Warrick glanced at me and immediately stopped when he saw the expression on my face. He rushed over to my side of the bed and crouched down, tucking a strand of hair behind my ear, "I will be back tonight, love. I promise."

I nodded my head unable to say anything. He finished getting ready then held out his hand to me, "Come downstairs with me for a moment? I'll make you breakfast."

"Okay," I said grabbing his hand and shuffling out from the warm covers.

It was still dark outside. The storm had picked back up, the strong winds were a constant at this point rattling the windows. I walked up to one running my hands along the edges, "Is this going to hold up?"

"Yes," Warrick said with so much certainty I raised my eyebrows. He went on, "I did a check of the place when we first got here. This storm is going to test your house, but it'll stand. Come eat."

Warrick had managed to whip up some pancakes, eggs, and a bowl of fresh fruit without hardly making any noise. I sat next to him letting our bodies barely touch, "How do you move so quietly?"

"My brother may always have been faster than me, but I'm the master of moving silently. That's my advantage, love, just have to figure out how to use it against him," Warrick explained in between bites.

I nodded and started eating my food. The rest of the time we spent listening to the wind trying to force its way into the house. When Warrick finally finished, he stood up and gathered his coat. I met him by the front door where he kissed me so hard you would've thought it was the last time we'd be seeing each other. His thumb stroked my cheekbone then he was gone leaving me standing there shivering from the blast of cold air.

A stair creaked from behind making me jump. Lou was standing there holding his hands up, "Just me."

I shot him a look, "You're lucky I didn't have anything on me."

Lou rolled his eyes while trying not to smirk, "Yeah, because you could do so much."

"Whatever," I mumbled making my way back into the kitchen to clean up. "Want anything?"

"Why are you up so early?"

I momentarily paused what I was doing debating on what I wanted to tell him when Lou continued, "You don't have to answer that. I saw you and Warrick. Everything good between you two?"

Sighing, I turned back around meeting his concerned grey eyes, "Of course everything's good between us. Why?"

Lou leaned forward, "I heard some yelling coming from your room last night, and not the kind I expected."

I looked away from him, "I didn't realize you got off on listening to other people."

"C'mon, Val. Stop playing around. I need you to be honest with me, are you okay?"

"He didn't hurt or threaten me if that's what you're concerned about," I started. I closed my eyes, but quickly opened them again when Az's face sneered at me.

Lou was moving towards me at this point, "What's going on?"

I let out an exasperated laugh, "Az. That is what's going on. I can't get his smug face out of my head, and not that I really wanted to dive into my sex life with you, but when Warrick was between my legs, all I saw was Az staring back at me. So, I panicked and that ended the night."

Lou hugged me. I guess if Warrick wasn't here to offer comfort, Lou had no problem stepping into those shoes.

"You'll make it through. You always do," Lou quietly said into my hair.

I pulled back before I could start getting emotional. I rubbed my hands along my pants, "Anyways, you want a snack?"

"Didn't you just eat?" Lou asked me. We may have just had our breakfast, but I was in the mood to eat. I shot him a look that spurred him into action. "I'll take care of it. Take a load off," he said busying himself with grabbing food out of the fridge.

"Did you and Jennie get any action last night?" I asked trying to change the topic to something that wasn't what was troubling me.

His face instantly turned red, "What if I don't want to dive into my sex life with you?"

"That's only fair," I said, staring into the blizzard raging outside before refocusing my attention on him. "But, you know I'll find out one way or another. I always do."

"Fine," Lou sighed. "The answer is no. She was caught up in Mark being back and I wasn't really in the mood to jump into bed with someone."

"You know," I cocked my head to the side. "I've been so caught up in my own shit, I haven't asked you. How have you been holding up with everything going on?"

Lou ran a hand through his hair. *Oh boy, I guess I just asked a loaded question.* He jerked his head over to the couch, "Let's go sit over there."

We settled in, me with a blanket over my lap and Lou happily staring at his breakfast. I poked his arm, "Ready to tell me?"

He nodded, "I've been struggling if I'm being completely honest. Being back in the position of Warrick's second, even though it's not an official change, has stirred up a lot of shit I keep buried down. Although it is a little weird with how nice he's being. It's like I can't trust him."

"I can see that, especially with all the history between the two of you," I added.

"Yeah," he nodded. "And finding out I was just a test subject didn't help with anything. Then, his brother comes in and shakes everything up. And, you're probably not going to like this one, but there's still quite a bit I'm sorting through when it comes to you. It's hard not to lose my shit when Warrick goes crazy or when Az shows up."

I slowly brought my eyes to meet his, "You have to move past that, Lou."

"We're just being honest here, right?"

"Right," I nodded. "What gets discussed here stays between the two of us."

"Exactly," he said then took a few more bites. "When you told me you thought you made a mistake, man, it took everything I had not to just take you in my arms then and run away with you."

That one hurt. When I didn't say anything, he kept going, "You don't have to worry, though. I'm sticking to the friend zone and I'm good with that."

I let out a breath which Lou ignored, "Then, there's the topic of the war. I'm more nervous than I'd care to admit to be running headfirst into that, especially after seeing what Az is capable of. I'm used to being the wolf who's close to death after an encounter, but seeing Warrick like that ..." he trailed off shaking his head. "That scared the shit out of me, Val."

"I know," I said quietly. "I felt the same way."

"No one should be able to take him down like that. Add in how fast Az heals and moves, too? I'm worried about how this is all going to play out."

"Don't talk like that," I warned.

Lou closed his eyes before turning to me and placing my hands in his, "I know you don't want to hear it, but I need to get it out."

I held my breath waiting for him to continue. This conversation was heading down a path I hadn't let myself think about during this journey. There was only so much time, though, before it came up.

I forced myself to look in Lou's grey eyes as he started talking again, "I couldn't live with myself if anything happened to you or anyone else you hold close. You have to know I'd take a bullet for each of you, and yes, that includes Warrick despite how much I can't stand him. Val, if anything happens to me, I need you to take care of the pizza place – the thought of it being run by someone I don't trust hurts me more than I care to admit. I need you to promise me you won't be too sad and you'll carry on, okay?"

I swallowed allowing myself to start breathing again. His tone was so serious, his face somber. I opened my mouth to tell him he was going to make it through this, but I couldn't say something I wasn't completely sure of. Hell, I knew there was a good chance I'd probably die, too. I gave his hands a squeeze, "You got it. Although, you were starting to sound like I was going to have to look after your first born."

He dropped his head shaking it, letting out a soft laugh, "I thought it was obvious. That restaurant *is* my first born."

Smiling in return, I rested my head on his shoulder, "You would say something like that. You know? We haven't been around each other for that long, but I feel like its been a lifetime."

"Maybe that's because you've lived through things most people wouldn't even think about in their lifetime," he said quietly.

A peaceful silence blanketed us. I lifted my head up and moved so I was directly across from him again, my tone turning serious now, "It's my turn."

Lou started to protest. I gave his hands a squeeze, "Nope, you wouldn't let me stop you, so you're not getting that chance." I took a steadying breath, "If anything happens to me, and considering my track record, there's a good chance. I want, no, I *need* you to take care of my friends. Especially Jennie. I also need you and Warrick to get along. No more fighting between you two, and I'm not saying to join your packs together. I just want there to be peace. You've shown me that can happen. Also, I need you to make sure Warrick finds someone to love and doesn't stay hung up on me. He deserves happiness. You do, too, so no mourning me. If you miss me, pour yourself a beer and one for me while you munch down one of your pizzas."

As soon as I finished, Lou pulled me into a hug, "Deal."

"This doesn't leave here, okay? No making these pacts with anyone else, either. It's too sad," I mumbled into his chest.

He chuckled, "I think I can handle that."

"Am I interrupting something? I can go back upstairs," Mark said startling the two of us.

Lou shook his head, "No, just a moment between friends. Don't feel like you need to run away."

"Cool," Mark said. "I take it Bruce Wayne left for the day?"

"What?" Lou asked knitting his brows together in confusion.

I burst out laughing, "I knew it!"

"Can someone bring me up to speed?" Lou asked.

Mark grinned, "I'm talking about Warrick. He's, uh, pretty intense. Has the whole dark and moody vibe."

"Who's Bruce Wayne?" Lou asked with a little annoyance creeping in. He looked at me since Mark probably wasn't going to give him too many helpful details.

"A comic book character. He's a rich orphan who runs a huge company, but also doubles as a vigilante called Batman. He doesn't have any superpowers, but he's probably one of the most recognizable superheroes, if not the most recognizable. Very brooding, keeps to himself, that sort of thing. Know anyone similar?"

At this point, Mark had disappeared back upstairs. Lou slowly started smiling when Mark returned holding out a *Batman* graphic novel. Lou took it and starting skimming through the story nodding his head, "Yup, I can see it."

"Didn't you do you research? Back when we were hanging out with the vampires?" I asked Lou.

He shook his head, "I didn't really get a chance to."

I sighed, shaking my head. "To answer your question, Mark," I said turning to my friend anxiously watching Lou who was still flipping through the book he had been handed. "Yes, Warrick is gone for the day, but he'll probably be back tonight."

"You can read it if you want," Mark offered, ignoring me.

"Thanks, man," Lou said setting it down on the couch. "I'll dive into it later."

I poked Mark with my foot, "You really brought a comic?"

He shrugged, "I figured I would have something to read if we all needed a break from each other during the weekend."

"I don't blame you," I responded.

Mark ran a hand through his hair, "Can I ask you two a couple of questions?"

"Ask away," I said gesturing for him to go on.

Mark looked between Lou and I, "Was there a thing between you two?"

Lou stifled a laugh and glanced at me. I smiled at him before looking at Mark, "Yup, but I did what I always do and overreacted."

"So, there's nothing going on now?" Mark asked waiving his hand back and forth in our direction.

"No," Lou was the one to answer this time. "Figured we'd be better off as friends since there's no arguing with fate. She and Warrick are simply meant to be."

Mark slowly nodded his head, "Cool, cool. And what exactly is Warrick doing?"

"Trying to find the witch leader," I blurted.

"Why?"

"So he can get their support and make our side stronger when the time comes to fight Az," Lou said.

"He's not going to find her," Mark mumbled.

Both Lou and I sat up straight with our full attention on Mark, now. We glanced at each other and I started talking, "Mark, if you know something about the witch leader that could help Warrick get to her faster ..."

He squeezed his eyes shut, "I'm not going there, Val."

"Please," I encouraged quietly. "The sooner we can get out of here the better, and that's not going to happen unless Warrick gets to talk to her."

"She's not a pleasant person," Mark said looking at me. "If she can get her hands on someone who will strengthen her powers, she won't let them go. That's all she wants. She doesn't care about the greater good or helping others. She barely cares about people here, even those in her coven. I hope Warrick knows what he's doing."

Worry erupted in me. If I was understanding Mark correctly, he was hinting that Warrick may not be making it out of this place. It didn't help that a nagging voice was telling me the witch leader was most likely already on Az's side. It's too coincidental that Az showed his face so quickly after we got here. Lou must have been thinking the same thing judging by how he was looking at me. He slowly turned so he was looking at Mark, "Do you have a way of getting ahold of this witch?"

"I was hoping you wouldn't ask that," Mark sighed.

"Please, Mark," I cut in. "I don't like the thought of Warrick having to go out there every day only to run into dead-ends. It would help us out so much."

"Fine," Mark huffed. "I'll see what I can do."

"Just don't put yourself at risk," I said.

Mark finally looked at me, "There's no way in hell I'd let that happen again. I will say, though, I'm going to need some time. She won't agree to a meeting overnight."

I threw myself at Mark suffocating him with a hug. He let out a grunt followed by a laugh, "Thank you, Mark. If you start running into any troubles, let me know. I'm more than happy to help you out."

"Don't worry about it," he said giving me a little squeeze before pulling away from the hug.

He tried to keep a smile on his face, but the moment he thought no one was looking, fear took over. Immediate regret filled me after asking him to put himself out there like that.

We eventually went back to chatting about anything not related to potential deaths or what these witches could do if they got their hands on you. Mark was laughing and cracking jokes in no time and Jennie eventually joined us. They all scarfed down some food then decided to go out. The three of them were by the door, bundled up ready to brave the wind when Jennie looked back at me, "You sure you don't want to go?"

"Yeah," I nodded. "I have my hot chocolate, my book, and plenty of blankets. I'm more than happy to hang at the house. You all go enjoy the bar."

Jennie gave me a thumbs up then led the way out of the house. Lou was the last one to leave watching me for a moment, "Are you sure? I can hang back if you want some company."

"Absolutely. Now, go before you let too much of that frigid air in here," I shooed him, pulling my blanket up to my neck.

The less I left the house, the smaller the chance would be for me to run into Az and that makes everyone breathe a little easier. Plus, I don't have to worry about any potential wrath from Warrick. I stared down at the cover of my book as Lou shut the door behind him. *Alone at last.*

I cradled the mug of hot cocoa savoring the warmth it provided while watching the never-ending onslaught of snowflakes attacking the house. I sat there for a while until I was ready to dive back into my book. Having been afraid of the silence in the past, I was surprised when I felt at home for the first time in a *very* long time.

Time flew by, and as the sun started to set, my eyes grew heavy until I eventually drifted off into a light nap. Lips gently pressed on my forehead startling me awake. When my eyes snapped open, they met the icy blue gaze of Warrick. The corners of his eyes crinkled from a smile lighting up his face, "Hi, love. You have no idea how happy it makes me to see you safe and home."

I stretched as he came to sit next to me on the couch, "When did you sneak in here?"

"About five minutes ago," he said situating my legs on his lap. "You looked too comfortable so I didn't want to wake you up quite yet. Where's everyone else?"

"They went back to the bar," I yawned. "I just didn't feel like dealing with the weather, or being a third wheel."

"So the Jennie and Lou plan is working I take it?" he asked cocking an eyebrow.

I chuckled a little bit, "Kind of? Lou's feeling pretty conflicted."

"I'm sure," Warrick said directing his focus out the windows.

"Make any progress?" I asked.

His face grew serious as he responded, "A little. I found a few witches and tried talking to them, but they didn't give me much to work with."

"What would you say if I told you that Mark could use his connections to get you to the witch leader?" I watched Warrick very carefully.

He pulled me into his lap, "I would greatly appreciate that, love. I don't want to spend more time here than we have to."

We sat there letting the silence settle on us, Warrick resting his head on my chest while I ran my fingers through his hair. My stomach decided to end this sweet moment with a growl so loud that Warrick snapped his head up to look at me, "Have you eaten today?"

I shook my head, "Not since our breakfast."

"Love," he started to scold me. I put a finger to his lips getting an amused twitch of his lips in return, "I haven't been hungry until now, so don't start with me."

Warrick moved me to the spot next to him before getting up and moving towards the kitchen. He worked in silence filling the house with mouth-watering aromas. Curiosity got the best of me leading me to look over Warrick's shoulder. I had no idea what he was making but I was looking forward to devouring it.

"If you would like, I brought home a nice bottle of wine we could share before everyone else descends on the house, love," Warrick jerked his head towards the island without taking his cycs off the pan in front of him.

"How very fancy of you," I joked earning a soft laugh from Warrick. For someone who was having to deal with the worst parts of this world, he sure was in a good mood.

As I poured our glasses, I studied him. Warrick was talking about whatever popped into his mind, completely carefree. Then it hit me. It was like we were back in Cian's world tucked away in Warrick's cabin. I came up behind him placing his wine glass to the side of the stove then hugged him, "You know what this reminds me of?"

"I do, love," Warrick smiled.

"Can we just stay like this forever?" I smiled in return.

He turned around to face me tugging me closer to him, "If I could freeze time, I would."

I lifted myself up to kiss him. There was no hesitation from Warrick's side as his hand became entangled in my hair tilting my chin up for a deeper kiss.

A throat cleared from behind us making me jump. Warrick sighed, "Welcome home. Dinner will be ready in a few minutes."

"Didn't mean to interrupt," Lou mumbled.

"Don't worry about it," Warrick waved him off.

Mark turned on the music again as I found my way to a chair on the other side of the island. I sipped on my wine watching Mark pull Jennie into another dance then Lou taking his turn. Mark joined me at the island after grabbing a beer, "How was the quiet house?"

"Apparently something I needed," I said. "How was the bar?"

"Busy as usual. I'll probably keep my shifts until it's time to go, but the owner knows," he explained.

"Do you work every day?"

"Yup," he nodded. "I figured it could be a way to get everyone out of the house for you."

We talked a little longer then Warrick served up the food. The mood was light with everyone laughing and conversation flowing freely. We hung out a little longer after we finished our meal then went to our rooms for the night. The next few days played out the same way: Jennie and Lou accompanying Mark to the bar, Warrick trying to get a meeting with the witch leader, and me staying home.

On the fourth day of this new routine, I was fully invested in the book I just started when the doorbell rang. I froze, any semblance of peace leaving me. Anyone who should know we're here doesn't need to ring the doorbell. They all know how to get in. As far as I know, we've all kept to ourselves maybe except for Warrick, but I highly doubt anyone wanting to talk to him would be stopping by the house.

I waited a couple of minutes before slowly making my way over to the front door. I peeked through the peep hole to find the porch empty. There were too many footsteps from everyone coming and going in the snow to distinguish anything, so I cracked open the door. When nothing happened, I stepped out once again scanning the area. The coast was clear, but when I turned to go back in the house, something bright red caught the corner of my eye. A giant bouquet of roses were tucked in the far corner.

"What?" I asked myself, moving to grab them. There were at least three dozen if not more. The heavy glass vase had an intricate design from what I could see as I set it on the island. I went back to the front door to do one more quick check for signs of life and to make sure the door was locked.

"Alright, what's going on here?" I stood on my toes to look around the forest of flowers for any type of card or indication who they might have come from. For all I knew, Lou was upping his game and got something as a surprise for Jennie when they get back to the house today.

I finally spotted the cream colored corner belonging to a small card. "Ah-ha," I plucked it out turning it over. Neat writing scrawled across the card: *Love, these roses don't make up for everything you've endured the last few weeks nor do they fix the way I reacted. I hope they lessen the frustrations of being locked in your house every day. May they remind you of the promises I made.*

Smiling, I checked the water levels and went back to my reading. Every now and then, I would glance at the flowers letting myself feel like a giddy teenager. I could get used to Warrick's grand gestures.

Lou burst through the front door on one of my flower admiring breaks. He was shaking the snow off him when I asked, "Everything okay?"

His head popped up, "Yeah, just wanted out of the damn cold."

"Where's everyone else?" I asked while patting the spot next to me on the couch. As soon as he sat down next to me, I threw part of my blanket over him.

Lou rubbed his hands together blowing some warm air into them, "They'll be coming home in a little bit. Jennie made some new friends at the bar, but I was ready to get out of there. I can only take looking at wood paneled walls for so long before I go crazy."

"You're welcome to join me in my prison of choice," I gestured around the house.

Lou grinned looking around the house, pausing when his eyes landed on the roses. "When did you get those?" he pointed at them.

"Uh, not too long ago actually."

Lou walked over to them. He picked up the card raising his eyebrows when he looked at me, "May I?"

"Go ahead," I beamed. "Maybe Warrick's coming around after all."

"Yeah, maybe," Lou mumbled as he finished reading the card and put it back. I watched him for a moment as he stared down the flowers with suspicion. Before I could ask what's running through his head, the door slammed open again with Warrick being the one to barge right in.

"Is the storm really that bad now?" I asked getting up.

"Sorry for slamming the door, love, and yes, the storm picked up," Warrick said. His attention was immediately drawn to the flowers. He pointed his finger, "When did you get those?"

I furrowed my brow, "You mean you didn't send them?"

"I don't even know where to find a florist," Warrick mumbled taking the card Lou was holding. "Have you left this house?"

"What?" I asked.

Warrick calmly set the card down. With a cool tone, he slightly raised his voice and talked at a slower pace, "Have you left this house, love?"

"No," I shook my head. I glanced at Lou who was closely watching Warrick, "What's going on?"

"Has Mark mentioned any progress?" Warrick now asked Lou.

"Briefly today, but he said he'd tell us more at home," Lou said keeping his answer short.

"Hello? Will someone please fill me in?" I asked taking a step closer to the two.

Still keeping his attention on Lou, Warrick asked, "As far as you know, Val hasn't left the house since that first night?"

"Correct. Every time we've come home, she's been sitting in the same spot we left her," Lou kept his tone businesslike.

"*She* is standing right here," I huffed.

Warrick started at the flowers with a face full of contempt, "Sorry to disappoint you, love, but Az is behind this romantic gesture."

Chapter 9

"How?" I glanced between Lou and Warrick.

"No idea," Lou mumbled crossing his arms. "My best guess is that he followed us after the run-in at the bar."

"Did you keep one eye over your shoulder?" Warrick asked. It sounded as if he was talking to a couple of kids with how he asked that question as if we didn't know to check behind us.

"Yes, and we didn't see anything," Lou said.

Warrick finally looked at me, but was cut off by the door flying open again. We all whirled around ready to defend ourselves. Jennie and Mark froze when they saw us. Mark slowly closed the door and locked it, "We interrupt something?"

"Where are you at with getting me a meeting with the leader?" Warrick asked wasting no time getting down to business.

Mark walked up to him placing a folded up piece of paper in Warrick's hand, "Follow these instructions. Don't deviate, don't try to take shortcuts, and don't share this with anyone. There's a spell on there that'll kill anyone who looks at what's written or if you try to read it aloud. It's for you and you only. I'm sure you already know this, but I have to say it anyways so I can sleep tonight. Try to keep your emotions in check. Remain neutral or they'll attack, especially someone with the amount of power you have. It'll take you a few days to get through this list, so you'll have to be okay with leaving here for a while."

Warrick nodded reading through the note. I wish I could've seen everything he was going to have to do, but that wasn't a chance I wanted to take. Besides, I had bigger fish to fry.

"I'll have to head back out tonight," Warrick announced. My world lurched forcing me to grab on to the counter to try to keep myself steady. He tilted my chin up, "I know you're scared, love, but I'm going to take care of this and we'll be able to get out of here soon."

"How do you know Az isn't going to try to pull something?" I asked unable to keep the tremble out of my voice. "You've hardly been around since that night. It's like you're handing me to him. Fuck, it's like Cian all over again except I'm not doing anything wrong. Do you know how terrified I've been?"

His thumb stroked my cheek, "I can't stand here and make empty promises, love. What I can do is ask Lou to stay with you."

"Empty promises? Is that what you made the other night when you said you'd come back here every day?" I asked, my tone creeping towards anger.

Warrick stilled, but kept my face in his hands, "I chose the wrong words there. That wasn't an empty promise. I meant it with everything in me. Circumstances have changed, however, and we need to be able to change with them."

I swallowed, glancing at Lou over Warrick's shoulder, "I'm sorry." I looked back at Warrick, "How is Lou going to stand any chance against someone like that?"

"Ouch," Lou mumbled. "No offense taken, though. Warrick, she has a point."

"It's better than nothing, isn't it?" Warrick growled in Lou's direction. Lou just held his hands up.

I turned Warrick's head back towards me, "It has to be, right?"

"This hurts me as much as it hurts you, love. I hate the thought of leaving you when Az keeps finding ways to mess with you, but if I can get everything wrapped up here within the next couple of days, we can put some distance between us and him," Warrick said.

I closed my eyes, swallowing and nodding my head. He kissed my forehead then whispered, "We'll continue this conversation upstairs, okay?"

"Okay."

Warrick turned around to Lou, "Please stay with Val. If she has to leave the house for any reason, go with her and don't let her out of your sight. Az is less likely to approach with you around."

Jennie crossed her arms, "So now you're taking away Lou's freedom, too?"

"Sorry to put some delays on whatever's going on between you two, but you're going to have to deal with it. Unless, you'd like to be courted by Az, then by all means, join Val," Warrick shot back at her.

Her eyes widened before narrowing in my direction. Jennie didn't have to say anything for me to receive the message. I was once again getting in the way of her life, and this was yet another sacrifice she had to make for me.

"Hey, what's wrong with the buddy system, Jennie?" Mark nudged her with his elbow.

"Nothing," she muttered. Mark rolled his eyes.

"It'll be fine," Lou finally agreed. "We all just need to survive until we get the green light to jump."

"With that, I'm going to grab a few things then get out of here," Warrick said. He turned around to me extending a hand, "Come with me?"

"Sure," I said reluctantly placing my hand in his. I wasn't happy with how this was all unfolding, but this would give us the chance to continue our conversation.

As soon as we were back up in my room, Warrick shut the door and turned on the TV at full blast. He pulled us as far from the door as he could, "Talk to me, love."

"About what?" I asked.

"Everything that's running through your mind right now," he said sitting on the edge of the bed and wrapping his arm around me.

I laughed a little, "Where do I even start? My first thought when I got those flowers was that you maybe had something else on your mind besides getting things taken care of here. Then, when I found out Az was behind that, I was scared shitless. That told me he knows I've been staying cooped up in this place while also somehow staying out of everyone else's sight. I want to know what the hell he's even doing here anyways. Does he have a way of following us? Does he already have the witches on his side and he's been sending you on wild goose chases day-in and day-out so he can have a chance to grab me?

"And I can appreciate you ordering Lou to be my protection, but you and I both know that he stands no chance when it comes to Az. You also know I can't stand the thought of being so limited. It hasn't been a problem for me to stay in the house up until now, but I'm getting antsy and we're getting low on food. Then there's Jennie. She's now pissed because I'm once again getting between her and the guy she wants to be with. I don't know how much longer we can keep doing this dance. Add this all on top of the worry I have for you. You're going out there and risking your safety. I don't want to see you like Mark, all sad and tired and like you've had your life sucked out of you. What happens if you don't show back up here? If they're really as powerful as everyone says, then there's a good chance they could take you down," I took a breath to keep going but Warrick stopped me.

"Love, everything you said is valid. I can't answer all your questions like I couldn't make a promise I couldn't keep down there. Know I'm taking all the necessary precautions – they aren't going to take me down; I've been preparing some fail-safes that will get me out of there if I need to use them. Lou can stand up to Az long enough for you to get away if you need to. As for Jennie, she can get her head out of her ass," he snarled. "I'm sick and tired of her attitude when things don't go her way. Mark should be able to keep her entertained enough."

"I guess," I shrugged.

Warrick stood up and pulled me into him, "I really do need to start working on this list, but know I love you, Val. Don't for a second think I'm not going to come back home to you, love. Trust in this process and stick with Lou."

His lips crashed into mine before I had the chance of saying anything else. Warrick's tongue traced my bottom lip igniting a fire within me. I moved my hands to the bottom of his shirt, inching it up. Before I could go any further, Warrick's hand held mine, "As much as I'd love to stay here for this, I can't lose any more time."

"I love you," I whispered.

He kissed me one more time, then I watched as he flew around the room gathering whatever he needed. Warrick jogged down the stairs and out the door which Lou locked the minute it closed. Lou looked back up at me, "It's just you, Mark, and myself for dinner tonight."

"Did Jennie leave?" I asked now heading into the kitchen to grab a drink.

"No, but she's turned into a whiny baby who's locked herself in her room for the night," Mark scoffed. "When did she turn into such a killjoy?"

"When I became the one ruining all of her fun," I quipped.

Mark sighed, "She's just jealous you're getting all of the attention."

"No, she's just having to go through shit. I get it, I have my moments where I need a breather, too. Let her get the space she needs and she'll come around," I said. "What do we want to eat tonight?"

"I'm making my specialty," Lou said getting all the ingredients out for his pizza. "We'll need to run to the store tomorrow, though, which means you're getting a break from this house, Val."

"Yay, field trip," I said into my beer bottle.

That got a chuckle out of Mark who settled on to the couch to watch a movie. When I was certain he wasn't paying attention to us, I moved to help Lou, "Sorry to get you stuck with me."

"It's not as much of a problem as you think," Lou said working the ingredients together. "You want me to get rid of those?"

He nodded toward the roses and my gaze followed, "Yeah, probably. They are really pretty though."

"I'm sure they cost a pretty penny," Lou observed. "Az really wants to get your attention."

I reached out to touch some of the petals, "Or he's making sure he's as convincing as possible when trying to be Warrick."

"That too," Lou agreed.

"Hey, I'm sorry about all of this," I said finally addressing the elephant in the room.

"About what?"

"About putting you back on babysitting duty," I said watching as Lou worked the pizza dough.

"Don't be, Val," Lou shook his head. "It's nice to have something to do again and I need a little bit of space from Jennie."

"I hear that!" Mark shouted from the living room.

"Anyways, it'll be nice to hang out a little again," Lou grinned at me.

I threw a playful punch at his arm, "Careful, you might actually convince me that I'm not half bad to be around."

"You two make a cute couple," Jennie casually said walking up to the fridge. She grabbed herself some of the curry leftovers and warmed them up. Mark started to say something, but I shook my head to tell him to keep quiet. No sense in giving in to what Jennie wants right now.

She moved close to Lou, her hand barely touching his arm. He pursed his lips and tensed clearly not wanting any part of this interaction. We sat in silence waiting for her food to finish warming up.

The minute she retreated back upstairs, the tension lifted and the three of us were able to go back to joking around. We brought the finished pizza over to Mark to watch *Halloween*. I sandwiched myself between the two of them giving their arms a squeeze, "Thanks for putting up with all this nonsense."

"There's nowhere else I'd rather be right now," Mark said resting his head on top of mine.

Lou shot him a look, "Watch it, buddy."

"Not in a romantic way," Mark's eyes widened. "I'm not inserting myself in her complicated love life. You kidding me? I don't stand a chance against you guys. Totally meant that in a non-romantic, strictly platonic way."

"Good answer," Lou mumbled. "And no need to thank us, Val. We've been over this."

The movie ended and Mark got up to put a new one in, "How do we feel about the *Scream* series?"

I winced, "That's a little close to home, don't you think?"

Mark cocked his head, "What do you mean?"

"Well," I fidgeted with the edge of the blanket. "Considering I have someone playing games with me, someone who's deciding to follow me around, and has threatened my life, I'd say I have some things in common with Sidney Prescott. Although, not for the same reasons."

"Are you saying you're scared of a little old movie?" Mark teased.

I sighed, "No, I'll get the Jiffy Pop going."

Lou leaned over to me, "You don't have to watch it if you don't want to."

I waived him off as I stood up, "It's not big deal. Just found it ironic, that's all."

We ended up having a *Scream* movie marathon, but all fell asleep during the fourth one. We must all have really needed the sleep because we didn't wake up until Jennie started slamming cabinets around. I jumped awake, Lou doing the same thing while Mark just yawned and stretched.

"Oh, did I wake you?" Jennie asked nonchalantly. "Whoops."

She was clearly still working through things.

Jennie moved so she was standing in front of us with a hand on her hip, "I'm going out today. The snow's calmed down and I want to explore. Just figured I'd report in just in case you cared."

"Thanks, Jennie," Lou said standing up. She became hopeful Lou was going to be joining her, but as soon as he changed directions to head towards the kitchen, Jennie quickly became annoyed. She turned on her heels making a dramatic exit. Mark and I stared after her. "When did she learn to throw Lilly-style tantrums?" Mark asked.

"Good question," I said still staring at the door.

"We really need to get food," Lou noted.

I stretched then stood up to join him. There was enough food to last us a couple more days before we really needed to go grocery shopping. "We'll be fine for now," I responded.

"If you say so," Lou grabbed some eggs and veggies for a quick breakfast of omelets.

Snuggled back into the couch, the three of us chowed down while we finished the rest of the *Scream* movies. Lou and Mark decided to play a few rounds of pool, and thankful to have some time to myself, I changed into some workout clothes. I joined the guys in the basement to use what little workout equipment was down there, not missing the subtle glances Lou threw my way.

Moving my body in a way I haven't in a while did wonders for my mind. I wasn't feeling as anxious and took care of disposing the roses. One less thing to remind me of the looming threat of Az. I was also able to leave behind any frustrations related to Jennie. If she wanted to act like a baby, that was on her. She made the choice to join us fully knowing the chaos that follows everywhere I seem to go lately. I'm sure the weather isn't helping anything either. We've gone from places that are much sunnier and not as snowy to dark, gloomy, and nonstop blizzard. Then, there's Warrick. I hated that he had to leave, but he's getting so close to his goals of building the army he wants to be able to put up a fight against his brother. I'd be doing the same thing. I'd do whatever it takes to finish this, especially now that Az is applying more pressure.

I left Mark and Lou to their never-ending rounds of pool to get cleaned up. I was halfway through my shower when Lou poked his head in, "Hey, Val. Jennie just texted and needs me to go meet her. Apparently, Az showed up and was giving her a hard time."

"Yeah, do whatever you need to," I said.

"You'll be fine here with Mark?"

"Yup," I answered. I didn't dare tell him I was worried Az was only trying to get Lou out of the house. Instead, I chalked it up to being paranoid.

"Okay, keep everything locked up," he ordered then left.

I wrapped up my shower getting back into my pajamas then rejoined Mark downstairs. He was watching another movie series I couldn't remember the name of, but I still joined him. His movie finished and he turned to me, "I have to head into the bar, but Lou isn't back yet."

"Go," I smiled at him. "I'll be fine. You're not on babysitting duty."

"You sure?"

"Yeah, honestly. Lou should be back any minute," I nodded.

Mark gave me a nod then got ready to head into work. As he was getting ready to leave, Lou came back in, "You know? This is about the best damn weather we've had since arriving here."

"It looks like it," I observed. "Where's Jennie?"

"Oh, she apparently just needed me to walk her across the street to the bar and join her for a drink," Lou sounded annoyed.

I raised an eyebrow, "Any signs of Az?"

"None. She wasn't even the slightest bit anxious when I got to her. When I mentioned Az, she started to ask me why I brought him up, but then remembered why I was out there in the first place," Lou said shaking his head.

Mark ran past him out the door, "See ya!"

"Where's he going?" Lou asked jerking a thumb over his shoulder. He turned to make sure the door got locked then sat at the island.

"He had to go into work," I answered. "Do you think Jennie just dragged you out of the house because she was wanting some alone time with you?"

"Yeah," Lou chuckled shaking his head. "She's not doing anything to make me want her ... I don't think she realizes that."

I played with the edge of the blanket again, "No, she never has. Jennie just thinks she's being cute and that every guy wants to save a damsel in distress which I don't blame her since that's what she's been seeing. I mean, every time I'm in trouble, either you or Warrick come running. But, in the end, she pushes away every guy that thinks they want to be with her. Although, this is a new record. I've never seen it happen this quick."

"And yet she judges you for your romantic choices," Lou said coolly.

"Not that I can always blame her," I looked up at him. "I've made plenty of my own questionable choices, one of which has been haunting us. Anyways, I'm assuming it's just you and I tonight?"

"Yup, seems like it," Lou nodded.

I threw him a thumbs up. We pulled out some of the leftover pizza, talking about whatever popped in our minds eventually landing on Az. Lou chewed on his food for a little bit then took a sip of his beer, his eyes narrowing in thought, "What attracted you to Az?"

I choked a little on my food, "What do you mean?"

"Jennie told me a little bit about the history between you two, but I want to hear it from you," Lou said watching me carefully.

"The whole thing?" I asked trying to delay the conversation that was about to happen.

Lou nodded, "The whole damn thing."

"Why?"

"Maybe I'll get some insight into what's going on in his head," Lou shrugged.

"Good luck," I scoffed. "Not even his own brother can do that."

"If I can crack the code a little bit, maybe I'll be able to help Warrick a little more."

I held my bottle up to my lips smirking at him, "I didn't realize you cared to go for extra credit."

Lou paused for a moment then said, "I want us to end this war as fast we as can. Whatever I can do to give us an upper hand, I'll do it. Now, stop procrastinating and tell me everything."

"So bossy," I rolled my eyes. When he didn't show any signs of a smile or laughter, I cleared my throat, "Alright. Your question is a good starting point. There were a lot of things that attracted me to him: his smile, his accent, his eyes, his body, the tattoos, the fact that he rode a bike, he had a successful career, he took care of himself, he was kind and understanding. The list goes on."

"Alright, how did you two meet?"

I sighed, "At work. He was representing the tech company he worked for at a meeting I was in. He was sitting across from me and kept looking my way. Eventually, I got curious.

We could message each other despite not being in the same company thanks to the meeting invite, so I reached out to him asking if there was something on my face or in my teeth. Az tried really hard to keep a straight face when he responded. Apparently, I had made his day by reaching out because he was intimidated by me and had no idea what to say."

"I can't see him being shy," Lou noted.

I shook my head, "Me neither."

"What happened after that?"

I took a sip of my beer then continued, "He played it up, and it worked. We ended up exchanging numbers before the meeting was over. When everyone was schmoozing each other, Az walked up and didn't hesitate to ask me out."

Lou nodded and grabbed us a few more beers, "How did you know you wanted to be in more of a relationship with him than any of the other guys you dated?"

"Good question," I said leaning back in my seat. Lou smirked, throwing an arm over the chair next to him. "Why are you looking at me like that?"

"No reason," he said as he shook his head.

I shot him a look of disbelief and he laughed, "Fine, I'm just impressed to see you not anxious when you're talking about Az."

"I guess I'll take my small wins where I can get them," I said.

"Anyways, you were just getting to the good stuff," Lou said before taking another sip.

I rolled my eyes at him. Clearly, the beer was doing its job and making him feel good. I set my bottle on the table, "There was one night in particular that changed everything for me. Most of our dates we spent goofing around not really talking about anything which was my specialty at the time. I just wanted to have fun and not dive into a serious relationship after what happened to Gabriel. Other times, we'd go on rides with our group, but it was usually one or the other when we hung out. It just so happened to be a ride day. I had hardly slept because Gabriel kept popping up in my dreams. My emotions were all over the place and I really wasn't in the mood to go riding. Az shows up at my place with his goofy smile all ready to go, but as soon as he saw me, he immediately took me in his arms. Az listened to everything I had to say without making me feel like I was crazy, and trust me, I was saying a lot of off the wall things. He didn't push me to go on a ride, he let me make that decision for the two of us."

"Let me guess, you still went on the ride?"

I nodded, "Even when we got back, he took care of me. Az wouldn't let me get off the couch. He made my favorite meal, watched my favorite movies with me, gave me tissues when I cried, and didn't pressure me to do anything I didn't want to. That was when I realized I could have an actual relationship instead of just hooking up a few times. Don't get me wrong, though, the sex was pretty great, too, but this was the first time I wasn't focusing on that aspect of the relationship. I wanted to get to know this guy. I was happy with him, and not the fake happy I was around everyone else."

Lou was listening intently at this point, "So, what happened? What ended things?"

I gave a shaky laugh as I played with my hair. The emotions were creeping up at this point thanks to me opening the door wide open. I glanced at him out of the corner of my eye before staring into my hands, "Things with the war were getting more intense, so I chalked it up to our relationship being too much on top of that, but now there's too many possibilities. Anyways, the last time I had seen him, he was sleeping over at my place. We had a crazy night together, in a good way. Az was whispering promises until we fell asleep. I now know he had no intention of keeping those. When I woke up, he was gone. There was no trace of him and it was like the entire time we had been together was a dream. His number was disconnected and there was no other way of getting ahold of him. Our friends hadn't seen or heard from him. Az was just gone. So, I did the only thing that was going to help me cope. I did my best to forget – drank too much, slept with I don't know how many other guys, deleted pictures, distanced myself from the friends we made together. Anything and everything to get his face out of my head. I didn't have room for him *and* Gabriel, so I chose to remember the one who meant more to me."

"Shit," Lou said. "Is that why you didn't recognize him at the pizza place? Because he walked out of your life so suddenly and you didn't want to remember that?"

"Maybe," I sighed. We let silence blanket us. Lou had finally run out of questions and I felt the sudden urge to pick up my drinking pace.

I finally looked up at Lou, "Do you think me being fated to Warrick had anything to do with me being drawn to Az?"

He shrugged, "Could be. I mean, they are related, but it also could have been Az targeting you before you knew it."

"Sucks to think that what we had was all fake," I said into my almost-empty bottle.

"No kidding," Lou stood up. He took our empties to the sink which ended up being way more than I thought. Lou checked the fridge for any more and sighed, "We're out of beer."

"I guess it's time to call it a night," I glanced towards a clock. "Shouldn't Jennie and Mark be home by now?"

"Yeah, they should," Lou furrowed his brows. He moved towards the front door and I followed him. We stood outside bracing ourselves against the cold only to be surprised with a clear night. No wind, no snow. We had a clear view down the street to the bar that was still very much alive when it's normally closed at this point. My eyes drifted up towards the sky to see green ribbons of light dancing with the stars. I elbowed Lou and pointed up, "Look."

"Wow," he said breathlessly. "I've never seen anything like this."

"We have something similar on our world, but I've never seen them in person before. Absolutely gorgeous," I said in wonder.

Giggling and crunching snow snapped our attention to in front of us rather than on the sky. Jennie and Mark were finally making their way home, and it seems like Mark was able to pull Jennie out of her funk. She would stumble every now and then, but the only thing that came from her was laughter. They finally made it to the front door and Mark was fully smiling at us, "What's up, guys?"

"Just hanging out," I answered. "Glad to see you made it back home safely."

I opened the door leading the way into the house with everyone following behind me. Lou, being the last one in, made sure the door was locked. Jennie crushed me into a hug catching me off-guard, "What's this for?"

"I'm such a bitch to you, Val, but you never take it out on me," she mumbled into my hair.

"No worries, I guess," I patted her back. I pulled away, "I'm going to head up, though. I'm pretty wiped."

She jutted her lip out, "Boo." Turning to Mark, she asked, "You'll stay up with me, right?"

"Sure thing," he answered with a nod.

"How about you, Lou?" Jennie craned her neck around Mark to look at Lou.

Lou shook his head, "I'm in the same boat as Val. Goodnight, guys."

We made our way upstairs, Lou following me into my room. I flopped on my bed, "Isn't your room down the hall?"

"I just wanted to say thank you," Lou said sitting next to me.

I propped myself up, "For what?"

"For being so open with me."

I raised an eyebrow, "So did it help with trying to figure Az out?"

"No," Lou shook his head letting out a small laugh. "It did confirm he's hard to predict and understand his motives."

"I figured that would be the case," I mumbled.

Lou clapped a hand on his leg then made his way over to the door, "Anyways, goodnight, Val. Hopefully you get some decent sleep tonight."

"Thanks, Lou. I hope you do, too," I replied.

He stood in the doorway for a moment debating if he was going to say something. When I sat up, though, Lou left closing the door behind him. *I wonder what that was all about.*

I flopped back on my bed running through the conversation we just had. Was that relationship even real? Did Az genuinely have feelings for me or was that all for show? I rolled over, the questions not letting up their barrage. My eyes squeezed shut willing the onslaught to stop. Eventually they did and I was able to drift off to dreamland.

Chapter 10

"Val," Jennie whispered gently shaking me awake. "Val, I need to talk to you."

Groaning, I rolled over and opened my eyes. Somehow I got under the covers, but didn't get out of my clothes. I rubbed my eyes, and with a voice still very groggy from sleep, asked, "What's up?"

"I'm sorry about what I said," Jennie couldn't look me in the eyes as she said that.

I sighed dropping my head back on the pillow, "Aren't you tired of going in circles all the time?"

"What do you mean?"

"This has been the same routine for years. I do something, directly or indirectly, that pisses you off. You throw some verbal daggers hoping to do damage then go run away to cool off. Once you feel better, you come crawling back groveling with the hopes I'll move past what you said," I explained. "I'm getting tired of it. Either you want to be around me, accepting me for everything I am, or you can leave. I'm not the one forcing you to follow me in this journey. You've made that choice time and time again."

My focus has shifted and now I'm tired of her excuses. There's no more mental capacity to handle Jennie's flip-flops. I glanced in her direction. No surprise, she looks like she's been slapped. Her mouth opened and closed a couple of times until she finally figured out what she wanted to say, "If you didn't want me around, you could've just said so."

"That's not what I'm saying. At all. The things you say hurt, and this is going to be selfish, but I'm having to deal with so many other things right now that are taking up my pain capacity. I don't want any more," I said sitting up now.

She gave a few small nods, "I guess I have some things to think about."

Jennie moved to stand up as I asked, "Can I get your honest opinion?"

"On what?" she asked, her voice sad.

"Do you really mean what you say about me?"

Jennie closed her eyes, "There is some truth behind them, yes, but it's also a knee jerk reaction. I let my emotions dictate what I say which is something I apparently need to work on. Before you try to say anything else, know you're not the only one who's told me that."

My mouth closed. She walked away as soon as Lou came in the room with breakfast ready to go. He looked over his shoulder in Jennie's direction then back to me, "Everything good?"

"Yeah," I sighed rubbing my eyes again. "I just called her out. Who knows what's going to happen now."

He sat on the edge of my bed offering me the plate he had prepared. Pancakes and eggs. My stomach rumbled at the sight of food. I started digging in as Lou said, "Well, I'm glad someone finally said something. Anyways, I know you said we could wait a few days, but I'm overruling that. We're going today because I need some more alcohol if you and Jennie are going to start a war of your own."

I raised my eyebrows, "Oh really?"

"Before you go making any judgements, I'm not an alcoholic," Lou said defensively.

I shook my head, "I never said you were. When are we going?"

"I was thinking soon, if you're good with that?"

"Sure," I took another bite.

"Have you heard anything from Warrick?" Lou asked suddenly changing topics.

My body tensed a little bit. I searched the covers for my phone scanning the screen once I found it. There was a new message from Warrick making my heart beat a little faster: *Just wanted to let you know I'm still alive, love. I hope you're doing okay.*

I typed out a quick response: *Thanks for checking in. All is well over here.*

"Well?" Lou impatiently asked.

"Yeah, he just texted to let me know he's still alive," I nodded still focused on my phone.

Lou let out a breath, "Good."

"Lou?"

"Yeah?"

"Do you think I ma – "

He cut me off, his tone serious, "Do not ask me again if you made a mistake, Val."

Setting my empty plate on my nightstand, I asked, "Why?"

"You really have to ask that question?" Lou stared at me. "Let me turn it around to you. Why do you keep asking me this? Why me?"

I blinked a couple of times trying to process what he was asking before I regained my composure, "My intention is not to jerk you around. You're the only one I can have this kind of conversation with. I'm not asking to imply that we should be together. It's felt like a lot lately and I've been wondering if I walked away from all of this, if I'll be able to live a somewhat normal life. A life without constantly getting hurt, physically and emotionally. A life where I'm not always under attack."

His grey eyes softened, "Where would you go?"

Not where I was expecting this to go, but okay. I shrugged, "No idea. My first thought is to stay in the werewolf world, but in a different city. Far away from where Warrick could easily get to me. Someplace unknown so his brother can't find me."

"I get it," Lou said. "But, I think no matter what, you'd always be drawn back to Warrick somehow. It might be unavoidable now."

Sighing, I said, "I guess you have a point."

I started getting ready, hiding behind my bathroom door when it came time to get dressed, "Have I told you that I appreciate being able to have these honest conversations?"

"No, I don't think so," Lou answered with a little sarcasm.

I grabbed the plate giving Lou a playful shove as I passed him then headed downstairs, "Don't let it go to your head."

"Hey, I view it as a privilege. Same goes to you, by the way," Lou said following me.

Jennie was sitting with Mark, zoned out and completely ignoring whatever movie he had playing. She snapped out of it to join us by the island. In a lowered voice, she said, "Please tell me you guys are going somewhere."

"If we were, would you be joining us?" Lou asked her matter-of-factly.

"Would it be alright if I did? I'm getting so antsy here," her eyes widened with hope.

Lou glanced at me waiting for my subtle nod knowing I wouldn't turn down Jennie in a plea of doing something that might help her out. A small part of me wanted to make up for the conversation we had first thing this morning. When he got the signal, he said, "Alright, we're heading out to the grocery store in a bit. Mark, you good with hanging back here?"

Mark was so engrossed in the movie that he barely gave us a thumbs up. Jennie gave a couple of excited claps then ran upstairs to get ready. Lou nudged me, "You sure?"

"I'm not going to stop her. Again, this is her choice, so if she tries to pin it on me, I'll point that out to her again. Besides, she can go wander around on her own. She's not the one who needs a bodyguard," I answered.

"Works for me as long as you two play nice."

Jennie bounded back downstairs, "So, when do we leave?"

"We can head out now," Lou looked out the window. "Looks like we're still having a break in the weather, so might as well take advantage."

The grocery store was at the end of the street we were on. Thankfully, there was no wind. The downside – it was still so cold it felt like nothing was going to help keep us warm. Any hopes of a quick walk were dashed since there was at least two feet of snow we were having to trudge through. Every now and then, I scanned the surroundings noting there were very little people out. A lot of the buildings were closed up, looking devoid of life.

As soon as we walked through the doors to the grocery store, Jennie left us to wander on her own. Stomping the snow off my boots, I mumbled to Lou, "Thank goodness for some heat."

"I hear you there," Lou said waiting for me to lead the way.

I gestured for him to start, "You're the one who knows what we need. I'm along for the ride just enjoying some time out of the house."

Lou started wandering up and down the aisles slowly filling the cart with various ingredients while I kept my head on a swivel. *No wonder I was fine with staying in the house. I wasn't having to constantly look over my shoulder and could relax.* The store was surprisingly big in contrast with how it looked from the outside. Fluorescent lights cast a cold glow over the never ending shelves and freezers full of food that sprawled towards the back of the store.

"How are we going to pay for all of this?" I focused my attention back to the cart.

Lou nodded in Jennie's direction, "Grabbed the money from Jennie a while ago."

"So, you're the one holding the purse strings now," I observed.

"Couldn't hurt to lift a little bit of the responsibility off her."

We went back and forth a little longer, throwing some jokes and carrying light conversation. Just as it was outside the store, there was hardly another person in sight. All the employees kept their heads down and kept to themselves.

"Damn, this place is depressing," I mumbled under my breath.

Lou cast a glance out of the corners of his eyes, "You can say that again."

We got to the wall of beer, Lou taking a step back to study the options in front of him. I positioned myself next to him taking in the various labels. He stood there for about five minutes without moving. I leaned closer, "Any idea what you're looking for?"

"Nope," he shook his head. "I'm hoping something pops out at me."

"While you're waiting for that moment, is there anything else we need?" I moved towards the cart.

Lou followed me and started rifling through everything. He started to say something then stopped, putting more of an effort into checking what we had in the cart. "Dammit," he muttered. "There's a couple things missing."

"Since this place is relatively empty, I'm probably in the clear. Hand me your list and I'll get the rest," I stuck my hand out.

"What list?"

"The one you've been using this whole time," I answered, confused.

He tapped his head, "It's all been up here."

I rolled my eyes, "Will you tell me what we need, then?"

"Sure. Grab a couple of green onions, a couple types of cheese – don't forget the mozzarella, and grab a few packages of whatever pasta calls out to you," Lou instructed.

I gave him a little salute then headed in the direction of the produce, "Got it, boss."

As much as I've enjoyed being in Lou's presence, this little minute of independence worked wonders for me. It took me no time to grab the green onions and cheese, so I made a quick run back to the cart to empty my arms and check on Lou. He was right where I left him studying the beer choices, although, there was one six pack in the cart. *Progress is good.*

"How are we going to get back with everything if we're walking?" I asked staring into the pile of food.

"We should be able to carry everything," Lou answered not breaking his concentration. "Don't worry about the heavy stuff, either."

"Okay," I said skeptically. I kept my fingers crossed hoping the weather would still hold out for us so the trek back wasn't any more miserable than it needed to be.

I turned on my heels to start my search for the pasta aisle. The one thing this store didn't have was any signs to indicate what we'd find in the aisles, so I was making my way up and down each row again. Humming to myself, I got distracted with the baked goods section. *Maybe I can make us all something to munch on tonight.* I picked up a box of cake mix to see if I was going to have to add to the load we'd be carrying back when I heard footsteps approaching me. I tucked myself in closer to the shelf to make sure I was out of this person's way when the steps stopped right behind me. "Excuse me," I shuffled a little out of the way.

An arm grabbed the shelf immediately to the left of my head. I turned to go the other way when the other arm did the same thing. Panic erupted. I was trapped. I could call out to Lou, but he's also on the opposite side which meant I'd have to yell pretty loudly. I had no idea where Jennie was, but I wasn't sure if I could count on her anyways given how quick she was to leave us the moment we stepped foot in here.

"I was wondering when I'd see you again," Az purred in my ear.

I flipped around pushing my back into the shelf. Az's face was much closer than I would've liked. He was leaning over, using his arms to hold himself up so we were eye level. Seeing the gold and green flakes this close brought back so many memories of our time together. His black hair was a mess as usual falling into his face, but I hated to admit he looked put together with his black wool coat, black jeans and boots. A smirk snaked its way across his face when terror took over mine.

Az moved a little closer so his lips brushed my ear sending shivers down my spine, "What, no babysitter? When Warrick's gone, the cat comes out to play?"

"How did you know?"

"Know that Warrick's out of the house?"

"Yeah," I kept my attention focused on the bags of flour across from me.

"Besides the fact I keep an eye on your place? It was easy. I know all about the little mission he's on," Az brought his face in front of mine again. He cupped my cheek, "Did you like my gift?"

I smacked his hand away from me, "Not at all."

Anger flashed across his features, but never came back, "Such a shame. I thought roses were your favorite."

I steeled myself for whatever was going to come next, "What do you want, Az?"

"I'm just stocking up on my food like everyone else," he swept a hand towards his cart.

"Looks like you're planning for company," I observed.

He cocked his head to the side, one corner of his lips turning up, "Am I?

Something about the way he said that filled me with suspicion. Az pressed against me, the metal shelves now digging into my back, "Do you remember that time we went grocery shopping before going to cook at your parents?"

A hand came up to the back of my neck, lightly touching it, but poised for pulling me into him. I clenched my jaw shut not allowing myself to participate in his games. He let out an annoyed sigh, "Well, we had just finished with a ride and you always got turned on whenever we went out. We were in a store very similar to this one. Quiet, not a lot of people. In fact, I think we were in the baking aisle, too. Funny how things play out. Anyways, you pulled me into you in a position much like we are now. I thought we were going to have to ask the store to erase some security camera footage with how you jumped me."

I swallowed. Now would be a really good time for Lou or Jennie to come looking for me.

Az jerked my head towards him. I squeezed my eyes shut as I resisted as much as I could. He only chuckled, "You know? I could grab you right here and now. No one would know where you disappeared to and that would give us all the time in the world to pick up right where we left off."

My eyes sprang open. He didn't kiss me like I thought he would, but the idea of him kidnapping me was even worse.

"Don't like the sound of that? Disappointing," Az said in a mocking tone.

"I will scream."

His grip on the back of my neck tightened as he snarled, "You make a sound and I will make you watch as I kill everyone around you, including your precious Warrick. Ah, that's how I'll get you to listen. Did I tell you I know exactly where he is and who he's with?"

My eyes widened and I gave up the fight. I don't need to be the one to cause anything to happen to him.

He stroked my hair, "That's better."

"What happened to you, Az?" I asked sincerely. If there wasn't an easy way out of this, I might as well try to get answers to the questions running through my head since he showed back up.

"Nothing," he kept his face neutral.

"Sure, nothing," I shook my head. "You're a completely different person from who I remember."

"You just ignored me when I was like this," Az smirked again.

I narrowed my eyes at him, "Stop gaslighting me."

"Hey!" Lou shouted.

It took you long enough.

Az slowly lifted his head in Lou's direction still keeping me trapped. "Can I help you?" he asked in a disinterested tone.

"What's going on?" Jennie asked coming out from behind Lou. "Shouldn't we go pay?"

She froze when she saw who Lou was yelling at. I turned my head the other way earning a low chuckle from Az. He focused back on me, "Trouble in paradise? This really is like old times."

"Drop it, Az," Lou started moving towards him.

He stood up rolling his shoulders back finally freeing me. I turned to run, but Az grabbed my hair pulling me back. I let out a gasp, my hands flying up to my hair to try to get him to let me go. He pulled me next to him, "And what are you going to do if I don't?"

"I'd hate to spoil the ending for you," Lou rolled up his sleeves. "Jennie, go find some pasta." He dropped into a fighting stance.

Az let out a bark laughter, "Ha! You're kidding me, right?"

When Lou took a step closer, Az tightened his grip and lifted me up, my feet kicking out, "If you want me to let her go, I'd suggest taking a few steps back. Just like you, I need food to survive. We can't all feed off of souls in this world. Val and I were just reliving old memories, that's all. Have you told him about us, yet?"

"Yes," I whispered still trying to get him to let go. My head was pounding at this point, but he showed no signs of stopping.

"Share any of the juicy stuff? Lou looks like a guy who'd get off on that."

Lou growled, no longer sounding human. That only made Az laugh more, "Oh, this is good. Too good. Val, did you sleep with Lou, too?"

"I said drop it, Az," Lou warned through clenched teeth.

"Drop it or her?" he sneered up at me. "Be careful what you wish for."

Lou shifted his focus on me before looking back at Az, "I'm serious. You need to let her go."

"Okay," Az shrugged. He swung his arm throwing me back like I weighed nothing. I crumpled on the ground, the wind getting knocked out of me, but I was free. This was my chance to run. I started crawling away glancing back at the two. Lou was now starting to run at Az who was now laughing, head thrown back.

"Shit, why am I about to be stupid?" I pushed myself off the floor and ran in their direction.

Lou was just about to reach Az when I jumped between the two of them. I threw out my hands connecting with both of their chests, "No."

"What's this? The damsel is now coming to the aid of her rescuer?" Az sneered. "By the way, I never got an answer to my question."

I ignored him, turning to look at Lou, "Don't put yourself at risk. Walk away."

"You don't get to order me around, Val," Lou said between clenched teeth still watching Az's every move.

Az lowered his voice, speaking in a dangerous tone, "You should listen to her. You never know what people may bring to a fight."

I glanced back at him noticing he was reaching in his coat pocket for something. He barely pulled it out, but I saw enough to know he was armed with his knives. I pushed against Lou, "We should go."

I gave him another shove and he finally took a step back, "Fine."

Lou walked backwards toward the front of the aisle making sure not to turn his back. He stopped when he reached the end of the aisle. I whirled around on Az, "What the fuck are you doing, huh? What's your endgame?"

The smile he gave me turned my stomach, "Pretty soon, I'll be doing you, but I can't divulge all my secrets."

I walked away the same way Lou did. No way was I going to turn around and end up with a knife or two in my back. I bumped into Lou, "Where's Jennie?"

"Right here," she answered out of breath. "I wanted to get back as soon as I could. I wasn't sure what we needed."

Lou was still staring down the aisle at Az so I took a look in the cart. "How much pasta did you grab?" my eyes widened as I took in the mini mountain of various types of pasta.

"Lou wasn't specific, so I just grabbed whatever," Jennie shrugged.

Lou took a quick glance at the cart before returning his attention to Az, "I think we'll be fine. Fuck, where did he go?"

I looked over my shoulder at the now empty baking aisle, "I don't know, but let's get the hell out of here."

Lou kept me in between him and Jennie as we made our way to the register. Loaded up with our bags, we made the trek back to the house just as it was starting to snow again. I helped Lou put things away, Jennie disappearing into her room with the snacks she got. I rolled my eyes, "Guess she's still keeping her distance."

"You okay? He threw you pretty hard back there," Lou watched me, face full of concern.

"Oh," I paused what I was doing. I gave him a small smile, "Yeah, I'm fine. Just knocked the wind out of me that's all."

Lou crossed his arms leaning against the counter, "Why'd you decide to run in between us?"

"I didn't want to see you get hurt," I mumbled.

"You really think you could've stopped a fight between two alphas or whatever the hell Az is?"

"No, but after seeing what he did to Warrick, I couldn't let that happen to you too," I glanced up at him.

He dropped the tough guy act and went back to putting away our food, "I appreciate it, Val. My job is to look after you, though, not the other way around."

"It goes both ways, Lou."

We finished putting away the groceries in silence. I decided to knock out a workout while Lou joined Mark for some video games. As I headed up to my room to take a shower, I paused outside of Jennie's door. I wanted to see if she was okay, but I also wanted to respect her space. It felt weird not talking to her about all of this.

Sighing, I made my way into my safe haven to get cleaned up. When I got out of the shower, the blizzard was back in full effect, howling winds and all. I checked to make sure my balcony door was locked before heading downstairs to join the guys. Lou already had some dinner going, the tantalizing smells wafting over from the kitchen. I checked every door and window to make sure they were locked then sat on the couch. Lou gave me a quick glance, "What was that all about?"

"Just making sure the boogeyman can't get in here," I said wrapping a blanket around me.

"The boogeyman?" Mark asked.

"Did you not tell him?" I asked Lou only to get a quick shake in return. Sighing, I started to recount what happened in the grocery store, "We had another run-in with Az."

"What happened?" Mark kept his attention on the screen in front of him, but sounded concerned.

"Just the usual head games like what you saw in the bar," I answered. "He trapped me in one of the aisles trying to relive parts of our relationship. I had to step in between Lou and Az and then we all left. No idea where he went, though."

"That guy gives me the chills," Mark pretended to shiver.

Lou and I both chuckled in response. They finished their game and Lou served up dinner, Jennie deciding to join us. We all kept the conversation light. No one said anything about Az anymore. No one asked about Warrick or wondered where he was at on his list. Lou pretended to laugh at all of Jennie's jokes while Mark supplemented some of his own comedy every now and then. Lou made it known he was happy to have his beer back while I happily drank down some wine noticing my mind had finally stopped replaying the events that took place in Warrick's apartment before coming here.

Mark's phone lit up and he groaned, "Damn it. I was hoping I didn't have to go in tonight."

"What changed?" I asked.

He rubbed a hand over his face, "A lot more people than what was anticipated." He sighed standing up, "Jennie, want to join?"

"Sure. I got nothing better to do tonight," she shrugged then downed the rest of her wine. They headed out leaving Lou and I alone again. I checked the front door to make sure it was locked, letting my nerves settle a bit once I confirmed no one was going to be walking through there.

As I was walking back to the table to snack on another piece of garlic bread, music started playing. The notes from a familiar slow song danced out into the room. I took a sip, a grin on my lips at the memory of dancing with Lou after the summer solstice ball. It's crazy to think that times felt simpler then. Warrick was the enemy, I was scared of the feelings I was getting for Lou, and worried about Daryl.

Lou started slow dancing on his own, holding his arms out like he was with someone. I laughed, "How many beers have you had?"

"Plenty," he closed his eyes. The corners of his mouth started twitching because he was probably starting to realize how funny he looked. He opened one eye, "You going to finish your wine and join me or just leave me hanging?"

I cocked an eyebrow as I gulped down the rest of my glass. I placed myself in his arms earning a lazy smile from Lou, "Before you say anything, this is strictly platonic. I'm not trying to make a move on you, just enjoying the dance and the memory associated with it."

I gently laid my head on his chest while we slowly spun around the living room. After the next couple of songs played, I raised my head to look up at him, "Can I ask you something?"

"Anything," Lou mumbled.

"When fated, shouldn't you have a bond or something?"

He paused for a moment, "Why?"

"I haven't felt anything like that with Warrick. I mean, right now, I can't feel anything that's supposed to be like this magical bond between the two of us," I explained.

Lou resumed leading us around, "There should be a bond."

"What should it feel like?" I started growing concerned. *Has Warrick been playing me this whole time?*

"I can't speak from experience," Lou cleared his throat. "But, what Raf has told me is that you should be able to feel your other half's presence even if it's only a little bit. You should be able to communicate through your minds, no one else should be able to hear you. You'll know what each other is feeling, if the other is in pain, if they're okay, and anything else. You're sharing the most intimate parts of yourself."

"Oh," I nodded my head. I pulled away and headed for the wine bottle to help myself. I definitely didn't have any of that with Warrick. I tried reaching out in my mind only to get my own thoughts and feelings back. Lou followed me over helping himself to another beer, "What's running through that mind of yours?"

I shook my head, "Just worried Warrick's not being completely honest with me. Did Raf mention if it happens automatically or is there something that unlocks the bond?"

Lou let out a soft laugh, "You talk like it's a game."

"I'm serious."

"Okay, got it. He didn't mention anything about that, so I would imagine it's different for each pair," he said sipping his beer. "Look, you've got nothing to worry about."

I studied him for a moment. He was avoiding eye contact with me and I wasn't sure if he telling me the truth or just wanting to be done with this conversation. There was something else there, though. He wasn't sharing a part of the story. I cocked my head to the side, narrowing my eyes, "What aren't you telling me?"

He nervously laughed running a hand through his hair, "I've told you what I know."

I stepped up to him jabbing a finger into his chest, "Tell me right now."

"What are you going to do, Val?" his voice dropped to a hushed tone, his hand wrapping around my finger while he looked at me with those grey eyes of his.

"You don't want to find out," I said trying to keep my voice even.

Lou sighed, "The bond is active on Warrick's side."

"What?" my mouth hung open in disbelief. *Why wouldn't he tell me something like that?*

Lou took a step back and gestured for us to go sit on the couch, "Judging by your reaction, he hasn't said anything to you."

"Nothing at all. Radio silence in that department," I settled on to the couch. I graduated from my wine glass to just drinking from the bottle at this point since I was going to be finishing it anyways. "Tell me what you know."

"Remember that night with Az in Warrick's apartment?" Lou asked like he already knew the answer. I shot him a look and he continued, "Well, before he got to his apartment, he could tell you were in trouble. He felt your panic the minute he got back to Lupusantha. Warrick heard all your thoughts, too. It fucked with him pretty bad."

"Why didn't he say anything?" I asked in a quiet voice.

Lou shrugged, "I have no idea. He hasn't given me insight to that, but he did say he felt it after the incident with Cian. The bond, I mean."

"Does that mean going through something traumatic does the trick?"

"Like I said, it's different for every pair, Lou reminded me. "I just don't know why you're not feeling it."

"I don't know either, and quite frankly, I don't have enough brain power to analyze that too much," I held up the wine bottle. I took another sip and blurted the next question, "Is there any way I can keep Warrick out?"

"I think that might come with you feeling his side of the bond, and it's probably a question for him. Although, he's not going to like it, but cross that bridge when you get there," Lou grinned at me. "Ready for another dance?"

I nodded taking his hand. We went back to swaying back and forth slowly getting more drunk as the night went on.

Chapter 11

I lost track of how much we drank, but by the time I laid down in my bed, I could feel the world spin. It wasn't hard to lose track of everything when we were just hanging out. Things were easier with Lou.

After helping me up the stairs and into my room, Lou was getting ready to leave, but I wasn't ready to be alone yet. I lifted up my head, "Wait."

"Yeah?"

"Stay with me?" I asked. He thought about it, so I continued, "No strings attached, I just don't want to fall asleep alone in this room."

"Alright, as long as it doesn't put me at risk of Warrick ripping my throat out," Lou sighed.

"No," I shook my head. "I'll make sure of it."

He closed the door, shut off the lights, and crawled into the bed with me. I settled in under the covers while he laid on top of them. We laid there just staring at each other. There was no way I was going to let myself go down the rabbit hole of what-ifs to imagine a life with Lou, especially now that I know Warrick can peek in whenever he wants.

I searched his grey eyes, "I'm really sorry."

"For what?" he asked slightly furrowing his brows.

"For how I acted. Back in Cian's world. I was a bitch and you didn't do anything to deserve that."

Lou softly laughed, "You're fine, Val. I'm not dwelling on things in the past, and neither should you. Let's go to sleep, okay?"

"Okay," I nodded. We laid there watching each other a little longer. When my eyes finally fluttered closed, I felt Lou brush some of my hair out of my face, "Goodnight, Val."

"Goodnight," I murmured back to him.

Scents of leather and sweat filled my mind as Az pushed me against the exposed brick wall in my apartment. My legs were wrapped around his waist, ankles locked together while desire pulsed through me. Any distance between our bodies made me scramble to pull him closer as I arched into him. I couldn't stand letting there be any space between us, not when all I wanted was to feel his body against mine. We were holding on to each other like this would be the last time we saw each other. He nosed my head to the side to expose my neck, his lips kissing every inch of exposed skin while I fumbled for the zipper on his jacket. He moved us over to the bed, stripping my riding gear from me as I did the same to him marveling at how his body looked. It was as if his muscles were sculpted. We couldn't get enough of each other, our kisses and moans growing more passionate as the seconds ticked by. His hands were all over me while I moved his body to be on top of mine, the two of us synchronizing our movements in a well-practiced dance.

My core filled with the anticipation I've come to know with Az and he knew it judging by the look he was giving me. Rain started tapping on the glass reminding me we didn't bother to close the curtains, but I didn't care. I was too consumed by the man on top of me giving my body what it craves.

Az's fingers slowly traced the outlines of my thong. All the frantic groping and kissing from earlier replaced with his slow determination. I tried to roll my hips to get his hand where I wanted it, but he already knew what I was going to do, holding me back. "Patience," he whispered in my ear, his lips a smile on my neck. "You'll get what you want soon. Let me enjoy this."

"How very interesting," Az's cool voice snapped my eyes open. "The minute my brother is gone, you crawl into bed with the next closest wolf."

I sat up looking down at a still-snoring Lou then brought my stare to Az. He was leaning against the wall opposite of the head of my bed, his arms crossed and a smug, knowing grin on his face. A few beats passed. He cocked his head to the side, "Were you having a wet dream?"

The heat rushed to my cheeks while I willed Lou to wake up. I slowly inched my hand over to Lou tapping his arm. Nothing.

"Oh, don't tell me, Val," Az said, pushing off the wall starting to close the distance between us. With every step he took, the more I clutched the blankets to my chest. "Were you dreaming about us? That's why you're at a loss for words, isn't it?"

Sense finally caught up to me and I started trying to shake Lou awake, "Lou, I really need you right now. Wake up. Now."

Az watched us amused at the scene playing out in front of him. *How the hell did he get in here? I swear, if Jennie and Mark left that damn front door unlocked ...*

All I got from Lou was a grunt before he rolled over moving away from my hands. Az chuckled then aimed a gun at Lou, "Guess he had a bit too much to drink tonight, huh? If you get him to wake up, though, I will shoot. This is supposed to be just you and me."

I slowly turned to look at him again, my throat dry. Az moved closer to me still keeping the gun trained on Lou, "You're coming with me tonight." Nothing indicated there was another option.

"No," I whispered.

"You really don't have a choice in this matter," he caressed my cheek. "There's two ways we can go about this. You come willingly, which is the preference, or you don't. If you don't make this easy for both of us, well, I'll take care of that. Now, get up. A bag is already packed."

When I hesitated, he shook his head, "I'm giving you one last chance to make it easy."

I still didn't move which pissed him off. The glint of the gun made me worry he was changing his target. He curled his lip as his other hand shot out of his pocket with a needle he thrust in my neck. I didn't have any chance to react or fight back. I felt a sharp pinch as he pushed down on the plunger. My world faded to black as he threw me over his shoulder.

My head was throbbing as I tried peel my eyes open. I had no idea what year it was. All I could tell is that it was still dark out. Judging by that, I hadn't been asleep for very long, yet I felt like I could sleep for a couple of days. *How much did I drink?* I swung my arm behind me to see if Lou was still there, but the bed felt empty. *Guess he went back to his room.* I rolled over and was now staring at a wall, not my closet doors. I turned back over to my other side expecting to look out a window or see my balcony door, but was looking at a black, leather couch. I was as awake as I could be at this point despite the fog blanketing my mind.

I rubbed my eyes to help them focus a little better, but gave up when the fuzziness around the edges wouldn't go away. I had no idea where I was, but it looked pretty similar to my apartment back home. The bed I was in had black silk sheets with a cozy black comforter and I was comfortable. The only light was coming from the kitchen where the smell of cinnamon and vanilla wafted over me. Sharing the same wall as the headboard were floor to ceiling windows where I had an unobstructed view of the northern lights dancing across the sky. The furniture was simple, all black and modern. The walls were all exposed brick with minimal decorations.

"Where – ," my memory finally caught up to me. Az.

"Good morning," he sauntered over pulling a chair up and flipping it around before sitting down. He rested his chin on his forearms on the top of the chair's back. "I should've taken into account the fact you were drinking."

"Why am I here?" I slurred, my tongue suddenly feeling too big for my mouth. I took a quick glance under the covers to make sure I was still clothed. A small sigh of relief escaped me when the clothes I had been wearing before Az grabbed me were still on.

"I missed you, that's all," Az grinned at me. "I was hoping to pick up on where we left off all those years ago."

"What did you do to me?" I tried lifting my arms, moving my legs, something. Everything felt too heavy and clumsy.

He stood up and headed towards the kitchen, "I gave you a choice. You chose the harder one."

I rolled onto my back, staring at the ceiling, "How long have I been out?"

Az came back setting a plate and a glass of water on the nightstand, "You slept the whole day. It's about twenty-four hours after I brought you here."

He tried to put an arm behind my back making me tense, "Don't touch me."

"Okay," he held his hands up. "Figured you could use some help with sitting up, but you're a strong, independent woman."

Az settled back into his chair watching me closely. The memory of what happened came rushing back in. Az there with a gun threatening a sleeping Lou. The needle he jammed into my neck. I reached up to feel the spot he had stuck the needle wincing at the thought. I sighed and tried to move my arms back so they could lift me up only to fall right back to where I was. I tried a couple more times, but ended up with the same result. Here I was, completely useless, unable to defend myself. I had been unconscious for a full day and who knows what Az did while I was out. Just because my clothes were still on me didn't mean a thing at this point. Tears sprang into my eyes as I screamed, "What the fuck did you do to me?"

He was by my side in an instant, lifting me up and guiding me into a sitting position, "You got hit with a potent drug. Again, I wasn't accounting on you having a shit ton of wine otherwise I would've lowered the dosage."

His tone was gentle and didn't contain an ounce of threat, almost as if he regretted doing this to me. That didn't keep the anger from rising in me.

"I hate you," I said through clenched teeth.

Az had his back turned to me as he moved towards the kitchen. He slightly turned his head, "There was a time where you wouldn't have dreamt of saying that to me. Now, drink some water and eat something. It should help you feel better."

I was caught off-guard by his stern, but quiet voice. I think this has been the truest version of the Az I knew since he reappeared. He disappeared behind the wall and I glanced at what he had placed next to me. A perfectly made cinnamon roll was sitting next to a glass of water. I looked back towards the direction he walked to before attempting to pick up the glass. My hand shook and I was surprised this small glass felt heavy. I lifted it to my mouth with both hands. Water had never tasted as good as it does now.

Az slowly came back holding up a fork as I gulped the water down, "Forgot this."

"Az, what did you really do to me? How did you get into my house?" I asked returning the empty glass back to its spot.

He turned his chair back around and sat down to start eating his own cinnamon roll contemplating what he could tell me. He shook his head not bothering to look in my direction, "Unfortunately, I am also bound to secrecy. Although, I am enjoying having your feisty company to myself. Its been too long. All I can tell you is that Warrick currently can't check in on you in any way. To answer your second question, you forget how well I knew your parents' house when we were together. I learned where the weak points were, and much to my delight, they were still there. Your balcony door happens to be one of them."

"Do I have to worry about the food being drugged?" I asked staring down the plate of gooey goodness still on the nightstand.

"No," he placed the plate on my lap. "Eat."

I watched him a little longer. He was acting different than he had been. Maybe he doesn't feel the need to put on a show where there's no audience, but that doesn't explain how he acted that night in Warrick's apartment. I sighed and did as I was told. My stomach was growling at this point, anyways.

Az studied the northern lights across the sky in between bites. He looked tired. Seems like everything he's trying to do is wearing on him more than he's letting on. There was something else there, though. Az looked like the man I remembered dating. The one who would goof around and be sweet. I tapped my fork against the plate, his attention snapping back to me, "Why the cinnamon rolls?"

"They're your favorite, right?"

My brows furrowed, "Is this another one of your games?" I hated that he remembered this about me. What I hated even more was the thought of him changing his strategy to get to me. If Az was planning on being the same person he was when we were together just to flip the switch again ... I shuddered unable to finish the thought.

Az let out a laugh, "Call it what you want, Val."

I continued watching him, not quite trusting what he would do next, while I finished what was on my plate. Unpredictable behavior seems to be his M.O. lately.

He got up, taking both mine and his plate to the kitchen before grabbing something from the couch. Az threw some clothes at me and jerked his head towards the door, "Figured pajamas would be more comfortable than what you're wearing now. You can change in the bathroom if you can get yourself over there."

Unsure of how much one cinnamon roll would really help, I swung my legs over the edge of the bed to try standing. No way was I going to give Az more opportunities to see me naked, and you can bet I wasn't ready to let him get his hands on me. As soon as I put any weight on my feet, though, I collapsed to the floor. Az poked his head around the corner, "That's a shame. I'm happy to help you get undressed."

"I'm sure you are," I mumbled as I tried and failed multiple times to get myself off the cold floor. "Can you help me get back in this damn bed?" I hated I felt helpless, and it couldn't have come at a worse time. It was one thing to have Lou and Warrick constantly taking care of me, but I had no chance at fighting Az off if he decided he wanted to go after me.

He smirked as he slowly walked over to me. Az crouched down so his face was filling my view, "We're going to have so much fun together."

The bed was back underneath me, my change of clothes thrown at me. Az returned to the kitchen giving the perfect opportunity to change without him seeing me. One problem, though, my body was unable to match the speed I wanted it to move at. I was halfway out of my pants when Az came back in. He crossed his arms leaning on the wall between the bed and the kitchen. Feigning disappointment, he asked, "Starting the show without me?"

Tsking as he walked over to me, Az ripped the covers to expose me then gently worked my pants off followed by my shirt. The moment he reached for my underwear, I grabbed his wrist. "Don't," I warned.

"I'm not going to do anything to you. You're in no state to fight back and it gives me a little thrill to have that added challenge," he sighed continuing with his efforts.

"Is that some sort of kink for you?" I asked letting him completely strip me.

Az started to put my pajamas on, buttoning the top with care, "We'll just say it's a new development. My wolf enjoys the chase."

I set my jaw while he finished dressing me. Az was showing glimpses of the guy he once was tonight with some of the care he took when handling me. There were no forced attempts to touch me or sleep with me. I watched as he headed into his bathroom getting ready for bed. I couldn't help but go back to noticing how tired he seemed. It was almost as if I could see when he removed the mask he wore when he was trying to inflict pain. I could see it in the way he carried himself; the tired facial expressions versus the ones that were nothing but smugness, the slouched shoulders versus the confident posture, the slower steps in contrast with the way he walked with purpose and speed.

When he emerged from the bathroom shirtless, I forced myself to look away. This man was a lot more muscular than I remembered, something I brushed aside when I was trying to get away when we were back in the werewolf world.

Az pushed me to the side of the bed against the wall then climbed in to join me, "It would be a shame if Warrick knew his love was checking out his brother."

"We're not sharing the same bed," I protested completely ignoring his comment while I turned my back to him. "Why do you put on such an act? Where did that even come from?"

"I've been meaning to ask," he started, his breath warm on my neck, ignoring my questions. "What were you dreaming of that turned you on like that?"

"I don't know what you're talking about," I said hoping I sounded more convincing than I felt. My thighs clenched together and I could feel my nipples hardening at the mention of that memory now flashing through my mind. Az started drawing lazy circles on my skin chuckling as he saw the goosebumps erupt.

He pulled me back into him so there was no space between us, "Sure you don't, but I bet I can guess. Get some sleep, Val. May your dreams be filled with visions of me."

Az kept his tight grip on me, but his breathing slowed and I was sure he was asleep now. I let out the breath I had been holding. *I'm fucked.* There was no hope of Warrick coming to find me. Lou had no chance. I was truly alone this time.

The warmth coming from Az's body made my eyelids heavy despite not wanting to let my guard down. At least he didn't try too much which made it easier for me to be okay with closing my eyes. If he kept this up, I'd be able to make it out of here. Even though it was small, there was a little bit of hope in this situation which is enough to allow myself to sleep.

L*ou – One Day Earlier*

The soft light woke me. “Val, wake up,” I groaned rolling over. My head erupted in pain, “Shit, I drank way too much last night.”

Her lack of response must mean she’s still sleeping. I glanced over to her pillow. Her empty pillow. I blinked a few times trying to let that process. She must be downstairs already.

I rolled out of bed clutching my head trying to catch up with the fact I was awake sooner than I wanted to be. Sitting there a few moments, I willed the world to stop spinning, and when it did, I stood up. I stumbled my way down the stairs not caring if I woke Jennie and Mark up.

“Val?” I called out before I reached the bottom of the stairs. The lights were still off, but that didn’t mean anything. She could just be reading on the couch enjoying the quiet of the morning. I squinted until my eyes focused. Still nothing. I went downstairs, but found the same result. *Where the hell is she?*

My gut was telling me something was wrong. Very wrong. Yet, I kept pushing that feeling away. She had to be here. There’s no way she would’ve left after what happened in the grocery store yesterday and I know this house was locked up tight when we went to sleep. Unless ...

I turned to check the front door. Locked. *At least that eliminates that possibility.* As I climbed back up the stairs, I noticed the bottles from last night were still scattered all over the kitchen and living room. *If Val were up, she would’ve taken care of those already.*

It took a while after I knocked on Jennie’s door, but she finally cracked it open. Her eyes were barely open and her hair was a mess, “Lou? Why are you pounding on my door right now?”

"Is Val with you?" I asked not hiding the urgency in my voice.

"No," she yawned then moved to close the door.

I threw my hand against it making her eyes pop wide open, "Have you seen her at all?"

"All I've seen are the inside of my eyelids. Now, if you'll excuse me, I have a hangover to sleep off," Jennie huffed and slammed the door.

"What's going on?" Mark asked in a groggy voice. I turned to where he was poking his head out the door, eyes half open.

"Have you seen Val? Is she with you?" I asked again.

"Nope, haven't seen her. Why?"

My head dropped back, my eyes closing, "Fuck."

Here we are again. Val is missing and there really isn't any way to know where she's at. *Why does this keep happening? I swear if she went out on her own ...*

We don't have access to Warrick, not like the last time we couldn't find her ... I patted my pockets pulling my phone out once I located it. I started typing out a message to Warrick, but thought better of it. If he knows where Val is, I could go get her. On the other hand, there's a good chance he has no idea where she's at and I'd just set him off. No way was I dealing with that wrath especially when he was caught up in something else. I've learned that lesson already.

I slipped my phone back in my pocket as Jennie padded across the hall to the bathroom, "Val's missing."

She stopped, "You're kidding, right? This is a test. There's no way she could be missing again."

"We locked the door last night," Mark added looking between Jennie and me.

I threw up my hands, "Well, she's not in this damn house and there's no note. Nothing. I have no idea where she could be."

"She didn't say anything?" Jennie asked now moving closer to us.

I shook my head, "No. We drank, danced around, then went to sleep."

I immediately tried to remember if there was anything from last night that stood out to me. Warning signs, any red flags from our conversations, anything. I kept coming up empty, except there was something weird that stood out to me ... During one of my dreams, I heard her say something, but it was so faint I couldn't pick up on the specifics.

I ran downstairs and threw on my coat. "Where are you going?" Jennie and Mark called out in unison.

"I need to start crossing things off my list," I answered. "If she's not anywhere, I think we have a bigger problem on our hands."

The two of them ran downstairs and threw on their coats to join me. There was no hesitation. *Val will be happy to know that.* I glanced at my phone again to check the time. It was the afternoon which meant we slept way too long. Who knows how long Val has been gone. If Az got his hands on her, too much time has passed. I pressed the heels of my hands in my eyes trying, and failing, to keep the images of what he almost did to her in Warrick's apartment out of my head.

"Ready?" Jennie asked putting a hand on my arm.

"Yeah, let's go."

Our first stop was at the bar. Mark wasted no time talking with the owner and showing him a picture of Val. Jennie and

I hung back. I was afraid of how I'd react if I didn't hear what I wanted when I'm already very much on edge. However, watching wasn't helping much either. The moment the owner shook his head, I wanted to throw a table. Instead, I took a few breaths and forced myself to focus on where we'd go next.

Mark looked defeated, "He hasn't seen her since that first night you guys showed up. I checked to see if he's seen anyone matching Az's description and he hasn't seen Az either."

"Well," Jennie turned to me. "Where do we go next?"

I clenched my jaws together as I turned towards the exit. The breathing may have helped take the edge off, but that didn't mean anger and worry weren't dominating my emotions. We trudged to the next building, Jennie taking the lead on this one. She held up a picture of Val only to be met with a confused look and a shake of the head from the employee. Much to my disappointment, this was the result we got in the rest of the buildings lining the street.

We got back into the house and a growl erupted from my throat, "You've got to be fucking kidding me!"

To make things worse, my phone buzzed. Pulling it out, I groaned the minute I saw Warrick's name.

"Everything okay?" Jennie asked cautiously.

I shook my head, too focused on the message to answer. I went numb reading what he sent me: *I can't feel her anymore. Is Val with you?*

If Warrick couldn't feel her through their bond ... I couldn't let myself go down that path.

Chapter 12

Val

So warm. The amount of comfort I felt in this moment was something I hadn't felt in a while. I cuddled in closer to the source of the warmth not quite ready to open my eyes, my face pressing into a bare chest. Our legs were entangled and there wasn't a lot of space between us. His fingers were running up and down my thighs occasionally playing with the hem of my shorts.

I stretched into him, "Good morning, War – "

All I could see were tattoos now that I finally opened my eyes. This chest didn't belong to Warrick. This was Az. I slowly brought my eyes up meeting his amused gaze. His lips formed a lopsided grin, "Morning. Not who you expected?"

I tried to push back to get as far away from him as I could only for him to hold on to me tighter. Chuckling, he said, "Too late, Val. You're already wrapped up in me and I'm not quite ready to let you go. Besides, this is nice."

Az's hand went underneath the fabric of my shorts gripping my ass. I started to move my hand towards his to remove it from my body, but stopped. There were handcuffs attached by a medium-length chain that limited my ability to bring my arms from where they were resting behind Az's head. I jiggled the chain, "What the hell is this?"

"It's exactly what it looks like," Az sighed closing his eyes again.

"It looks like you're trying to keep me restrained," I was irritated. I wasn't happy being wrapped up in him nor was I happy about having my movements restricted.

"Bingo," he muttered.

"No," I wiggled from him trying to put distance between the two of us. "You do *not* get to fall asleep right now."

Az popped an eye open, "I don't think you're really in the position to order me around."

"Will you at least explain what's going on? Why the hell am I here?" I asked.

He rolled on top of me, the chain draping against the back of his neck. If I could only just ...

Az brushed my hair out of my face, "Is it not enough that I wanted the company? I saw an opportunity and took it."

"I don't believe you."

"Of course you don't," he shook his head. Az dragged his hand so that it was back up under my shorts, "Enough with the questions."

Az's thumb started to trace the top of my thigh, and the minute he started that, I wrapped the chain around his neck pulling with everything I had in me. I may have been a little disoriented this morning, but everything caught back up to me the moment I laid eyes on Az. He drugged me and brought me to his damn apartment. Now he was trying to take advantage of the situation, and I wasn't going to let that happen.

Instead of making choking sounds, he threw his head back and laughed. When he looked down at me, he said, "I didn't think you were into this kind of stuff. What a pleasant surprise."

As soon as I opened my mouth, he yanked down on the chain bringing me within inches of his smiling face, "You could've told me you like it rough. I would've handled things a little differently."

He untangled himself from the chain dropping me back on the mattress. I watched as he disappeared into the kitchen then examined the handcuffs. They were standard, so I shouldn't have a hard time getting out of them as long as I have the chance when he's not around.

Az rounded the corner leaning against the wall with a hot cup of coffee in his hands. He took a sip, his hazel eyes never leaving mine. When he was done, he asked, "How are you feeling?"

I furrowed my brow, "How do you do that?"

"What?"

"Flip back and forth between crazy and serious so easily," I explained.

Az smirked, "Just keeping you on your toes, that's all. Now, answer my question."

I pulled my knees to my chest, "A lot better than yesterday."

Az's face filled my vision as he started examining me. I hadn't even heard him move towards me. He lifted my chin focused on my eyes, "Any grogginess?"

"No."

"Feeling weak anywhere?" he asked, going through his mental checklist.

"No."

"I'd agree with that considering how hard you were pulling on that chain," he chuckled. "Anyways, guess that means it's time for another dose."

I tried to pull away, "What are yo – "

There was no chance for me to finish that question. Az shoved another needle into my neck. I gasped, but it wasn't long before the edges of my vision went fuzzy. I was out like a light as soon as he finished emptying the syringe's contents.

The apartment was filled with a flickering orange glow by the time I woke up. It was night again, and instead of using any lights, there were just candles spread around the room. I felt out of it, but not in the same way I did when I first woke up in Az's apartment. My shoulders were killing me and something was biting into my wrists. That's when I realized I was no longer laying in the bed. I glanced up, groaning when I figured out what was causing the source of my pain. Az had hung me up by the chain between the handcuffs.

"Oh, good. You're awake," Az said casually from his table. He was eating something that smelled delicious. Leaning back in his chair, Az studied me, "You know? I think I like this new addition to the artwork in this place."

Words were not coming to me, so I let out another groan. My head dropped down and I groaned again when I saw I was in nothing but my bra and thong. I rolled my head to the side to shoot him a glare earning an amused chuckle. He pushed his chair back to approach me. Caressing my face, he said, "Can't risk Warrick being able to reach you through that bond of yours. I'll save you the effort of trying to speak – yes, I know you two are actually fated and that means you can communicate mentally. This little drug I've been using blocks that bond, and that's all I'm going to tell you about that."

"Why am I up here?" I finally croaked out. The fact I was able to speak again meant I was coming to faster than I had yesterday.

"Can't risk you trying to choke me again, now can we?" Az responded with a mocking tone. "Besides, there are some things I need to take care of first."

He turned back to the table unrolling what I thought was just a napkin. Boy, was I wrong. Knives of various shapes and sizes were mixed with other tools used for torture. Panic clawed at my throat. I still had no idea what I was doing here, but being tortured was not high on my list of guesses.

Az plucked a small knife and headed back over to me. He waived it at me, "Just need to make a few marks on you. Draw out your pain and suffering." Az stopped putting an arm's length of distance between us running his fingers over the scars covering my body from the last time I was hung up like this. He tsked his tongue then said, "Looks like someone beat me to the punch, though. Oh well, I'll make sure to add my own flare."

He started moving the knife in my direction and my legs shot out, one connecting with his groin while I broke his nose with the other. I must've caught both of us off-guard. Given how I was currently feeling, I didn't think I was actually going to be able to do anything. Az stumbled back clutching his bleeding nose and his family jewels with a bewildered expression. He set his nose, regaining his composure. I watched as Az set the knife back on the table and used an actual napkin to wipe away the blood that had now stopped, "You're full of surprises, aren't you?"

He stood up straight then walked back over to me, no knife in his hand, "Care to bring me up to speed on who put all these scars on your body?"

"No," I answered firmly.

"Clearly whoever did that to you got under your skin for you to have a reaction like that," Az sighed. "Guess I'll have to change up my strategy. Are you hungry?"

"No," I repeated myself. As soon as I answered his question, my stomach betrayed me with a growl that Az picked up on.

He shook his head, "Sure." When he moved towards my wrists, I flinched. Az dropped the act he was putting on, his tone serious, "I'm just bringing you down so you can join me at the table."

My body was still tense as he held on to me while unhooking the chain. Az carried me over to the table then threw one of his hoodies in front of me before prepping a plate of food in the kitchen. I sat there staring at the piece of clothing. He was clearly going to have to release me in order for me to put any clothes on.

The sound of a plate sliding over to me snapped be back to reality. My eyes rested on a burger, freshly made with a lot of cheese. Fries were sitting next to it and my mouth instantly started watering. I no longer cared about wanting to cover myself as I dived into the food. Az took up his seat across from me, leaning back and crossing his arms across his chest, "I'm happy I still know your favorites."

"Just a coincidence that my preferred diet is that of a teenager," I mumbled between bites.

"So icy," Az commented. "You can just accept the food without the chip on your shoulder."

"I don't know that I can," I watched him carefully. "You've been playing games ever since you decided to reintroduce yourself, Az. How can I afford to let my guard down for even a moment?"

"Because I'm not going to attack you while you're eating," he answered matter-of-factly. Az headed back into the kitchen grabbing a couple of bottles and glasses. He set down a wine glass with the bottle next to it then put the other bottle down in front of where he was sitting a moment ago. He gestured for me to hand him my wrists. I hesitantly lifted my hands up for him to release me, "You should be able to put on the sweatshirt now."

I wasted no time throwing the oversized hoodie on, curling my legs into my chest. Az went back to his chair and took a long swig from the bottle, a familiar looking blue liquid sloshing around as he set it back on the table. I rubbed my wrists noting the handcuffs had started cutting into me already, "What's with the act?"

He momentarily bristled at that comment, "Don't know what you're talking about."

"Oh, I think you do, otherwise you wouldn't have reacted to that question," I said pouring myself a glass of wine. Thankfully, it was a screw top that hadn't been opened yet, so I didn't have to worry about him spiking it. *One less unknown drug entering my system.*

Az took another drink wiping his mouth with the back of his hand before responding, "There is no act. What you see is what you get."

I nodded my head even though I didn't believe him. He wore the same tired look on his face from yesterday. The mask he puts on when he's being an asshole is completely gone and he's not trying to make a move on me. He also didn't dive right in to torturing me when he saw what Cian had done. *Maybe there is a heart in him after all.*

I took a sip of my wine noting he hadn't taken his eyes off me. As soon as the liquid hit my lips, I knew he remembered what kind of wine I liked, too. Az grinned knowing he had hit the mark again. I scowled at him, finishing the food on my plate when he asked, "You gonna tell me what happened to you?"

"Someone like you should already know," I shot back. I was already in an anxious state, but him trying to get me to talk about the time I practically begged to be killed was only making things worse. I chugged down some wine refilling my glass.

Az leaned forward on the table, his voice dropping to a dangerous level, "What's that supposed to mean?"

I dropped my gaze to my empty plate, fidgeting with the edge of it, "I-I mean you've probably been keeping tabs on everything, right? That's what you do."

"Not everything, Val. So, tell me who took the fun away from me."

I paused then reached for my glass of wine. Probably not the best idea right now to keep playing into what Az wants, but it was a welcome distraction. I set the glass back down on the table still not looking at him, "I decided to be stupid and the vampires didn't like it, so they strung me up to bleed me out. Much like you just did."

"Interesting," Az rested his chin on his hand. "Is that all you're going to say about that?"

I raised my chin, "Yes."

"Fair enough," Az reached for his bottle. "Tell me. Did you miss me?"

And we're right back to where we were. The mask was slowly coming back up and I don't know if he had enough of a break or if the alcohol could be blamed for that. It was time for me to toughen back up. I cocked my head to the side, "Why do you care? Like I said before, you were the one that left."

He scoffed, "I'll be honest with you, Val."

"Please," I crossed my arms.

Az shot me a look of annoyance, but continued, "You may think I used you, but that relationship was as real to me as it was you. The reason I left was because I knew we were never going to last."

What he said didn't sit right with me. I was expecting something along the lines of just needing a good time or that he got bored, but not that. Noticing my reaction, he brought his bottle up to his lips then said, "Ah, not what you were thinking I was going to say, was it?"

"You better not be trying to play the game where you say what I think I want you to," I warned.

"Please, tell me what you'll do to me if I am," Az challenged. He waited a few beats then continued, "That's what I thought. Anyways, you and I didn't have that connection, we weren't fated. There was nothing I was going to do that would change that, so I left. Simple as that."

"Asshole," I grumbled into my glass.

He leaned towards me, putting a hand to his ear, "What was that?"

"You heard me," I said.

"It sounds like you had feelings for me," Az guessed.

"Bingo," I rolled my eyes. "But, I bet you knew that the whole time."

"Actually no," he said, a shadow crossing his features. "I had no idea, but nothing I can do about it now. You found who you're supposed to be with, and it just so happens to be my brother."

"Good sleuthing, detective," I mumbled and finally took a sip.

Az stood up a little too quickly for my comfort. He casually took my empty plate to the kitchen and I padded over to the bed. I finished off the bottle as Az came around the corner. He gave me a warm smile when I set the empty bottle down, "Good girl."

Ignoring him, I laid on my back happy my arms were free to move however they wanted to while Az finished cleaning things up. I glanced out the window noting the northern lights were out undulating across the sky in an attempt to get everyone's attention. Az blew out the candles joining me in the bed. He was hovering over me, but I still didn't turn to look at him as I noted, "They really are beautiful."

"So are you," Az said in a low voice. He gently put a hand under my head and I brought my eyes to meet his, "Don't say things like that."

"Like what?"

I swallowed, "Things that take advantage of how I'm feeling right now. Things that speak to the side missing being loved."

"When was the last time that side of you was satisfied?" Az asked, his pupils dilating.

I shook my head, "No, we're not doing this. It's wrong and I don't want to sleep with you."

He lowered his face enough so our noses were barely touching, "You sound like you're having to convince yourself more than me."

I sucked in a breath and pushed against his chest, "I'm serious."

"About?"

"I don't want to sleep with you," I repeated.

"I'm fine with there being no strings attached. We'll keep it between us," Az said, his voice barely above a whisper.

I tried to move back only to have Az follow me, "There's no such thing as no strings attached with you."

A smile slowly filled his face, "You know me so well. You should also know I have unfinished business."

Az dipped his head closer to mine, the smell of alcohol assaulting my nose. He hesitated the moments our lips brushed. I knew this was him baiting me into a response that would dictate how the rest of the night unfolds. If I pushed away again, not that I have a lot of options for getting away, he'd probably lose it. On the other hand, if I just stayed here, there might be a slim chance he'd back off. That slim chance diminished as I replayed his words through my mind. Mentioning his unfinished business just meant he'd be picking up where he left off in Warrick's apartment, except I don't have anyone who'd come to my rescue this time.

"Good answer," he whispered before pulling me into him. Az's lips were greedy, full of too much want. His hand moved under his hoodie gripping my rib cage and I knew the moment my body tensed, I messed up. Az pulled away from me, "What's wrong?"

"N-nothing," I stammered.

"Something's clearly bugging you," Az laid down next to me. I'm surprised he wasn't immediately trying to force me into something I didn't want to do. "Talk to me, Val."

I kept my mouth shut afraid of walking into a trap. Picking up on my hesitation, Az sighed, "Alright. Why don't you tell me what you were dreaming about when I picked you up?"

"You mean, kidnapped me?" I asked then continued. "I was thinking about one of the last days we spent together."

"Ah, that's a good one," he responded. I could hear the smile in his voice. "No wonder I could smell the arousal on you. Why were you dreaming about that?"

"I've been wondering the same thing," I answered while fidgeting with the edge of the only piece of clothing I had protecting me at the moment. I rolled over so my back was facing him and I was now facing the brick wall, "Why do you care so much? You're just going to do what you want with me anyways. What are you waiting for?"

Az rolled over wrapping an arm around me, "Don't tempt me."

"Can you answer a question for once?" There was no chance of me thinking about what I was going to say with how fast those words escaped me. I clamped a hand over my mouth, eyes widening as I stared at the wall in front of me.

Az's low chuckle vibrated against my back, "There's the Val I've grown accustomed to. You're right, I am going to do what I want, but I care because I still have a soft spot for you, for whatever reason. I'd like for you to enjoy a little bit of it."

"I hate to break it to you, but I don't know that I'll enjoy anything right now. You have me so tense waiting for the ball to drop."

"Finally," he muttered against my neck. "Honesty."

Then he was gone. He headed towards the kitchen to rummage through his cabinets for a second then came back to join me. I had rolled back over just in time for him to hand me another drink. I nodded towards the glass, "What is that?"

"Another glass of wine. I don't have any other clean glasses, so this is what you get. Want it?" he held it out to me.

I tentatively took the glass. The liquid was a light pink with a little bit of glitter in it. I glanced back up at him skeptically, "What kind of wine is it?"

He ran a hand through his hair, "I forget the name of it. It's something they make special here, though. If you don't think it's safe, hand it to me."

I did just that, except instead of taking the glass back to the kitchen like I thought he would, he took a sip. When he finished swallowing, Az met my gaze, "If there was something wrong with it, you think I would've taken a sip?"

My memories flashed back to the night in the club when Chris did the same exact thing. The only problem is that when Chris did that, there *was* something wrong with the drink. I shook my head, "I'm not falling for that again."

Az shrugged, "Fine, we'll lay here for a bit to rule out any reactions then you can decide if you want to drink it."

He set the glass on his nightstand and resumed laying next to me. Az lightly grazed my exposed legs with his hands and I hated the goosebumps that formed in response. I tugged the sweater down as far is it could go then stared at him. For once, he wasn't saying anything, so that's how we were for a few minutes.

"See?" Az started. "Nothing different."

"Walk around a little bit," I ordered.

He got out of bed laughing, shaking his head, "You sure are paranoid, you know that?"

I chose to ignore him focusing solely on how he was moving. Nothing had changed in how he was carrying himself to indicate that anything was wrong or off. Az finished his circle and did a little spin while holding his arms up, "See? Perfectly normal."

"Fine," I sighed reaching for the glass. I took a sniff. It smelled like a rosé, so I took a long drink. It must have had a higher alcohol content with how it immediately warmed my body, but that was the only thing that stood out to me. I placed the glass back on the nightstand as Az settled back next to me. He didn't hesitate to reach for my face, and when I didn't immediately recoil, I knew something was off. My outward reaction didn't match what I was feeling internally.

He pulled me in for a slow kiss. His tongue traced my bottom lip forcing me to open my mouth more deepening the kiss. The moment he pulled away to move to my neck, I asked, "Are you sure there was nothing wrong with that wine?"

"Why?" Az asked between kisses.

I gently pushed against his chest, "Because I'm not able to fight you off."

"Maybe you changed your mind."

"Maybe I didn't, but my body is no longer on the same page. Az, stop," I tried my best to muster as much authority in my voice as I could, but it only came out in a hushed tone.

He moved us so he was back on top of me playing with my hair, "Tell me what page your body is on then."

I could tell he already knew what the answer would be. This was all a part of his games. I drank another spiked drink like an idiot, and now I was losing control. The words fell out of my mouth before I had a chance to stop them, "It's on the page where you fuck me into oblivion to make sure your needs are satisfied."

My eyes widened and I clamped a hand over my mouth to keep from saying anything else. I shook my head while Az laid there, a sinister grin inching across his lips. *What the hell is wrong with me? That's the last thing I want.*

"Since you've decided to be honest with me lately," Az started spreading my legs apart. "I'll return the favor. That 'wine' over there was actually a special concoction I had made for the occasion. It helps to have friends in high places here. Anyways, I knew you weren't going to want to have sex with me, so I figured I would help take the edge off."

"What do you mean?"

He picked up the glass swirling its contents as a way to tease me, "Some powerful witches brewed up a potion to make you want me."

"A *love* potion? What the hell is this, Az?" I asked incredulously.

"Eh, more of something to make you lust after me," he shrugged. "Something to make the sex a little more enjoyable because the tears weren't doing it for me the last time."

I opened my mouth to throw an insult back at him only to have him forcing me to drink, yet again. He didn't pull away until the glass was empty. Not even a single drop remained. Satisfied with the empty cup, he tossed it aside, the sound of glass shattering ringing in my ears as his hands went back to roaming my body and his lips went to work kissing my thighs. His admission sucked the air out of me. The kindness and gentleness he had been showing me up until this point was all a game to get me to be more pliable. The real Az is showing his face now, the one who wants to use me as a way to torment his brother on the path for more power and influence.

Az planted kisses all over me. I wanted so badly to push him away, to fight, to do anything that would get him off me. I was a prisoner in my own body, forced to watch Az get his way. Despite my mind screaming out in protest, my body wanted the exact opposite. It was like I craved his touch and he would be the only one to satisfy it.

"There you go," Az said in a husky voice. He inched his hoodie off me, the cool air blanketing my skin. He removed the rest of my clothing leaving me completely exposed without so much of a fight from me. I gave it one more shot as he kept me trapped, "No. Please, Az. I don't want this."

"Your body would say otherwise," he observed as he rendered me defenseless.

"Please, stop," I begged. I made several more attempts only frustrating him. His hand shot out pinning my neck down.

Az snarled at me, face inches from mine, "You can beg all you want, but that's not going to change things."

I reached for his hand that was slowly tightening its grip, "You never used to be mean when you were drunk."

The expression on his face changed to something remorseful, but was back to crazed determination in a blink of an eye. I had clearly gotten through to him even if it was for a short moment and I pocketed that small win to get me through this pain as Az carried out his fantasies.

I dropped my head back to the bed, the fogginess in my mind getting worse. Whatever potion he forced down my throat was now reaching its full effect, and it was harder to keep myself from wanting the man in front me despite what he just did. Az got what he wanted, and in return, a piece of me shattered.

When Az finally finished, he grabbed something from his nightstand. I couldn't see what it was from the way he was holding me. Az laid back on top of me, stroking my face. I didn't recognize the pinch in my neck or register what he was saying, unconsciousness quickly approaching. Before my world faded to black, I felt his smile against my lips knowing he had won.

Chapter 13

Lou

We had been looking for Val every chance we got. There were no signs of her anywhere and my lack of response to Warrick didn't help anything. I was hoping he'd be busy enough with whatever task list Mark had given him, but that apparently wasn't enough to keep him from sending me nonstop messages demanding status updates on Val.

Sleep was a rare occurrence for me. Between the barrage of messages and trying to figure out what stone I left unturned, I didn't get much of an opportunity to rest. Mark and Jennie were doing their best to help, but there was only so much they could do. Hell, there was only so much I could do.

I was sitting at the island, my phone in front of me, rubbing my face with my hands. Jennie set a glass of water in front of me, "Has Warrick let up at all?"

"No," I mumbled in between my fingers. I took a sip just as my phone started buzzing. "Speak of the devil."

"It's not a text this time," Jennie observed, worry edging her voice.

I sighed picking up the phone, "Warrick."

"Lou, you better tell me you've found a lead on Val," Warrick's voice was angry and impatient.

"I've been looking nonstop for her. I've hardly slept, hardly eaten. I have no idea where she is, but I'm still going out day and night to search for her. Jennie and Mark have been helping, and still nothing. What the hell do you want from us, Warrick? We're running into dead ends everywhere we go," my voice grew louder as I went on. Jennie motioned for me to calm down.

There was a long pause on the other end of the line making me second-guess how I just reacted. I clenched my jaw together waiting for the backlash only to be met with a sigh, "Look, I know you've been doing everything you can. Hell, I've been trying to find her when I have some free time. She's off the map."

"Have you been able to feel her through your bond?" I asked.

"No," Warrick sounded emotional, his voice wavering as he went on. "The bond has been locked down tight."

I lowered my voice earning a concerned look from Jennie. I turned my back to her as I asked, "You okay?"

"I should've never asked her to come here, Lou. This one is entirely on me and I don't know if I'll ever be able to earn her trust back. There are so many things she wouldn't have gone through if she hadn't been associated with me," he finished with another sigh. The silence on the other line seemed to come through my phone and hang in the air before he asked, "Can I count on you? I'll give you anything you want."

Who knew what Az was getting away with having Val tucked away where no one could bother them. I'm sure it was eating Warrick alive knowing that's where she was at. Add in the past between the two of them? That served as a reminder as to why Warrick wouldn't let me sleep.

I found myself running my hand through my hair, "Hey, Warrick, we'll get her back."

"I sure hope so, Lou."

The line went dead after that. I stared at my phone while Jennie asked, "What was that all about?"

"That's the first time I've ever heard that man be emotional," I answered still staring at my phone. "We have to find her."

"I know, Lou," Jennie's tone was soft. "Let's go."

I nodded following her to the door as she called up the stairs to Mark. He finally ended his job at the bar, along with our nightly trips, which meant we had more time to focus on finding Val. We braved the cold heading to our coffee spot, my head on a swivel. This was one evening when the skies were finally clear giving me a good view of the buildings along the street. I thought I had seen Az's face in a window, but I wasn't so sure. It just so happened to be across from the coffee shop that had turned into our new spot and the best lead we had.

I took up our usual spot next to the door staring up at the windows hoping to see something, anything again. Mark and Jennie came over to the table with our drinks not saying a word. I had just taken my first sip when I could've sworn I heard a scream. Judging everyone else's reactions, they must've heard something, too. What got me was everyone rushing out of this place after hearing that keeping their heads down and out of everyone's business.

"What was that?" Jennie looked scared.

Mark glanced to me for an answer I wasn't sure I had. I turned my attention back towards the windows across the street, "I think you know exactly what that was."

"Why'd everyone react like that?" she asked. When I didn't show any signs of answering her, Jennie asked, "Mark? You've lived here."

In a grim tone, Mark answered, "It's not uncommon to hear someone scream like that around here."

"But what does it mean? Do we need to get out of here?" her tone was more urgent this time. I took a break from watching across the street to see she was getting herself ready to bolt out of her chair if she needed to.

Mark took his turn to stare out the windows, "It usually means the witches are out picking their next victim. That's why everyone runs. I don't think that's the case here. That scream sounded different."

I jumped in before she could respond keeping my attention on Mark, "Do you think that came from over there?"

"Yeah," he nodded.

I knew that scream, too. It was one I had heard more than I'd like to admit after we came back from Cian's world. Val was over there, but it wasn't clear how we'd get in the building. "We need to check that place out," I said quietly.

"Nope, we're not doing that," Jennie protested still panicky.

"We got you, Jennie. We'll wait it out a little bit to make sure the coast is clear, then we'll check out the door to see if we can get in. If we can't, we'll head right back to the house, right, Lou?" Mark looked at me expectantly.

"Yeah," I answered.

So, we waited. Jennie kept muttering complaints under her breath, but they fell on deaf ears. Mark was scanning the streets for any sign of witches in case we were wrong in our unspoken hunch. After several more minutes, Mark nodded his head. The coast was clear and it was time to move.

Jennie tucked herself in right behind me. With Mark on the other side of her, we quickly made our way across the street. I didn't have high hopes – the door had a locking mechanism on it that required a key card which was probably only given to residents. If we were back home, I'd take my chances with tampering with it, but we weren't and I didn't want to put any unwanted attention on us.

I tried the door to see if there was any chance of it not being locked. It didn't budge. I let out a frustrated breath when Mark tapped on my shoulder, "We got to go. Someone's coming."

I looked in the direction Mark had indicated. There was plenty of time before the approaching person reached us, but it wasn't worth the risk. I tugged on Jennie's hand, "C'mon."

V*al – The Same Morning*

A faint whistling brought me out of my sleep, if you could call it that. I couldn't lift my head this time. My eyes wouldn't open. My mouth felt like it was filled with cotton balls once again. Everything hurt and I had no idea why, where I was, or what was going on. I was so disoriented, and something was telling me this wasn't the first time either, yet I couldn't remember why I knew that.

The whistling moved closer and a hand brushed some hair out of my face before lifting my head up for me. The haunting tune stopped replaced by a familiar, accented voice, "Rise and shine, sweetheart."

Only a groan came out in response.

"Unfortunately, we're on a little time crunch. Wake up."

My head dropped back down to the pillow. I managed to force my eyes open only to be looking at a picture that wasn't there before, perched on the nightstand. I blinked trying to process what I was seeing. When it came in to focus, I realized I was staring a younger, happier version of myself. I was laughing, my eyes closed, with Az's arms wrapped around me. He was laughing with me, too, a huge, open-mouthed smile that mirrored mine. We were on a mountain, the city a speck in the distance. Our bikes were behind us which meant we were on a ride with our group. A couple of people who rode with us were in the background wearing smiles of their own. Who knows why we were laughing like that. Maybe a good joke?

I let out a grunt getting Az's attention. I tried moving my head in the direction of the picture. I wasn't happy if he was trying to use this as a way to play another mind game. He pointed at it, "What? That? That's been there, Val."

I glanced at him. Az was studying the picture now. He seemed to be mourning what he had lost, but his expression changed the moment he knew I was watching him. Az motioned for me to get up, "Time to get moving. Now!"

The order was followed by a punch in my gut. I coughed, curling in on myself from the pain. Az grabbed me by the chain from the handcuffs dragging me over to the wall he had hung me up before. It was as if I weighed nothing as he lifted me and hooked the chain in the same spot as before. This time, however, Az made quick work of restraining my legs with their own cuffs and chains.

It was hard for me to form a coherent thought or a way to protest. I could hardly remember what happened or why I was hurting so bad. All I knew was that Az had become more intense, but there was something else there. He seemed to be at war with himself. About what, I wasn't sure. I had nothing to clue me in on the specifics since all I had running through my mind was static.

Az casually walked towards the table while I blinked myself back to reality, getting rid of the remaining fuzziness lurking around the edges of my vision. He was examining something on the table in front of him, but I couldn't tell what. Az glanced over his shoulder at me, "You really know how to make a guy feel special."

"What?" I asked sounding about as groggy as I felt. At least being able to say something was a step in the right direction.

He plucked something up, a knife maybe? Az was blocking my view just enough so I could hardly make out anything. He walked back over to me pointing the object in my direction, "You don't remember?"

"Remember what?"

It was most definitely a knife, the tip just barely poking into my nose. Az leaned in whispering, "You fucked me into oblivion. All night."

"I feel like I'm going to be sick," I mumbled. My stomach threatened to empty its contents at the thought of sleeping with him. There was no way I would've agreed to that, would I? The more I tried to remember, the more my head screamed in protest.

"No time for that," he turned his back to me. "We're just getting to the good stuff. You see this?" Az held up the knife admiring it, my gaze following his, "Did Warrick ever tell you what I did?"

My eyes went back to him and that was all he needed for an answer, "I thought so. Little baby brother so torn up over something he had no control over."

"Why did you do it?" my words came out with a slight slur. My tongue still felt too large for my mouth.

"Good question," he turned away starting to pace in front of me. "They got wind of a plan I was hatching and didn't like it. Of course they didn't like it, because it would mess up their squeaky clean image. They didn't want to see me get stronger. They didn't want me to push the boundaries. Oh no, they had to try to keep me caged. And I knew. I knew they were the only ones who would be able to stop me if I didn't do anything right then and there. They had contingency plans in case we got involved with the wrong people, and by that, I mean the wolves."

"You had just been changed," I chimed in, Warrick's words replaying in my mind.

"And my world got a thousand times better," Az turned to face me holding his arms wide. "I had never felt stronger, more *alive*. The moment I got in the house, I knew what I had to do. And this little knife here is Old Faithful. She's been with me from the start."

I started piecing together what Az was saying. That was the knife he used to kill his parents. His parents who were the only ones who could have stopped him from starting this war. *Has Warrick checked his childhood home for anything on his brother? Notes, instructions, anything?* Tucking that thought away, I braced myself as Az came back in front of me. I could only hope I'd get another chance to see Warrick again to ask him if he's taken that approach.

"Enough of that," Az put his hands on either side of my head giving me a sinister smile. "Let's have some more fun, shall we?"

I tried tugging my arms, but that only got the hand cuffs to dig further into my wrists. Az laughed as he dragged his knife down the length of my arm. I don't think I will ever forget the bite of a knife into my skin after Cian. I screamed out, more out of fear than pain. Az's hand clamped down over my mouth, "Shhh, it's too early for that. Besides, I didn't even dig in like I wanted to. I'll give you something to scream about in a little bit. Meanwhile, I'm still trying to figure out where I really want to dig into, what designs I want to make on this beautiful canvas."

He pressed the knife into my stomach cutting swirls into my skin adding pressure as he went so the knife gradually got deeper. This time, it was the pain that made me scream out. Az pushed so hard against my mouth he ended up slamming my head into the brick. A white flash filled my vision momentarily before going back to the scene of Az's apartment. He made more cuts using precise movements, blood starting to trickle down my naked body with every new slice.

Az walked away for a moment giving me a break from his torture. He returned tying a gag around my head, "There, can't have anyone hearing you scream and I need both my hands to operate. Now, where were we."

He took a step back examining my body. I tried to wiggle myself free again with no luck, the chains mocking me through their metallic rattle. The knife was back in my side, deeper this time. Az moved it so slowly as if to draw out the pain. He was kneeling down, but I had enough give in my leg restraints to get the kind of movement I wanted. I jerked my knee up connecting with his stomach and knocking the wind out of him. He stumbled back a few steps doubled over gasping for air. He recovered, a little too quickly much to my dismay, storming over to me. Az thrust the knife in my thigh, the blade completely disappearing.

My head fell back as I screamed from the pain, pulling against the hand cuffs and the leg restraints. Az regained his composure and walked over to the rest of the knives laid out on the table. He grabbed a couple of the bigger ones. Kneeling in front of me to tighten my leg restraints, "I'm done being nice. This is payback."

He swung at my face breaking my nose. Unlike Az, I wouldn't be able magically heal this wound. I barely had time to register what he just did when the knives were cutting into me again. There was no more snide remarks or slow, torturous cuts. No, Az was being methodical. His cuts were deliberate and deep, made in a way to draw the most blood, the most pain. He pulled out a small knife driving it into my arm leaving it there like the one he left in my thigh. Tears streamed down my face. Az was making this hurt way more than I ever thought he would based on the show he was putting on just moments ago. I tried to beg and plead with him, but my attempts were muffled by the fabric covering my mouth. It didn't matter anyways, Az was ignoring every sound coming from me.

My throat was raw from all the screaming I was doing at this point, but the gag Az had placed was doing its job. No one was going to hear me. Az looked like he was in his element knowing where he was going to cut me next with the precision of a seasoned surgeon. Occasionally, I would feel him carve his name as if to brand me. I willed myself to try to see the results of his handiwork, choking back a sob as I did. My memory was flooded with images of being back in the cathedral, bloodied and hanging there to die. Cuts and blood covered my body. Az's name was on one of my arms, my chest, and the inside of my thigh. Where there wasn't blood, there were the faint purple marks of an early bruise forming where he had hit me with the butt of his knife.

I managed to get the gag loose after shaking my head. "Please," I begged. "Please stop. You've had your fun. You've made your point."

Az slapped me, the sting of his hand burning my face, "Shut the fuck up. I told you I was done being nice. Does Warrick really put up with all this whining and bitching?"

I tried screaming knowing I wasn't going to get Az to change his mind earning another slap. If I could only get someone outside to hear me, then maybe I'd be able to get out of here. I knew the chances were next to nothing, but I couldn't give up quite yet. Az let out a growl as he pushed away from me and went digging through the cabinets again. He wasn't gone for long, reappearing with a fully loaded syringe and a glass with some pink, glittery liquid. My memory may be fuzzy from last night, but I do remember him forcing me to drink the pink stuff.

I violently shook my head, "No, please not that."

"Just a little to take the edge off," Az smirked. He jammed the needle into my neck, but only emptied a quarter of its contents. Then, the sickly sweet taste of the pink liquid hit the back of my throat. I jerked my head away from Az causing him to drop the glass and the majority of what he was forcing me to drink.

"Damn it!"

He yanked the gag back up when a knock sounded. We both tensed. Az dropped the knives on the table as he headed to the door not bothering to cover me. I dropped my head. Whoever was there was going to see me bruised, bloodied, and naked hanging here with knives sticking out of me.

"What?" Az demanded, ripping the door open.

"Hello to you, too," a woman's voice responded.

"Get on with it."

"I see you're progressing with things nicely."

"Why are you here?" Az snapped.

She sighed, "It's time. She sent me here to pick you two up."

"Come in," Az grumbled moving out of the doorway to let his visitor move past him.

I struggled to lift my head to get a good view of the newcomer, but what I did see was enough to tell me that she's a petite woman with short blonde hair and dark blue eyes. She looked confident, oozing strength as she sauntered over to me. She was someone who was clearly aware of her beauty with her perfect makeup, glowing skin, and symmetrical features.

Az took a seat at the table wiping my blood off his precious knives while the woman kept approaching me occasionally glancing in my direction. Whatever Az had forced into my body was now taking effect. My head lolled forward, my vision losing the focus I had worked so hard to get back. The weight of my body pulling against the cuffs as I felt the moment when I no longer had control over myself.

Her perfectly manicured fingers dug into my chin as she yanked my head up. Recognition filled her features and she broke out into a wicked laugh, "Oh, this is rich. Az, you didn't tell me you were shacking up with Val."

Lilly. I tried to ask her for help, but the gag had other plans. Hearing the garbled sounds, she cocked her head to the side giving me a pouty face. In a mocking tone, she said, "Poor wittle Val reduced to begging. I never thought I'd see the day. Oh, how the mighty have fallen."

She took a step back releasing my head to let it drop as she went on, "I can see why all those men would want to sleep with you. Well, before all this anyways. Az, why'd you keep this such a secret?"

I rolled my head to the side so I could watch Az out of the corner of my eyes. He had moved over to the bed setting the picture of us face down on his nightstand. Lilly was still focused on me, so she didn't see him do that. Az's shoulders dropped when I returned my focus on him, but as he turned around, I could see when he transformed his character. He smirked at Lilly joining her in front of me, "I'm not a fan of ruining surprises. Although, this is news to me. How do you know Val?"

She slowly turned to look at him, "How do *you* know Val?" The wheels were turning in her mind at this point. She was trying to piece together if him and I had history.

Before Lilly could jump to any conclusions, Az threw an arm around her shoulder and booped her nose, "We all have our part, Lilly."

She regarded him with suspicion. Lilly opened her mouth to call him out, but Az tilted her chin up to him. "This is none of your concern, stay in your place."

Az truly knew how to play the game. He never answered the question, but I watched as there was a shift in Lilly. Her eyes softened as she moved to be closer to Az. She tilted her head, but as she moved in for a kiss, Az walked back over to the table. He was back to messing with his knives, "Now, you were just going to tell me how you know Val."

Lilly cleared her throat still watching Az, "Right." She turned back to me examining the intricacy of the cuts, "I knew her best friend, Jennie, who brought me into the ever sought after friend group. Val was one who always pissed me off. She was carefree and easy going, getting whoever she wanted. I always hated it."

"Why'd you stick around then?" Az casually asked.

"For Jennie. She had a hard time spending time with me outside of the group or work because she kept herself so busy. I can't forget Mark. He absolutely adored Daryl," Lilly said turning to join Az at the table. She sat down crossing her legs and busying herself with examining her nails, "Did you dose her?"

"Yeah," Az shot a glance in my direction. "Looks like it has kicked in."

"Then what are we waiting around here for?" Lilly asked in a bored tone.

Az shot her an annoyed look then sighed as he stood up to stand back in front of me. Lilly started yammering on about something, but Az ignored her. He started releasing my legs first then moved up to my arms. Az leaned in lowering his voice to a level I could barely hear, "You're going to do exactly as I say, got it? You do everything I say when I say it. If I say kiss me, you kiss me. If I say go, you go. I didn't hit you with enough of that drug or the potion to make it impossible for you to move on your own. In fact, you barely got any of that potion in you which means you're going to have to sell the act. The witch leader is powerful and will feed off your despair the first chance she gets. I'm going to keep that from happening because she will kill you."

I lazily nodded my head. When he removed the gag, I asked, "Are you telling me all of this because the great and powerful Az is feeling scared?"

Az chuckled and jammed another knife into my side. I yelped from the pain. He brought himself closer, "I love that fight you still have in you, Val, but you might want to think about the next things you say. Now, let's see if you were listening earlier. Kiss me and kiss me in a way that'll make Lilly blush."

He was holding me up while he worked on releasing me from the last restraint. I painfully wrapped my legs around his waist, grimacing as I did so. I draped my one free arm around the back of his neck watching Lilly as I did so. *At least she was finally honest.* She immediately became focused on what was playing out in front of her: Az finished what he was doing and I used my newly free arm to pull his face to mine. I gave him a kiss full of passion and heat. He pressed me against the wall, moaning into my mouth as I deepened the kiss. Az reluctantly pulled away, still clutching on to me throwing Lilly a look over his shoulder, "See? Whatever you all put in that potion, it's potent."

"Clearly," she said standing up and moving towards the door.

Az sat me on his bed then wrapped me in one of his longer wool coats. "Keep that up, and I may not want to let you go," he whispered.

"Just doing what you told me to," I hissed.

He forced me to look at him jerking my chin towards his face, "I'm serious, Val. You do need to keep that up."

"What's taking so long?" Lilly demanded. "Her screams cleared the roads so we won't have too many people in our way, but that's only going to last for so long."

"Can you walk?" Az asked.

I clutched the jacket to myself trying to stand on shaky legs. It was a fight, but I did it. I started to reach towards the various knives still sticking out of me, but Az stopped my hand. He slowly took the knives out of me causing a whimper to leave my lips, but left a few of them in me for dramatic effect. Az didn't bother to stop the bleeding as he guided me, putting a hand on the small of my back, and we followed Lilly out into freezing cold. The two of them were going back and forth, so I focused on how I was feeling. My body was heavy, the edges of my vision blurry once again. Thankfully, I had more movement than what I had before and I could think through everything that was happening.

I wasn't expecting Lilly to show up, but based on what Mark had told me, I'm not surprised. I'm also not surprised with what she was saying. It's about time she came out with the truth. But, what caught me off-guard was Az. He gave no indication he knew me despite her prodding, even hiding the picture he had of us. He gave me a warning about how to carry myself because he knew I was able to think for myself and I'd be snapping back at him. *Why? What's his angle with this one?* Could it have been how Lilly was acting? He did act a little weird when I was trying to get him to talk about the picture. Maybe he was hung up on what we were.

My train of thought was interrupted as I started shivering uncontrollably. Az didn't miss a beat with his conversation with Lilly while he scooped me up and made sure I was covered.

We were approaching a dilapidated building in the center of the town. There were several loose wood slats giving small viewpoints to the interior of the building. The wood was grey and the building was leaning. It looked as though another strong gust of wind would knock it over. All the shutters were closed, and even though a couple were hanging on by their last screw, you couldn't pick out any details from the inside. As we got closer, I noticed that you couldn't actually see anything on the inside through the various holes. There was only black like a shadow was covering each space.

However, when Lilly led us into the building, I was caught by surprise. It was warmly lit, the walls painted a deep shade of blue. Ornate furniture and decorations dotted the hallway leading to a main room. In between the furniture were several doors, all shut. It was dark in this building, but it was warm and well-kept. Every now and then, I'd see a woman strolling from door to door looking calm and collected. Realization dawned on me: this is the coven's headquarters.

Chapter 14

Az set me down watching to make sure I could walk on my own. Lilly looked at us impatiently tapping a finger on her crossed arms. I leaned on Az as he started moving us closer to the main room. It was surprisingly quiet, only the sounds of a faint violin coming from somewhere deep within these walls.

I gaped at the main room when we got in there. A massive, intricate chandelier lit up the space in a warm glow, the crystals sparkling from every angle you looked at it. The plush carpet was perfectly warmed and so soft you could lay there for days getting the best sleep of your life. The walls seemed to shimmer as you passed by. There were three chairs on the far wall aligned with the center of the room that looked like the matching pieces to what was in the hallway. Lilly led us up the couple of steps gesturing for Az to sit in the chair next to the one in the middle.

He settled in the chair then patted his lap for me to sit on it. My momentary hesitation earned a glare, and as soon as I settled in, he aggressively positioned me to look like I was all over him. Lilly, now satisfied, left the room. Keeping his voice low, Az said, "You need to listen."

"What is this place?"

"I think you know," Az said stroking my hair.

I turned to look at him, "What was up earlier?"

"What do you mean?" Az asked keeping his attention focused on the doorway that led to the hallway.

I reached out stroking his cheek in case anyone was watching, "Why didn't you tell Lilly about us?"

He finally slid his eyes over meeting mine. Az reached his hand up to mine, "It wasn't information that was going to help her. Besides, I have a feeling she'll be finding out soon enough. Now, kiss me again."

I was about to question him, but Az tangled his hands in my hair as his lips found mine. He stuck the knives back in and I pulled away gasping. "What the fuck is this, Az?" I asked checking my body. He had somehow managed to stick the knives back in their original spots without tearing any new holes in my skin.

Az pulled me back to him, "All a part of the show."

We were kissing again much to my dismay. The sound of heels approached followed by someone sitting in the chair next to us. There was a soft giggle, "Nice to see things have been working so well for you, Az."

Az smiled against my lips, "Nice to see you again, Abria."

Az shifted me so I was now facing the newcomer. Her appearance was breathtaking with her silky, red hair in perfect waves and make up that accentuated the best parts of her face in all the right ways – her high cheek bones, plump lips, expertly shadowed eyes with thick lashes. Her blue eyes popped and I couldn't help but wonder if every witch in this world had the same eye color. Abria's body was curvy, but she was thin; she wore a corset and black skinny jeans with stilettos. She sat in her chair with such grace, looking relaxed and in control. While Lilly was looking radiant, Abria outshone her. It must be the amount of power she had flowing through her right now.

She gave me a sickly sweet smile, "And who do we have?"

Az was fully putting on a show, now. He tucked a loose strand of hair behind my ear, grinning, "Exactly who you asked for."

"So, this is the woman who's captivated Warrick's heart? Val, right?" she directed her question at me.

"Y-yes," I stammered.

"Well done, Az," Abria nodded. She turned to Lilly who was standing at attention in front of us, "Bring him in."

I felt Az's grip on my waist slightly tighten. I had no idea who she was referring to, although my bets were on being reunited with Warrick.

Lilly nodded turning to leave the room, barking orders to other witches that had filtered into the space. While we waited, Abria turned to Az again, "You were right about her. I can *feel* the despair pouring off Val. You must have done a number."

"All thanks to you," Az said keeping his answers short. There had to be a reason why he wasn't offering up more information, but I didn't know enough about Abria to pick up on anything.

Abria tapped a finger to her lips, "About that. You think I should fix that now or later?"

"Let's wait a little bit," Az answered returning his attention to the doorway. I followed his gaze not quite able to see or hear anything yet.

"Fine," she pouted.

The clanking of chains faintly floated to me, but I still couldn't see anything. I squinted my eyes and waited a few more moments. The clanking gradually became louder until a group of people entered the room. There were at least five witches being led by Lilly around a man in the middle. I sat a little taller craning my neck to get a better view of the mystery man. My eyes widened as I recognized the black hair and icy blue eyes. I whipped my head back to Az who gestured for me to stay quiet then turned my attention to Abria.

She was practically salivating watching her witches drag Warrick in. Any movements were completely restricted with how they had him restrained. It didn't look like it mattered anyways – he looked defeated. Warrick's skin was pale, his cheeks sunken in with dark circles under his eyes. He looked as though he wasn't even present in this world anymore. Warrick's movements were slow and laborious, stumbling every now and then.

"Warrick, how nice of you to join us this evening," Abria held her arms out wide as she approached him. "We have a little surprise for you tonight."

Shaking, I watched as Abria forced Warrick's tired face to look at me. It took him a second, but as soon as realization dawned on him, his eyes widened and he lurched forward, "Val!"

Az pulled me back into him. "Don't move a muscle towards him," Az instructed, his voice barely a whisper. "You need to look disinterested. When I tap you twice, turn and kiss me."

"I have to say, your energy has been some of the best for us, but Val's might just top yours," Abria said nonchalantly as she made her way back to her chair. "Although, from the looks of it, I may have to fight Az for a chance to touch her."

"Hello, brother," Az said, words dripping with poison. I didn't have to look to know Az was giving Warrick his signature sinister smile. "Glad to see you survived your trials."

"Val!" Warrick shouted again, ignoring Az and Abria. "What did he do to you? Are you okay?"

It pained me to look at him like this, all chained up and vulnerable. The stark contrast from how he normally carried himself made me sick. I hated these women and Az for what they did to him, and yet, I couldn't do anything about it.

"Please, love," Warrick changed his tone to something softer, filled with concern. "Talk to me."

I turned my head into Az's neck so I could take a second to steady myself. Az chuckled, "She's a little indisposed at the moment."

"I swear if you hurt her, I will fucking kill you," Warrick spat. "I will rip your throat out. I'll shred you to pieces. There will be *nothing* left of you when I'm done!"

"Because you're clearly in a position to do that," Az said smugly. "Besides, Val and I were having so much fun rekindling our old flame."

Tap, tap. I lifted my head up to find Az staring down at me expectantly. He tapped again, his fingers digging into my side, and I slowly brought my lips to his, hating myself in this moment. The last thing I wanted Warrick to see was me being a damn puppet.

I heard the chains again followed by several gasps from the witches holding on to Warrick. I whipped my head in the direction of the sound seeing Warrick trying to regain his freedom. A couple of the witches were on the ground and he was lurching in our direction, a snarl fixed on his face.

Abria clapped her hands, "That's enough. Warrick, if you don't behave, I'll have to feed off Val's energy, and that would be such a shame. She's too pretty to be sucked dry. Anyways, that's not why we're all here, now is it?"

Warrick dropped his shoulders in submission not willing to take his eyes off me. Az let out a laugh, "Isn't it nice to know you're working with someone who's focused and not a love-sick wolf who's lost direction on what he needs to do?"

I stiffened at that remark. Warrick's eyes slightly widened, and in that moment, we both knew Warrick had no chance of getting the witches on his side. They made Warrick jump through hoops for nothing and I was tortured for the hell of it. Tears started forming as I glanced up at Az. He tightened his grip on me again, but that was the only indication he was paying attention to me.

"Az," Abria scolded. "You ruined all the fun."

Az looked at Abria, "Not all the fun. You got a much needed refill for your magic while I got to have a reunion of sorts. I hope you also got to enjoy yourself."

"Abria," Warrick started. His tone was commanding, taking what little strength he had left in him, "Just to be clear, there is no deal?"

"No," she smiled at him. "This was fun, but I think we're done here. Az?"

Az moved to stand up, sliding his arms under me when Warrick shouted, "Why the hell did you make me jump through all those hoops?"

"I wanted to see what you had in you to know if I made the right choice. Your actions here today made it very clear what I should be doing. However, your only use to me would be refilling my powers. Az, on the other hand, can provide me with a little more. He's focused and has a plan he can execute on. I mean, all of this was his idea and it played out exactly the way he said it would," Abria answered in a businesslike tone. "Don't think you never had a chance, Warrick. I was just hoping for a little more. Well, a little more outside of what you already gave me."

"You *bitch*," Warrick spat through clenched teeth. "We could've had a civil conversation days ago without all this bullshit and could have come to the same conclusion."

Abria leaned forward in her chair, "Where's the fun in that? I like to see how potential partners work under distress."

"First come, first served," Az cut in. "You might have had a better chance if only you got here earlier."

"Would coming here sooner have improved my chances?" Warrick asked. He wasn't letting go of getting her on his side. I knew this was going to put us at a disadvantage, but she seemed too focused on the wrong things. Her goals were more aligned with Az's and it didn't seem likely Warrick would have ever convinced her. Hell, he would've lost her at the first mention of Az.

Abria shrugged, "Maybe, but there's no going back to change that now. You gave it a valiant effort, Warrick, that's for sure. I mean the sex was out of this world, but I'm sure it was nothing compared to what Val experienced with Az."

My throat went dry. I slowly shifted my focus to Warrick. He looked conflicted about whether he wanted to be angry at Az or remorseful. I started to open my mouth, but Az tapped my waist once to make sure I didn't say anything. As she leveled her blue eyes on me, a smile inching across her lips, she asked,

"Were you trying to provide as much of a distraction to Az as you do for Warrick, you little minx?"

"It almost worked, too," Az cut in saving me from having to speak. "Except your updates kept me on track, so thank you for that, Abria. It would be nice, though, to have you back at my side, Val. Or should I start calling you 'love' like Warrick does?"

My blood went cold. I couldn't play this game anymore. I pounded a fist against Az's chest, ignoring the pain coursing through my body, "You asshole. I'm *sick* of these fucking games! I'm done. I'm over this. I want to go."

Abria's eyes widened, but she still looked amused, "I guess our time is up. Good to know our concoctions have limitations. Ladies, I think we're safe to let Warrick go. I can only toy with my food for so long before I get bored."

Az curled his lip at me, standing up. Abria stood up with him and was about to say something when Warrick, finally freed, straightened his shoulders, "We'll get out of your hair, Abria. Az, nice try, but let her go."

"Finally, some respect. Thank you, Warrick," Abria said coolly.

Az set me on my feet then shoved me in Warrick's direction. I stumbled, but did everything I could not to fall since I still had the knives in me. In doing that, Az's coat flew open exposing my beaten and battered body. Warrick caught me, a growl ripping from his chest, "Explain this, Azrael!"

"Oh, that," Az chuckled. "I also had strict orders, Warrick, so you should really be demanding answers from Abria. It took me back, though. I have to say, I haven't had this much fun carving someone up since our parents."

Warrick lunged at Az, dropping me. I watched in horror as Az broke out into crazed laughter the minute Warrick's fist disappeared into his gut. Warrick yanked his bloodied arm back, but the hole in Az healed instantly. Warrick swung again, but his fist was stopped. Az leaned in, "That was a cute party trick, but how do you like mine?" A sinister grin crept across his face as he pushed Warrick away, "I suggest you grab your *whore* and leave."

Warrick didn't listen, trying to throw another punch with his free hand. Az caught that, too, and kneed Warrick in the jaw. I screamed out as Warrick fell to the floor worried he'd be unconscious. Instead, he rolled on to his back swiping Az's legs out from under him. As soon as Az hit the floor, Warrick jumped on top of him aiming for his throat.

"Enough," Abria ordered freezing everyone in the room. "There will be no more blood spilled here. I'm already going to have to spend extra time getting rid of the spots from Val."

She moved her arms sending Warrick sliding back to me. She released Az who stood up and brushed himself off then leveled her gaze on Warrick, "You have five minutes to take Val and get out of here. As much as I love all this anger, fear, and sadness, I can't risk anyone who's here. Don't be mistaken, I am not involved with your petty conflicts."

Az straightened his jacket, hazel eyes staring down at me, "It's been fun, Val. I'm looking forward to the next time we can connect."

Warrick helped me up and tensed when Abria started talking again, "One more thing. Val, I love the emotions you carry with you, especially right now, but I can't let that beautiful energy of yours go to waste. Can't risk you going numb before I need you to."

I had no idea what she was talking about, but with a wave of her hand, the majority of my pain was lifted. I no longer felt the grogginess associated with whatever Az kept injecting me with nor the weird feeling from the potion. I glanced down at my body finding that most of the cuts and bruises had been healed. The ones that hadn't were the ones where the knives were still in. I was happy there wasn't going to be any more scars until I spotted one of the spots Az branded me: his name on my inner thigh remained there, the skin raised with an angry pink color.

"I, of course, had to leave you with a parting gift. You'll thank me later," Abria giggled. "Time's ticking, Warrick."

"C'mon, love," Warrick said scooping me into his arms being mindful of the knives. I let him carry me out of there, looking over his shoulder at Az. Expecting him to look triumphant, Az kept his expression serious. Maybe Warrick showed him something he wasn't accounting for in his master plan with that last attack.

I tucked my head into Warrick's neck. He held on to me tighter as he asked, "Are you okay, love?"

"I don't know," I croaked. And I genuinely didn't. When Abria healed me, she removed all the effects from the drug and the potions that had been impacting my memories. I saw everything that happened last night clearly, but she did something that affected my emotions, because I couldn't feel anything one way or another when I relived what Az had done. He raped me over and over, my judgement impaired by that damn potion, and I felt nothing. I was numb in a completely different way.

"You don't have to say anything," Warrick whispered as he brought us back out into the cold. I wrapped myself tighter in Az's coat to stay warm as Warrick continued, "I'm so sorry I brought you here, love."

"Please, don't say sorry," I told him. "I can walk if you need me to."

"No, let me do this for you."

We fell into an easy silence for the rest of the walk back. It was reassuring being in his arms. It seemed to be the only thing holding me together. I stared up at Warrick taking in the torture the witches had put him through. Seeing him up close was worse. He looked moments away from death, but still didn't have any troubles carrying me. I reached up to touch his face, "Please let me walk."

"Are you sure?" Warrick asked in a quiet voice. He slowed his steps coming to a stop in the middle of the empty street I've come to recognize. We weren't that far from the house. I could've easily let him carry me all the way back, but I didn't need to make his life any harder than it was at the moment.

I gave a quick nod. Warrick gently set me on my feet watching me with a worried expression. I hugged the coat tighter around me before taking a couple of steps to show him I was okay to walk. I glanced over my shoulder, gesturing for him to join me. We were soon walking side by side, still not saying anything to each other. Maybe we were saving the conversation for the barrage of questions we'd be facing in a couple of minutes, or maybe it's because we were exhausted with everything we went through. Hell, it's probably accurate to say it's a combination of both.

I stumbled a few feet away from the front porch out of my own clumsiness and Warrick hastily scooped me back into his arms carrying me to the door. I opened my mouth to protest, but he cut me off, "Don't. I know she healed you and you're fine. Just, please, let me do this, love."

I sighed as Warrick tried the door handle. To no surprise, it was locked. "At least they kept their wits about them," Warrick mumbled reaching for the doorbell. As soon as the chime sounded, Lou ripped open the door poised to attack.

His eyes widened once he realized who was standing in front of him. Warrick readjusted me, giving a little grunt, "You gonna let us in or just stare?"

"Right," Lou stepped back. Warrick headed straight for my room. Following us, Lou said, "You have no idea how relieved I am to be seeing you two alive."

Warrick set me on the bed then ran a hand through his hair before turning to Lou, "We'll be leaving first thing in the morning."

"Why?" Lou's brows knit together. "What happened?"

Before Warrick could answer Lou, Jennie and Mark burst through the door. Jennie rushed over to me, Mark not far behind her. She knelt in front of me, "I never thought I'd be seeing you again. Are you okay? Are you hurt? You're covered in blood again."

"What happened, Val?" Mark asked.

At the mention of blood, Lou snapped his attention to me. I pulled the coat tighter, focusing on the floor, "I'm fine. Looks a lot worse than it is."

"I think we need some space," Warrick stepped in between me and everyone else. "Give us a little bit to get settled. We'll come downstairs when we're ready."

Jennie nodded, turning to leave while Mark said, "You got it."

Lou was the last one out, keeping his eyes on us. It was almost as if he didn't trust Warrick to be alone with me.

As soon as the door closed, Warrick headed into the bathroom to start the shower. He came back out working his way out of his shirt. I sat there staring, unable to move. He squatted down in front of me, "Are you okay with sharing the shower with me, love?"

"Sure," I mumbled.

"Want to talk?"

"I'm not sure if I can yet. I feel weird, Warrick. I don't feel like my body is mine anymore," I mumbled finally bringing my eyes to meet his.

"Let's move this to the bathroom," he stood back up and I followed.

Warrick closed the door softly behind us. Every movement he was making was calm and gentle to avoid scaring me. I appreciated him for that, but whatever Abria did managed to suck all of the emotions out of me. It wasn't like I was numb, I just couldn't easily conjure up emotions like I normally do. It was hard to describe.

I leaned against the counter, Warrick taking a step closer to me while his eyes searched mine. He placed his hands on my waist, "Will you be okay if I take the jacket off?"

I quickly nodded my head. I wanted to get the smell of Az off me as soon as possible. Warrick stood up slowly pulling me to him and slid the jacket down my arms. He had turned me so I was facing the mirror, my mouth opening at the sight of me. There was a lot of blood covering my naked body showcasing what I went through in Az's apartment, but it was all dried. The knives Az had left in me were still sticking out, yet I couldn't feel them. At all. I reached up towards the hilt of one and wiggled it to test if I truly couldn't feel anything. All I could notice was the blade moving around. There wasn't any pain.

"Let me," Warrick reached up to my hand brushing it out of the way while he closed his fingers around the knife I was just holding. He gave a quick tug releasing the knife and leaving a fresh wound in its wake. Warrick repeated this motion for the rest of the knives growing angrier each time. When he got to the last knife sticking out of my thigh, he paused. At first, I thought it was because it was right next to the only spot Abria had left Az's name carved into me, but then I remembered this was the knife Az had used to kill their parents. I reached out to Warrick, "Hey, I can take care of this one."

He pressed his lips into a thin line taking a step back. Warrick turned so he was facing the shower, no longer looking in my direction as he worked his way out of his clothes. I held the knife for a few moments after removing it then quietly placed it on the counter with the rest. *He's probably going to want those back.* Unsettled by the thought, I opened the bathroom door, "I'm going to check on something. I'll be right back."

I didn't give Warrick the chance to respond. I immediately headed to the balcony door to make sure the lock was secured then wandered around the room searching for anything else that might make it harder for Az to attempt another break in.

While I was doing that, Warrick leaned against the bathroom doorframe, "What are you doing, love?"

"I'm making sure Az can't find his way back in here," I responded still grabbing various things.

"Is that how he got in?"

I paused then gave a quick nod. As I was walking back to the balcony door, the door leading out into the hallway opened revealing Lou. I jumped, scrambling to cover my body with anything. Warrick moved in front of me ready to attack. Seeing our reactions, Lou looked away, "S-sorry about that. I thought you guys would be in the shower by now."

"What do you want, Lou?" Warrick sounded annoyed.

"I was just coming to tell you that we have food ready and to see how long it would be so I can keep it warm for you two," Lou answered.

Warrick let out a sigh while I went back to the balcony door. I secured it shut and rigged it in a way where we would know if it got open, if Az could open this, while keeping my back to Lou so he couldn't see me. I could tell Warrick came back to shield my newly scarred body from Lou's view as he said, "Go ahead and eat without us. We'll be down in a little bit."

"Got it," Lou said shutting the door behind him.

We returned to the bathroom, Warrick guiding me into the warm shower and following me in. I watched as most of the blood ran into the water down into the drain. Warrick turned me to face him holding up a loofah, "Would it be alright if I helped, love?"

"Sure," I said quietly. "Can I return the favor?"

He nodded then gently started scrubbing me. When he was finished, I took the loofah from him and got to work. As I did that, I felt his hands work shampoo into my hair. I finished cleaning him, resting my head against his chest while he continued to massage my scalp. When he was done, he lifted my chin forcing me to look at him. Warrick still looked exhausted, like he was barely hanging on, yet there was a fight in his icy blue eyes. He moved us so the water would start rinsing the shampoo out but kept us in the same position. He traced a thumb along my cheek, "Are you okay?"

"I will be," I croaked out. "I always find a way to be, right?"

Warrick helped rinse the remainder of the shampoo out of my hair not saying anything else. He helped finish getting me clean while I did the same for him. When his head was back in the water and his eyes were closed, I asked, "What did they do to you?"

He ran his hands through his hair a couple of times to rinse the rest of conditioner out, "I was planning on sharing those details when Lou is around so I don't have to live through that twice, if that's okay?"

"Yeah, I get it," I watched as he turned off the water. Warrick handed me a towel and we both dried off as he asked, "What happened with Az?"

"I'd rather not live through that twice, either," I explained.

Warrick nodded then disappeared back into my room. I went back to the mirror examining the fresh cuts. It was the weirdest feeling to know they were there and not having any pain. I traced the knives thinking back to what happened. *Would the pain come back? Will I ever be able to feel again?*

"Come here, love," Warrick said softly. I did as I was told, stepping over to him then letting him get to work dressing my wounds so I didn't get blood all over everything. He held up pajamas and I got dressed making sure I didn't look at the knives anymore. We made our way downstairs finding everyone at the table. It didn't look like they've eaten yet. I started to head into the kitchen, but Lou stopped me. I watched him get the food out then went to sit next to Warrick.

Jennie got up and brought over a couple of warm mugs filled with tea. I offered her a grateful smile as I wrapped my hands around the comforting warmth. Lou served us all a plate of warm, cheesy pasta. I could tell the three of them wanted to start hitting us with questions, but they kept themselves quiet to give us the chance to eat. The food was filled with herbs and cheese, somehow putting me at peace. Warrick had already finished a plate, Lou bringing him another one. As he set it down, Lou said, "Look, I don't want you guys to feel rushed. We're all sitting on the edges of our seats to know what happened, though."

Warrick leaned back in his chair wiping his face with a napkin. He looked at each person, ending with Mark, "Are you good if we head out of here?"

Mark swallowed his bite, "Yeah, don't have to ask me twice."

"Good," Warrick gave a nod. He took a steadying breath setting his fork down next to his plate then started, "Let's just say we were unsuccessful with what we came here for."

"No witch leader?" Lou asked.

Warrick shut his eyes and shook his head.

Lou tensed, "What does that mean for us?"

Chapter 15

Warrick waited a little bit to answer. I thought Warrick was messing with Lou like he always does, but when I glanced over at him, Warrick's brow was furrowed making it obvious he was struggling with what to say. He's not one that typically meets failure and when he does, he blames himself. I put a hand on his arm and Warrick relaxed a little. He sat up a little taller, "It means we're at a little bit of a disadvantage, but it doesn't mean we've lost."

"Why do we need to rush out of here?" Lou asked.

Warrick set his fork down then leaned on his forearms on the table, "We're no longer exactly welcome here, so there's a time limit for how long we can stay."

Lou ran a hand over his face, "Shit ... want to catch us up on what happened to you two? How did Az get in here?"

My hands dropped into my lap. *I guess it's my turn to talk.* I met everyone's expectant gaze, took a sip of my tea, and started explaining, "You guys know I have a past with him at this point. Well, part of that past including him learning the weak points of the house so he could spend time with me whenever I stayed with my parents without them knowing. One of those weak points happens to be my balcony where he broke in the other night."

"The night we got a little carried away," Lou ran a hand through his hair. Realization dawned on him, "You tried waking me up, didn't you?"

"You could've kept this from happening?" Warrick asked in too calm of a tone.

Lou immediately dropped his head, "I don't know how much of a fight I could give Az."

"Calm down you two," I scolded. "There was nothing Lou would've been able to do anyways. Az had a powerful drug on him that he used to knock me out, and he wouldn't have hesitated to use that on Lou, or worse."

The gun Az aimed at Lou that night flashed in my mind. It most definitely would've been worse, but they didn't need to know that.

Warrick and Lou both let the tension drop from their shoulders. Warrick went back to eating while Lou motioned for me to go on. I took another bite then continued, "When I came to, I was in the apartment he has here. It started off not that bad, surprisingly. We spent the time mostly talking. He tried to torture me, but then held off. Az was smart. I started to feel like I could let my guard down, but that was when everything changed. He hit me with some sort of love potion."

Warrick stiffened, but I kept going, "Then, he got exactly what he wanted. Az picked up where he had left off at Warrick's apartment. Over and over again. I had no control over my body, so he took full advantage of that before drugging me again. He waited until I woke up to start carving into me, being more methodical than what Cian did. When I screamed out, he gagged me so no one would get suspicious. Eventually, Lilly showed up and that's when we went to the witch leader."

Jennie's hand went up to her mouth, tears starting to form in her eyes. Mark was staring at me in disbelief while Lou clenched his fists trying to reel in his anger. Through clenched teeth, Lou said, "That was the scream we heard. We heard you, and we were so close, but couldn't get into the fucking building."

I didn't register what Lou was saying. Instead, all my focus was on Warrick. He looked ready to kill, but there was something else there. He looked full of regret, sadness etched into his features underneath the rage. Warrick leaned closer to me, "Is that why you were all over him back there? Because he had you under the influence of that fucking witch's magic?"

"Yes," I dropped my gaze into my lap. I didn't want to talk about it anymore. I still couldn't feel any emotions towards anything, including the memories that wouldn't stop replaying in my mind, but that didn't mean it was something I could casually chat about.

"Can you talk about what you had to do now?" Lou asked Warrick. I was thankful he changed the topic to take the attention away from me. Warrick finished the food on his plate giving us all the chance to do the same. Jennie got up to clear the dishes and set out dessert, although, I don't think any of us were really wanting to eat that.

"That grocery list of tasks was all a waste of fucking time," Warrick spat. "It was all a rouse, a game. It gave Az the time he needed to get his hands on Val while it gave those damn witches time to use me. It didn't take them long before they locked me up to siphon my energy whenever they damn well pleased. The chains they used were laced with their leader's magic so I never got a break. Then, they brought me before her only for me to see Val all over Az, and while my mind was preoccupied with the idea that I might be losing her, I had the news broken to me that the witches were already working with Az. We had no chance. We didn't even need to come here which means this would've never happened to Val."

"You didn't know," Lou cut in. "You didn't know they were already working with Az, and there was no way you could've known. Even if you flat out asked your brother, he would've just toyed with you."

Warrick was watching me closely at this point. He wasn't breaking eye contact. I reached out towards him, "It's okay, Warrick. I'm not blaming you for anything that happened here."

That seemed to help. His eyes closed and he let out a breath. When he opened his eyes again, he looked at Lou, "Thank you for the food. I think it's time for us to rest."

He stood up holding his hand out to me. I took it letting him lead me towards the stairs as I glanced over my shoulder, "Thank you, guys."

When we got back up to my room, Warrick triple checked what I had done to make the door more secure before sitting on the edge of the bed. He hung his head in his hands. I kneeled in front of him, "Hey, stop beating yourself up, okay? We can't let Az break us like this. That's what he wants. That's what is going to give him the advantage he's been looking for. Az wouldn't be showing his face like this if he wasn't feeling threatened."

"I could've kept you back home, love. I could've kept you safe," Warrick mumbled into his hands still not looking at me.

"Warrick," I forced his chin up. "Stop. We can't change what happened. We can only move forward. I need you to stop wallowing."

I studied him for a moment. Warrick wasn't saying anything in return. Something started telling me he didn't explain everything that happened to him down there. I moved to sit next to him, crossing my legs, "What aren't you telling me?"

"What do you mean, love?" he asked staring at the wall in front of him.

"Look at me, Warrick. You're not explaining everything that happened while the witches had you. What are you leaving out?"

He squeezed his eyes shut, "They used that time to start figuring out a wolf's weaknesses."

"How?" I asked. I wanted to hear what they did to him. I don't know why, but I wanted to know.

"Silver, poking me with various things, the works," Warrick forced out, keeping his answer short.

I put a hand back on his arm keeping my tone low, "There's something Abria and Az said that doesn't sit well with me. They alluded to something else going on. Would you be willing to tell me?"

Warrick turned his head the other way, "They used that same potion on me to iron out its kinks before sending it over to Az."

I felt sick to my stomach. That explains the look he gave me before when I was explaining what happened. He knew what that potion did to people. Yet, I couldn't imagine what he had to go through being their test subject. I couldn't bring myself to ask him who was taking advantage of him, not because I didn't want to know, but because I could see how much it was hurting him to keep talking about this stuff. I gave his arm a squeeze, "Thank you for telling me."

He only nodded his head. I crawled into bed, "Let's go to sleep. Hopefully that'll help you feel better and maybe we can find Sarind to see what she can do to help us heal."

"Thank you, love," Warrick stood up to go to the bathroom. I settled in, pulling the covers up. It felt like heaven to be back in my own bed knowing Warrick would be next to me. It would be bold for Az to try anything, but this could also be a good time with Warrick not being at his top strength. I glanced nervously at the balcony just as Warrick was coming out. He followed my gaze, "We can sleep somewhere else if you'd like."

"It'll be fine," I said shaking my head.

He held out his hand, "Come on, love."

I took his hand following him as he led us to the basement. He was taking us to the most secure place he knew of in this house where we could still get some good sleep.

We passed Lou, Mark, and Jennie on our way down getting confused looks. Warrick waived them off and we headed all the way down to the bunker. The last time I had been down here to sleep was when this whole mess started. I stopped at the bottom of the stairs, Warrick giving my hand a tug. When he realized I wasn't moving, he turned, "What's wrong, love?"

He glanced up behind me and I followed his gaze. Everyone else had followed us into the basement wanting to know why we were coming down here. I returned my focus to Warrick, "You do realize the last time I slept down here was when I got transported to your world where you killed Daryl who comforted me as bombs were falling, right?"

Warrick put his hands on my shoulders, "This is the safest place we can be in this house right now unless you'd rather sleep up in your room?"

"I-I don't know if I can," I stammered.

"We don't have to stay in the same room, love. We don't even have to stay down here."

I met his icy blue gaze, "I'll be okay. Just caught me off-guard for a moment."

Warrick nodded then took me down to the last room. Jennie was right behind us, "I'll stay down here, too."

"Yeah, we all will," Mark added.

"Thanks, guys," I responded. "I'll be fine. You don't have to do something just because of me."

"It'll be better anyways," Lou mentioned. "Anything we can do to help?"

Warrick stood in front of me, but talked to Lou over his shoulder, "Just make sure this house is locked up tight. Goodnight."

Warrick was good at being the person to wind things down. He ushered everyone out closing the door behind them, then coming back over to where I was standing, "Let's go to sleep, love."

"Alright," I said getting settled into the bed. It wasn't the same as the one upstairs, but as much as I didn't want to admit it, I did feel safer down here.

I thought Warrick would be jumping in right after me, but he headed out instead. I had no idea what he was up to, so my mind drifted back to being back under the house.

The irony was not lost on me. I was going to be sleeping next to a man who I cared deeply about while knowing there was an unhinged, power-hungry wolf who wouldn't hesitate to kill in order to get me alone. Something started stirring within me. Sadness? Panic? Both or is there something else there? I had no idea, but I did feel some relief that I was finally able to start feeling things again. *Maybe there's a time limit on Abria's magic.*

The door opened, Warrick saying something over to his shoulder to Lou as he came back in. He closed the door then slowly walked over to me, "What's wrong, love?"

"What?"

Warrick nodded for me to get up. Doing as I was told, I watched as he replaced the blanket on the bed with the one from my room. He was straightening it out as he asked, "You look like something's eating away at you. What's wrong?"

"Oh," I cast my gaze down to the bed. "It's nothing. I'm focusing too much on the past. Let's just go to sleep."

Warrick guided me to sit down lifting my chin to look at him, "Is it the fact that we're down here? Is that what's going on?"

Sighing, I answered, "That's part of it."

"The other part?"

"I don't like the idea of the witches taking advantage of you like that," I shook my head. "I also don't want to make you feel like you have to keep talking about it when I see it hurts you."

Warrick cradled my face, "Look, love, I can't change what I did, but know that I'm not trying to bring you down here to torture you or get in your head. As for the other thing you mentioned, there will be a time I'm ready to talk about it, but that time isn't now mostly because I would like to get some sleep to hopefully get the last of her damn magic out of my system, okay?"

"Okay," I nodded.

He kissed my forehead then moved to turn the lights off. I laid down facing the wall and Warrick came in behind me. He started to wrap his arm around my waist to pull me into him, but stopped when I stiffened. I took a deep breath using the methods Raf equipped me with after what Cian put me through. *This isn't Az and I'm not going to be held against my will. Warrick will stop if I tell him to. He will let me go if I need him to.* I pulled on Warrick's arm to tell him it's okay. He gave me a quick kiss in between my shoulder blades then fell asleep. I laid there for a few moments thinking about Warrick. He was one who needed to come to terms with things before talking about them, and that was okay. I have to be more patient when it comes to getting details.

I shook my head and shifted my focus to my breathing. I took slow, deep breaths to calm myself while also working on slowing down the thoughts running at full speed through my mind. I needed sleep. The more I slept, the more I'd be able to heal, and most importantly, get back to myself. Repeating I was safe, I was finally able to close my eyes.

I had no idea how long I had been asleep. When I rolled over, my head was pounding, my mouth dry, and I was being hit with way too many emotions all at once. *I'm getting sick and tired of waking up like this.* The room was still dark, so I patted the bed next to me to feel for Warrick only to find the space empty. I laid there a little while longer until I was able to persuade myself to get up. Clutching my head, I slowly made my way over to the door, stumbling every couple of steps. When I cracked open the door, I noticed there wasn't a lot of movement happening in the house. Inching out into the hallway, I paused every now and then trying to see if anyone else was awake. There was only one other room that looked like it had been slept in but was now empty. *Must've been where Lou slept.* I kept my steps quiet as I continued to the stairs leading up to the basement. No one was in that part of the house so I ascended the stairs to the main floor.

I paused the minute I heard hushed voices talking. I couldn't make anything out from where I was, so I went up a couple more steps to sit in the doorway leading to the basement. It was Lou's voice I heard first, "You've hardly slept, Warrick. You got to stop blaming yourself."

There was a long pause with someone setting down a coffee mug, before Warrick mumbled something I couldn't quite make out. I shifted so I was at a better angle while still remaining hidden when Lou said, "Wanna talk about what happened?"

"When?" Warrick grumbled.

"Between you and the witch leader," Lou sounded annoyed like it should have been obvious what he was talking about. *Was he about to get Warrick to open up about what happened before me?*

The coffee mug was set back down on the island again followed by a sigh, "I hated it there. Sarind, the fae leader, warned me about coming here, but I didn't listen. I thought I would have a chance to persuade her. I'd do anything to get that power on our side."

"I know who Sarind is," Lou said, annoyance firmly in place. He let out a breath, his tone changing to something more kind, "What did she warn you against?"

When there was no answer, Lou repeated his question, "Warrick, what did she warn you against?"

"She said I would find nothing but darkness. I'd put everything at risk," Warrick sighed. "She was right, and I almost lost everything, too."

I sat straight up. Every part of me wanted to storm into the kitchen demanding to know what happened that would make him say that, yet I stayed rooted to my spot because as soon as I walked in there, he would keep the nitty gritty details to himself. Why? I don't know. Maybe it was to protect me or to avoid burdening me. Either way, Warrick was clearly being cryptic, but he was finally starting to open up about his experience being cooped up with Abria and I didn't want to be the one who stopped him from talking.

"You're gonna have to give me more than that," Lou said.

A chair quietly slid back as Warrick said, "I'm going to need more coffee first."

"While that's brewing, you want to talk about why you're up here and not down there with Val?" Lou asked.

"You like to ask the hard-hitting questions, don't you?" Warrick groaned. Clearly, this wasn't a topic he wanted to touch on this morning, but Warrick continued, "Let me ask you this, Lou – do you think it's fair I'm fated to her? And you better answer honestly, not what you think I want to hear."

"No retaliation?"

"None," Warrick promised.

"Alright. Honesty," Lou sighed as if he were hyping himself up. "I don't think it's fair. If it were up to me, I'd be the one fated to her. You're hardly around when shit hits the fan. You often leave me to clean things up and take care of her. You aren't the one having to see how lonely she is and how much she wants to be with you. You also don't get to see the conflict raging inside of her. I hated learning you two were fated after everything you did to her. The thing I hate the most, though, is that I will *never* get the opportunity to hold her the way you do at night or love her the way you do, and it kills me."

More silence followed. Not being able to see Warrick made it hard to gauge his reaction. I was completely caught off-guard by what Lou said, though. Tears sprang into my eyes. I had to bring my hand up to my mouth to keep any sounds from escaping.

Warrick blew out a breath, "Well, fuck. I appreciate your openness, but I wasn't expecting that."

"You get what you ask for. Can you tell me why you asked that? While you're at it, can you tell me why you're so scared to be around Val?" Lou asked while refilling Warrick's coffee.

I heard Warrick take a sip before answering, "I don't think it's fair I'm fated to her, either. Val deserves better than me. She deserves someone who will take care of her and actually keep her out of harm's way rather than thrusting her into danger. As for your other question," Warrick paused. He let out a quick chuckle before turning serious again, "You really are observant, aren't you? Well, you've heard as much as I have about how serious, how intense fating is. Everyone I've loved in my life, I've lost. The fact I both love and am fated to her can be too much at times. I guess a part of me thinks that if I push her away, she'll move on and then I don't have to feel like I'm the reason her life is a living hell."

"Shit, Warrick," Lou whispered. His voice was so quiet I almost didn't hear it. I leaned closer to try to give myself a better chance at hearing what the two wolves were saying.

"Yeah," Warrick said in the same low tone. "It would really help to have Raf here right now."

Lou scoffed, "You know? I'm not all that happy with you being as close to my second as you are. Has it always been that way?"

There wasn't any vocalized answer. Instead, Lou just muttered, "Thought so."

Hearing Warrick say those things made it hard for me to want to walk into the kitchen. All those times I told myself Warrick was away to help our chances in this war partly had to do with staying away from me. He hasn't been the only one struggling with the idea of being fated, but the least we could do is share our fears with one another rather than keeping them bottled up. Hell, I could do that if Warrick would stay around me for more than a day or two. It would be nice if we could get alone time where we weren't sleeping either. The more he's away from me, the more danger I'm in because we're going up against beings I don't stand a chance against. I mean, look at Az and Abria.

My thoughts were cut off by Lou clearing his throat, "Now that we've aired it all out, want to go back to my first question about what happened to you out there?"

"Not really, but I guess you're not going to give me a chance to get out of this," Warrick said, his tone muffled enough to tell me he was talking into his mug. "I had to meet up with Lilly. That was the first time I had that fucking love potion forced down my throat. She took me back to her apartment and she forced herself on me. After that, she drugged me with what I'm assuming is the same drug Az hit Val with because when I woke up, I was naked and chained to Abria's bed. How do I know it was her bed? Well, she was sitting at a vanity in some pretty lingerie getting ready to join me. Those damn chains burned like hell. I had no idea what was going on, but she later explained to me that she laced the chains with her magic to suck out whatever the hell she wanted to in order to fuel her magical abilities.

"She kept the chit chat short, though. Abria's intentions were very clear – fuck with me a little bit because of the intel Az had fed her. And I went along with it with the hopes I was doing what I needed to in order to make progress. I shoved aside the thoughts of Val while Abria rode me nonstop. They had several iterations of the potion they tested on me to help make it less painful. There were so many times when I was alone I apologized to Val. Everything that was happening to me was so wrong. In between our sessions, if you will, her witches came in taking blood samples, poked and prodded me with who knows what, and ran all sorts of tests," Warrick's tone was filled with sadness at this point.

"It's not like you could've changed what happened to you," Lou said. "Same thing with Val. You both went through something you shouldn't have with horrible people taking advantage of you guys in a vulnerable state. What I don't know is how you were able to keep in contact with me during that."

"Abria made sure I did. I didn't know it at the time, but she knew what was going on with Val. She wanted to see me in more pain so she could lap it up like a cat getting its first taste of milk," Warrick explained. "Lou, I hate myself for what happened back there."

"If you keep wallowing, you're not going to be able to move forward."

"No," Warrick started. "You don't get it. There were times I enjoyed what was happening, and I *hated* myself for it."

"Fuck ... that was because of the potion, wasn't it?" Lou asked keeping his voice low again.

"That's what I'm telling myself. It has to be," Warrick trailed off.

My heart may have been struggling with what he was saying before, but now it feels like someone punched me in the gut. Again. The breath had been sucked out of my lungs, my world was spinning. Now I see why he didn't want to talk about what happened with me. I also get how he feels when he sees me with someone else because jealously freely flowed throughout my body at the thought of him sleeping with someone else. I was angry someone else got to be with Warrick. More importantly, I was angry I couldn't have done anything to stop it.

"Those times you enjoyed it, was that after they gave you some of the potion?"

There was no answer I could hear from Warrick once again, but Lou's response filled in the blanks for me. "It was the potion, then. Clearly, I haven't had that forced on me, but if I had to guess, it sounds like it takes away your thoughts and emotions to replace them with pleasure."

Breath filled my lungs. Lou had a point. That love potion could make something as awful as assault pleasurable.

"Or, they could've been using me to help find ways to strengthen Az," Warrick hypothesized sounding more like himself now.

"Is that how he's untouchable? The witches' magic?"

"Spot on, Louis."

Chapter 16

They paused their conversation for a few beats before Lou said, "Look, I know you're trying to shove what happened into a box to tuck away, but it will feel better to talk about it. You should tell Val. She may not like it, but she'll appreciate you opening up to her. You also have to stop being so scared when it comes to talking to her, especially because you two are fated."

"I know," Warrick said then the two of them fell silent. After what felt like hours, Warrick started the conversation again, "Lou?"

"Yeah?"

Warrick let out a loud sigh, "If anything happens to me – "

"We're not having this conversation, Warrick. Nothing's going to happen. It's you we're talking about," Lou said hastily.

"No, I need you to hear me out," Warrick commanded. "If anything happens to me, you need to take care of Val. You need to love her, help her through the loss, and make sure she lives out her best life. I don't want her to mope just because I'm no longer here."

My heart instantly shattered at the thought of losing Warrick, but I took this as my cue to head into the kitchen. Still being quiet, I stood up and took a deep breath to shake off the storm brewing inside of me from all of Warrick's confessions.

"You can count on me," Lou promised. "Although," Lou continued. "We probably had company that entire time, so that'll save you a step with the truth telling part at least."

I turned the corner earning a nod from Lou. Warrick slowly turned to face me, his face pale and filled with guilt. "Good morning," I croaked out.

Warrick opened and closed his mouth a couple of times trying to find the words to say. I don't know how he didn't notice me, but maybe it had something to do with Abria's magic still having a hold on him. I gently laid a hand on his back while graciously accepting a warm mug of coffee from Lou.

Lou looked between us a couple of times, but when it became clear neither of us was going to say anything, he turned his focus to me and asked, "I may not be as good as Raf, but therapist Lou is not too bad of a stand-in."

"I guess it is nice to know I don't need to have a one-on-one session with Warrick later," I answered, jabbing Lou in the ribs with my elbow.

Warrick ran a shaky hand through his hair, "Shit, Val. I didn't mean for you to hear any of that."

"It's okay. I think I've told you before I appreciate the honesty," I quickly responded. "I'm not here to pick a fight."

His mouth opened and closed a couple more times, but Lou jumped in before Warrick could say anything else, "Warrick's confessions have that much of an impact?"

I shifted my attention to Lou, his grey eyes intently staring at me, "Some of Abria's magic may have a time limit."

"What do you mean?" Lou asked.

"If you remember, Warrick," I turned my head slightly towards him to bring him into the conversation. "Abria worked some of her magic to remove the pain I had felt from Az's little torture session. In doing so, she also removed the emotions I would've normally felt from everything he put me through. I was numb, but not in the way that concerns everyone. I was a robot."

"That's why you couldn't tell me how you felt. I thought you were just doing that to keep me from asking too many questions," Warrick whispered.

"I couldn't tell you how I felt because I couldn't feel," I added.

Lou leaned on the island resting on his forearms, "What does that have to do with her magic having a time limit and how you're feeling right now?"

I looked between the two as I answered, "Everything is back, now. I can feel again, and let me tell you, that's the last thing I want to be doing right now."

"I'm sorry, love," Warrick reached out to me.

I pulled away, raising my voice, "Stop saying sorry, Warrick. I know you didn't mean for this all to happen to me. I know you didn't intend for me to hear everything you confessed to Lou. We're good. I don't need you to treat me like I can't handle things. You have your own shit to process, too." I took a deep breath, "Look, you didn't need me to go off on you like that. I'm sorry. For the sake of being honest, if you really want my opinion to be tossed out there with Lou's, it hurts me knowing you had sex you enjoyed with another woman when we're together. Yet, you didn't have control over yourself. I'm not faulting you for any of that. I'm not blaming you for bringing me here and making it easy for Az to grab me. He would've done it either way and I'm pretty sure he's going to try it again."

Warrick gave my hand a squeeze, looking like a million pounds got lifted from his shoulders. He stood up and started heading towards the stairs leading to the upper floor, "I'm going to freshen up a bit before everyone else is awake and we jump."

"Wait," I said, reaching for his arm.

He turned around slowly, those icy blue eyes filled with emotion I probably wasn't supposed to see, "Yes, love?"

"One of the times Az was spewing his bullshit, an idea popped into my head," I glanced back at Lou then returned my gaze to Warrick's. "Your parents were the only ones who could've put a stop to him. You *and* Az said that. I'm wondering if they left something behind outlining what the key is to taking Az out. Is there any possibility of something like that existing?"

Warrick closed his eyes taking a few breaths then answered, "The house is still in the family, but it's owned by Az. I don't know if he got rid of all their belongings or if everything's still there, and before you ask, I don't know if I could bring myself to go there to check."

"I could go in," I volunteered. "You could wait outside and I can check things, but I think it's worth a stop before we head to my world."

"I don't know, love," Warrick shook his head.

I dropped my hand, "If we don't check, then we may be missing out on the biggest advantage we could give ourselves. If we truly lost out on a power that would've given us an upper hand, then why wouldn't we take this one last opportunity to get an advantage we desperately needed?"

"What if he shows up there?" Warrick asked.

"And what if he doesn't?" I countered.

"What if it's not there?"

I sighed, "We could play the 'what if' game all day, but I have a strong feeling in my gut this pit stop will be worth our time."

Warrick turned and continued heading upstairs, slumping his shoulders, "Fine."

Lou and I sat there staring after Warrick even though he had tucked himself away in my room. I slowly turned around as Lou turned on the faucet. He leaned on the island to be closer to me, dropping his voice, "I am sorry about what you heard. I didn't want him to stop, though. That's been the only time he's shared what's going on in his head. If I would've let on I knew you were sitting there, he would've clos – "

"You and Warrick wouldn't have had such an honest therapy session," I cut in. "Why is he so worried about being that open with me? It would save us all a lot of trouble later on."

Lou shrugged, "I don't know. I figured it wouldn't help anything if I kept talking about my true feelings and pining after you when you're trying to build something with Warrick. As for him, he's always been closed off. Are you okay, though?"

"Yeah," I rested my chin on my hand. "I'm upset Warrick had to go through all that, but I'm even more upset he felt the need to push it all aside to help me. I'll recover. I've been given some good tactics from Raf, I know I have an incredible support system around me, and I'm only going to get stronger." In a quieter voice, I said, "I have to."

"You good to keep talking about things?" Lou asked, glancing upstairs to make sure we didn't have someone listening in.

I nodded. He grinned at me, "Good, because knowing that Abria's magic has a time limit could actually play to our advantage."

"What do you mean?" I furrowed my brows. I wasn't following where he was trying to go with this. I sat up a little straighter and patted a seat next to me.

Lou settled into the chair so we were facing each other, knees barely touching. He had turned off the water since it was clear Warrick was showering and there wasn't a risk of him being able to hear what we were saying. Still keeping his volume low, Lou responded, "Well, since they're feeding magic into Az to make him unstoppable, I'm betting that magic has a time limit, too. He probably didn't intentionally follow us here. Az most likely needed a refill and it just happened to be a happy accident we were here, too."

I tapped his knee as I was processing what he was saying, "You might be on to something there, but how do we capitalize on that? Az isn't going to risk his main power source. That's what he's going to be protecting the most."

"Even without that magic, Az is someone who would be hard to stop," Lou trailed off, thinking.

"Everyone has to have a weakness. We could exploit that, if we knew what his weaknesses were," I said trying to think of anything that would hit Az hard.

"That man doesn't have a weakness," Warrick's cool voice settled on to us. Lou cleared his throat putting more space between us. He looked over towards the sink while I turned my attention to Warrick. Warrick stared at Lou, an unreadable expression on his face, as he continued, "He trained himself not to have any."

"That's impossible," I shook my head. There's no way someone has hardened themselves so much that nothing gets to them. Despite my mind telling me not to, I started analyzing the time Az and I spent together when he took me. There wasn't a lot of time where I wasn't drugged, but there were things standing out to me now. The tired expression he wore when he thought I wasn't looking. The night where I was convinced he was going to cut into me like Cian had, but stopped when he realized I was hungry. The picture of us by his bed. His admittance of having a soft spot for me. The way he tried to look out for me before we met up with Abria. *Wait, you've got to fucking kidding me. Why am I always the one these guys focus on?*

Warrick cocked his head to the side, now studying me, "What's running through that mind of yours, love?"

I sighed, pinching the bridge of my nose, "There was something Az said when I was cooped up in his apartment. It may not be a true weakness, but he admitted to having a soft spot for me."

Lou's lips thinned while a shadow crossed Warrick's features. We sat there silently, the wheels turning in each of our minds. Warrick was the first one to break the silence, "Are you sure that's what he said?"

"Unfortunately, yes," I nodded.

Lou rubbed his face, "I don't like what I'm about to suggest ..."

"Then don't," Warrick and I spat back in unison. Warrick pulled up a chair, "We'll find something else to focus on."

I stared Lou down, "Is that the first thing that jumps in your mind whenever it comes to getting an advantage?"

Lou held his hands up, dropping his gaze to his feet, "Sorry. Just figured we don't have a lot of time and this would be the easiest option."

"I'm not putting Val at any more risk than she already is," Warrick growled. "She's gone through enough."

"Got it," Lou mumbled getting up to start pulling out food. "We'll figure something else out, then. You better hope there's something at that house, though, because I really have no idea how we stand a chance against Az."

Warrick let another growl rumble low in his throat before disappearing back upstairs. I whipped my head around to face Lou as I stood up, "You really couldn't think of anything else?"

Lou shrugged, "I wasn't the one who brought up something that could potentially help us."

"I didn't want to fake a relationship the first time, remember?" I hissed. "*You* were the one who pushed me into that then instantly regretted that choice. Now, you want me to do the same thing, but with someone a hell of a lot more dangerous than Warrick. Let's not forget about the fact I'm fated with Warrick. That shit isn't even a possibility anymore."

"Silly me, I guess," Lou sighed.

"What's not a possibility?" Jennie asked, emerging from the basement.

I started making my way upstairs as I responded over my shoulder, "Lou can bring you up to speed while he gets us back to Lupusantha."

"Where?" I heard Jennie ask. Lou explained what I was talking about, but I didn't stick around. I headed to my room to find Warrick staring out the balcony window, brooding. Slowing my pace, I hugged him from behind, resting my cheek between his shoulders.

His body tensed, so I moved to sit on my bed. "Why haven't we jumped yet?" Warrick asked, still staring out the window.

"We should be going soon," I answered quietly.

Warrick looked over at me. His eyes were no longer his. The bright intensity burning into me belonged to his wolf. I sucked in a breath, knowing I'd have to be a little more careful in my movements to not set him off. He took slow steps until he was standing in front of me, placing his hands on either side and lowering his face to be inches from mine, "Did you tell him to go to Earth?"

"No," I whispered. "We're going back to your world."

Warrick didn't move an inch as he said, "I'm not all that thrilled to be going back there."

"I know."

"But you have a point," Warrick started, finally turning away from me and going back to his spot to look out the balcony door. "Lou is out of his damn mind if he thinks I'm going to let you whore yourself out to Az. We need to find something, and if we get lucky, the answer will be in whatever my parents left behind."

I flinched at his word choice. Warrick was back in front of me in an instant, "You know we're already going to be taking a huge risk by going to my childhood home. We'll likely have a run-in with Az."

I met his gaze, not thinking about being careful with how long I looked him in the eyes when he's like this. Warrick studied me carefully, fighting what his wolf was telling him to do. I quickly dropped my gaze as we jumped worlds. When I could finally breathe, Warrick caressed my cheek, his voice taking a dangerous tone, "Tell me. Do you still have feelings for him like he does for you?"

My head snapped up, the sudden motion causing Warrick to tighten his grip on the sheets. I looked into his eyes, not hesitating with my answer, "No."

He studied me, almost as if he didn't believe my answer. I put my hands on his chest, "There is nothing there but hate, Warrick. I want nothing to do with Az."

He brought a hand to my thigh, pushing the hem of my pajama shorts up to reveal the name there. Warrick brushed his thumb over the letters and it took all I had in me to stay still. With him so close to me, I didn't want to do anything to risk setting his wolf off more than I already have.

"You're mine," Warrick said, his breath hot against my throat. "He will not go unpunished for what he did to you. I will kill him for that, love."

"I know," I whispered, remaining motionless.

"Food's up," Lou knocked on the door. Warrick froze, but didn't move from where he was. Neither did I. Sensing the tension, Lou slowly asked, "Am I interrupting something?"

Warrick curled his lip, turning his head, "No." He stood up straight, his wolf suddenly tucked back away, "We'll be down in a minute."

Lou glanced between Warrick and me, his eyes landing on my legs where my newest scar was still exposed. Lou's stare didn't linger, but he clenched his jaws, tapped the doorframe, then left.

I started to stand up and Warrick stuck out a hand to help me to my feet. I didn't say anything, but accepted the help. As I was adjusting my shorts to cover myself back up, Warrick dropped his shoulders, "I'm sorry about the way I just acted, love. My head's all over the place."

"Don't worry about it," I muttered gesturing for him to lead the way. I'd be lying if I said I wasn't terrified. Warrick was doing better, but he was still a loose cannon. There was no telling what he would've done when he was not entirely himself, especially when he was focusing on what he saw between Az and I back at Abria's.

We joined everyone else down at the table, filling our bowls with oatmeal. When we were all seated, Warrick looked around the table, "We don't have a lot of time here. Check in on the pizza place to see if Joe and Bev would like to come with us. Me and Val have an errand to run, but as soon as we get back, we'll need to jump again."

"To Earth, right?" Mark asked in between bites.

Warrick only nodded to answer his question. I glanced at Lou who was still watching me a little too carefully. I looked back over at Warrick, "Lou and I have a theory. About something that could help us."

"Please, share," Warrick said.

I sat up a little straighter, "With Abria's magic having a time limit, we may be able to capitalize on Az's reserves running low *if* we can get the witches away from him long enough."

"The problem with that, as I'm sure you already know, is that he's not going to let that kind of power source just disappear," Lou started.

Warrick jumped in, "And we don't have a definitive answer for how long the effects of the magic last. If it takes twelve to twenty-four hours, the chances of getting him to put distance between him and the witches are next to none."

"Hmm," I tapped my spoon on my bowl. "We don't know if the time limit applies to all of their magic, either."

"Good point," Warrick nodded.

"During your time there, Warrick, did they give any indication about that?" Lou asked.

"No, Lou," Warrick said in a sarcastic tone. "It didn't come up with Abria riding me, gloating about her victory."

I set my fork down, my appetite suddenly gone. Jennie and Mark looked between Warrick, Lou, and I with wide eyes. I forgot they hadn't overheard the conversation this morning so they had no idea what had happened during the time Warrick was gone. I mouthed to Jennie that I would tell her later.

Lou dropped his gaze as Warrick dismissed himself from the table. Before he walked away, Warrick put a hand on my shoulder, "Will you be ready to go within the hour? I don't want to spend more time here than we have to."

"Sure," I nodded.

The rest of us sat in silence. I tried to eat more of my breakfast, but I couldn't stomach it. Warrick was on edge. You could tell he wasn't trying to take it out on everyone else, but he's having to fight hard.

Lou nervously fidgeted with his fork before looking up at me, "I'm sorry for barging in earlier."

"Don't worry about it," I pushed away from the table.

"You don't have to answer this," Lou started. *He was going to ask about the scar.* "And feel free to tell me if I'm overstepping. Why was Warrick fixated on one of your scars?"

I debated how I wanted to answer, if I wanted to just come out and tell him about that part of the Az experience or if I just wanted to brush it off. Sighing, I turned to face him, "Because Az took things too far, as he's been doing lately."

"What do you mean?" Jennie asked, now feeling comfortable to speak up since Warrick left the room.

I looked at the floor, "Az wanted to claim certain parts of me. Leave a reminder for Warrick."

"We're still not following," Jennie shook her head, confused.

I squeezed my eyes shut then lifted up my shorts to reveal Az's name on my thigh. I heard Jennie gasp and Lou let out a growl. A fork clattered against a plate, most likely Mark's. When I opened my eyes again, Lou met my gaze, "There's more of that on you?"

"No," I swallowed, hiding the scar again. "The witch leader removed all but one in her sick game."

I didn't wait for anyone else to add to the conversation. My throat was starting to close and my stomach turned thinking back to the joy Az had when he branded me. "I need to get ready," I mumbled.

When I got into my room, Warrick was sitting on the bed, head in his hands. "I'm sorry for how I handled things earlier, love," he said into his hands.

I still couldn't bring myself to talk so I squeezed his shoulder and started getting dressed. I bundled up, wearing a hoodie and started grabbing my riding gear. "Are the roads clear?" I asked quietly.

"Why?"

"I need to clear my head a little bit. Are you okay if I follow you there?" I turned to face him.

"I'd prefer if we could go together, but we'll drive separately. Might help if we need to split up," Warrick walked over to me. "What's wrong?"

I cast my gaze to floor, not wanting to look him in the eyes after our earlier interaction, "Just having to deal with some memories, that's all. Ready?"

"You can talk about these things with me, love," Warrick said, his tone gentle.

"Maybe later, I just need some air," I made my way to the door, brushing shoulders with Warrick. There was a little bit of electricity, but that faded as quick as the feeling passed through me.

The rest of the group still hadn't said anything, finishing their breakfast in silence. Warrick followed me into the garage to help me push my bike out, and once I was on the street, I took a deep breath in before donning my helmet, grateful we weren't in an eternal blizzard anymore. There was a sense of relief in knowing the weather here wasn't being controlled by any sort of magic.

Warrick pulled up next to me, "Good to go, love?"

"Lead the way," I nodded then put on my helmet. I zoomed after him feeling appreciative he was in the mood to drive fast. We navigated through the city then got on the familiar road that led to the oceanside restaurant. Instead of going straight, we turned left and went up the coast for a little ways. The houses were big, spread apart from each other. People who live here clearly had money.

Warrick slowed as we passed a beautiful white and grey house with intricate stonework, a grand entry leading up to the front door, and plenty of windows to give a perfect view of the soft hills and the ocean behind them. The house looked empty, but I was assuming this was the place Warrick grew up.

We turned around at the end of the street. Warrick rolled down his window and waved for me to pull up next to him. "I'm going to park at the restaurant and head back over here."

"I can follow you there and drive you back to save some time," I offered.

He nodded. I could tell he was tense just being here. I was getting ready to ask if he was okay even though I knew the answer, but he sped off. Shaking my head, I followed closely until we got to the restaurant. He barely gave me the chance to come to a stop before he hopped on the back of my bike. I took a second to get adjusted to the change in weight, then we sped off back to the house. I parked a little further down the street as he instructed and matched his pace as he headed up to the front door.

"Are we worried about surveillance equipment?" I hissed behind Warrick.

"No, there's no need," he gestured around the street. There were no other houses on this block and no sign of life other than the two of us. We reached the front door. Warrick took a deep breath before working on the lock. He turned to me once we heard the click, "You'll have to go in. I'll stay out here. I-I don't know that I can go in there, love." His voice had dropped. This was one of those rare times he showed his fear. Warrick's face was pale, his lips drawn into a thin line, his muscles rigid from how tense he was.

I put a hand on his arm, "It's okay. I don't want you to do something you don't want to. You've already made it this far which is a huge accomplishment. Can you tell me where I should start looking? Where should I go? What should I be looking for?"

He swallowed, closing his eyes, "Head up the stairs and go to the last room at the end of the hallway. Just head straight back there. Don't go anywhere else. We don't have time. Maybe try finding a journal. I have no idea what to expect, but you'll be going into my dad's office. If there's anything that even mentions Az, just grab it. We'll sort it out later."

I nodded then gave his arm a squeeze as I gripped the doorknob to head in. Warrick grabbed my arm, stopping me, "Thank you for doing this, love. Be careful."

I gave him a quick kiss on the cheek then headed in. I don't know what I was expecting, but it wasn't an airy open space. White was everywhere. The cream-colored furniture looked comfortable, a picture-perfect place to relax and unwind. There were pictures of a happy, smiling family lining some of the walls. I'm surprised to see all these photos of a young Warrick and Az surrounded by proud parents considering how Az had brutally murdered them.

I shook my head. I needed to focus on what we came here for. I quietly ascended the steps listening for any sounds to indicate I'm not the only one here. So far, it was silent.

When I got upstairs, there were quite a few doors lining the hallway. *Thank goodness I only need to head into the one at the end.* I started to head in that direction glancing in the open doors to see nicely decorated bedrooms. It looks like they haven't been touched in ages. The one room I needed to go into was the one room whose door was closed. Reaching out for the door handle, I hesitated for a moment listening only to be met with silence again. I glanced to the room on my right. It had to be the primary bedroom judging by the size, but what made me stop, was the framed picture of Az and I on the nightstand. It was the same one he had back in the witch world. My blood went cold as realization dawned on me. *Az has already been back here.*

There was a part of me that wanted to turn and run back out of this house. It may seem like a happy house, but I could start to feel a dark presence creeping in.

Instead, I set my shoulders and opened the door. There were so my books lining the shelves behind the large, ornately carved oak desk, but I couldn't take in any more of the office. My hands started shaking, my throat closing. *We're too late.*

"Miss me?" Az smirked, giving a little finger wave.

I started to back away, shaking my head. Az stood up and crossed over to where I was. He managed to close the distance in no time, cupping the back of my neck and pulling me back into the office with him. "Sit with me for a second, Val. Let's have a little chat. Is your boyfriend with you?"

"He's waiting outside," I said tersely.

"Of course he is," Az smiled as he lifted me up and sat me on the desk. When he settled into his chair, he put a hand on my knee. I tried to jerk away, but he held on tightly. "So, welcome to my home."

"Cut the shit, Az. You can let me walk out of here, no questions asked. Warrick and I will get on our merry way," I did my best to convey confidence despite wanting to scream.

"Alright, alright," Az held up his free hand. "So touchy today. But," his tone suddenly serious, "how have you been holding up?"

"Why do you care?" I spat.

All humor in his face left. Az looked as though he was genuinely worried about my well-being. This had to be a part of the game he was playing, to get into my head and drive a wedge between me and my friends. Especially me and Warrick.

"I didn't like how things were left back in Frigusmada," Az moved closer to me. "As much as I enjoy getting to play with knives, you're the last person I wanted to carve up."

"Really didn't seem that way when you decided to brand me," I said.

He ran his hand up my thigh to the only one left on me. I tensed, but that didn't seem to deter him. Az brought his brows together, "I only did that to play the part. Anyways, you clearly came here for something. What is it, Val? Maybe I can help you."

He shook off the emotions he was showing to put his mask back on. I was too close to him and I didn't trust how he said that last part. *Az knows what we came here to look for.* I looked around the surface of the desk scanning for anything that would give me a clue. My eyes lingered a little too long on a worn, brown leather journal that looked like it had just been placed on the desk. Az caught on to what I was looking at, his sinister smile creeping along his face. He picked up the journal, "This old thing? It's just my dad's journal. What would you need with it?"

"Warrick's been feeling a little homesick lately. Thought he could use something to remind him of better times."

Az let out a bark of laughter, "Really? You think that's going to work on me?" More laughter ensued. "Cut the crap, Val. You're here because you think this might be the one way you can stop me. Very good, I might add. You picked up on me saying my parents were the only ones who knew how to stop me, and you hoped they documented that somewhere. What? Did you, Warrick, and Lou hatch up this plan? You convinced Warrick you needed to make a stop here before your next destination to get the golden ticket with the hopes that I wouldn't be home yet. Is that it?"

It was like he had been sitting in the room when we all talked about it. I wouldn't let him see my shock, though. Instead, I nodded my head towards his room, "Why do you keep that picture close to you? Miss me or something?"

"You could say that," Az answered, not fully biting my bait. He stood up, our faces now inches from each other, "I haven't been lying when I've said you were the best I've ever had. Is it a crime to miss you?"

"Careful, Az," I dropped my voice. "You might actually show you have feelings."

He tucked a strand of hair behind my ear, "Would that be another crime? Because if it is, lock me up."

"That's what you're going to say?" I asked pulling my head back a little bit so I could breathe. No part of me wanted to be this close to him. And yet, I had to take advantage of this distraction. My hand started inching towards the journal while I said, “You never really answered my question.”

“Because, waking up to your beautiful face helps me get through,” Az whispered, bringing his face even closer to mine.

“Do you enjoy being a walking cliché?”

His hand slammed down on mine as soon as it grasped the journal. I let out a whimper from the pain that shot up my arm. I’m pretty sure he just broke a couple of my fingers from how hard he smacked my hand. “I don’t think so. You’re not getting out of here without giving me something in return.”

“Step away from her, Az.”

Hearing that voice sent relief throughout my body.

Chapter 17

Az chuckled, the sound low and menacing, "Of course you're coming to her rescue. Can't stand the thought of seeing us kiss again? Too afraid of losing her? Val and I had something special. Is it the fact there's a chance she'll remember how good she had it with me and leave you?"

He knew exactly what buttons to push. Az probably had this whole speech planned from the minute I walked out of Abria's with Warrick.

"Shut your damn mouth," Warrick started lunging in our direction.

"I wouldn't do that if I were you," Az said suddenly controlling my movements. He got me to my feet and turned me around to use as a shield. There was a quick kiss on my neck then Az continued, "I'm sure you'd like to kill me, especially here, as a way to get revenge for our parents, but you'll have to go through Val first. You wouldn't kill the woman you're fated to, now would you?"

Warrick growled, his wolf back at the surface. I still didn't trust they couldn't change on command, especially with how Warrick has been lately. I glanced up at Az to find him looking at me, his eyes different, too. I had never seen him as a wolf, but I wasn't expecting his eye color to completely change. Warrick's and Lou's eyes became more intense, almost like the color of their irises glowed. Az, on the other hand, now had violet eyes.

There was no sign of the color glowing, but they were different enough to know I really had no chance to get out of here on my own. Warrick would have to free me from Az's grasp.

Az smiled at me, almost a smile that matched what he used to give me during our relationship: a soft one radiating love. "We were starting to get somewhere when we were in my apartment, weren't we?"

I was going to be sick. I immediately shook my head, "No. We weren't." I looked back at Warrick who had silently moved closer to us. "Don't listen to him, Warrick. He's just trying to get in your head."

"I know, love," Warrick responded. "Az, there is no reason for Val to be in the middle of our fight. Let her go."

"Well, I can't quite do that," Az yanked me closer to him. He held up my hand still holding on to the journal, "She owes me something in return if I let her walk out of here with this."

"And what would that be?" Warrick asked.

Az stroked my jaw with his thumb, "Haven't decided yet. I could keep the sex-theme going, or I could demand some information in return of the same value."

Shit, I didn't have anything like that. We were all scrambling to come up with something to give us an upper hand against Az. I'm pretty sure he already knew all our weaknesses and how easy it would be to take us all out. The whole reason Warrick and I came here was to get the one thing that would change who owned the power in this conflict.

When neither Warrick nor I said anything, Az clicked his tongue while shaking his head, "How unfortunate. I was really hoping to get an insider's scoop as to what's going on behind enemy lines. Oh well, I guess I know what the choice is now."

Az moved us out from behind the desk. He kept me in between him and Warrick, but Az must've made some sort of adjustment, opening up a window of opportunity, because Warrick launched himself into his brother.

Az staggered back before Warrick pinned him against the wall. I stumbled a few steps noting I still had the journal in my hand. Warrick looked at me over his shoulder, "Val, run!"

"What about you?"

"I'll be fine, love. Get out of here," he grunted. Az was starting to come back to his senses. Warrick returned his full attention to his brother. I could only take a few steps back. Something was keeping me here despite my mind screaming at me to put as much distance between myself and Az as possible.

"Figured you would want these back," Warrick said between clenched teeth. He pulled out Az's knives one at a time, driving the blades into Az.

Az laughed, "Weren't you going to kill me, baby bro? Isn't that what you said the last time we saw each other?"

When Warrick was down to the last one, the knife Az had used to kill his parents, he smiled, "Oh, I'll stay true to my word, but now is not the time."

Before Az could say anything else, Warrick buried the knife within Az's neck. Those violet eyes of his widened in shock. Apparently, Az wasn't expecting that from Warrick, but we didn't stick around to see the aftermath. While Az was scrambling to remove the blade, Warrick grabbed my hand leading us out of the house. He took the journal, tucking it away, and practically threw me at my bike. I had recovered enough from my own shock to launch us out of the neighborhood.

I sped over to the restaurant for Warrick to retrieve his car, leaving the minute he was off my bike. I didn't look back, lowering myself closer to the body of the bike while increasing speed. We made it back to my house in no time, and as soon as we ran into the house, Warrick shouted, "Lou, we gotta go now! Get us to Earth!"

Lou ran over to the kitchen where he had left the device then ran out on the street to transport us. Warrick and I stood rooted to our spots, staring each other down while we returned to my world. Once everything had settled, Lou rushed over to us, "What the hell happened? Why'd we need to get out of there that fast?"

"Are Jennie and Mark here?" I asked Lou without taking my eyes off Warrick.

"Yeah, they're here, but – " Lou started answering.

"Were you able to check in on the pizza place?" Warrick asked before Lou could finish his first answer.

"I had just gotten back, but – "

"Good. Now if you'll excuse us," Warrick reached out for my hand. I placed mine in his as he led me upstairs.

"Will one of you two just answer my damn questions?" Lou called up after us.

"Later," was all Warrick said. He continued leading us to my room, closing and locking the door behind us then moving to turn on some music. Warrick stood in front of me, his hands cradling my face, "Are you okay, love?"

I nodded, "Just shaken up, that's all."

He turned my head in both directions scanning for any signs of injury, "I don't trust we were able to get the journal that easily."

"I don't either, but we might as well check if there's anything in there that points to what may actually bring Az down."

"How were you able to distract him?" Warrick asked. The words came out slowly and I knew he was worried I had crossed a line.

"All it took was for me to ask him about a picture of us he keeps on his nightstand. I just had to do something that reminded him of our previous relationship," I answered.

His grip tightened, "Nothing physical?"

"No, nothing like that," I said. "Just talking. That's all we did. I promise you."

Warrick got quiet as he kept watching me. I started to open my mouth to ask what was running through his mind when I felt a slight pressure in my mind. My hand instinctively reached up to my head. Warrick cocked his head to the side, "You okay, love?"

Even though his question was one of concern, Warrick's tone and facial expression didn't match. I nodded my head, "Yeah. Maybe I'm getting a headache or something from all the excitement."

Warrick didn't say anything, but the pressure was back. It wasn't painful, but felt like something that didn't belong to me. I brought my gaze back to Warrick's to study him. He was staring at me too intently for someone who was genuinely worried about my health. "Why are you looking at me like that?" I asked.

Instead of answering, Warrick took a step closer. He knew I didn't like when he acted like this. It very much felt like he was starting to toy with his prey, and that prey was me.

"Warrick," I warned. I put a hand on his chest to push him back, but his expression didn't change. The pressure grew stronger, so much so that I brought my hand back up to my head. *What the hell is going on?* I didn't have a lot of time to run through the possibilities of what this pressure was since Warrick pulled me against him. His heart rate was starting to pick up, his pupils growing larger. Now was not the time to get close and personal. Maybe I had a migraine going on or I was going to black out, but I was in no condition to do anything but nap. That was the only thing I could come up with that would counter the pressure I was feeling.

I gave Warrick's chest another push, "I should lay down."

Nothing. He gave me nothing in return except for the same expression on his face.

Talk to me, love.

My eyes widened. It was Warrick's voice in my head.

Can you hear me?

"Yes, but what is this?" I asked out loud.

Warrick smiled at me. *It's our bond. Try talking to me in your mind.*

I swallowed. I had no idea what I was doing. I tried to say hello, keeping it simple. Warrick's facial expression didn't change which must have meant my attempt wasn't successful. I tried again with no luck. I shrugged my shoulders.

Try again.

I took a deep breath setting my shoulders. I brought my eyes to meet his icy blue gaze and tried again. *Can you hear me?* Warrick showed no signs of being able to hear my attempts. I threw my hands up, "What's wrong with me?"

Warrick gave my shoulders a squeeze, "It's okay, love. You don't need to beat yourself up. The fact you can hear me now is more than enough."

"Were you the pressure I was feeling?" I asked.

"My guess is yes. It could have been caused by me trying to break through your mental barriers," Warrick brushed my hair out of my face. "As I understand it, we should be able to reach a point where it'll be second nature. We'll be able to communicate feely, be able to feel what the other is feeling. It may just take time."

"Why? Shouldn't this be something that's automatic?" I asked.

Warrick shook his head, "I don't know. It's different for every person."

"Have you asked Raf? About his experience?"

"Not yet," Warrick answered. "We'll get a chance to. In the meantime, we'll just keep working at it, okay, love?"

I nodded my head. I wish I wasn't adding one more thing to his plate for him to worry about. There was enough going on. Just look at what happened when we were retrieving a journal. Az knew we were going to be there somehow, and yet, he virtually let us walk out of there.

I moved away from Warrick heading to the bathroom. Even though his mood was lighter from the breakthrough with our bond, there was something dangerous still lingering under the surface. I knew better than to wait to see what happens.

As I was peeling my clothes off, Warrick leaned on the doorframe. I glanced at him, turning my back to him to shield myself a little bit. I couldn't trust how he would act the minute he saw Az's name on my thigh. "Why'd you come into the house back there?" I asked quietly.

He was watching every movement a little too closely for comfort as he answered, "Too much time had passed. Something was telling me to suck it up and get in there."

"I had it under control," I countered, noting the slight protest in my voice.

Warrick took a step closer to me and I held my breath. His eyes flicked down to the now exposed scar left there to cause contention. Warrick tilted my chin up, his voice calm, "What did you do to have a hold over him?"

"I have no idea, and before you go making accusations or running with wild theories, I have done everything to push him away. The *only* explanation I can come up with is that I'm fated to *you*. Az clearly wants to get under your skin. That's what he's been doing even before he showed his face. It has nothing to do with me," I explained.

Warrick chuckled, "Oh, but I think you have a little more than nothing to do with it, love. You've haunted him as much as he's haunted you in this reunion."

"What do you want from me? What are you trying to get at here? We came out of there unscathed and with a journal that could give you what you want. You even got to stab him in the neck before we got out of there. So, tell me, Warrick, what is it that you want from me?" I asked, my voice barely above a whisper.

When he didn't say anything, I went on, "You keep accusing me of trying to run away from you and into the arms of others. That's the farthest thing from the truth. I've been doing what you've asked of me. I'm helping you. I'm trying to figure out what the hell is going on to fill in the blanks to give us the upper hand. But, I'm tired. I'm tired of the constant head games and the constant back and forth. There hasn't been a break in the tension. It's taking a toll on me. Now, please let me shower so I can at least get the smell of Az off me. Use that time to start reading through the journal and see what you can find out."

Warrick dropped the hostility. *Guess he didn't realize I wasn't trying to jerk him around. How long has he been holding on to that?* I started the water then turned back to him, "Why do you always have to convince yourself that I'm scheming against you?"

"I'll be in your dad's office," he said, dropping his shoulders as he turned to leave.

I watched as he left and didn't move to get in the shower until I heard the door close. I was reminded of the conversation I'd overheard between him and Lou about how Warrick was scared I'd succumb to the same fate as everyone else he's loved in his life. He's trying to push me away to protect himself. Warrick forgets I'm scared of being fated, too. I never thought I'd be in this kind of relationship. Sometimes it stings, knowing I'd never be able to make that choice of who I get to spend the rest of my life with. I mean, I could make the choice, but I'd always be drawn back to Warrick. He'd pop back up in my life and cause complications. Despite that, though, I know deep down I do love Warrick. It would break me not to be with him.

I grabbed my head, the water pouring over me. My tears blended with the water as I slid to the ground. *Everything okay, love?* I knew I'd be okay and this was one of those moments where I needed to let everything out. I wasn't expecting

Warrick to pop in my head at that moment. Apparently, he was already able to pick up on what I was feeling through our bond. I took a deep breath to calm down and made another attempt to send him a silent message.

I focused on Warrick, on trying to find him in the house. My eyes closed. I imagined myself reaching a hand out to him, picturing his back facing me. As soon as I flattened my palm against the warmth of his back, I extended the reach from my mind to his. *Can you hear me?*

It was like Warrick was standing right next to me, letting out a sigh of relief. The image of him in my mind turned around, a smile on his face. *Yes, I can.* My eyes snapped open. I don't know what changed this time, but our bond was open. It was weird being able to have this place reserved in my mind for him where I could feel what he was feeling, talk to him without opening my mouth, and I could almost see what he was seeing. He repeated his question: *Are you okay?*

Yes, just needed to let some things out, I answered.

I'm sorry I've been such an ass, love, his tone filled with remorse.

Let's put it behind us. I'm happy we don't have the stress of trying to figure out this bond anymore. I grinned at that. I knew he still had his own feelings to sort through, but we finally made progress on something. It wasn't lost on me the advantage this would give us, either. Warrick and I didn't have to share our plans with anyone now. We didn't need to worry about the risk of unwanted ears listening in anymore.

A surge of warmth travelled down the bond through my mind until it settled in my heart, then Warrick left me to finish my shower. I got dressed, taped up my broken fingers, and headed downstairs, pausing in the doorway of the office to see if Warrick was there. When I didn't see him, I assumed he was with everyone else. Light-hearted conversation filtered up to me as I finally convinced myself to descend the stairs to join everyone else.

"There she is!" Mark called out.

I gave a quick wave then stopped when my eyes landed on Joe and Bev sitting at the table smiling up at me. I jogged down the last couple of steps, "When did you guys get – dad?"

I froze. My dad had stepped into view clutching his hat, "Hey, Val-pal. How you holding up?"

I ran over to him, throwing myself into his outstretched arms. The tears were back, and as I squeezed him a little harder, he lowered his voice, "It's good to see you standing. Warrick and Lou caught me up on the stunt Az pulled. It's taking everything in me not to hunt him down. He doesn't get to mess with all the women in my life and get away with it."

Mom. I can't believe I had almost forgotten about her loss. Immediately flooded with guilt, I pulled away, "I miss her."

"I know," he patted my arm. "We're having a funeral for her in a couple of days. A quick turnaround for you, I know, but I'm just happy you're here now. I figured I'd bring over the details while checking on the house. Glad to see it's still standing."

We moved to join everyone else at the table. I took my seat in between Warrick and Lou, my dad settling in the seat across from Warrick. Jennie, Bev, Mark, and Joe filled the remainder of the seats watching as my dad and Warrick got down to business.

"Az follow you here?" My dad asked.

Warrick shook his head, "I don't think so, but I'm not ruling it out. He got back to Lupusantha a lot faster than I thought he would."

"You had talked about retrieving a journal while you were there?"

"We did," Warrick confirmed.

Did you find anything in there? I tried to see if I could pick up on any other indicators in our bond. I could feel Warrick's disappointment and knew what his answer was going to be.

"Well?" my dad prompted.

Warrick dropped his shoulders, "There was nothing in there that would give us any sort of upper hand against Az."

"Damn," my dad leaned back in his chair rubbing a hand over his face. "Well, I guess we're back at square one in that department."

"Az doesn't have any clue that you're working with us, right?" Warrick asked, his tone shifting.

If Az had a clue my dad was crossing him – I couldn't think about the consequences of that. Picking up on my worry through the bond, Warrick gave my knee a squeeze under the table.

"None," my dad answered with confidence. "And I plan on keeping it that way."

My dad was about to say something else when his phone started buzzing in his pocket. He pulled it out, looking at who was calling him. My dad raised his eyebrows, answering the call, putting the phone on the table.

"Are you available to meet tonight?" asked a familiar voice.

"I can be in about thirty minutes. Where do you need me?" my dad answered watching Warrick and me.

"Downtown, the usual place. As soon as possible."

The call ended. My dad clapped his hands together, "Well, duty calls. I need to head out."

I reached out to Warrick through our bond, but Warrick beat me to it. *We need to be careful here, now, love. We can't put your dad at risk. Az is too close already.*

I gave a subtle nod only for Warrick as I moved to walk my dad to the front door. He pulled me into a warm hug, "We'll make it through this, Val. Just a little longer."

"Be careful out there."

"You need to be careful, too. I don't want any more reports about you getting hurt," he lectured.

"I'll keep an eye on her, James. I won't let that happen anymore," Warrick promised, placing a hand on the small of my back.

My dad nodded, then left. I turned to Warrick as soon as the door closed, "Do you think Az knows?"

A muscle twitched in Warrick's jaw, "I don't know, love. Your dad may be confident, but Az tends to know too much. He shouldn't have even known we were going by the house back in my world."

"Is that what happened?" Lou asked, directing our focus back to the table. "You had another run-in with Az?"

"Yes," Warrick started. I put a hand on his chest before heading back to my spot.

Jennie brought me a fresh mug of tea as I looked at Lou to answer his questions, "We knew there was a pretty good chance of running into him there, but it wasn't set in stone. Warrick stood guard while I looked for anything that might help us, but the minute I stepped into his dad's office, Az was waiting. Warrick eventually joined us and managed to get a couple of blows in, creating the opportunity for me to run with the journal we've been talking about. We both knew it was too easy to get the journal, but there wasn't any chance for us to go looking through anything else there. That's why we came back in such a hurry."

"So, what do we do now?" Lou asked Warrick.

Warrick lifted his shoulders in a shrug, "I don't know. We hope that Val's dad manages to find some sort of hint for any kind of weakness Az has. In the meantime, we need to try to find where he's hiding out, what kind of arsenal he has, and go from there."

Jennie distracted me from the conversation between Lou and Warrick, "Val, are you going to your mom's funeral?"

Az could be there, Warrick warned, not missing a beat with Lou and his questions.

I sat there quietly, more so I could respond to Warrick. *I know that's a risk, but this is something that's non-negotiable.*

Want me to be there, Warrick asked.

Please. I met Jennie's concerned gaze, "Of course I am. It would mean the world if each of you could be there, too."

She offered a reassuring smile, "We wouldn't miss it for the world."

I turned my attention to Joe and Bev, "What made you two want to join?"

"We were more curious about seeing what it was like back home. It'll help us while we're deciding where we'd like to end up," Joe answered.

"Well, I'm happy to see both of your faces here," I said, smiling.

Love, let's go upstairs.

Okay, I answered back.

I gave Jennie's arm a squeeze as I stood up, "I think I'm going to turn in for the night, though. See you all in the morning."

Several goodnights rang out. I grabbed my comforter from the basement then climbed up to my room. After getting my bed all setup again, I stared out the balcony door. I hadn't had too much time to take in the scenery since we landed here, but it was nothing like the place we had left. A lot of the surrounding buildings had been burned down to nothing. The landscape was charred and pockmarked, scars from the many bombs that fell that night. Even the skyline of the city below us had changed, only a few of the towering skyscrapers still standing. Any semblance of home was gone now, destroyed by greed. *I can't live here anymore.*

I rested my head against the cool glass when I heard the door click open then quietly close. It wasn't long before Warrick's strong arms wrapped around my waist. His lips brushed against my ear, "How does it feel to be home, love?"

I sighed, "This isn't home anymore. Az made sure of that."

He turned me so I was facing him, those icy blue eyes of his soft, "That's what he does, but enough about him. There was something I didn't like about today."

"Just one thing?" I tilted my head to the side, rubbing his arms. Being this close to him without feeling an impending argument coming or Warrick fussing over any new injuries covering my body made it hard to focus.

"There were a lot of things," Warrick's voice dropped to a low level. "But, the one that stood out to me the most was seeing another man in between your legs."

I lifted my chin while holding my ground, "I don't like knowing another woman was on top of you, either, but here we are."

A growl rumbled in his chest, but Warrick tampered that down, "Since we've taken care of the bond problem – "

I cut Warrick off, "Didn't realize that was so much of a problem. I thought it was something that could take time."

His arms squeezed me tighter as he pushed me against the wall, "Let me finish, love."

I nodded for him to continue. His gaze dropped to my lips before meeting mine again, "I was starting to question if we truly were fated, but the bond was the last thing I needed to fall into place to know for sure. You're *mine* and I never intend to let you go."

"Are you finally going to let go of that fear, of that doubt?" I challenged him.

His nostrils flared as he pushed up against me even more, "It's gone."

I put a hand on his chest despite the lack of space between us, "No more running away?"

"Never again," Warrick promised.

"No more flipping a switch and making me feel threatened?" I asked.

He brought a hand up to trace my jawline bringing his lips inches from mine, "I wouldn't dream of it, love."

"Good," I whispered. The butterflies threatened to take flight with all the promises Warrick made. Saying the words was the easy part, I reminded myself, but he needed to prove it. Don't they always say actions speak louder than words?

Chapter 18

Warrick moved his face closer to mine so our lips were barely touching. Any hesitations from earlier had left me, replaced with the desire to feel his kiss while his body catered to my every need. I arched into him, my heart beating faster while I watched his pupils dilate. Warrick leaned in to kiss me, my eyes closing. *It has been far too long.*

That's why I plan to do something about it tonight, love.

A knock sounded from my door shattering the perfect little bubble we had created for ourselves. Warrick's lip curled as he whipped his head in the direction of the distraction. "What?" he demanded.

Lou poked his head in, "Uh, everything okay in here?"

"What the hell do you want, Louis?" Warrick asked, annoyed and inpatient.

"Jennie wants to go out tonight to see if her favorite club is still around and wanted me to check if you two were still awake."

"And?" Warrick prompted. *If he doesn't get the fucking question out in the next five seconds, I'm kicking his ass out of here.*

Won't hear me complain.

I felt him chuckle. It was weird seeing him remain serious on the outside when that didn't match what was going on in his head.

"Want to come with us?" Lou finally asked.

Considering how the last club adventure went, I wasn't too sure. The chances of that incident repeating were very little, but I couldn't rule anything out with Az being here. *Do you want to go?*

I looked up at Warrick who was turning to face me. This could be the first time I test if he truly meant what he had committed to earlier. Plus, it would be an added bonus to let loose for a little bit. The corner of Warrick's mouth turned up, "This could be the last time in a while we get to just have a night."

"What are they saying?" I heard Jennie hiss out in the hallway.

Lou raised his eyebrows at us waiting for an answer. Warrick nodded his head and Lou called over his shoulder, "They're in."

There was a happy squeal in response and we all started moving to get ready. I knew the dress code for this club, so I grabbed a skintight, black minidress with several slits along the sides showing a decent amount of skin. Unlike the last time we all went out together, I didn't have to worry about flashing anyone. I styled my hair in big, loose curls after throwing on some simple makeup. I came out of my bathroom expecting Warrick to be sitting there, but found the room empty.

I was on my way downstairs when I noticed Jennie was still getting ready, so I knocked on the doorjamb, "Hey."

"Damn, Val. Look at you!" she gushed. Jennie ran over to grab my arm and pulled me into her room. As soon as she got the door closed, she lowered her voice, "We haven't really talked since everything happened. Are you doing okay?"

Sighing, I sat on the edge of her bed, “I don’t know.” A chuckle escaped my lips, “It doesn’t feel like any of this is real, you know? Or, at least, that’s how I’m able to make it through all of this.”

“Az really forced himself on you?” Jennie asked.

I slowly nodded my head, “Yeah.”

“That doesn’t seem like him,” she said in a faraway voice as she sat next to me.

“He’s definitely not the Az we knew. Although, there were a couple of times he was nice to me. He even looked out for me a little bit before we went to the witch leader,” my voice trailed off.

Jennie looked as if I had a third head, “You’re not trying to justify his actions, are you?”

“Oh, there’s no way in hell I would try to do that,” I shook my head. “Just throws me off a little, that’s all.”

“So, how are you, really?” Jennie directed the conversation back to her first question.

“Barely holding it all together, Jennie. It’s hard to know what to feel and when. I can’t tell up from down anymore. I found out this morning that Lou wishes he were in Warrick’s shoes. My mom is gone and I haven’t even had a chance to process that, but now I’ll be going to her funeral. I still don’t know if I can trust my dad even though Warrick can. Then, I’ve been dragging you guys through all of this,” I brought my eyes up to hers. “Speaking of you guys, why are Joe and Bev here? I thought they were going to be staying in the werewolf world.”

“It feels like all of this has been going on for years,” Jennie laughed pushing her hair out of her face. She started to get back to work on putting it up, so I reached over to help her out.

She shot me a grateful look over her shoulder then continued, "I seriously don't know how you handle any of this, Val. I would've given up a long time ago. I mean, I kind of did in Cian's world. I just went about establishing my new life without even thinking there was a possibility I would be able to see home again. Although, there's nothing really here anymore, is there?"

I joined her in a soft laugh, "Not really."

"Anyways," she sighed. "Stop feeling bad for us. I mean it. As for Joe and Bev, Lou mentioned we'd be coming back here and they decided they wanted to come after all. They said it would help with their decision-making. I think they're going to check on their house, jobs, and all that tomorrow, and if things aren't still standing, then they'll probably move to the werewolf world. They've asked what they missed while we were gone, but none of us really wanted to get into that, so I guess be prepared for questions."

"Fair enough. I'd want to check on things here, too, if I were wanting to make a decision on where to spend the rest of my life."

I put the finishing touches on her hair. Jennie turned around to face me, brows furrowed, "You talk like you don't have one."

I messed with the hem of my dress a little bit, "I have a choice, but I don't, if that makes sense? The thing about being fated to a wolf is that no matter where I go, who I date, or what I do, I'll always be drawn back to him. Warrick will keep showing up in my life."

"How do you feel about that?"

I lifted my gaze to meet hers, "I love him, Jennie, I really do. For once, I'm not looking for an excuse to run away. It's more what I have to move past. You know things have been pretty rocky, but I'm ready to move on from those things."

She tilted her head to the side, "Are you? You sound like you're having to convince yourself."

I couldn't help but let a little bit of laughter slip from my lips, "I am, aren't I? Well, I guess you can say tonight is a bit of a test. Warrick made a bunch of promises to me just now and I want to see if he can stick to them."

She nodded, letting things soak in for a moment. After a few beats, Jennie asked, "Is Az really here?"

"Good question," I pushed my hair back again, noting the slight shake in my hands. I glanced down at the edges of his name poking out from my dress and frowned. When I looked back up at Jennie, I caught her staring at the scar, "Probably, and there's a good chance we'll run into him tonight, but I don't want that to ruin our fun, okay?"

"Okay," she nodded. Jennie reached out to the scar, her fingers lightly touching the raised portions of my skin, "It makes me sick that he did this to you."

"Me too," I agreed quietly. Letting out a breath, I squared my shoulders grabbing her hands and standing both of us up. I fixed a smile on my face, "That's enough serious talk. We have a club to get to, right?"

Jennie mirrored my actions, nodding vigorously. She led the way out of her room, "Let's get our asses down there."

The rest of our group was waiting around the island for us. I beamed at Warrick when I could see him, the same smile being returned. I took my place next to his side, Warrick tossing an arm around my shoulders as he tilted my chin up to him, "You look ravishing tonight, love."

I gave him a quick kiss on his cheek, "You don't look half bad yourself."

Jennie clapped her hands together dragging my attention away from Warrick, "Alright, Joe and Bev are driving, but we need one more car. Val?"

"Sure," I nodded.

"That settles it. What are we doing standing around here?" Jennie motioned impatiently, her arms hastily pointing to the door, "Let's get a move on people!"

When Lou, Warrick and I settled into my car, Lou let out a chuckle, "Jennie sure does take her partying seriously."

"Don't take away that girl's good time," I warned.

Warrick followed Joe and Bev's car. As much as I wished Warrick could've seen this drive and the city before half of it was destroyed, there was no changing the destruction his brother caused. People were wandering around aimlessly, despair etched into their features. The buildings that were still standing were covered in soot, pieces crumbling to the ground. For the buildings no longer there, very little remained. Stubs of posts were barely sticking out of the ground, the remaining pieces of walls showing evidence of the severity of the blasts that came through. We made the drive in silence, my heart breaking at the thought of so many people displaced. It would take way too long for this place to recover.

Their car ahead of us slowed before pulling into a parking lot. The club was still standing, but for the first time since this place has been open, there wasn't a line of anxiously waiting club-goers wrapping around the building despite the full parking lot.

We all got out, Jennie leading the way to the door. The usual bouncer was at his post. As soon as he saw Jennie, his eyes lit up and he spread his arms out wide. Jennie ran into them, his thunderous voice sounding out, "It has been far too long! How's my favorite partier?"

"You have no idea how much I've missed seeing your wonderful face!" Jennie exclaimed straightening her skirt out after the bouncer set her back on her feet. "I've been doing good, just traveling on an extended vacation."

"I can't even begin to tell you how worried I was that you may have been caught in a blast, but forget about talking to me. You all get in there," he pulled the door open.

We all filed in with me bringing up the rear. I gave the bouncer's arm a squeeze, "I'm so happy to see you're still standing."

"You too, Val," he smiled down at me. "Enjoy."

Music washed over me the second I crossed the threshold. It was like I was transported to someplace else entirely. The lighting matched the music, currently soft and moving in slow, lazy circles around everyone crowded on the dance floor. The slow pace didn't last for long, though. The lights started flashing in time with the beat that was steadily gaining speed. The crowd of people moved with it. I had never seen this dance floor like this. Everyone was completely lost in the music, dancing as if this truly were their last night.

Unlike the one we went to in Warrick's world, there was no lavish decorations. It was pretty bare bones with the bar in the far corner opposite of the door and tables hastily strewn around the edges. There were bathrooms next the bar, but no other visible doors or hallways for people to get into precarious situations.

Jennie grabbed Mark's hand pulling him out on the dance floor with her. She motioned for the rest of us to follow. I looped an arm through Warrick's and was just starting to do the same to Lou when Lou leaned down to talk to me, "I'll camp out at a table for a little bit."

"You sure?" I asked.

"Yeah," he nodded. "Now, you two crazy kids have fun. Make up for lost time."

Warrick took the lead now, tugging me out to join the rest of our group while I watched Lou. He was trying to keep up his usual light-heartedness, but I could tell he was feeling lonely. I made a mental note to have one dance with him, minimum. Warrick quickly got my focus back on to him as he looped my arms behind his neck and pulled me close. I let him direct our movements just enjoying the proximity of our bodies. We swayed with the rhythm, his hands resting on my ass. He leaned down, his lips once again brushing my ear, "You have no idea how much I want to take that dress off you, love."

I buried my fingers in his hair pressing up as much as I could against him, "You could've had me all to yourself in an empty house, but you were the one who wanted to come here."

"Maybe I wanted the satisfaction of seeing you all dressed up again just so I can take it all off," he turned me around, my back so close to him there wasn't a chance for even air to find its way through. We danced like we had back in the club in his world, grinding to the rhythm of the music. One of his hands started inching my skirt up, "There are so many things I want to do to you." My core tightened at the thought. Warrick picked up on my reaction, chuckling a little bit, "Let's see if I can show you."

Our bond was wide open at this point, my mind instantly flooded with images of us tangled up in one another. As each image flashed, I felt the heat rising and knew my cheeks were beyond red at this point. I could feel my nipples harden, the anticipation making me wet with desire. It had been far too long since Warrick and I could enjoy each other's company, my body aching at the thought.

I turned back around in Warrick's arms only to be met with his lips crashing onto mine. The familiar electricity was back growing more intense with every second. We were hungry for one another, our kisses filled with a ferocity we haven't had in a while. We were the only two for miles and I wanted him *now.* I felt Warrick harden against me. A soft moan only meant for us to hear escaped my lips and I pulled away, struggling to catch my breath as I remembered where we were. I rested my forehead on his chest, "We need to save some of this for the bedroom where no one else can see."

"As much as I would like to say I could be discreet, love, you're right," Warrick breathed. "I'll go cool off and get us something to drink."

He reluctantly left the dance floor, but the minute he was out of sight, Jennie tugged me to her, "What was all *that* about?" She fanned herself, "It was hot."

I laughed, throwing my head back. I was about to respond when Lou pulled me over to him. He gave a wink to Jennie then pulled me further into the crowd where we had no choice but to be close to one another. He leaned down so he didn't have to shout, "Mind if I have this dance?"

"Do I have a choice?" I nodded towards him.

"No," he shook his head. "Not really."

The way we were dancing was nowhere near what Warrick and I were doing. Our movements were respectful of one another despite the close proximity, but not in a way that was sexual. Lou's calloused hands found my exposed skin tightening their grip as they did so. His warmth spread despite me already starting to sweat from all the movement in the short time we had been here. *Remind Lou not to get too handsy with you. I don't share.* I blushed at the sudden sound of Warrick's voice in my head.

"What's on your mind?" Lou asked.

"What? Nothing," I answered.

Lou smirked, "You and Warrick get that bond figured out?"

"What made you ask that?"

"You looked like you were focused on something else going on and then blushed, so either you were thinking back to what you and Warrick were about to do in front of everyone or he was talking to you," Lou tilted his head. "So, which one is it?"

I shrugged, "You caught us red-handed, I guess. The blockage finally moved and we can use our bond."

Even though he tried to hide it, I caught the little bit of disappointment that flashed across his features. He quickly smiled at me, "Guess that means my chances of being with you are next to none now, huh?"

"Guess so," I nodded.

"What do you think changed?" Lou asked getting back to business.

I looked over his shoulder at Warrick who was watching us very intently, "I don't know. Maybe it was the last run-in we had with Az and Warrick was confident I wasn't going to run from us as soon as I got the chance. Maybe my body was tired of all the fighting it's been doing and I finally let my walls down. Maybe it was overhearing the conversation between you two. Who knows."

Lou swung me around so Warrick was no longer in my line of sight, "Either way, I'm sure it's a relief. For both of you."

I studied his grey eyes debating on what I was about to say next. I cupped his cheek, "You'll take care of him, right? You'll take care of Warrick for me after I'm gone?"

"Not again," Lou groaned. "Why are we all acting like we're not going to make it out of this?"

"Need I remind you, you were the one who started it," I scolded. My tone immediately softened as I went on, "But, you will, won't you? No going back to the constant fighting you two were doing before me."

Lou leaned into my touch, "I've already made that promise. I'll even look after all your friends, or at least those who choose my world as home."

"Thank you," I pulled him into a hug. "Now, if you'll excuse me, I have someone impatiently waiting for my return."

I walked away, leaving Lou to join up with the rest of the group. The music had changed to something more happy and upbeat so that the couples were no longer paired off. I watched all of them dance together looking free of the stress occupying our lives. Warrick wrapped an arm around my waist while he watched them all, too, "This was a good call tonight."

"Yeah it was," I leaned my head back on his chest savoring this moment. It wasn't one I wanted to forget. Happiness was a rarity these days, so being able to see it on each of my friend's faces wasn't something I was going to let go of.

We stayed there a couple more hours, Warrick and I resuming our dancing every now and then. We honestly needed to pace ourselves – it was getting too easy to get caught up in one another so when those breaks rolled around, we took advantage of them to catch our breath and cool off. One of the bartenders I was friends with eventually stopped by our table to say hi. It made me feel better to see at least a couple of people I knew still around, but it only reminded me of how much was at stake.

After our last round on the dance floor, Warrick and I were ready to head back to the house. I leaned over to Lou, shouting over the volume of the music, "We're heading out. Want to ride with us?"

"With how you two have been all over each other?" Lou raised his eyebrows. Shaking his head, "No way. I'll squeeze into Joe and Bev's car. I don't think we'll be too far behind you guys, so enjoy your alone time while you can."

"Suit yourself," I said, but was relieved we'd be doing the drive home without anyone else in the car.

Warrick put a guiding hand on my lower back practically shoving me out of the club. *If you don't let up, I'm going to trip.*

Sorry, love. Just excited.

When I looked up at him, I found him staring down at me with nothing but love. We settled in the car, Warrick's hand immediately resting on my thigh. I put my hand over his then moved it up earning a raised eyebrow from Warrick. I gave him a wink then turned to look out the windshield as he left the parking lot, slamming on the gas to get us home as fast as possible.

As the city flew past us, Warrick inched his hand higher up on my thigh until his fingers were within reach of their intended destination. His pinky finger barely brushed over me, the sensation sending shivers throughout my body. My hand reflexively went to his arm. I glanced over to him to find Warrick smirking. He knew he had me right where he wanted me. His fingers continued teasing me, and the more they did, the more I had a hard time containing the moans. The first signs of pressure started building low within my core, but I wasn't ready to lose myself here. Not yet. "Warrick," I said breathlessly.

He slammed my car into park in the garage wasting no time with taking me in his arms to carry me into the house. He ran us up the stairs, taking them two at a time, then slammed the door to my room as he laid me on the bed. Warrick leaned in like he was going to kiss me, but stopped so he was hovering over my face. I grabbed his shirt to pull him closer, but he was bracing himself so well there was no chance of him budging. Warrick gave me the same smirk he wore in the car, "We've waited far too long for this, love. I want to make it last."

I opened my mouth to protest, but his lips were finally on mine. He dragged his tongue along my bottom lip before pulling it into his mouth to give it a little nibble. A hand cupped my neck, his thumb under my jaw to tilt it up. While he was working to deepen the kiss, I took advantage and teased his mouth with my tongue. I dragged my hand from his chest to his hips, reveling in his tight muscles before I rubbed my hand along his shaft, moaning at the thought of him in me. Warrick pulled back from the kiss to let out a moan, his eyes closed. I kept rubbing in a slow motion to draw the pleasure out of him until he put a hand on mine to stop me. He opened his eyes again, the glacial blue just poking around the black of his pupil, "You, love, you are an incredible creature who knows exactly how to make a man want more."

"I love you, Warrick," I said pulling him back to me. Our lips found each other again, our hands clinging to each other. One of his hands gripped my side, inching between my skin and the fabric of my dress just enough so his thumb could brush the bottom of my breast. The movement caused me to involuntarily arch into him, spreading my legs, and that was all he needed to move his fingers in between my legs. I moaned loudly getting lost in the sensations Warrick was sending throughout my body. When he stopped, my eyes snapped open, "Why?"

He chuckled, "Because I'm tired of this dress being in my way."

Before I could say anything, the sound of fabric tearing filled the room. He made quick work of my dress, now tossing the ripped pieces on the floor. Warrick's lips were back on my neck as he fervently kissed down my body. I entangled my hands in his hair, my voice husky, "I liked that dress."

I felt him grin against my stomach, "I can always buy you another one."

I was bracing myself for when his lips made their way in between my legs, but the feeling never came. I lifted my head finding Warrick staring at Az's name, a scowl fixed on his face. I immediately sat up, cradling his face, "Look at me, Warrick."

When he didn't listen, I moved my face closer to him, "Look at me." His eyes lifted to meet mine, now cold and distant. Very contrasting of what they were seconds ago. I rested my forehead against his, "This is exactly what Az wants. We can't let him win. Please, Warrick, let's pretend that damned scar doesn't exist and fuck until the sun comes up, okay?"

"He's going to pay for everything he did to you, love," Warrick responded, his voice cold and angry.

"We're not bringing him into the bedroom, okay?" I said.

He squeezed his eyes shut, slowly nodding. "Good," I said quietly. I moved my hands down to his shirt as I kissed one side of his neck followed by the other, inching the fabric up and pressing into his body to feel his skin on mine. I stood up, moving him to the bed underneath me. Warrick kept his eyes shut, but the tension oozed from his muscles as I continued to strip him.

I settled on top, gently sliding on to him. I marveled at the fullness now that Warrick was in me. I slowly started to move my hips, adding the occasional roll. He had completely forgotten whatever was going through his mind moments ago, his thoughts now consumed with the pleasure he was feeling. Warrick shared some of those feelings down the bond and I almost lost my control there. Sensing that, he flipped me under him, grinding his hips into me as he palmed my breasts, alternating from one to the other. Despite our slow pace to start, we both succumbed to our climaxes at the same time. Warrick collapsed on me, pulling me into him. Breathless, he said, "You are the most incredible woman, love. I never want to leave here."

"Let's freeze time, then. Let's stay entangled in one another for as long as we can," I mumbled into his chest. I hadn't felt so warmed and loved in a long time. Things would have to calm down eventually, right? I couldn't stand the thought of having any more interruptions to cause as long of a hiatus as this one.

Chapter 19

We were a mess of limbs the rest of the night as we continued getting lost in one another. It's safe to say we didn't get the most sleep, so when the sunlight poured into the room, we both groaned. Warrick turned his back towards the windows and I threw an arm over my eyes, "Why didn't we close the curtains last night?"

Instead of a verbal response, Warrick opted for using our bond. *I don't know, but I do know I'm going to sleep for a little while longer.*

I laid there for a few more moments letting my eyes adjust to the light before getting up and throwing on Warrick's shirt. I scrounged up some shorts that disappeared under his shirt after I slowly stuck my legs into them. Tying my hair up in a messy bun, I made my way downstairs, grimacing with each step. I wasn't entirely surprised to find Joe and Bev talking quietly amongst themselves when I got down there. Bev raised an eyebrow at me as she lifted her coffee mug to her lips, her grin poking out from under the edge of the mug.

"Morning," I mumbled making my way over to the coffee pot to get a mug of my own.

"Sleep well?" Joe asked.

I waited until I was settled in a chair across from them, swallowing my first sip, to answer with a chuckle, "Not a wink."

Bev giggled, "We know."

A giggle escaped my lips. I brought a hand up to cover my mouth. Joe shook his head, "I'd be surprised they didn't hear you tearing up your room all the way down in the city."

We all collected ourselves, sipping on our coffee. Bev let out a sigh and reached across the table to put a comforting hand on my arm, "Jennie wouldn't give us the details, but are you okay talking about what happened in the witch world? I see we got Mark back, but there's no Lilly. Whenever I asked them for more details, everyone just clammed up. Also, what happened to your mom?"

Jennie wasn't kidding about these two having questions. I blew out a breath, "That's a tough one."

"You don't have to talk about it if you don't want to. We just noticed everyone's super tense, too. Well, at least you all were until last night," Joe said.

"No, you guys should be brought up to speed," I shook my head. I tucked a foot under my legs then dove into the story, "I guess I should start from before we left for the witch world. So, you guys remember Az?"

"The asshole at Lou's?" Joe asked, frustration creeping into his tone.

"That's the one," I nodded. "Anyways, I decided to head over to Warrick's after our girl chat that night. Instead of finding Warrick, I ran into Az who tried to assault me. Luckily, Warrick got into his house at the right time. He shot Az, but that didn't have any effect on him. Az eventually left and Warrick made the decision that it was time to go. Before you all got to his office, we had a meeting with the world leaders and I got to see my dad. That's when I found out Az murdered my mom, hence the funeral coming up.

"Fast forward to when we got in the witch world. We found Mark pretty quickly, but there was no Lilly with him. He explained that she went to the dark side, literally. The witches do awful things to the people in their world and Lilly just dove right in."

"She's a witch, now?" Bev asked.

I slowly nodded, "Yup, and she had a grand old time when we were there, but I'll get to that in a second. After Mark and I caught up, Az made an appearance to flex his muscles a little bit. Thankfully, he backed down, but that put us all on high alert. I hunkered down in the house to minimize the chances of running into Az again while Jennie, Mark, and Lou got to enjoy the very few things to do in that world. Warrick ended up having to go on a solo mission to try to get a meeting with the witch leader, so Lou was left in charge.

"Eventually, we needed to venture out to get groceries which led to yet another Az run in. We managed to get away, but that night Az broke in here and kidnapped me."

Joe was leaning into the conversation fully engaged, "How was he able to do that with Lou being in charge? There's no way he would've left you if he felt the risk level was too high."

Bev nodded in agreement and I pinched my nose, "Lou and I got carried away with how much we drank that night. We fell asleep up in my room, but when Az showed up, Lou wouldn't wake up. I tried waking him, but then Az pulled out a gun aiming at Lou. I definitely didn't want Lou to take a bullet when he couldn't defend himself, and by making that choice, Az had the perfect opportunity to grab me."

That was the one detail I was wanting to keep to myself because I knew this would cause tempers to flare. I turned my head slightly in the direction of the stairs to see if there was any movement. I let out a breath when I didn't hear anything. *Why didn't you say anything about this sooner?* Warrick asked through the bond.

I did my best to keep my facial expression the same as I responded, *Because nothing happened and we don't need to worry about that right now. You know Az has access to weapons, this isn't anything new.* I gave my head a subtle shake to focus on the couple in front of me and went on with my story, "Az took me back to his apartment where he continually drugged me, then was able to finish what he had started at Warrick's. After that, he had some fun with knives and took me to the witch leader where I was reunited with Warrick. Come to find out, the witch leader and Az were already working together and just wanted to toy with Warrick. During the time Warrick was on his mission, he was apparently locked up by the witches where they assaulted him, Lilly included. Lilly, who was also enjoying seeing me in pain, is fully on their side, unfortunately.

"After the witch world, we popped back into the werewolf world, as you know. Warrick and I went to his childhood home to try to find something that would lead to a way to take Az down. The reason we went down that path was because it had been mentioned before that their parents were the only ones who knew what Az's weaknesses were. The hope was that they would've written that down somewhere, but when we got there, Az was already in the house. Him and Warrick had a scuffle, but we came away with a journal. We knew Az handed it over too easily which we confirmed why after we didn't find anything in there that hinted at a weakness. Now, we're here and you're all caught up."

Joe ran a hand through his hair leaning back in his chair while Bev swiped at her eyes, "We missed so much."

"It's okay, Bev," I started with the hopes of keeping their guilt at bay. "We're happy you were in a safe place. We were able to rest easier knowing that. Did Raf give you the all-clear for jumping when you're trying for kids?"

They looked at each other, a silent message passing between the two, when Joe answered, "We're putting a pause on trying for kids until after this war. We wanted to be available to help. I would lose my mind if Bev was pregnant right now, and you know how she is. She isn't going to want to sit on the sidelines."

"I get it," I nodded, putting a hand over Bev's. "You know you guys have already helped, right?"

"You know that's not what I mean, Val," Joe closed his eyes. "I know we're only two people, but that's two more people to join the effort."

"We appreciate that, but before we agree, I need to know your background. How can you contribute in a way we need it the most?" Warrick asked, his voice making us all jump. I glanced over my shoulder watching as he sat in a chair, shirtless but not looking as tired as I would have thought. I blushed a little thinking back from last night, but my focus was quickly redirected back to the conversation.

Joe cleared his throat, sitting up a little straighter, "I've been out for a while now, but I was in the military. I have some combat experience."

"You do?" I asked. "Daryl never mentioned that."

Joe waived me off, "Like I said, it was a while ago and not really a time I like to talk about. Either way, I have experience."

Warrick nodded in his direction before looking at Bev, "And you?"

Bev twisted her hands together, glancing over to Joe who gave her a nod, "Actually, Joe and I met in the military. I was combat medic, so I have a medical background."

Warrick gave another nod, his tone businesslike now, "We'll talk more about that later. Thank you for letting me know."

I studied my friends a little more carefully. For them to not talk about the time they served, it must've been brutal. Before I got the chance to say anything else, Jennie and Lou emerged talking quietly. They looked happy and closer than usual. Warrick threw an arm over the back of my chair and leaned back, smirking in their direction, "Have a good time last night?"

Jennie blushed, not able to say anything as she made a beeline for the coffeemaker. Lou casually sat in the chair next to Warrick then brought his grey eyes to mine before shifting them to Warrick, "I should be asking you the same."

Mark stumbled out of the basement, yawning, before Warrick could clap back, "Love was in the air last night. Makes me feel left out."

Jennie's mouthful of coffee spewed all over the sink. Fighting a laugh, I asked, "Something you want to share with the class?"

"No," she answered, her tone higher than usual. I gave her a wink thinking back to a conversation we had about Lou earning a blush in return. Bev thankfully changed topics and started talking about something random. The conversation didn't drift back to how the rest of last night went or what we needed to focus on for this war. We eventually started getting ready for the day, people filtering out of the house to take care of whatever business they wanted.

A couple of days passed following the same pattern: We wake up and enjoy breakfast then everyone leaves the house to do whatever they needed to. My friends had all made the tough decision to move on from Earth and call Lupusantha home. They figured out there wasn't anything really left of their homes and their jobs had already been filled for the businesses that were still around. As the day of the funeral approached, I could feel my grief settling in. I didn't want to spend a lot of time with people, locking myself away in my room or venturing to my parent's room across the hall to hold my mother's things close. Warrick made sure to keep me fed and keep people away if I didn't want to be around them.

I was getting ready for the funeral, taking a break to sit on my bed to watch the light snow fall when my dad knocked on the door. He was in his formal uniform, hat in his hand, "Hey, Val-pal. How're you holding up?"

In a distant voice, I answered, "I think it's finally settling in that she's gone. I'll never see her roll her eyes at one of your jokes again."

My dad had joined me on the bed, dropping his head as he let out a soft laugh, "I'll miss that. There's so much about her I'll miss, but we're giving her a good send off today. I just wish I could've been around more."

I looked at him, "What do you mean?"

My dad sighed, "I've been so caught up in this damned war I hardly had any time to spend with her. If I hadn't been so consumed with everything, maybe I could've prevented it."

"Unfortunately, there's nothing we can change," Warrick said quietly from where he was leaning against the door. "Don't beat yourself up, James. She should've never had her life ripped from her like that. It's unacceptable and we'll make him pay for what he did."

"You're right," my dad nodded, closing his eyes. He took a deep breath then stood up, holding out a hand for me, "Ready?"

"It's time already?" I glanced between my dad and Warrick.

They only nodded. I took my dad's hand, straightening out my black dress. My dad led me over to Warrick who held my coat out for me. I graciously accepted it and let him lead me down the stairs. We all piled in the cars waiting for us outside, my friends in the ones behind us. I rested my head against Warrick's chest focusing on keeping the tears at bay.

You can let them out, love, Warrick's gentle voice filled my mind.

Not yet, I replied.

He tightened his comforting grip on me. The drive to the cemetery wasn't long, but it felt like it took ages. Despite all the destruction around the city, the cemetery had been untouched. *At least Az had enough sense to respect the dead.* There was already a crowd gathered around the site we'd be lowering my mother's casket into. When our cars pulled up, they all turned watching us expectantly. My dad was the first to get out of the car, buttoning up his jacket and coming around to open our door. My friends all piled out of theirs leaving me as the last person to step onto the grass.

Warrick turned around to help me get out of the car. I kept my gaze trained on the ground because if I looked at any of their faces, I would've lost any semblance of control I had. Every step we took closer to the rows of chairs made me grip Warrick's hand even tighter. I felt Lou's fingers brush against mine, but when I glanced in his direction, Jennie had already tugged him closer to her. Warrick gave my hand a squeeze to let me know he picked up on that, too, and directed my dad to my other side where we grabbed each other's hand.

We made our way to the front row, everyone taking their seats as we sat down. The service started, but I couldn't focus on what was being said. Instead, I kept my attention on the white roses surrounding her casket. Every now and then, Warrick would squeeze my hand bringing me back to the present as a way to get me to pay attention when something new was happening. A couple of people sang a beautiful song my mom loved and would often hum around the house, several people said some kind words, and our pastor guided the service along.

When it came time for us to place roses on top of her casket, I was able to lift myself out of my seat. My dad went first, the tears dripping from his face. Some of his close military buddies clapped him on the shoulder and pulled him into a hug after he returned to his seat. My dad motioned for me to go, and as I placed the rose on the wood, I whispered, "I hope you find peace, mom. I love you. There won't be a day I won't miss you."

I glanced up, taking in the sun starting to set and caught a glimpse of a grim-looking Az watching on. He had tucked himself in between some trees, barely visible. Catching me staring, Az gave a subtle nod then went on staring at the ground. I returned to my seat scanning Warrick's face to see if had any idea Az was here. He gave nothing away on the outside, but I could pick up on his alertness through the bond as he moved to place his rose on the casket despite never knowing my mom. Everyone else filed from their seats to do the same thing until it came time to lower her casket in the ground. We all watched as it made its slow descent into the freshly dug hole, the tears finally breaking free. Everyone was sniffling, wiping tears with the tissues that had been distributed prior to the service.

The pastor announced where the reception was going to be held, signaling the end of our time here. People made their way to their cars. Warrick started to pull me towards him to walk with my dad, but I reached for our bond, *I'm going to stay here for a couple more minutes, but you two head to the car. I won't be long, I promise.*

Warrick hesitated but eventually headed to the car. I watched him until the door closed knowing he was keeping an eye on me. As soon as I was sure I was alone, I squatted down in front of where we had just lowered the casket. Keeping my voice low, I said, "Mom, I'm sorry for all the hell I put you through when I was a teenager and in my adult years, especially all the attitude I threw at you when you would catch me sneaking back in. I'm sorry for all the late nights you stayed up waiting for me. I'm especially sorry I wasn't around a lot in your last days. I hope dad at least put your mind at ease and told you I was safe. I'm going to miss you like crazy. I love you and hope you're finally at peace."

I slowly stood up, wiping more tears away. I caught a glimpse of Az out of the corner of my eye. I straightened my shoulders and turned my attention to him. Az made no move to come closer much to my relief. Instead, he stayed in the same spot I had seen him in earlier still wearing the same grim expression. He met my gaze, giving me a little finger wave. All of a sudden, I felt a new presence poking at my mind. It was similar to the pressure I had felt before Warrick was able to talk to me through the bond, but this time, I had no idea what was causing it. My hand went up to my head, unsure of what was happening when Az's voice came through loud and clear, *It's not going to make up for what I did, but I'm sorry.*

Panic flooded me. I couldn't move, frozen to my spot. I was now a sitting duck completely exposed. Az had every opportunity to attack if he wanted. There's no way he should be able to talk to me like we have a bond. I can't be fated to him *and* Warrick. Seeing my reaction made Az grin, and if he could talk to me through my head, then he could likely sense how I was feeling. He started to take a step towards me, but Warrick shouted, "Val!"

I heard the car door slam, the sound of feet pounding the ground, but I couldn't look. I could only keep my attention on Az who was no longer making a move towards me. He scowled at the sight of Warrick right as I felt Warrick's arms wrap around me.

"It's time to go," Warrick said softly guiding me towards the car.

"He talked to me," I said, my voice quiet and distant.

Warrick scooped me into my arms, "I know."

"How can he talk to me?" I asked finally able to look up at Warrick. He shook his head, brow furrowing. He didn't know, either. Warrick got us settled in the car and we headed in the direction of the reception.

My dad's voice cut through the fog, "He has some nerve showing his face here, of all places."

I looked over at him. His shoulders were tense and he was clenching his jaw as he stared out his window. My dad slowly turned to me, "What was that all about?"

"Warrick and I are fated," I blurted. "I kind of told you about this back at Warrick's office."

"The werewolf tradition?"

"Yes," I nodded. "Part of that entails being able to communicate non-verbally, through our minds. Warrick and I just had a breakthrough with that not too long ago, so I'm still getting used to it. Apparently, though, Az is now able to do that."

My dad looked from me to Warrick, "Is that why you ran out of the car?"

"Yes," Warrick answered.

"Does this mean you're fated to two wolves?" my dad asked, returning his attention to me.

"I-I shouldn't be. It's not possible, right?" I looked at Warrick.

His brows were still furrowed, the gears in his mind turning to process what this could mean. My dad, being impatient, asked, "Does this mean you two aren't truly fated?"

Warrick ran a hand through his hair, "We're definitely fated to each other. I didn't think it was possible for two wolves to be fated to the same person, but there's not exactly a lot of information out there about fating since it's so rare."

"So what the hell does it mean?" my dad raised his voice, making me jump. He's never done that, always one who's calm and composed. Seeing my reaction, my dad sighed, "Sorry, Val-pal. My head's all over the place right now and I'm not liking the chance of you being linked so closely with the man who murdered my wife and has threatened my daughter."

"It's okay," I mumbled quietly. Warrick gave my hand a squeeze.

"We'll figure it out, James," Warrick said. "I don't know how, or when, but we'll get it figured out and I'll keep her safe in the meantime."

The car pulled up to where the reception was being held, ending our conversation. We made our way in, everyone falling silent as my dad thanked everyone for showing their support during this time. You know, the typical things people say after losing a loved one. The two of us stood together while everyone formed a line to share their condolences. Every now and then, I'd pick up on the whispers and side glances. No one knew what happened to me. All they knew was I had gone missing for an extended period of time, then showed up after my mom was killed with two mystery men. My dad grew more tense as the night went on only telling me he was picking up on what people were saying, too. All I wanted at this point was for the night to be over, to curl up in Warrick's arms and shut the world out for a little while.

Once we finished eating, I rested my head on my dad's shoulder, "I think I'm ready to get out of here. Is that alright with you?"

He only nodded before going back to the conversation I had interrupted. I grabbed Warrick's hand, *Time to get out of here. I can't stand listening to people's gossip.*

Warrick didn't hesitate. He quietly told Lou we were heading back to the house before following me out. I gave a couple of hugs to the people I was closest to outside of my friend group, but that was it. As soon we got outside, I took in a deep breath. Warrick started leading us towards the car as he asked, "Tired of hearing people talk about you?"

"You have no idea," I mumbled getting into the car.

We started heading in the direction of home. I leaned my head back against the headrest and closed my eyes, "The people in there have always been nosey. They know my mom was murdered, but now that I'm back, I'm sure all they think is that I had something to do with it."

"James was getting upset, too, I'm assuming for the same reason," Warrick observed.

"Yeah, it's not what anyone would like to hear when they're putting their wife in the ground."

We spent the rest of the ride back in silence. By the time we got into the house, I was starting to fall asleep. Warrick carried me up to my room, helping me get settled into bed. He pulled up a chair to my side looking lost in thought. I reached out for him, Warrick entangling our fingers, "Thank you for being there for us tonight."

"I wouldn't have had it any other way, love," Warrick said, giving me another one of those soft smiles. "Now, rest. You need it."

He leaned back in his chair not quite letting my hand go as I asked, "What are we going to do about Az?"

"That's a problem for another day. Rest," Warrick ordered.

I sighed to show I wasn't happy with being ordered around, but all the fight left me and I quickly fell into a light sleep. At some point, I heard my friends come back home. They each filtered in one at a time checking in on me. Warrick would tell them each the same thing – I was doing as expected and just needed some rest before falling asleep at the reception. He didn't mention anything about Az or what people were whispering, although I'm sure they heard it to since the whispers weren't exactly discreet.

The last thing I expected was for the bomb sirens to be going off. I was jolted from my sleep, Warrick carrying me down the stairs. He kept muttering under his breath, but I wasn't awake enough to pick up on what he was saying. I heard my friends running around to close the house down like we had done the last time. Curtains were drawn, lights were shut off, and we all ended up down in the bunker. Everyone had gone to individual rooms to start, but eventually joined me and Warrick.

I blinked the sleep away. At least this time everyone wasn't looking as worried. We all knew by now we'd be transferred to the same world if we were in the same room, so Jennie and Mark pulled in a couple of mattresses, lining the floor in case we were going to have to sleep in here again. When they were done, Jennie put her hands on her hips, "It's a good thing we like each other so much."

Joe and Bev laughed a little at that, nervously looking between Lou and Warrick. Warrick sat next to me while everyone else got comfortable. He ran a hand over his face when Lou asked, "What happened back there?"

"Where?" Warrick responded.

"At the reception," Lou answered.

I let out a small laugh, "I got tired of everyone's bullshit and wanted to leave."

"What was going on?" Jennie asked.

"Everyone there kept gossiping about me," I told her, not wanting to get into specifics.

"They didn't have anything nice to say, Jennie. At all. I'm surprised you didn't hear any of it," Bev sighed.

"Warrick," Lou started. "Was there something else that happened?"

"What do you mean?" Warrick asked back.

"When I was asking about what happened, you asked 'where.' Does that mean something happened at the service?"

Warrick didn't answer right away. We both weren't sure if wanted people to know about Az showing up and what he was able to do. While he debated on what to say, we felt the rumble of bombs hitting. They weren't too far from the house which meant there was a very real possibility we would be sucked from this world to somewhere else. Probably a way for Az to buy some more time by keeping us from getting closer to having an advantage. *I wonder if my dad had any idea this would be happening tonight.*

Probably not, love, Warrick added. I didn't realize my thoughts were not entirely private, but I shouldn't be surprised. Warrick continued, *I think this is all Az.*

"Are you guys going to loop us into the conversation?" Lou asked impatiently.

"What are you talking about? No one's saying anything," Mark said.

Lou scoffed, "Perks of being fated, you can talk to each other telepathically. They're trying to figure out what to tell us."

Annoyed, I said, "I was actually worried about my dad with these bombs falling around us. He's typically looped in, but he most likely wasn't for this one."

Warrick put a hand on my knee to calm me down. "After you all left to go to the reception, Val spotted Az who was able to utilize a bond," Warrick explained.

"Shit," Lou said running a hand through his hair. "He's fated to Val?"

"That's what we're trying to figure out," Warrick answered, his voice quiet.

I hadn't considered how this would impact him, but as I studied Warrick, I could tell the potential of me being fated to him and Az was starting to eat him alive. This had to be another one of his head games. It had to be. Az was the one person who truly scared Warrick, and Az was more than aware of the effect he has on his little brother. He was also the one person who could rip the people Warrick loved out of his life. I tentatively reached out with our bond to have my suspicions confirmed: Warrick was terrified of Az getting closer to taking me away from him.

Chapter 20

The bombs thankfully didn't last all night. When we emerged from the bunker, there was a collective sigh of relief seeing the same landscape outside the windows as what we had yesterday. Sirens wailed in the distance presumably heading towards the multiple plumes of smoke we could see coming from the city, the first responders and military to help take care of the aftermath, serving as another reminder of what was going on around us.

Lou watched Warrick and I carefully. I don't know what was running through his head, but it couldn't be anything good judging by the way he was watching us, and more specifically, me. It was almost as if he couldn't trust I wasn't going to reveal all our secrets to Az. Little did Lou know, Az could get his hands on just about whatever information he wanted regardless of whether or not I volunteered any of it.

Warrick put his hand on the small of my back, leaning closer to me so I would be the only one to hear him, "Meet me up in your room in a couple of minutes, love. There's something I need to talk to you about."

I gave him a quick nod then a kiss on his cheek. He disappeared up the stairs while I stared down the clock to make sure I waited. Jennie's concerned face filled my vision, "What does it mean, Az being able to talk to you through a bond?"

I shrugged, "I have no idea. Trust me, Warrick and I aren't withholding anything about this. It's throwing us off as much as it is you guys." I glanced in Lou's direction only for him to quickly redirect his gaze out the window. I went on, bringing my focus back to Jennie, "I just have to be careful with what goes through my mind, no matter what. Right now, I don't feel him there, just Warrick."

Her eyes widened a little bit, "Is that part of the bond? Feeling them?"

I nodded, "Yeah, just enough to let me know he's there. Look, you have as much information as I do. I'm gonna change."

I gave her arm a gentle squeeze then made my escape. I walked into my room, pausing in the doorway. Warrick was sitting out on the balcony, the curtains fluttering with the slight breeze. His icy blue gaze rested on me as he motioned for me to join him. I grabbed a throw blanket then settled into the empty seat next to him. Warrick turned his attention back in the direction of the smoke rising in the north. There were a couple of small fires not too far from the house in the pockmarked ground. That was the extent of the damage near us, but who knew what the places further away looked like.

"Everyone else will soon be popping up here," Warrick mumbled.

I watched him a moment before asking, "Where will they go?"

"Up the road a little ways. I had Lou scope it out. There's no one out there and he found a few empty, relatively untouched buildings they can sleep in. My plan is to have Lou gather some supplies so they're comfortable. We'll need to meet with them soon, but I'd like to get a handle on the Az situation before you get pulled into that meeting," Warrick explained.

I sighed. Here I was going back to being one more thing Warrick had to worry about. I played with the edge of the blanket a little bit, "Right, the Az situation. Any ideas on how we can tackle that?"

"A few," Warrick answered. "But, I also wanted to see how you were doing, love. After yesterday."

I squeezed my eyes shut, "I'm not going to lie, Warrick, it still stings. I'm sure my dad is in the same boat. Whatever meeting you pull together, make sure you give my dad some time."

His hand was on my knee, his face now occupying my view, "You don't have to worry about that. Besides, everyone will need some time to adjust. I just more wanted to give you a head's up that Liam will be back."

I gave a cold chuckle, "Just one more thing."

Warrick and I talked strategy for a little while longer until I was too cold to stay outside any longer. We joined up with everyone downstairs, a heavy silence sitting on our shoulders. It didn't take long, however, for Mark to do his thing and start cracking jokes. Pretty soon we were all laughing and feeling back to our lighthearted selves, the ones we thought we left in the club.

We let a couple of hours go by where we didn't have a care in the world. After we had finished eating lunch, I got dressed and had my hand on the doorknob to go out to the garage when Jennie's head popped up, "Where are you going?"

"I figured I'd go check on my apartment. If it's still standing, then I'm hoping I can grab a few things so they don't get destroyed in the next attack," I answered. "You guys all got to go check on things, so now it's my turn."

"Want some company?" Jennie asked.

"Sure," I nodded. Warrick started to stand up, but I waved him off, "You stay here. Relax. It'll be good for me and Jennie to have some girl time, anyways."

Warrick narrowed his eyes a little bit before shaking his head, "Let me know if you run into trouble, love."

"Aye, aye, captain," I gave him a little mock salute.

On the familiar path to my apartment, I kept telling myself not to get my hopes up in case the building wasn't accessible or just wiped off the map. I didn't care so much about the clothes and things like that, but I did care about all my pictures and all things Gabriel.

"You were right," Jennie said, snapping my attention back to the present.

I quickly glanced at her before returning my attention back to the road, "What are you talking about?"

"About being with a werewolf," she smiled. "There's nothing like it."

I laughed, "And?"

"It was probably the best night of my life. Lou really knows how to pay attention to what a girl wants," Jennie said.

I patted her knee, "Well, I'm glad you two had a good time."

We pulled up to the parking garage, relief washing over me at the sight of the building still standing untouched. I parked in my usual spot, "It shouldn't take me too long. You good with just waiting down here?"

Jennie nodded, "Yup!"

It was like I had only been gone a couple of days rather than months on end with how quickly my old habits came back to me. I shook my head as I slid the key into the lock then pushed open the door. I scanned the tiny studio apartment only now realizing how much I had missed this space. I loved my parent's house, but nothing beat my own place. Except, it felt a little off. I started to chalk it up to how similar Az's apartment back in the witch's world matched this space, but that wasn't alleviating the uneasy feeling growing in my stomach.

I slowly stepped in, closing the door behind me. Almost everything looked the way I had left it except for a leather jacket draped over the back of one of the dining room chairs. It wasn't mine and it wasn't Gabriel's either. Brows furrowed, I walked over to the fridge in the galley kitchen. It wasn't full, but it wasn't empty, either, which is how I left it. I whirled around, my senses on full alert, now. I walked over to the set of drawers I kept all my clothes in, opening one at a time starting at the bottom. Each drawer was filled with my clothes still folded neatly, until I got to the top two drawers. They held clothes that definitely didn't belong to me. I pulled out a black shirt to hold it up. It was a man's shirt, bigger than anything I'd wear.

"What the hell?" I muttered to myself. I put the shirt back in the same way I had found it then closed the drawer as I continued to scan the space. I walked over to the bathroom finding someone else's toiletries scattered about. Someone else was living here, but who? I walked over to the bed, sitting on the edge of it. I know I haven't been around and everyone thought I was missing, but if my landlord gave the space to someone else, wouldn't he have trashed all my things?

The questions kept piling on as I continued looking around from my spot on the bed. As soon as my eyes landed on the couple of shelves I filled with pictures, I knew exactly who was in here. I got back to my feet, reaching for one of the frames that didn't belong to me. It was the same picture I stared at back in the witch world, the one in the bedroom across the hall from the office where we ran into Az: the one of me and Az laughing while we were out on one of our rides. My fingers traced our faces before I set the frame down. I could feel the panic rising in my throat. Who knew how long I had to grab things with Az living here. He could come back at any moment and then it would be the witch world all over again.

I shook my head then went rifling through the drawers again. "Where is it?" I muttered over and over again while shoving my clothes to the side.

I was ready to focus my search elsewhere when my fingers brushed the key to my storage unit. I held it up, smiling. If there was only one thing I grabbed out of here today, this would be it. I put everything back the way I found it then ran back down to the car. When I jumped in and hastily turned the car on, Jennie looked at me confused, "I thought you were grabbing things."

"I really only wanted one thing," I started, intentionally leaving out what I had discovered about Az living there. "We're going to my storage unit. I have a couple of boxes in there, but most importantly, I have Gabriel's bike and I'm not leaving that here to get destroyed. Besides, I'll come back for the rest later."

"You still have that thing?"

"Sure do," I nodded, gradually increasing speed to put as much distance between my apartment and us. "Are you good with driving my car back?"

"Sure?" Jennie answered. "Can you even drive his bike?"

A nervous laugh escaped me, "We'll find out."

"Wait," Jennie put a hand up. "Have you never driven his bike?"

"Nope, only had the luxury of riding on the back," I said. I knew his was more powerful than mine, but there was no way I was leaving it behind. Not when I spent so much time maintaining it. Despite the nerves, I couldn't help but smile at the thought of finally getting to drive it.

"You're crazy, you know that?"

I smiled at her, slowing as I pulled in front of the storage unit. It was hard not to contain my excitement at seeing this place untouched, too. With how crazy things have been, these little wins felt like major victories.

I made quick work of the lock while Jennie took her time getting out of the car. I yanked the door up to reveal Gabriel's bike still covered along with the few boxes I had lining the sides of the unit. Jennie started loading the boxes into the car while I inched the cover off the bike. His Ducati Panigale V4 gleamed, with its all black paint job. It was in perfect condition as if we drove it off the lot yesterday. I ran my hands along the bike then did a little happy dance. Jennie shook her head, laughing at me.

When she finished loading up my car, she stuck her hand out, "Alright, Val, give me your keys."

I gladly handed them over then ran over to my car to throw on my extra set of gear. As I was sliding on the helmet, Jennie started my car, calling out the window, "Be careful! I'll see you back at the house."

"Thank you for coming with me!" I responded as she pulled away. I pushed the bike out of the unit, closing the door behind me. I threw my leg over and settled into the seat. The second I turned the key, the engine roared to life in a way that convinced me it was happy to be ridden again. I patted the tank then eased the bike towards the office building. It definitely had more power than mine, wanting to fly rather than move at a snail's pace.

After I had let the office know I was done using the storage unit, I pulled the bike into an empty parking lot. The engine still running, I rolled my shoulders back tilting my head to one side then the other to stretch out. It wasn't a huge jump, but I wanted to take a moment to get a little more used to Gabriel's bike before speeding home. I eased out of the friction zone, shifting into the next gear as I picked up speed. I took a couple of laps around the parking lot focusing on building my confidence with how this bike worked versus the one that has essentially become an extension of myself.

It started getting darker, the sun dipping below the horizon, and I ripped my helmet off cursing I didn't have a clear visor to change out. *Love,* Warrick's voice purred in my head. *It's a full moon tonight and you're not home yet.*

Shit ..., I sent back. *I'm on my way.*

He didn't have to say anything, but we both knew how big of a risk Az is. My mind immediately went back to what Az did to Warrick the last time they had changed. There is no way in hell I wanted to be trapped out here with a wolf who could cause that much harm. Besides, I could only run for so long.

I threw my helmet back on glancing in the direction of the moon. Warrick wasn't wrong, but why hadn't he said something earlier? Why hadn't he at least given me a warning not to stay out so late? I shook my head to clear my thoughts turning my attention to the road ahead of me. As I eased out of the parking lot, a howl pierced the air. It was a lot closer than I would've liked. I felt for our bond, but something was off about it. Our bond felt more angry, chaotic than the calm, warm place I've become familiar with. I guess this is what happens when he's a wolf.

I gave the engine a rev then started the trek home. It was time to be a big girl – I could handle this bike. I kept my speed lower, still not fully comfortable with opening up. I made it halfway back to the house when I caught something moving in one of my mirrors. Something large and black was coming at me quick. At first, I thought it was Warrick coming to escort me back to the house, but as the wolf approached, I very quickly realized I was wrong. This wolf may have had a black coat, but there were bands of white fur circling his ankles. The blue eyes I've come to love weren't the ones staring me down; rather, this wolf had violet eyes that practically glowed. I knew without a doubt this was Az.

"Quit checking him out, it's time to go," I scolded myself as I pulled on the throttle, shooting forward. I hadn't been quite comfortable going at this speed when I was driving around the parking lot, but now wasn't the time for that.

Az picked up his speed to match me, his paws thumping in a steady rhythm on the ground. I kept watching as the number on the speedometer ticked up in between the glances over my shoulder to the wolf running next to me. He snapped at my leg a couple of times making me wobble. Az's teeth were bared, saliva flying out of his mouth, as he motioned to snap at me again. His teeth grazed my leg and I gunned it. Az tried to pick up his speed even more, but he was quickly distracted by two other wolves jumping out: Lou and Warrick. I kept an eye trained on my mirrors watching as the three wolves seemingly blended into one, a mess of fur and teeth. I could hear the snarling and fighting over the sound of the bike, but it quickly faded the more distance I put between myself and them.

I pulled into the garage, already opening, practically beckoning for me to hurry up to get inside. I ran inside throwing the helmet towards the couch before examining my leg. The one thing I didn't want to happen was to get bit by a werewolf. I could take the torture, the cuts on my body. What I couldn't take was being changed into a creature I didn't want to become. That would be the last straw.

Jennie's steps thudded up the stairs from the basement, "What's wrong?"

My head snapped up, "What?"

"I heard a noise and wasn't sure what it was," she said, glancing at my helmet still spinning on the floor. "Now I know. You good?"

I followed her gaze down to where my hands were checking my leg. Thankfully, there was nothing there, only a small rip in my pants. My skin was untouched. Az's teeth didn't have the chance to make it through. I clutched my heart, standing up now, while breathing a sigh of relief, "Yeah, I am now."

She gave me a puzzled look, "Tell me more about your ride home downstairs."

Mark and Joe were in the middle of a pool game while Jennie and Bev were snacking and watching the guys. I pulled up a seat, collapsing into it. I closed my eyes, catching my breath, but Jennie didn't want to wait for me any longer, "Lou and Warrick were chilling out in the backyard keeping an eye on things then suddenly ran off. You come in the house looking like a bat out of hell. Was Gabriel's bike that much different than yours?"

With my eyes still closed, I answered, "No, well, I mean it's more to handle, but I was getting the hang of it. I would've been fine coming home, but Az showed up chasing after me."

"You were faster than him, right?" Jennie asked, eyes wide.

"Not at first," I shook my head, sitting up now. "I wasn't comfortable with going that fast yet, but then he started trying to bite my leg so I wasted no time with getting out of there. He almost got me to wreck the bike with his snapping, so I figured it would be better if I wrecked from going too fast rather than from being attacked by a wolf."

The sound of the balls hitting against each other stopped, the guys now paying attention to me. Jennie shook her head, "He didn't get you, did he?"

I lifted up my leg to point out the small tear in my pants, "Nope, just my clothes. Lou and Warrick showed up at the right time to let me get out of there."

"I'm glad you made it home safely," Bev smiled at me. Jennie nodded in agreement, popping a chip in her mouth.

"You have a new bike now? Can we see it?" Mark asked. Joe pretended to roll his eyes, but I could tell he wanted to see it, too.

I grinned at them, "Sure."

Me and the guys headed up the stairs while Jennie and Bev resumed their conversation. As soon as they could see the bike, Joe and Mark ran over to it, admiring every little detail. We talked a little bit about it then they went back to their pool game. I joined up with the rest of them for a while then moved up to the living room to have a moment to myself. I was still shaken up from having Az pursue me like that. I was too close to having my life completely changed in a way I didn't want. Again. I knew I didn't want to be a werewolf. I also knew I didn't want to wreck Gabriel's bike when I had just gotten my hands back on it.

I ran a shaky hand through my hair just in time for my thoughts to shift to Lou and Warrick. Worry flooded me. There was no way I wanted to see Warrick in the condition he was the last time he had a face-off with his brother. The closest hospital was still too far away and it would take too long to get Raf here. Then, there was Lou. He couldn't afford to get hurt either for the same reasons. I had to worry about two wolves, now, which meant I was in for a long night.

I spent the entire night on the couch staring out the backdoors watching for any signs of Warrick and Lou. My friends had all made their way to their rooms several hours after I had gotten home. Bev offered to sit with me, but I waived her off. I didn't want to bring her any more into the craziness than what she already was.

I nodded off a couple of times, but any bump or sound startled me awake. When the first rays of sun poked up, Warrick and Lou were walking back, no marks on them. They were unscathed. I yanked the door open, catching them both off-guard. Running out there, I pulled them into a hug, mumbling into their bare chests, "You have no idea how happy I am to see you both standing, not a scratch on you."

Warrick's arm tightened, pulling me more to him as he chuckled, "Az was more trying to be a nuisance than an actual threat, but it's good to see you, too, love."

"It's a little hard to believe that when he was snapping at me," I said.

Warrick held me at arm's length, his eyes scanning my body for any scratches or a bit. When I glanced at Lou, he was doing the same. I put a hand on Warrick's chest, "I'm fine."

"He didn't bite you?" Lou asked.

I turned to lead the way back in the house, "No. He just snagged my pant leg a little bit."

They both let out a breath of relief. The two of them headed upstairs to get cleaned up and dressed while everyone else was still sleeping. I sat on my bed waiting for Warrick to come out of the bathroom while watching the snowflakes start falling.

The door to the bathroom opened. I kept my focus outside, but asked, "Why didn't you give me a head's up that it was going to be full moon last night?"

"Didn't think I was going to have to worry about you being out, love," Warrick calmly answered. "The important thing is that we're all okay."

I turned to look at him. He hadn't bothered to cover himself, his strong muscles fully on display. Something stirred low inside me, but I had to keep it together. Warrick smirked, "Like what you see, love?"

I slowly nodded and he started making his way over to me, a predatory grin on his face. His lips were on mine and we fell back onto the bed, consumed with each other.

Warrick and I headed downstairs after he confirmed everyone else was down there. The minute my foot hit the first step, I looked over my shoulder at him, "I have to get the rest of my stuff, Warrick. I don't know how long my apartment is going to be there."

"It's just things, love, they can be replaced."

"There are some things that can never be replaced," I shot back.

We made our way over to the table where everyone else was sitting, trying to act like they weren't listening to every word. Warrick continued over to the island where there was still some food laid out grabbing both of us a plate, "I don't want you going back over there and giving Az another chance to grab you."

"This isn't the time for that conversation," I said quietly. I made a motion in the direction of everyone else and thankfully Warrick picked up on the signal.

Lou glanced between us, but I shook my head and he kept quiet. Mark eventually broke the silence, throwing out a couple of jokes while he asked Warrick and Lou what it was like to be a wolf. Jennie and Bev picked up where they left off in their conversation, and I leaned back in my chair closing my eyes again.

I must have dozed off, the lack of sleep catching up to me, because my eyes opened to a cleared table and poker chips being stacked into neat piles in front of everyone, including me. I glanced over to Bev, "How long had I been out?"

"A couple of hours," she smiled at me. "You good with playing a round?"

"Sure," I yawned. "Just need a moment to wake up."

"You'll have that time, love," Warrick said, sitting next to me. "Lou's just about to explain the rules."

"Mmm," I said, rubbing my eyes.

Lou pulled out the cards and was just about to dive into how to play my chosen game when Warrick's phone started buzzing non-stop. Lou eyed him carefully as he asked, "Everything good?"

Warrick studied the screen, brows furrowing. Once he read through the messages, he ran upstairs. "Where's the device, Lou?" Warrick called over his shoulder.

"What?" Lou asked, starting to frantically look around.

"The device!" Warrick yelled. He was already coming back down the stairs throwing a jacket on.

Remember what we talked about, Warrick's voice said softly through our bond.

Just give me an Oscar for the performance I'm about to deliver, I sent back.

"What's going on, Warrick?" I stood up, concerned. I headed over to the couch, tossing the device to Lou.

Warrick came right up to me, pocketing the device Lou handed him, then cradled my face, "Some shit's going down and I need to head back for a little bit."

I put my hands over his, "Will you tell me what's going on? Please? I don't want to think you're running straight back into a dangerous situation. What if Az is laying a trap?"

"Holly's just being a pain in the ass. I need to go help my pack out so she leaves the company alone," Warrick answered, thumb stroking my cheek. "Come with me, love. Az shouldn't be there and I can keep an eye on you."

Stick to the plan, love, Warrick reminded me. *I need you to keep selling it.*

I gave my head a small shake remembering the script we went over, "No, I should be here in case my dad needs me."

"Lou can help him," Warrick's gaze flicked to Lou before returning to me.

"You know I was hoping to take care of things around my apartment, too. Who knows when there will be another raid?" I asked, worry creeping in my voice.

Don't linger too long in there, and make sure to have your weapons on you, Warrick instructed.

Warrick's eyes searched mine, "I don't know what's going on, but I don't exactly have the time to fight your excuses. Are you sure you're okay with me leaving? I can try to take care of things from here."

I nodded, "Yes."

"I don't want you thinking I'm breaking my promise," Warrick started.

"You're not," I responded. When he opened his mouth, I shook my head, stopping Warrick from saying anything. "I don't feel like you're abandoning me. Go, take care of what you need to and give Holly hell."

Warrick pursed his lips then let out a sigh, "Listen to Lou, love. I won't be gone for long."

He kissed me before I could say anything else. "Be careful," he whispered into my ear. I shivered a little more from the thought of what I was going to walk in to rather than the sudden rush of air from Warrick leaving. He jogged out the door, urgency in every movement he made.

As soon as the door closed, Lou whirled around to me, "Why didn't you go with him?"

I lifted my chin up, holding my ground as Lou started stalking over to me. "I have things I need to take care of here, Lou," I answered.

"Right," Lou shook his head, not quite believing me. "*Things*. Look, Val, I don't think this is a good idea right now."

I started to move around him ignoring what he just said, but Lou's arm shot out stopping me. I froze as he said, "At least let me go with you."

"No, Lou. I need to do this on my own."

I shook my arm loose and jogged up the stairs. Lou wasn't going to let this one slide, not with the high chances of Az not chasing after Warrick. I started shoving some clothes, knives, rope, and a toothbrush in a bag just in case I'd end up staying there longer than I planned when Lou stood in the doorway, "Why are you instantly running the minute Warrick leaves?"

"Lou, I just need a little time to myself to grab some small things I left back at my apartment. That's all I'm asking for," I explained, throwing my bag over my shoulder.

"I'll give you your space," Lou started to protest. "Just stay here, Val. Please."

"No," I shook my head. "I need this time. I shouldn't be gone for too long, but I'll give you a call if anything seems off. I promise. And I do appreciate the offer. Enjoy this time with Jennie, okay?"

I brushed past him heading out to my car so he wouldn't have another chance to try to stop me. The snow had picked up throughout the day covering the roads, so the drive was a little dicey. I gripped the steering wheel a little tighter earning a small groan – it wasn't the roads making me anxious, it was knowing I was about to confront the last person in the world I wanted to see right now. I reached out to our bond to see if Warrick was there, but got nothing in return. Even the feeling of it was more faint than usual. I was going to be getting what I wanted – some uninterrupted alone time to carry out Warrick's insane plan. *Just remember what we talked about, Val,* I thought to myself as I pulled out of the garage. *Get in there, get some information – doesn't matter if it's big or small, then get out. Don't give Az the chance to hold on to you.*

I parked my car in the same spot Jennie and I had the first time we came over here, taking a moment to check the spots I tucked my knives into as a way of reassuring myself they were still there before I headed up to my apartment. I was sure Az would show up despite his bike not being in here, which meant I'd probably have to endure another torture session like what had happened back in the witch world if I weren't careful. My hands started shaking at the thought as I pulled my phone out to let Lou know I had made it safely. *This would be different this time*, I told myself. *I have my phone, I'm armed, and this is my turf.*

I didn't wait any longer to give myself a chance to back out. I needed to pack my things up, load my car, and then enjoy one night, if I got that lucky. I took my bag and headed up the stairs.

The apartment was the same as it was the last time I had been here: clean, organized, but sprinkles of Az here and there. I sighed, getting to work on emptying my drawers and grabbing the things I cared the most about. I finished up a lot quicker than I thought I would, so I set my bag by the door and went into the kitchen to grab some water. I reached into the cabinet above me, pausing when I saw the bottle of wine on the counter. It was a good one, but it had a pretty price tag to go with it, so it was rare for me to have a taste of it. I didn't hesitate, filling my glass with that bottle. When my glass was full, I pulled out the vial of liquid Warrick told me acted as a truth serum. I twirled the small vial in my fingers, observing its clear contents. I removed the cork, holding it up to my nose for a sniff. It was odorless, too. Warrick had mentioned something about how hard it would be to detect. As long as this doesn't change the color or impact the flavor of the wine, Az should have no idea. I dumped the contents of the vial into the rest of the wine in the bottle before tucking the empty container away in my bag. I patted my pocket to make sure the second vial was still there, smiling to myself when I felt it.

I shot off another quick update text to Lou then started scrounging through the fridge for any food.

The door quietly opened and closed, making me stand up. I casually walked back over to my glass, taking a long sip willing my panic to stay quiet. I raised my eyes to meet the hazel ones of Az who was standing at the door, his hand still resting on the door handle. He didn't make any move to come over to me as he flicked his gaze to the open wine bottle on the counter before looking back at me, "I was saving that for a special occasion."

Chapter 21

I regarded him coolly, "Well, then, it's not every night your most sought-after prize waltzes into your life so willingly. Consider yourself lucky. Want a glass?"

Still not moving, Az cocked his head to the side assessing me, "What are you up to?"

"Nothing, just needed to grab the last of my things," I shrugged.

Az smirked, straightening a little bit, "Let me guess – your big, bad boyfriend popped back over to Lupusantha to take care of business and you knew this would be the perfect time to come back into your apartment. You didn't mention, however, that public enemy number one was living here and you'd likely run into him. Does that cover it?"

I nodded, raising the glass to my lips, "Yup. What are you doing living here anyways?"

Az pulled out a bag of takeout from his backpack then walked over to where I was standing in the kitchen, setting the food down on the table in the process. He reached above me into the cabinet, grabbing a glass. I scooted out from under him to look at what was in the bag, the mouth-watering smell of Chinese food making my stomach growl. He didn't answer me, but only grinned at my reaction. I pulled the bag a little closer to me, "Is this Liu's?"

"I had a hunch you might be showing back up," Az turned, leaning against the counter and taking a sip. He closed his eyes, savoring the smooth flavors. If he could tell I spiked his drink, he wasn't showing it. Watching me again, Az smirked, "You forgot how hard it is to resist my charm, didn't you?"

I rested against the table, swirling my wine around, "You didn't answer me, by the way."

His hazel eyes met mine, "You were gone. I needed a place to stay. It was pretty easy to convince the landlord you weren't coming back when the articles about you missing started popping up."

I shot him a glare, "Well, I'm not happy about it. You being here, I mean."

"Would you have rather had your apartment going to someone else? A stranger?"

"I guess not," I mumbled.

"Figured that was the case," Az said, moving to get plates out. "Now, eat."

I put a hand over his, stopping him, "Let's catch up first."

Az glanced down to my stomach then slowly dragged his gaze back up to my eyes, "You sure you want to wait?"

I nodded my head, pulling him with me towards the couch, "Grab the wine."

I settled into the worn piece of furniture, Az taking the seat right next to me. My phone buzzed with another check-in text from Lou. I responded back, glancing up at Az who was watching me very closely. I set my phone screen down on the coffee table, "What?"

"Why are you really here?" he asked, suspicion laced in every word.

"You already said it," I answered. "I'm here because it's the perfect time, but you had to interrupt that."

"Cut the shit, Val," Az said, folding his fingers together. "You knew I'd be showing back up. Your scent was all over the place yesterday, driving me wild. You forget I know you. You're not as innocent as you like to pretend you are. You're not stupid either. You wouldn't willingly walk into another situation like the last time. So, why are you really here?"

I leaned into him, getting some satisfaction when I saw his nostrils flare to take in my scent, "I needed to grab my things. I knew there was a good chance I'd be running into you, but I was hoping you weren't going to walk through that door. In fact, I was hoping you'd be chasing Warrick back to Lupusantha."

He studied me as I sat back and it took everything I had in me not to back down. I started to feel the same pressure I had the day of the funeral, but I kept still. *I don't know whether to call you stupid or brave for risking the chance of running into me,* Az's voice filled my mind.

I took a sip, turning my attention to the glass debating on asking him how he was able to do that. I lifted my eyes to meet his, looking at him skeptically, "What are you going to do about it?"

Az shook his head, "Haven't made up my mind yet."

I set my jaw, swallowing the panic. If I freaked out too much, he might start to get even more suspicious than he already was. On the other hand, if he picked up on me trying to maintain a calm exterior, he'll think he's got an edge. That's the one I want – the path that will lead to the least number of questions from Az.

I finished off my wine then set my glass down, refilling it, earning raised eyebrows from Az. I had to be careful now – Az wasn't the only one who would be under the truth serum. There wasn't a lot of the wine in my glass, so I tossed it back.

I caught him downing the rest of his glass when my gaze returned to his, and mumbled, "Bottle's empty."

"I know," he said, standing up. "That's why I'm getting another one."

I watched every move he made closely to make sure he didn't tamper with the bottle he was opening. I couldn't let him take that opportunity away from me. Az caught on to what I was doing, so he angled himself to give me more visibility almost as if he was trying to call a truce. Bringing the bottle over to where we were sitting, he said, "This still doesn't make sense to me."

"What do you mean?" I asked.

He filled my glass before his. As he leaned back, he answered, "It still doesn't make sense why you're over here. Aren't you scared I'm going to try something?"

"Will any answer satisfy you?" I asked.

"The honest one will."

I stiffened for a second. His words hinted at him knowing something was up. I watched him a little longer, but Az didn't give anything else away that indicated he knew I tampered with the wine letting me relax a little.

"Fine," I huffed. I tipped my glass back and forth watching the wine get closer to spilling with each movement, "I want to know why you're able to talk to me through a bond. The only way I was going to get that answer was by talking to you, one-on-one."

Az sat back, swallowing half his glass in one sip thinking about how he was going to answer. He looked at me, his face calm with a trace of something else. Happiness, maybe? "I don't know if it's the wine or if I'm feeling generous, but all I'm wanting to do is be honest with you tonight."

"Maybe, deep down, you're feeling guilty," I threw out. *Thank goodness it's working.*

"Guilty for what?"

"You really have to ask?" I asked incredulously.

Az closed his eyes, "It was too much to hope for you to forget about all that."

"You've got to be kidding me, Az. You really think I was going to forget about how you raped and then carved into me?" I shook my head. "What, did you hit your head last night?"

I caught myself off-guard with how calm I was being. I should've been yelling and screaming at him for what he did to me, but something was holding me back. Maybe it was the fact that Az was showing no signs of hostility. We were having a civil conversation without any hints of him flipping that switch. Yet, I wasn't sure if I should feel relieved or worried. With him, it could only be a matter of seconds before he flipped.

"I know, I know," Az held up his hands in defense. "I'm being stupid. Maybe you're right, maybe I am guilty. I know you thought I enjoyed all that, but I really didn't. Well," he chuckled. "Maybe I enjoyed it a little once that potion was in your system. Anyways, I've told you before – I had a part to play."

My palms started to sweat a little as my stomach turned from his admission, "What does that have to do with my question?"

Az shot me an annoyed look, "It was the witches. They were able to concoct a little brew that mimics the effects of a fated bond thanks to Warrick. Abria had a field day knowing she had a fated wolf."

"So, you and I are not fated?"

Az shook his head, "As much as I want us to be, no."

"I want to go back to something," I tapped my finger against my glass.

"By all means," Az finished his wine then poured more.

"If you didn't like what you did to me, why the hell did you do it? Why not just let me stay with you until the meeting with Abria?" I asked, trying to keep the anger out of my tone.

He rubbed his face, "You forget I enjoyed some of it, which is one reason – it's been a while since I've been laid. I digress – I needed to bring you there in pain. Their magic feeds off that energy, so the more I could do to you, the happier Abria was which meant I solidified our partnership. It also meant she would be able to tell if you were faking it, so I had to do something."

I was going to be sick. I was just a pawn in their game to work together, and so was Warrick. I pushed down the anxiety again, still somehow keeping the mask of calm in place, "I've been through hell, but that had to be one of the worst things I've gone through. Guess it felt good to check that box, huh?" I shook my head, closing my eyes as I asked, "So, since we're not fated, will you stay out of my head?"

"I guess I can do that, but what will I get in return?" Az asked while bringing his glass up to his lips.

I set my glass on the table then rested my head on the back of the couch, "You're getting some time with me. Is that not enough?"

"Depends. Are you going to try to get revenge for what I did to you?" Az scooted closer to me.

Az was crowding my space now, his scent enveloping me with mint and pine. My gaze slowly drifted up from his chest to those hazel eyes that had a tendency to draw me in when we were together. I sucked in a breath, silently cursing myself for momentarily getting caught up in Az and pretended to scratch my lower back when I was really reaching for my knife. As I let it out, I said, "How many times do I need to tell you? I'm here for the rest of my stuff." It wasn't a lie, but I had to fight like hell to keep from spilling everything.

"And to get the truth," Az added, cocking an eyebrow. "Or is there something else you're not telling me?"

"One more thing," I said before I could stop myself. Damn this truth serum … "If it was a potion they gave to you so you could pretend you were fated to me, does that mean the witches are here?"

A knock sounded at the door making me jump. Az chuckled then made his way over there. He opened the door, accepted a bag from some kid. When the door was closed again, Az held the bag up, "Just some dessert. Figured you wouldn't mind."

"What did you get?" I asked, my curiosity overtaking my panic.

"A birthday cake," he answered, taking it into the kitchen.

I grabbed my wine glass, following him over there, "Why?"

"Grab the bottle of white in the fridge," Az ordered. He watched me out of the corner of his eye while pulling the small cake out of the bag, "Because you had a birthday recently."

"I don't understand why you're being so nice to me right now. Is this all part of your game?" I asked, not trusting how smoothly things were going right now.

Az casually walked back over to the table, grabbing the bottle of red we had been enjoying, and downed the rest of it before coming back into the kitchen. He set the bottle on the counter behind me, our arms brushing, then wiped his mouth with the back of his hand.

He quickly turned to grab us fresh glasses, "Stop looking for an ulterior motive, Val. I'm just wanting to enjoy the evening with my guest of honor or is this the part where you try to hurt me?"

Az gestured for me to start pouring before he busied himself with putting our dirty wine glasses in the dishwasher. I followed the silent command, ignoring his question despite the truth serum urging me to speak, and took my opportunity to spike this bottle with the second vial, "How did you know Warrick had left? And you still didn't answer my question about the witches."

I had to keep the questions going while he was under the influence.

"Believe it or not, I keep tabs on everything you and your little crew do. I know he's not going to be away for long thanks to my little distraction. I know he's got the fae, the vampires, the dragon riders, the elves, and you humans on his side and they're all waiting in the wings for his signal to come here.

I also know he's struggling with being fated, which surprises me considering he's with you," Az cocked his head to the side then turned to cut the cake. "And yes, they are here along with others."

I placed Az's glass next to him, standing closer than I should have. I thought about leaning on him, but decided against it, moving back to my spot on the opposite side. Az looked at me over his shoulder, "Do you miss what we had?"

"Do you?"

Az sighed, "I think you know that answer."

"And I can say the same," I shot back. I silently cursed myself for letting old feelings get stirred up despite everything Az had done to me recently. I guess things were still unresolved from how he just upped and disappeared all those years ago, and the wine sure wasn't helping anything, either.

He handed me a plate with a slice of cake, not saying anything else. Az took a step a closer to me, making me look up. Az reached toward me, tugging me into him, "Happy belated birthday, Val."

It must be the wine, but I wanted to stand up on my toes to kiss him. This night felt like one we had shared so many times when we were together – the nights where we had nowhere to go and the world outside these walls didn't exist.

He gripped me harder, the slight twinge of pain finally snapping me out of it. He may be opening up to me thanks to the serum, but I had to be careful. Az liked to flip a switch to let the crazy out with no warning. He could very easily catch me off-guard. I lifted the plate up, taking a step back, his hand reluctantly releasing me, "Thanks."

Az walked back over to the coffee table, his wine glass in one hand and a piece of cake in the other. I followed his lead, getting comfortable in my spot again.

I took the first bite and closed my eyes. It had the perfect ratio of frosting to cake. It wasn't too sweet and the buttercream was handmade. When my eyes fluttered open, Az was watching me, the corners of his mouth twitching upwards, "I'm thinking I don't want to let that reaction of yours go to waste. Maybe I'll have to have my cake and eat you, too."

"Where did you get this?" I asked, the sweet flavors suddenly sour on my tongue.

"Where do you think I got it?" he asked, watching me with those hunter's eyes.

"You didn't go to Sandra's, did you?" I responded, my gaze lingering a little too long on his mouth. *Play the part, Val, play the fucking part.*

He set down his cake and finished what was in his glass. Apparently, he was in the mood to drink tonight. Az stood up to get the bottle for another refill then walked over to me, wiping some frosting from the corner of my mouth with his thumb that he brought up to his mouth. His eyes were locked on mine as he sucked the frosting off his finger, then answered, "Again, it's one of your favorites."

Heat tried to blossom in my chest, but I shook my head. This has to be the wine. It has to be since I'm trying to keep up with him. I turned back to the few bites of cake I had left in front of me so he wouldn't be able to see me blush. I hastily finished it, then took my plate to the sink, "Trying to get me drunk?"

"Is it working?" he asked in a low, dangerous voice.

I was certainly feeling light, my world starting to feel unsteady. I turned to put away the leftovers and moved any other dishes into the sink to keep me busy. I held up the box holding the rest of the cake, "Thank you for this and the wine. Oh, and I can't forget about the food over there."

When Az got too quiet, I glanced over my shoulder. He was no longer in his spot on the couch. *Maybe he went to the bathroom ...*

Rolling my shoulders back and taking a calming breath, I turned to put the rest of the cake into the fridge, bending over to place them on the lower shelves. There was one more bottle of wine, so I pulled it out just in case. I was still straightening things out in there, but when I felt a hand on my lower back, I jumped. I whirled around, finding Az right there, not moving from where he was. He took his hand away from me, waving the sheathed knife, "Trying to pull one over on me?"

My face paled, but before I could stutter a response, Az lightly wrapped a hand in my hair, tugging my head back and moving us so he could trap me against a wall. Watching me closely, Az lowered his voice, "I'm going to look past this, but know you've used your one free pass. Try anything else tonight and I'll make sure Warrick and your pesky friends never see you again. Got it?"

"You wouldn't expect me to come in here unarmed, now would you?" I asked coyly, trying my best to show I wasn't scared of him when I very much was right now.

Az raised an eyebrow, releasing me, and I quickly waived him off. I grabbed the bottle then moved back to the couch. He took it from my hands to open it up, filling my glass in the process. He settled in the space next to me making sure to keep some distance this time. Az cleared his throat, "Did you really have a relationship with Lou?"

"Why are you asking?" I watched him carefully, not sure where he was going with that. I pushed past the slight tug I felt from the serum from not immediately answering the question.

"Touchy subject?"

"No," I shook my head. "I just don't know why you need to know that information."

"Can I not make conversation?" Az asked defensively, taking a swig from the bottle.

I let out a breath, "Fine." I glanced out the window, "Yes, Lou and I were together for a little bit."

"What happened?" Az asked, sounding genuinely interested.

I turned to face him, tucking my legs under me and taking another sip, "I overreacted in the way I always do."

"Please, tell me more," Az said trying to keep from smirking like he knew what happened.

I rolled my eyes at him, but went on, "We had just jumped to the vampire world, Stragairel, right?"

When Az nodded, I continued, "The house was outside the city, so we felt we were on our own. We got some time to spend together and everything was magical. We finally worked our way into town to a pub that became our frequent hang out spot."

"If I remember my notes correctly, you worked there," Az said in a distant voice.

I stopped, shocked by him knowing that detail. First, Az hinted at knowing what happened. Now, he fully admitted to knowing a piece of the story. He gave a slight shrug of his shoulders and brought the bottle back up to his lips, signaling for me to go on. I traced the rim of my glass, focusing on what was left in there and centering myself, "Anyways, the night Warrick actually decided to come back in my life was the night I threw everything out the window. Lou was getting cozy with his ex while Warrick was playing head games and giving me a few new cuts. I got a ride home from someone else, called Lou out on his shit, and ended things."

Az let out a whistle, "I can see why you lost it. I wouldn't have liked seeing my partner getting up close and personal with their ex. I mean, I haven't enjoyed seeing that, but things have been over for a while between us."

"Really? I tell you something that personal and you decide to throw shots at what we had?"

"Careful, Val," Az warned. "You're walking a thin line already." He jerked his head in the direction of the kitchen where my knife was still resting on the counter before taking another swig of wine.

I reached for the bottle, my fingers closing around the neck, "Maybe you should take a break from that."

Az tugged me to him, our faces inches apart. His pupils dilated, his breathing slowed. My heart started racing. His gaze dropped to my lips, his tongue darting out to wet his lower lip while his hand found its way to my waist again. I let out a shiver when part of his hand touched my bare skin. "Maybe I should drop my restraint," Az said in a low, husky voice. "We've spent enough time talking. I want to use my lips for something else. Besides, your racing heart is driving me wild."

He just proved to me I hadn't been doing as good of a job as I thought hiding my anxiety. I scowled at him, trying to tug the bottle away again without getting it to budge. He grinned at me, but for once it wasn't predatory. It was that soft grin I had grown so fond of while we were dating. *Damn it, he's changing his demeanor again.*

Az slowly moved towards me until our lips were barely touching. Fear kept me rooted where I was while I was trying to figure out how I could reach the other knife I had strapped to my calf. When I didn't move away, his lips pressed against mine. Az was being so gentle, almost as if he were asking for permission. He tugged on my lower lip while his hand tightened its grip taking my lack of response as the permission he needed. Everything about his actions told me he was holding himself back despite what he had said earlier. He was doing his best impression of Warrick with his actions and most of his words, making my heart confused. Caught up in the kiss, my tongue barely traced his bottom lip before I could stop myself. A soft moan came from Az and I took my hand from the wine bottle to let my fingers get tangled in his soft, thick hair. The bottle made a thump as Az set it on the ground. He pulled me more on top so I was straddling him. Az ran his hands up my thighs, but before he could cross a line, they settled on the outside of my legs.

His kisses grew more passionate, more needy. I was finding myself getting lost in them, dragged back to a time where my life was simpler. It was getting harder to distinguish between then and right now. When he brought his hand back to my waist and traced a scar, I snapped out of it. I pulled away, resting my forehead against his. Az was breathing heavy and I wasn't too far behind him. I sat back, sucking in the cooler air.

"What are we doing?" I whispered looking down at him.

"Enjoying ourselves," Az answered, light dancing in his eyes. Az was yet again getting exactly what he wanted.

I shook my head, shoving away from him, "I can't, Az."

He readjusted so he could pick up the bottle, forearms resting on his knees, "Right, you're already spoken for."

"What?"

Az took a swig from the bottle, squeezing his eyes shut, "Forget about it."

I started to put a hand on his arm, but thought better of it, "Talk to me, Az."

Maybe I'd get some more information out of him.

"Do you know how nice this night has been?" Az asked, those hazel eyes molten, desire still clearly at the surface.

I nodded, swallowing, "It's felt like old times."

"Then why did you stop?"

He couldn't hold the hurt back anymore. The small voice popped back into my head wondering if this was all a ruse to keep worming his way between me and Warrick. On the other hand, I felt like he was being so vulnerable, something I had hardly seen since he came back into my life. Was this the truth serum mixed with the wine talking?

I stood up, walking over to the window to look out at the city, "You do realize what you did to me, right?" I turned slowly, seeing him nod. I continued talking, "Then you know how hard it is to let myself get close to you like that. Plus, what is that going to do to Warrick and me? There are consequences to our actions, Az. Ones I don't want to face."

Az held up a hand stopping me. I was ready for a fight when he gestured for me to be quiet, his head angled toward the door. I couldn't tell what he was hearing, but I stayed where

I was. A knock rang out and I looked at Az, confused. He shook his head at me, walking over to where I was standing, "Don't let anyone know I'm here."

"What?" I hissed as another knock sounded. He moved into the bathroom not completely closing the door, but not visible either. I scanned the place, throwing anything indicating Az was here in the bathroom with him while I made my way to the door. I glanced out of the peephole. Lou raised his hand to knock again, his mouth opening, but I finally said something, "Give me a second, Lou."

I took advantage of this opportunity to reach into my bag, grabbing the rope I had tucked away in there earlier. It wouldn't keep Az down for long, but tying him up would give me a head start in getting out of here. Az was getting a little too comfortable around me for my liking and I was starting to question if he would let me go.

Lou's head whipped up, "Open the door, Val."

I opened it a crack, poking my head out, "What's going on?"

"You stopped answering my texts," Lou tried to peek in.

"You're sounding a little panicky," I observed. "Are you okay?"

"Can I come in?" he asked, dropping the urgency.

I nodded, moving to open the door some more. Lou headed straight for the table. He scanned the space again, his eyes landing on the bag of untouched Chinese food sitting in front of him, "You sure you're alone?"

"Yes," I said sitting across from him. When Lou looked at me skeptically, I pulled out my phone letting him know Az was here. He opened his mouth like he was going to say something, but I aggressively pointed at my phone where I had also typed out a warning for Lou not to say anything. "What's up?"

His brows knitted together. I held my breath waiting to see if he would play along with me or if he would blow my cover. Lou still looked concerned, but said, "Jennie and I were getting close again tonight. I very much wanted to get close to her, feel her skin on mine, but then she started getting weird."

Oh, boy. We were getting right into it. *It would be nice to have some popcorn in here if the conversation is going where I think it is*, Az chuckled in my head.

Hush, I shot back. *Aren't you supposed to be staying out of my head?* I rubbed my temples, hoping Lou wasn't picking up on me silently communicating with the last person I should be around. I didn't want him knowing that was still happening. Not yet, anyways. I looked back up at him, "What do you mean 'weird'?"

"We had just gotten naked and she was asking me to do all sorts of things. I'll, uh, I'll spare you those details," he paused. I nodded in appreciation that I wasn't about to hear some of my friend's kinks. Lou went on, "After I kept telling her no, her whole personality changed. Jennie started comparing herself to you and what we had. I couldn't take it anymore. I had to get out of there."

"That's ... that's a lot," I said. Lou nodded towards my phone and I handed it over to him. While he typed something out, I asked, "Are you okay? You didn't just leave her there, did you?"

He placed my phone in my hand where I quickly skimmed what he wrote, *What the hell are you doing here with Az? Why didn't you tell me?*

Lou cleared his throat, "No, I told her I needed to clear my head for a little bit before we could talk about what just happened, although, I didn't exactly tell her where I was going. I didn't even realize where I was headed until I was halfway here. I'm okay, though, just weirded out."

I deleted what he wrote to replace it with my answers, *Warrick and I will explain when he gets back. We didn't tell you at first because we knew you'd disagree and fight us on this. Please, trust me. I'll be out of here soon if things keep going my way.*

"Do you want a piece of cake? It's my go-to when I'm needing some comfort," I got out of my seat, walking towards the kitchen. I glanced over my shoulder to find Lou shaking his head at what I wrote, but letting out a sigh while his fingers tapped on my screen.

"Sure," he answered, not breaking his concentration.

"Does Jennie know you left the house?"

I set a small slice and a fork in front of him, swiping my phone from him at the same time. *I'm not happy with you two* – that was all he wrote.

I frowned at my screen as Lou answered, "No ... I probably shouldn't stay too long or I'll be going back to an even more upset Jennie than when I left."

He stabbed his fork into the soft sponge clearly not holding back his annoyance. I put a hand on his and showed him what I typed up, *I promise we have a good explanation. We will tell you as soon as Warrick is back.*

Lou shot me a glare, but his shoulders dropped. He reached for my phone, typing as soon as it was in his hands. He scarfed down a few more bites, almost finishing the piece when his phone rang. Lou pulled his phone out of his pocket, groaning when he saw the name on the screen, "Damn it."

He shoved my phone back at me, but I watched him a little longer. Lou placed his phone in the middle of the table, squeezing his eyes shut as he answered the call, putting it on speaker, "Hey, Jennie."

"Where the *hell* are you?" she screeched.

I winced with him then read what he wrote, *Even though I'm not happy about it, I trust you'll call me if anything goes wrong. Don't forget – you owe me an explanation the second Warrick's back.*

I gave him a nod to show I understand. He massaged his brow as Jennie kept going, "I've looked all over this house. Mark told me you stormed out of here. Was I really that bad?"

"No," Lou shook his head. "I'm headed back now. All I needed was some fresh air to cool off."

Jennie abruptly ended the call seemingly satisfied with Lou's answer for now. He stood up from the table, getting ready to take his plate back to the kitchen when I grabbed it from him. I shoveled the rest of his piece of cake in my mouth then dumped the plate in the sink. When I turned around, Lou laughed at me, "You look like a chipmunk."

I waived him off, swallowed the cake, then pulled him into a hug. "Thanks for checking on me, Lou," I whispered in his ear.

"Anytime," Lou answered in the same hushed, gentle tone. "Be careful."

"I will."

We pulled a part and Lou headed towards the door, "Thanks again for the cake and giving me a place where I could breathe."

"Drive safe, Lou. I'll see you in a bit."

The second he was out the door, Az stormed out of the bathroom, his wild eyes fixed on me, "You want to finally tell me what you're really doing over here, Val?"

Shit ... I needed to act now.

He stomped over to me, trapping me against the wall as he rested his forearms on either side of my head. I cranked up the seduction, batting my lashes at him and tracing a finger in lazy circles on his chest. Az glanced down at my hand, and when he looked back up at me, a slow smile started to replace the scowl he had there before, "Picking up on where we left off before we were so rudely interrupted?"

"Maybe," I breathed out.

"You won't hear me complaining," Az said, lowering his face down to kiss the sensitive spots on my neck.

I swallowed down my nausea, forcing myself to let out small moans instead. The sounds encouraged him, his hands dropping to my waist the same time he moved to kiss me. I slid a finger up to his lips, stopping him, "Why don't we take this to the couch?"

"Better yet," Az started, his voice low and laced with desire. "Why don't we take this to the bed?"

"Lead the way," I whispered against his neck before I placed a light kiss there. He shivered a little telling me I had hit my mark.

Chapter 22

Az bounded over to the bed, yanking his shirt off before grabbing the bottle of wine on the way over there. I made sure he wasn't looking as I snagged the rope off the table.

He tilted the bottle to his lips, watching my movements as he took a drink. He lazily pointed at the rope, "You have some new kinks I don't know about?"

I waved it at him, closing the distance, "I wanted to give you at least one surprise."

Az raised his eyebrows up as he looped an arm around my waist, "Where the hell have you been hiding?"

I reached for the bottle, Az happily obliging my request. I'm going to need all the alcohol I can get if I'm really stooping down to the tactics I used back in Warrick's office. I couldn't move past the irony of this – the wine, the way I jumped into action. Why did I always resort to using my body when it came to getting information out of powerful men? The thought of that memory made my heart lurch ... I missed Warrick way more than I thought I would ...

I set the bottle on the nightstand then tossed the rope on the bed. Az yanked my face to his, his lips desperately seeking out mine. Gone was the tenderness from the moment we shared on the couch earlier – Az was acting like I was going to bolt at any moment if his aggressive kiss had anything to say about it. In all fairness, I was planning on making my great escape, but I had to return the feverish movements if I wanted to convince him otherwise.

Az's fingers slid their way between the waistband of my sweatpants and my skin. My hands started to shake. I may have thought I was ready to do this, but I couldn't. Not after what he did to me.

I pushed against his chest, "Easy, there. What's the rush?"

"I don't want you to change your mind," Az answered. His fingers brushed over my thong then moved to the thigh where his name was still prominently etched into my skin. He stilled as he started tracing the raised letters.

"Is something wrong?" I asked.

"No," he answered with a strained voice.

"Are you sure?"

Az felt the rest of the area, "She said she would get rid of all the scars."

"Well, she didn't," I was bitter. I removed his hand from my pants, "You really think she was going to let me walk out of there without something to bring me negative emotions she can feed from? I thought you were smarter than that."

I moved to grab the bottle to take another sip, but Az grabbed my arm. Tensing, I waited for him to say something, anything, but Az just laid there, his jaw twitching. He dragged his hazel eyes to meet mine. In a low voice, he said, "I have never stopped loving you, Val. Seeing you again has stirred up all these memories, these feelings I thought I had moved on from. You can't tell me you didn't feel anything, too. There has to be something stirring in your heart."

It took everything in me to keep my composure. Where the hell did that come from? His admission came from leftfield. Az had to be messing with me, he *had* to be. It's the only thing that makes sense for why he would say something like that. What other reason would he have to open his heart to me in this moment?

After a few steadying breaths, I tried to shake him off, but that only seemed to bring him back to the present. Whatever had been haunting him disappeared, and whatever drove him to confess his feelings for me was erased. His hand released my arm to find the wine instead. He polished off whatever was left in there, wiping his mouth with the back of his hand. Cocking an eyebrow at me, Az asked, "Now, where were we?"

He roughly positioned me on top of him, yanking me back into another aggressive kiss. I blindly reached for the rope hoping my other hand was doing enough to distract him. I let him start trying to explore my body with his hands, but the second his fingers grazed my breasts, I pulled away and pinned his arms above his head, "Nuh-uh, not yet."

Az grinned and tried to bring his arms back down only to be stopped when I threw my bodyweight into keeping him where he was, "Is this where things get interesting?"

I nipped at his ear, fighting back the urge to empty the contents of my stomach. When I got my stomach back under control, I whispered, "Only if you let it."

"By all means," Az purred in response.

I started tying the rope around his wrists, looking for a place to attach it to in the process. I needed to make sure I gave myself every advantage I could which meant I needed to make this as hard as possible for Az to get out. The more he struggled with it, the more time I would have to put distance between myself and this place.

"If you would've shared these kinks with me all those years ago, maybe I would've been more open to staying," Az said as he watched me.

I faltered in my movements. I had to keep up my act, but it was getting harder and harder the longer I was here. I just wanted to finish this up so I could tuck myself away in the comfort of my own home. I shook my head a little, feeding a piece of the rope through one of the holes in the intricate metal design of my headboard before finishing the knot. As I tightened his restraint, I smirked at him, "Did you know you're obsessed with having sex with me?"

"And did you know," Az started. He bucked his hips under mine, knocking me off-balance, "Valerie sounds a lot like Valkyrie."

"What does that have to do with anything?" I asked, suddenly very confused and on high alert. Was he about to flip his switch? Was he just playing into my little game for a moment knowing full well he'd be able to free himself and grab me? It would be a very convenient time with me feeling light from all the wine while tucked in the corner of my apartment. But, why was he comparing me to something from Norse mythology? Especially something that has a lot of ties to death. Is this his way of hinting what's to come?

"Just an interesting thought I had," he answered, lightly testing my handiwork. I held my breath for a moment, readying myself to run if the knots didn't hold. The knots didn't budge – Az wasn't going to be able to break free any time soon. I released my breath, sitting back on my heels. The dangerous wolf lifted his head, smiling at me, "Were you planning to tie me up all along?"

"I couldn't deprive you of some fun while I'm here," I winked at him. Technically, I was planning on tying him up so I wasn't lying. There was nothing else in my bag of tricks that would delay Az's eventual hunt once he realized I was only here to get information out of him. This was my final showdown. Before he could say anything else, I pointed down to his pants, "Let's get these off, shall we?"

"What's my dear little brother going to think about his one and only running over to me the minute he jumped from this world?" Az asked, his tone cocky.

I unbuttoned his black jeans and started working them off his hips. He lifted himself up just enough for me to pull them down his ass. My mouth went dry and I had to pour all my concentration into keeping my hands from shaking as I stared at Az's naked body. Does this guy own a piece of underwear?

Catching on to my reaction, Az asked, "Like what you see?"

There was a little bit of a possessive growl in his question. He was fully convinced I was enjoying the sights rather than having the complete opposite reaction. I must've been doing better than I thought with my acting tonight ...

Forcing myself to resume, I yanked his pants off his legs and tossed them into the bathroom. When the time came, I knew Az wouldn't run out of this apartment naked. At least, I hoped he wouldn't. I was also banking on the fact that he probably didn't have a car, and if that truly is the case, he'd have to throw on some clothes to go riding on his bike in this weather. More and more things were starting to line up in my favor – his bike tires wouldn't have the kind of traction needed to chase me down in the snow which meant I was only adding to my head start when I made my great escape. I sent up a silent thank you to whoever was listening, feeling some of my worries ease for what I was about to do.

I stood up and gave him a half grin, "I do now." I turned on my heel heading for the table where the food was waiting. I snagged the bag, headed into the kitchen to grab what was left of the cake, and walked towards the door.

I heard the metal of the headboard groan a little as Az shouted, "What the hell do you think you're doing, Val?"

I slung my bag over my shoulder and lifted up the food as I fully smiled at Az, "Thanks for the chat and the food, but I think it's time for me to head back home."

"You're just going to leave me here? Like this?!" Az thrashed around some more. Damn, I did better on those knots than I thought.

I was reaching for the apartment door when I threw a wink over my shoulder, "Its been fun, Az, really. We should catch up like this again. Oh, and thanks for letting me know about the whole bond thing. It brings me some relief, and Warrick will be happy to hear there's nothing between you and I, either."

A growl ripped from his throat as he tugged on the rope again. Az was outraged at being caught in his own game. When I saw he was able to get a little more movement than before, I blew him a quick kiss then made my exit. I didn't wait for the door to close behind me as I sprinted towards the stairs. There were a lot of curses being hurtled my way, but I wasn't going to let my curiosity win out on this one. No, I had to get out of here and back to the house as fast as I could because Az would be chasing me down the second he got free.

I tossed everything in my car, taking a quick second to send a text to Lou letting him know I was on my way back home with the potential for a very, very pissed off Az chasing me. I turned my car on and sped out of the garage, tires squealing with every move I made.

Out on the road, I quietly cursed through clenched teeth every time my tires tried to slide. My eyes were constantly flicking to my rearview mirror checking for any signs of Az. I jammed my finger into the power button for the radio, shutting the staticky signal off so I could listen for any sounds of a bike. I can't believe I actually pulled that off. Sure, there were a few times where I wanted to throw up because of the time Az and I spent together on Frigusmada – the fact I didn't lose that composure and was able to restrain him won out. My head was spinning from that victory. That, and the whiplash Az put me through back there from going between the nicer side I knew and this new, darker version of himself.

I pulled up to the house, slamming the car in park and sprinting in. Lou was the only one in the living room. The rest of the house was dark which meant everyone else was asleep.

I dropped the food on the table, my bag thumping to the ground before I made sure everything was locked. I peered out the blinds for any signs of Az finally letting out a breath of relief when there was nothing except for the thick blanket of night. I slid to the ground quietly laughing to myself.

"Anyone tell you you're crazy lately?" Lou asked, squatting in front of me.

I opened an eye to take him in. He looked frustrated and like he was ready to laugh all at the same time. I dropped my head back against the wall, "Not enough apparently."

He sat across from me crossing his arms, "Care to explain why you reek of Az?"

I finished getting the crazed laughs out of me then wiped a tear from my eye as I answered, "Remember how I told you to trust me?"

"Don't answer my question with another question," Lou scolded.

I pointed up at the table towards the food, "Have you eaten anything besides cake?"

"No."

Pushing myself up, I grabbed a couple of the takeout containers, handing one to Lou then tossing him a fork. I settled back in my spot, loading my fork up. When it was clear I wasn't going to say anything else, Lou glared at me, "His scent is a little too strong for me to sit here idly."

"Remember what we did to Warrick? Besides, my answer will stay the same – I'll catch you up on everything once Warrick's back," I reminded him while I kept my attention focused on my food. I hadn't realized how much I had missed these sweet, tangy flavors of orange chicken.

"No, you're going to tell me what happened now," Lou argued.

I set my jaw, lifting my gaze to finally meet his. Anger was written all over his face. My shoulders relaxed, dropping the fight in them. It wouldn't hurt to give Lou some of the answers he's looking for. I can at least wait to share the little piece of information I got out of Az for when Warrick's here so I'm not having to repeat myself. I don't think Warrick wants to hear the nitty gritty details about how I was able to get that information – he'd be able to see it through our bond anyways.

I set my container on the ground, running my tongue over my teeth to clear the food out of them before I explained, "Az showed up as expected. He even got food from my favorite places, so he had a pretty good idea I'd be showing up at some point."

"And yet, you still walked in there ... Warrick let you walk in there," Lou muttered in disbelief.

"Hold on," I held up a finger. "Don't think I didn't go in there unprepared. Warrick gave me a couple of vials of truth serum to spike the wine to make Az more willing to give out information. Not only that, but I was armed with a couple of knives and was ready to restrain Az."

Lou's eyebrows raised in disbelief, "Don't take this the wrong way, Val, but I wouldn't really expect you to be the one who could keep Az down for long."

"He isn't here, is he?" I gestured towards outside.

"You have a point," a muscle in Lou's jaw twitched. "I thought you weren't going to be doing the whole spy-thing anymore."

I sighed, "We're getting desperate, Lou. Trust me, I didn't want to. Warrick has been running into dead ends everywhere he turns trying to get any info on Az, literally anything. Warrick knows Az has a soft spot for me, just like you knew Warrick had the same soft spot for me. He also knew I would probably have to get a little too close for comfort, so don't go jumping to conclusions that I cheated on him. Warrick actually encouraged this with his twisted mind despite my protests. I did what I had to do just like I did when we were trying to get info out of Warrick. That's what gave him this idea."

My phone dinged dragging my attention away from this conversation. I fished it out of my pocket to find a text from Warrick: *Are you back home?*

Yes, I responded.

I'll be there shortly, Warrick replied.

"So, you willingly slept with Az after what he did to you?" Lou asked, quiet rage inching its way into his words.

My head jerked back like I had been slapped, "No. I would *never* willingly jump into Az's bed for *anything*."

"Then why is his scent covering every inch of you?" Lou hysterically asked.

"Az and I shared a couple of kisses. I had to lead him on so I could get him in a spot where I could tie him up with that rope I brought, okay?" I defensively answered. "I got him naked then took my opportunity to bolt, and before you try to jump to any more conclusions, I was doing what I could to buy myself more time because I knew Az would try to chase after me."

A loud banging on the front door startled us. Lou looked between me and the door before getting up, "Stay there."

He checked through the peephole then ripped the door open, "You and Val are crazier than shit, you know that?"

Warrick barged right in searching for me. The moment his eyes landed on mine, he crouched down, grabbing my face to start his inspection. His lip curled once he caught a whiff of Az's scent, but pulled me into a hug, "You're okay, love."

"Was there really an emergency back home to make you leave?" Lou asked, shutting the door and joining us back on the floor.

Warrick let me go, turning to face an angry Lou, "Not exactly an emergency, more of nuisance I had to take care of."

"Why did you leave, then?"

Warrick sighed, "I didn't want to know what was going on between Val and Az. Besides, it just confirms our bond can't work between worlds. It's important to understand these kinds of limitations, Louis."

"What was the nuisance and how did you take care of it?" I asked, jumping into the conversation.

Warrick smirked at me, "Holly and there's no longer the possibility of her bothering us anymore."

"Val mentioned something about a truth serum. What was she talking about?" Lou asked.

"Turn off the lights. I heard Az's bike headed this way when I got back," Warrick said, gesturing to the switch. We all took a moment to get comfortable in the dark before Warrick dived right in, "It's not exactly a truth serum, but something that acts like it. It's a blend of various herbs and spices from Sarind's world. She made it for me before you lot showed up there because she knew I was going to need it. She didn't tell me when, only that I would know when the time was right. Now seemed like the right time so we had a chance to get something from Az." Warrick turned his attention to me, "Now, please, love. Tell me you got something we can use."

Lou also turned to look at me. I nodded my head, "Not a lot, but I was able to figure out whether or not Az is truly fated to me."

Warrick leaned forward giving me his full attention. I went on, "He's not. Turns out the witches were able to brew something that could mimic a fated wolf's bond thanks to the time they had Warrick shackled up. That's what he's using to be able to do that. On the plus side, I can get a sense of when he's about to pop into my head since there's a distinct feeling that's unique to Az, so I just need to be careful. The next thing I found out is the witches are here with him, as well as the rest of his army. I didn't press for too many details regarding who else has teamed up with him, but know that we were right about him not wanting to keep his power source away for too long."

"Damn it," Lou said quietly, sitting back and rubbing his face. "Was it too much to hope that him and the witches wouldn't be attached at the hip?"

"I think it would be," Warrick mumbled. "Go on, love."

Lou growled at him, but I ignored that, continuing, "The third thing I found out was that he knows everything you've been up to, Warrick. Everything *we've* been up to. He knows who you're working with. He knows when you leave and when you come back. Az also admitted to knowing you're struggling with being fated. There's no telling what else he knows, but we have to assume nothing is a secret."

"Az has to have a mole," Warrick said, the wheels turning in his mind. "Someone on our side has to be feeding him this information."

"Maybe it's Val," Lou accused.

It felt as if I had been slapped for the second time tonight. "Are you fucking kidding me?"

"You're the one with a history with Az. Who knows what happened while he tortured you. Hell, who knows what you even told him," Lou said.

"You're out of your fucking mind if you think it's Val," Warrick calmly said.

"How can you know for sure?" Lou snapped.

"Because I'm in her damn head. All the time, Lou. I know what happened between her and Az just by probing her memories. The only reason we're sitting here having this conversation is for your benefit, so I suggest you keep your fucking accusations to yourself. It's *my* responsibility to figure out who the mole is," Warrick explained. His tone may have been calm, but those blue eyes were filled with nothing but rage.

Lou started to grumble to himself, but was cut off when Warrick turned to Lou, "See why I sent her in there? You may not think it, but that's about some of the best information we could have." Warrick turned back to me, "I'll pass the relevant information along to your dad so we can change up our plan a little bit."

"I'd like to help with that," I offered.

Warrick pursed his lips, but ultimately agreed. "Thank you," I said. I turned to Lou, "We can't be bickering like this anymore. I have a hunch that Az is trying to work his way in between us to break the weak alliance we already have. We started at a disadvantage because of the strained relationship between you and Warrick. We can't let that be what breaks us. I can't let Az come between me and Warrick, either. I guess all I'm saying is it's a group effort."

Lou sighed, closing his eyes, "You're right. I don't like to admit it, but you're right. I'm all over the place with everything that's going on and it doesn't help you coming in here with another wolf's scent rolling off you in waves."

The rumble of Az's bike roared past the house, but didn't stop. We all paused, waiting for something to happen, but when nothing did, we let out a collective sigh of relief.

"About that scent," I drummed my fingers along my legs. "I need to take a shower."

"I'll be there in a little bit, love," Warrick said. "I need to catch up with Lou and give your dad a call."

I stood up, giving him a kiss on his forehead then left. If Warrick was truly in my head all the time, he knew I had my own internal war raging. The last thing I needed was for him to know the feelings Az stirred up.

Chapter 23

Steam was starting to waft from my bathroom where I had the shower going. I sighed, starting to peel my clothes off when Warrick joined me in the room. I glanced over my shoulder, standing there in my underwear, watching as he slowly walked over to me. I recognized the look on his face. It was one I saw quite a few times in the early days of knowing him. The scary calm set in his jaw had me immediately backing away, "Warrick, look, I'm sorry. I'm sorry for what happened between me and Az. He initiated the first kiss, but I did the second time. The only reason I did that was so I could keep him from realizing what was going on. He was acting weird and I – "

Warrick held his hand up, quieting me. We were against a wall at this point, his hands on either side of my head trapping me. His gaze flicked down to my lips before returning to my eyes, "I don't care about the kissing. I expected that. What I don't like is what he said to you and what those words stirred up."

"What?" I croaked out. We both knew what he was talking about.

Warrick traced my jawline, "Is it true? Do your thoughts match how you really feel?"

"No," I shook my head. "I was getting caught up in the moment. You know how I am, but I feel nothing but resentment towards Az. I wouldn't dream of being with him after everything that happened in the witch world."

"Don't fucking lie to me, Val!" Warrick shouted, making me flinch. He lowered his voice, but the anger was still there, "After all those promises I made you, after all your insisting you only have feelings for me. I can't be sitting here questioning if I'll be losing you or not."

Lou flew through the open door, breathing a little heavier. He took in the sight of Warrick cornering me and swallowed. In a calm voice, he started, "Warrick ..."

"Fuck off, Lou," Warrick said over his shoulder, teeth clenched.

Ignoring him, Lou took a deep breath, "Val said it back there. This is Az trying to get in between all of us, especially you. If he can get you and Val focused on what you two share then rip it apart, you're going to be so distracted from keeping the pieces moving. That'll give him the opening he needs. You need to trust her."

"I promise you there's nothing there, Warrick. I'm yours," my voice was shaky as I brought a hand up to his cheek. *I'm not going anywhere, Warrick. Az isn't going to rip me away from you. I won't let that happen*, I threw all the love I felt for Warrick through our bond to add extra reassurance.

Warrick squeezed his eyes shut, his chest still heaving with the emotions raging within him. When he opened them again, his icy gaze was on me, the anger gone now. He hung his head, pulling me into him, "I hate this. I hate how easily I let him get to me."

I rubbed his back, giving Lou a thumb's up to let him know I'd be okay. He nodded, backing out of the room closing the door softly. I held on to Warrick a little tighter, "I hate how he gets under my skin, too. It's not going to be easy, but we have to remind ourselves to see through his charades."

"It's only going to be getting worse from here on out, love," Warrick mumbled into my neck.

"I know. Look," I pulled away from him. I caressed his cheek, "We'll stick together. No more going off on our own, okay?"

Warrick nodded. Before he could say anything else, I walked towards my bathroom, "Getting his scent off me will help. I'll be out in a little bit. You should rest."

Warrick was still sleeping when I got out of the shower. I didn't want to wake him when he looked so peaceful, so I made my way downstairs, my nerves still rattled from that interaction with Warrick.

Lou was still the only one sitting in the living room, so I joined him on the couch. I rested my head on his shoulder, sighing, "We didn't wake anyone up?"

"No," Lou said. "Surprisingly, they're all still dead asleep."

I picked at a piece of fuzz on the couch before pulling a blanket over my lap, not responding. Lou put a hand on my knee, his voice quiet, "Did Az do anything to you? Anything that would've made Warrick react like that?"

I laughed, shaking my head, "No, nothing like that. Az briefly showed me the side of him I had come to know and love when we were together. He never forced me to do anything I didn't want to. And when you popped over, he made sure to stay hidden in that tiny ass bathroom as a way to keep me out of trouble. Warrick was more upset at the idea of me potentially wanting to be with Az more than him because old feelings got stirred up."

"And?" Lou asked.

"And nothing. It would've been easy to succumb to those voices telling me to run to Az, but I couldn't look past what he had already done to me *and* Warrick. Besides, it was just an act to drive a wedge between us," I answered, not breaking eye contact. "I'm not going to let that happen again."

Lou only nodded, letting the silence settle between us. We sat there staring out into the backyard, covered in a light dusting of snow. I got tired of us not saying anything, so I playfully punched him on the arm, "So, what's going on between you and Jennie?"

He pretended to rub his arm, shaking his head, "Nothing, Val. Tonight was all a little too much for me. I don't think it's going to go anywhere, but thanks for trying to set me up."

"It's just weird she acted that way. I mean, she's never given me a play-by-play, but I didn't think she'd do things to scare you away," my voice trailed off as I got lost in thought.

"You don't think," Lou said, keeping me from getting too lost.

"Think what?" I asked.

"Think that she could be the mole, do you? Out of all of us, she's the only other one besides you and Warrick who knew Az before things escalated," Lou theorized.

"No," I shook my head. "Just because she had one night that seemed out of character during this whole mess doesn't mean she's the mole. Besides, when Az walked into our lives at your place, he didn't even acknowledge Jennie like he knew her."

"He did mention he recognized her, but that was buried so deep in all the other bullshit going on. It could've been something they agreed upon before that whole mess went down. I don't know," Lou rubbed his face. "Maybe that's how they want to play it. What were they like when you two were dating?"

I thought back for a minute before answering, "Jennie wasn't happy at first. She thought Az was another bad influence, very much the same way she thought of Gabriel at first. She got over it, though, when she saw how good we were together."

Lou ran a hand through his hair, "Did they have a lot of alone time together?"

"As far as I knew, they had none," I slowly shook my head. "Actually, Az and I spent more time with each other and I didn't spend a lot of time with my friends. He never acted suspicious or like he was scheming behind my back, either."

"How would you know, though? He clearly showed you a side you had no idea existed," Lou pointed out. "Would you have really known if he and Jennie were working together?"

"I guess not," my voice quiet. I thought for a little while longer before asking, "You've been around her a hell of a lot more than I have lately. Do you think she's sneaking around and getting info to Az?"

"She wouldn't have to do much sneaking," Lou said, going back to watching the world outside of the glass doors. "She hasn't been on her phone a lot around us, though, but who knows what she's doing behind closed doors. Every time Az showed up or his name was mentioned, she did genuinely seem freaked out. I don't know," he shook his head. "Maybe we do leave this one to Warrick."

"I don't like you right now," I said, narrowing my eyes at him.

"Why?" Lou asked defensively.

"You're throwing one of my best friends under the bus then dropping the topic like it's nothing. Now that's all I'm going to be thinking about," I explained.

I hadn't realized the two of us fell asleep on the couch, but when we woke up, Lou glanced down at me, ready to say something only to be interrupted by a knock on the front door. Warrick jogged down the stairs, wiping the sleep from his face, mumbling, "I got it."

Lou and I slowly stood up, our defenses raised just in case the person on the other side of the door wanted to attack.

"Thanks for stopping by, James," Warrick said, moving aside. The two of us let out a breath of relief at the sight of my dad walking into the house.

He gave a nod to me and Lou then returned his attention to Warrick, "You mentioned you had information."

"Yeah," Warrick said, motioning to the table for us all to sit. "I'll let Val be the one to explain it all since she obtained it. Love?"

I went through everything I had learned from Az, Warrick jumping in to add in the potential for us having someone on our side feeding him information. My dad didn't like hearing that, his brows furrowing as he asked, "Any ideas on who that could be?"

"Lou threw out the hare-brained idea that our mole is Val, but I haven't had a chance to think on it anymore." Warrick turned his attention to Lou, "Any other ideas?"

Lou quickly glanced my way. I nodded my head, encouraging him to share the theory we had talked about last night. He took a deep breath, "What about Jennie?"

My dad looked at me, his face serious, "Your best friend?"

"Let Lou explain. I don't buy it, but I don't think we should rule anyone out. Except for me. I can guarantee I'm not feeding Az information. The only way he'd get anything out of me is if he's filing through my mind, but I can't feel his presence like I can feel Warrick," I said tapping my fingers on the table.

"Explain," Warrick ordered Lou, his tone serious and business-like.

Lou's jaw twitched, but then he dove into it, "Jennie is the only one in our group who knew Az, besides Warrick and Val, before this war went crazy. Well, and you, James. They could've established a connection during the time Az was involved with Val, even though Val pointed out that Az and Jennie didn't really spend much time together. However, in the time they did spend together, Az could've roped her in to help his cause. She has been around when we've talked about some of our plans and Az has popped up when we've least expected it. She very much could've been texting him when we weren't paying attention to her or when she would hide out in her room.

"On the other hand, Jennie has been freaked out whenever Az has showed his face. Val doesn't seem to think she could be the mole, but that could be the perfect opportunity for her to be gathering this information. She's someone we overlook which means we've had quite a few sensitive conversations around her. We also don't know if she's been lurking around when we would have conversations in the office upstairs. That gives her everything she needs to feed to Az," Lou finished by running a hand through his hair.

Warrick nodded letting Lou's words sink in. He tapped his fingers on the table a couple of times then said, "You have a good theory. We don't know how much information Az has for sure since he only gave Val a sneak peek, so if he knows things that happened before Jennie rejoined our group, that eliminates her as a suspect."

"Is there anyone else?" my dad asked.

Warrick shook his head, "That's something I need to dive into. I did eliminate one threat back in Lupusantha. Az did send Holly as a spy who was getting a little too close to getting her hands on crucial information."

My dad nodded then asked, "What's next, Warrick?"

Warrick met his gaze, "We need to get the world leaders who are on our side to meet up here. It's time we start transporting whatever weapons we have and storing them someplace close by, which means we need a place to put everything. While we work on that, we need people to start trying to locate Az's arsenal, but we need people looking that he doesn't know. If we're all of a sudden running around the mountains in obscure locations, that's going to raise flags. I'm sure he has his people watching who will gladly report back, but I think if we have people who live in the mountains looking, it would be less suspicious since they're already associated with the area.

"Beyond that, I think we need to expect him to mount his final attack on Earth sometime soon. If he's bringing everyone on his side here, something big is going to happen. Something bigger than the ground and airborne attacks. The faster we can move, the better. And yes, the other world leaders know it's time to come here."

My dad nodded, taking everything in, "I can do that." He checked his watch then looked back up at Warrick, "I have to get going again, especially with the new work cut out for me. Just so you all know, Az has requested a dinner with me tomorrow and insisted Val be there – hence why I stopped by rather than taking this all in via a phone call. I'm not sure what's going to happen with that, but it would be a good idea for you and Lou to be there just in case. If he truly knows more than we think, then I think my cover is blown."

"No," I protested. "He can't know that."

My dad looked at me, his expression softening, "There's a good chance he does, Val-pal, but I'm going to do my best to keep the act going. I just need you to show up at that restaurant across the street from your apartment tomorrow. I'll text you the time. Dress nicely and play along, okay?"

I nodded, emotion threatening to take over. My dad pulled me into a hug. "I love you," he whispered into my ear. "You and your mom have made this life so much more wonderful than I could've imagined." He moved to shake Warrick and Lou's hands not quite meeting their eyes. I'm sure he was fighting the tears as much as I was.

I collapsed into my seat, my face in my hands. The air was heavy with the realization of what could happen with Az knowing what my dad has been up to. Warrick and Lou both put a comforting hand on my shoulders, but neither said anything. We sat there like that, quiet and somber, until the sound of car doors closing and laughter came from outside. I had no idea when all our friends left, but they didn't need to know about anything we just discussed. I sighed, running a hand over my face and shaking my arms. Time to fake it. I looked at the wolves at my side, "We don't talk about any of this with them."

"We know," Lou said, answering for the both of them.

The next day rolled around after a night spent laughing and having a good time. Sitting up in bed, the sinking feeling in my gut had only grown stronger. Warrick joined me in the kitchen for a small breakfast since that was all my stomach could handle. I glanced out of the front windows, "I'm going to go for a ride today since the roads are nice."

"I'll follow behind you," Warrick said, picking up on me wanting to be alone.

Even though he didn't ask any questions, I felt the need to explain myself, "I need to clear my head before everything tonight and figured I might as well start looking for any signs of Az's hideout in the mountains."

"You don't have to do that, love," Warrick started.

I shook my head, cutting him off from what he was going to say next, "I need to start doing something that doesn't involve sleeping with the enemy. Anyways, has my dad taken care of everything you asked him to yesterday?"

I knew it was a long shot. Warrick hit him with some big asks, but I had to start getting a handle on any unfinished business in case something happens to my dad. Warrick nodded, catching me by surprise, "Believe it or not, he did. I've sent a message about the arrangements to the other leaders. They should be here soon. I've also sent Lou the location where we'll be storing our equipment which should be arriving any day now. There are also people who will start combing the mountains in a couple of days – people who are familiar with the area who can play it cool. I don't know how he managed to pull it off, but he did."

I gave Warrick a soft smile, "He probably already knew what was coming."

"That's the only thing I could think of," Warrick said. He scooted closer to me, his hand on my knee, "It's going to be okay, love."

"I keep telling myself that," I responded, my voice distant. I sighed then moved to clean up our mess and get dressed for the day.

There was no hesitation from me as I swung my leg over Gabriel's bike. I strapped the helmet on and pulled out of the garage, heading to the stop sign at the end of the street. I waited until I saw Warrick in my mirrors, taking a deep breath as the feeling of the engine helped calm my nerves. He kept sending reassurances down our bond, but I couldn't bring myself to answer.

I shot forward taking the familiar path into the mountains. It was the path I had gone on so many times with Gabriel, the one he had led us on in my dream, and it just so happened to be the same one I took with Az all those years ago.

My time was limited here, so I enjoyed what was probably going to be one of my last leisurely rides with these views. The trees zipped past me, the fresh air I've always associated with a higher altitude filling my lungs. I slowed my speed as I approached the pull-off at the top of a hill that serves as the backdrop of so many of my pictures. Turning my bike off, I removed my helmet. I sucked in a deep breath of air, taking in the smell of pine and snow, closing my eyes and letting my head fall back.

Are you okay, love? Did you see anything?

No, I answered Warrick. *Just taking a moment to enjoy the day, and get a good vantage point for anything that may be what we're looking for. Just stay parked back there.*

I heard the car turn off serving as Warrick's acknowledgment. I scanned the landscape below me, but as I expected, there weren't any buildings that would've been a place to store weaponry I could see or any suspicious activity going on. Not surprising considering we're not too far from the city. Az is smarter than that.

The sound of a loud engine pulled me out of my thoughts, approaching us. *Stay in the car*, I warned Warrick.

Why? Warrick asked, his tone telling me he was on high alert.

Before I could respond, Az's bike rounded the corner, slowing when he saw me standing there. He pulled up leaving a good amount of distance between us, cutting the engine.

Popping his visor up, Az took me in. He didn't say anything, just rested his forearms on the tank, watching the landscape stretch before us. I directed my attention in front of me, too. We were like that for a couple of minutes, not really acknowledging the other's presence, until gravel crunched and Az was standing next to me. He finally took his helmet off, examining the bike I was on, "This new?"

"No," I answered curtly.

Az scoffed then asked, "Traveling with a bodyguard now?"

I kept my gaze trained on the city below us, "He wanted to come with me, but I wanted to ride alone. That's all."

I felt an increase in the pressure I associate with Warrick in my head. He wasn't speaking to me, but I had a hunch he was trying to use our bond to see and hear what I was. He was going to have to teach me that trick later.

"You're awfully quiet today," Az observed. "Where's that fiery Val I saw in the apartment? I miss her."

I shook my head, finally meeting his gaze, "Just a lot on my mind that's all."

"Is this Gabriel's bike?" he asked, gesturing towards it.

I nodded, my throat tightening with emotions.

"Hey," he said, softly. "What's wrong?"

A tear trailed down my cheek, "I'm really missing people in my life, Az, people who shouldn't be gone."

That was the wrong thing to say. He pursed his lips together, tilting my chin up so I was forced to look at him. I knew the moment my eyes met his, his hazel eyes cold and hard, the switch had been flipped. That sinister grin of his replaced the concern that had been there moments ago,

"Sacrifices have to be made, Val. You should know that more than anyone right now."

I tried to jerk my chin away from him, but Az only tightened his grip. He clicked his tongue a couple of times, "You're so naive."

"What are you talking about?" I hissed at him, my lip curling.

A low laugh escaped his lips as he shifted, one hand still holding my chin while his other arm wrapped around my waist trapping me, "You make it so easy to target people, to get in your head. I bet you're still questioning if what I said the other night is true or if I was just saying those things."

"Well?" I demanded. I could feel Warrick's anger rising up, thankfully directed towards Az and not me.

Az's thumb stroked my cheek, "Lucky for you, not so lucky for me, they were. I meant every word."

"Then what the hell are you doing right now?"

"My plan was to enjoy the view, like you, but I wasn't expecting anyone else to be up here. I know you were just trying to get intel out of me. That wasn't hard to figure out when you left me tied up and naked. There's no way Warrick would've let you do that willingly if it meant he could lose you. I don't appreciate being taken advantage of like that."

"What are you talking about?" I asked, no longer able to keep the panic out of my voice. I had no weapons and with how Az was standing in front of me, I couldn't try to fight my way out of this one.

"You know exactly what I'm talking about," Az snarled, his face inches from mine. "You spiked my drink to get information out of me. You let me kiss you, say those things to you; things, I might add, that I very much intended to keep to myself. I'm not the only one who plays games here. You've fucked with my head and I don't appreciate it. But, I'll give you one more chance tonight at dinner. A chance to make up for that."

"Is that why you invited me?" I tried to pull my head back to get him out of my space with no luck. To be honest, I was surprised it took him this long to try to exact revenge for what I did to him.

"I have my reasons. I have to admit, though, I'm very excited to see you dressed up. I love how you look day-to-day, but there's just *something* about you when you clean up."

Az glanced in the direction of the car, something now pressing into my side. His smirk made me feel sick, nausea threatening to take over as his eyes slid back to mine. I glanced down discovering a gun was the source of the pressure I was feeling. My eyes snapped back to his, wide and full of fear. Az leaned in to whisper in my ear thinking Warrick had no chance to hear him, "You'll find I can be very persuasive, so keep an open mind tonight. Also, have fun explaining to your boyfriend why you're happily kissing his brother."

I started to ask him what the hell he was rambling on about when his lips were on mine. When I wasn't kissing him back, he cocked the gun. My lips instantly started moving with his. I had to remind myself this was all a part of the games he's been playing to get in between me and Warrick. A car door slammed, slow footsteps approaching, "You have five seconds to let go of her, Az."

Az pulled away, giving me a little boop on my nose as he answered Warrick, "That's fine. I was just leaving anyways."

We both watched Az saunter over to his bike then leave. As soon as he was speeding up the road further into the mountains, I whirled around to the nearest bushes just in time to empty my stomach contents. Warrick put a comforting hand on my back, "It's okay, love. He's back to his usual self."

Wiping my mouth with the back of my hand, I turned to Warrick beating a fist into his chest, "It's not okay! He just threatened to shoot me if I didn't kiss him back just to screw with you. He started this *fucking* war that ripped Gabriel from me. He *murdered* my mom. He almost killed you. Now, I have to go waltzing into a damn restaurant acting like everything's normal when you and I both know he's going to pull some shit in there! Az isn't going to let me go and I just want to go. I want to leave and enjoy what little bit of this life I have left because I have no idea how we're going to win."

Sobs wracked my body. Warrick pulled me into his chest, "Are you done now?"

"Fuck you," I muttered between tears.

"No," Warrick moved me so I was sitting on my bike. He put his hands on my shoulders, those glacial eyes meeting mine, "That's not what I meant. Get it all out, love. Whatever happens tonight, whatever happened in the past, will sort itself out. I know it doesn't look like it right now, but we have a chance to beat him, and you better believe me when I say I will kill him the first chance I get. Then, all this chaos will be over. We can go about our lives. But, in order to do that, I need you to have that same confidence you had when I first met you. That confidence when you waltzed into my office and drove a knife into my thigh. I need that Val right now, okay?"

I moved to wipe my tears, but Warrick beat me to it. I sucked in a deep breath to bring my emotions back in check then nodded my head. It felt good to get everything out, but I knew Warrick was right. Pity party time was over. Setting my shoulders, I said, "I guess it's time to go home and get ready."

It was hard to keep everything in check after my run-in with Az earlier. Warrick and I made our way back home and I was now in my bathroom putting the finished touches on my makeup. I put my curled hair up in a high-ponytail, admiring how perfectly the waves fell. I took a step back to admire my work – the whole look coming together with one of my many little black dresses hugging me in all the right places.

"If only I could be in Az's shoes tonight," Warrick purred from the doorway, dressed in his expensive business attire.

I closed my mascara, cleaning up the rest of my makeup I had scattered around the counter, "Why?"

Warrick tugged me to him, "Because you look incredible, love."

We shared a gentle, passionate kiss. I wiped my lipstick off his lips, "Thank you. You'll be there, though. With Lou?"

"Yes," he nodded. I followed him out of my room downstairs where Lou was ready to go, too. I did a double take – it's a rare occurrence for Lou to be dressed up, and it suited him well.

Warrick guided me over to the island where there were several knives laid out, distracting me from giving Lou a compliment. "You're not going in there unarmed. Not after this afternoon," Warrick started explaining. "It's going to be a challenge with that dress, but carry as many of these as you can."

"What's so special about these? You know a regular knife isn't going to do anything," I countered.

Lou cleared his throat, keeping his eyes trained on the knives, "Remember the knife you stabbed Warrick with?"

Yeah," I slowly nodded. "But I didn't think there was any more of that venom."

"I never said there wasn't. My team was able to replicate the venom by pulling a sample from my blood. I need you to drive these knives into Az at the first sign of trouble. It may not cause a ton of damage to someone like him, but it'll at least hurt and give you a chance to get away," Warrick explained. He held up a leather band, "You good with that plan, love?"

I nodded my head, taking the band and strapping it to my thigh. I tucked a knife, safely in its sheath, into the band, then tucked a few of the others in my purse. I took a step back, Lou and Warrick circling me to check if the knives were obvious. Thankfully, the material my dress is made out of is thick enough to hide anything. Combine that with the thin band, and you wouldn't even know I was carrying some sort of weapon on me.

We snuck out of the house before my friends could grill us with where we were going. The less they knew right now, the better. Warrick and Lou dropped me at the doors going into the restaurant then went to park a couple blocks away. I set my shoulders, walking into the building and letting the host guide me back to a private room.

Az was the only one in there casually sipping on his wine in his black attire, the first couple of buttons undone revealing some of his muscled chest and the sleeves rolled up exposing parts of his tattoos. His face betrayed him the minute he laid eyes on me, and I knew I had caught him off-guard. He stood up, pulling out a chair for me. As I settled into it, I watched him from the corner of my eye, "You like it when I clean up, so I had to make sure I wasn't going to disappoint."

"I don't think you ever could," Az responded with a quiet voice.

Before I could say anything else, my dad was escorted into the room, the host closing the door on his way out.

"James," Az nodded, switching into business mode.

"Well, isn't this a little bit like deja vu," my dad observed. "Too bad I'm missing my wife."

A heavy silence settled in the room. A server kept her head down, coming in to bring us all small salads and to fill the empty wine glasses in front of me and my dad.

"Well," Az cleared his throat. "I appreciate you two joining me tonight. I'm going to cut to the chase because, quite frankly, Val is making it incredibly hard to focus."

"Get on with it," my dad ordered.

"I'm giving you both one last chance to truly join my side," Az started. My stomach dropped. Az knew. My dad called it yesterday.

"And if we do?" my dad asked. I opened my mouth to question why he was considering this, but quickly shut it when my dad shot me a glare. His way of telling me to let him do the talking.

Az steepled his fingers in front of him, elbows resting on the table, "I pull out of Earth. I shift my focus to Lupusantha until I get Warrick to beg and plead for me to stop. Until I get full control of that world."

"Why are you doing this, Az?" I asked, no longer wanting to sit quietly.

"Doing what?" he asked. Az's tone was light almost as if he wanted me to ask that question.

I narrowed my eyes, "Don't play dumb. You know what."

"Enlighten me, Val. I'm doing a lot of things. You're going to need to be more specific," the corners of Az's mouth were starting to twitch into a smile. Everything about this felt too rehearsed.

"What is the purpose behind this war?" I slowly enunciated every word to convey my annoyance.

"Well, you should've just started with that," Az said, the sinister smile fully in place now as he leaned back into his seat. He swirled his wine glass around, "I'm going to bring these worlds to their knees, take out their so-called leaders if they resist me, and come in like the savior I am. You see, I've always been viewed as the enemy, so I'm going to make myself the hero. I've had to make every opportunity in my life, so why stop now?"

"That'll never happen," I said quietly.

"And that's where you're wrong, Val-pal," Az started. My dad's face reddened at Az using his nickname for me. "I'll get everything I want. I'll have the most power in this universe. I'll get rid of my little brother who has been a thorn in my side since the day he was born. As an added bonus, I'll even get *you* standing by my side. Everyone will cry out their thanks and love for me, and so-on and so-forth. You get the picture."

"How are you going to convince everyone of that when you started all this?" I asked. I had taken the conversation over now, but my dad didn't seem to mind. He sat back watching the exchange making a mental note of every word being said.

Az leaned closer to me, "That's the beauty of it – they don't even know I'm the one wreaking havoc in their lives."

"They will once the world leaders spread word," I countered, sticking my chin up.

"Not after the witches get ahold of them and wipe their memories," Az said.

"They can do that?" I asked, unable to keep the horror out of my voice.

He nodded slowly, "Yes, and if you two join up with me, I'll make sure they take care of those pesky memories of me only leaving the nice ones. Hell, they'll even make sure you forget you're fated to Warrick."

Panic gripped my throat. We may have been struggling with being fated to each other, but I wasn't going to lose Warrick. I couldn't ...

"Besides," Az continued, turning to stare down my dad. "You both have played me. The fact I'm even giving you this way out is a blessing. Normally, I would've killed you both on the spot."

"I don't know what Val may have done," my dad started.

"Cut the crap, James," Az interrupted. "I've known for quite some time you're feeding information to Warrick. You've been doing what you can to get people out of here so they aren't hurt by the war, including your daughter. Actually, you got her out of here right before I could pop back up in her life."

My dad remained stoic as he continued to deny these allegations, "I've been on your side since the start. I've carried out each of your orders without protest."

"Yet, you still continued to sneak around my back," Az calmly set his glass in front of him putting a hand in his pocket.

"Val-pal," my dad turned his attention to me. Tears started welling in my eyes. We both knew what was about to happen. "You have to keep going, okay? I love you so much and I've been so lucky to be your father. Give 'em hell out there."

"I love you, dad," I said.

"This is sweet and all, but I'm tired of it. Are you going to join up with me or not?" Az asked impatiently. "This is the last time I'll ask."

My dad hadn't even gotten the word out when Az sunk a knife into his heart. Wide-eyed, my dad stared down at the hilt sticking out from his chest. My hands shot up to my mouth to keep my scream contained. There were other people in this restaurant and I didn't need to put them at risk.

As my dad looked back up, Az threw another knife. It landed in his neck, taking away his ability to talk. My dad mouthed that he loved me one more time then Az threw his last knife, landing in between my dad's eyes. He slumped over, motionless, but Az jumped up to check for a pulse to make sure he had finished the job.

Az whirled around to me, his eyes wild. He started stalking over to where I was still seated, a predator going after his prey. My hands were shaking, tears streaming down my face. I just lost one of the pillars in my life, but I would have time to mourn my dad in a little bit. I needed to make it out of here on my own.

I finally found my legs, able to stand, backing against a wall. Az glanced at the table then looked back at me, "It's a shame we won't be getting our meal. I ordered your favorite."

He pressed his body against mine, pushing me against the wall. It hurt, how much weight he was pressing against me. Sneering, Az said, "You always have to take the hard way."

Able to move my arm a little bit, I reached for the knife between my legs. *Warrick!* I screamed through the bond. I would at least get him and Lou moving to where I was.

The door next to me started to open, but Az slammed it shut pressing his body weight against it while still reaching for me. I let out a choked sob. I'm trapped in here now. I knew Az was strong, but to keep the door closed on two other alphas like it was nothing terrified me.

"You just made me lose one of my most valuable assets. You owe me for that one," Az sneered as he caressed my face.

"No," I choked out. "I'm not coming with you."

"I've had you once, I can have you again. Just think of the life you'll live with me, Val. We'll be happy. You don't have to worry about anyone attacking you ever again. I'll keep you *safe*. You'll never feel unloved or unwanted."

"Get off me," I said as I shoved the knife info his stomach.

He doubled over, rage filling his features while he tried to grasp the knife, "What the fuck is this?"

I didn't bother to answer. I grabbed my purse, ripped the door open, and ran right into Warrick and Lou whose eyes were widening as they caught a glimpse of my dad slumped over the table, the pool of his blood growing larger. Warrick passed me to Lou, closed the door behind me, and we ran. We didn't look back as we sprinted to the car. I stumbled a few steps, the adrenaline starting to wear off, everything that had just happened starting to set in. Lou scooped me into his arms carrying me the whole way until he tucked me into the car. Warrick hopped into the driver's seat, and as soon as Lou got in, Warrick slammed his foot on the gas pedal. We sped off towards the house, the tires screeching. We passed the restaurant, Az nearly throwing himself in front of the car. He was still doubled over, the knife embedded in his stomach, cursing as we swerved around him. We were going to have hell to pay, and I just painted the world's largest target on my back.

Acknowledgements

I can't believe this series is more than halfway over now ... A huge, huge, HUGE thank you to my husband! I had so many doubts with how this one was going to go (much more than the previous books) and you helped walk me through each and every single one. You've dealt with the constant back and forth and the million "are you sure?" questions to help me get through everything the characters experienced in this book. You opened my eyes to the importance of not shying away from the hardships the characters face. And I am so beyond appreciative that you are willing to take the time (even if that means less time to read other books) to read through the early drafts of my books and giving such good feedback.

Thank you again to my mom for catching my typos and grammatical errors! I hope my typos and missed punctuation marks are getting fewer and fewer each time. Thank you for also dealing with my aggressive timelines – it's a lot to go through in a smaller window of time when you are already balancing so much. I can't forget to add that I always enjoy talking about who your favorite is and what you think about certain scenes, too!

I, of course, have to keep sharing my appreciation for the team at Miblart. You all make it so easy to work through changes and deal with my many changes to the smallest of details. Your patience and expertise is so appreciated and I brag about your services to anyone who will listen!

My family and friends – thank you to each and every one of you who has taken the time to read this. We've made it to four and you're still here! As always, I'm beyond thankful of your patience with me as I continue to keep my head down and right. I'm also so appreciative of you all taking the time to spread the word about my books!

For my readers, there will never be enough thanks and appreciation to capture what it means to me that you are standing by me and supporting this dream of mine. I do this to share stories with you. To see you all get so into the stories and the characters is amazing! It makes me smile so much when I hear about your favorite characters, or how maybe Val has annoyed you, or how your viewpoints change as you learn more. Not only that, but you all have been able to pick up on some details that I didn't think anyone would. Thank you, from the bottom of my heart, for being so willing to read what I have to write and for being engaged. That helps me feel like this is truly real and that I'm not dreaming. Thank you!!

Thank you again for taking the time out of your busy schedule to shove the world aside and escape into *Torn Between Times* I really hope you enjoyed it, and if you did, please leave a review!

Did you know?

Indie authors are small business owners (yay for supporting small businesses!). Reviews are our bread and butter, and mean the world to us. Fun fact - it takes 50 reviews *minimum* for exposure on Amazon. The best way to support an author (after reading their book, of course) is by leaving a review, even if it's just a few words!

Thank you sooo so much for your support!

Want even more content? Check out my website and socials to be in the know for all the latest and greatest updates:
www.toriegwriting.com
www.facebook.com/toriegwriting
www.instagram.com/toriegwriting

www.goodreads.com/torie_gaylord
www.youtube.com/@awkwardauthortg
www.twitch.tv/awkwardauthortg

About the Author

Torie is a passionate adventurer who finds inspiration in the beauty of the outdoor world, especially in her backyard of Colorado. When not hiking through the mountains or torturing herself with running, she enjoys the company of her loving husband and their two cats, who serve as her trusty sidekicks as she types away . A lover of engaging storytelling, she often loses herself in a good book, movie/tv show, or video game. Eager to create her own worlds, Torie is excited to share her adventures through writing, inviting readers to embark on journeys of their own.

Read more at toriegwriting.com.

www.ingramcontent.com/pod-product-compliance
Lightning Source LLC
LaVergne TN
LVHW020650110826
845149LV00012B/1959

* 9 7 9 8 9 9 2 2 3 8 9 7 6 *